rs03

D0571691

ALL THAT GLISTERS

A Selection of Recent Titles by Janet Tanner

DAUGHTER OF RICHES
DECEPTION AND DESIRE
THE SHORES OF MIDNIGHT
HOSTAGE TO LOVE*

* available from Severn House

ALL THAT GLISTERS

Janet Tanner

This first world edition published in Great Britain 2001 by
SEVERN HOUSE PUBLISHERS LTD of
9–15 High Street, Sutton, Surrey SM1 1DF.
This first world edition published in the USA 2002 by
SEVERN HOUSE PUBLISHERS INC of
595 Madison Avenue, New York, N.Y. 10022.

British Library Cataloguing in Publication Data

Tanner, Janet
     All that glisters
     1. Irish – Australia – Fiction
     2. Love stories
     I. Title
     823.9'14 [F]

ISBN 0-7278-5711-8

Typeset by Palimpsest Book Production Ltd.,
Polmont, Stirlingshire, Scotland.
Printed and bound in Great Britain by
MPG Books Ltd., Bodmin, Cornwall.

*Not all that tempts your wand'ring eyes
And heedless hearts, is lawful prize;
Nor all, that glisters, gold.*

Thomas Grey

Prologue

1852

'*In the midst of life we are in death; of whom may we seek for succour but of thee, O Lord . . .*'

The captain's voice rose flat and emotionless to be carried away on the stiff breeze that filled the sails of the *Gazelle*. Amos Rich – or 'Bully' as he was known to his officers and crew – had conducted too many burials at sea to be affected by them any more, and in any case, the deceased was not known to him personally. She was just another emigrant, one of the hundred and fifty who had been packed into the 'tween decks for the long and tortuous voyage from Dublin to Melbourne. Like so many others, she had contracted a fever in the cramped and unhygienic conditions; like so many others she had died of it. Such was life. And death. Bully Rich's only concern was to get the burial over as quickly as possible so that he could get back to the only thing that concerned him – ensuring as fast a passage as was possible for the *Gazelle*.

'*For as much as it has pleased Almighty God of his great mercy . . .*'

Towards the back of the crowd who had lined up on deck to watch the burial, Tara Murphy brushed the tears out of her eyes and slipped her hand into that of her husband, Patrick. She had not known the deceased either, except by sight. The poor woman had been just one of the milling crowd below who fought by day for the use of the cookers to prepare their meagre meals, and slept at night in the narrow cots which lined the walls of the cuddy. But as she looked at

1

the sailcloth bundle, covered by a Union Jack and lying on a rough trestle near the ship's rail, Tara felt she might have known her. She could, after all, have been any one of them. Like them, she had sailed from Dublin and the poverty and the hunger that haunted Ireland in these days. Like them she had been full of hopes and dreams for a better future in the new country. Well, there was no future at all for her now. Nothing but a watery grave in the Indian Ocean.

Tara blinked hard against the tears that were pricking at her eyes again.

It wasn't just pity for the dead woman and her family that was affecting her so, Tara knew. The words of the burial service had reminded her all too clearly of her own mother's funeral service.

That, of course, had taken place in the cemetery adjoining the Church of the Sacred Heart, not on the deck of a sailing ship. The wind that had swept dead leaves into flurries around the old headstones and into the shallow new grave had smelled not of salt but of damp peat, and the rain that had soaked Tara's worn-out boots and mingled with the tears on her face had been soft, like the clear springs from the mountains. But the words, oh, the words had been the same.

Oh, Mammy! Tara wept silently now. Why did you have to die? And just when you had the chance of a better life too? Just when you were so happy . . .

For all the blows that fate had dealt her, for all the hardships she had endured, Mary Reilly had never quite lost her cheerful optimism. She had still had the heart to sing as she washed and scrubbed, even though her hands were cracked and raw, and to smile even when her belly was aching with emptiness because she had dished up most of the meagre supper onto her family's plates. And she had been as excited as a child when Patrick and Tara had suggested she should go with them to Australia.

'Sure, you don't want to be burdened by an old woman

like me!' she had protested. But her eyes were alight in her thin face.

'Mammy, you're not old!' Tara had said emphatically, though the way she had seen her mother age rapidly in the years since the potato famine had taken hold frightened her. 'You'll never be old. Not even if you live to be a hundred.'

Mary had laughed shortly. 'Chance would be a fine thing!'

'And you'll have that chance if you come with us,' Patrick told her. He and Tara had been childhood sweethearts and he had grown up loving Mary almost as much as he loved his own mother. 'Don't you know they've found gold around Melbourne? Just think of it, riches there for the taking, and I intend to have my share if I have to work all the hours God sends to do it! I'll buy you new clothes, and all the food you can eat, and maybe even a carriage to drive around in. We'll have a fine house and . . .'

'Oh, Patrick, stop, stop!' Mary had laughed. 'What in the world would I want with a carriage? Sure, haven't my poor legs served me well enough these forty years?'

'Mammy, we *want* you to come with us and share in our good fortune,' Tara had said, taking her by the arm and wincing as she noticed again how thin it had become, nothing but skin and bone. 'Do you really think we could go off to the other side of the world and leave you here alone? And how would I manage when my babies come, I'd like to know? You have to come, or Patrick and I won't go.'

Mary had nodded, smiling. 'Now you're talking, Tara my girl. Fine clothes, carriages . . . you can keep them. But my grandchildren, that's something else. I'd like to be there to see them grow up.'

'Then you'll come?'

Another smile, brave and determined. 'Just try to stop me!'

They hadn't, of course, and the Government had not objected either when the family applied for their passage. Mary Reilly might not be of an age or constitution to survive the long voyage, she might be of little use in the new land, but that was not their concern. Those in power had long ago come to the conclusion that it was far cheaper to ship out the starving masses than to keep them in Irish workhouses. And so the plans had been made.

Except that Mary had collapsed and died the week before they were due to sail. The suddenness with which the end had come had shocked Tara, and the long months at sea had done nothing to ease her grief and terrible aching loss.

Tara, once as resilient and optimistic as her mother had been, was beset now by doubts and anxieties. It was almost as though Mary's death had been an omen, she thought, as she lay awake fretting night after night in the whispering cuddy.

The same thought occurred to her now as she stood on deck, listening to the all-too-familiar words of the burial rites.

This voyage, which they had set out upon with such hope and excitement, had turned into a terrible ordeal. The seasickness, the raging storms, the terrifying calm and tropical heat of the doldrums, the fevers, the hunger, the overpowering stench of unwashed bodies packed together like sardines, the sleepless nights, the endless days, all had taken their toll. Sometimes Tara had wondered whether they would ever reach Australia at all, and if they did, what they would find there.

And the deaths! At least thirty souls had gone to meet their maker, Tara knew, though she had long since given up counting.

Would her mother have been yet another one? Tara suspected that she would. Perhaps after all it was a blessing she had not survived to embark on the tortuous voyage. At least she lay now in the soft earth of the land she loved. At least she would never be food for the fishes.

'We therefore commit her body to the deep . . .'

The bundle was raised, the flag drawn back, and the body slid with a splash into the sea. As the waves closed over it a child sobbed. Tara's heart filled and she squeezed Patrick's hand so tightly that her fingers ached.

He turned to look at her, his blue eyes anxious.

'Don't upset yourself now, sweetheart. It's not as if we really knew her.'

'How can you say that?' Tara's own eyes were blazing suddenly, all her grief and apprehension turning to anger. 'She was somebody's wife and mother.'

'I know that, but . . .'

She wheeled round. 'We are going to make a success of our new life, aren't we?'

'Of course we are! When I find gold we'll be rich and . . .'

'Never mind gold!' Tara said passionately. The tears were still sparkling in her eyes but her pretty face, pinched now from lack of sunlight and months of deprivation, was the picture of determination. 'Never mind rich! As long as we're happy and content! We have to be, Patrick! Not just for us, but for them – all of them – who didn't make it to the new country. And especially for Mammy.'

'Of course. It's all going to be great,' Patrick said, squeezing her hand. But for all his quick assurances, Tara was not sure she believed him. Patrick seemed to think it was all going to be so easy; she was not so sure. For the first time in her life she looked at him and clearly saw, without the rosy tint of love, the sweet unworldly dreamer she had married. How would he fare in the new land if things were not as he expected them to be? A shadow of doubt assailed her. Then she thrust it aside.

If things went wrong, she would just have to be strong for both of them. She had inherited every bit of Mammy's indomitable character, and she also had youth on her side. Whatever it took, she would make sure that she achieved what Mammy, and all the others, had wanted.

It was a sentiment that was to keep Tara's resolve and courage high throughout all that was to come.

One

T he last rays of the setting sun were slanting through the mimosa trees as James Hannay turned his horse into the drive that led to Dunrae, his home.

After a long day in the saddle he was tired, thirsty and hungry. But he still sat straight and tall, a dark muscular man with the look of the outdoors. Though sweat-streaked, his shirt and breeches were obviously of good quality and his boots, under their coating of dust and grime, were the finest leather.

James Hannay was a farmer, one of the wealthiest in the rich pastureland that was Victoria. But he had been born and raised to a strict work ethic. He still rose early to check on stock and fences, and burned the candle late into the night as he pored over the accounts that detailed sales of the prized wool which came from his flock of merino sheep. With the help of his brothers Philip and Cal he managed Dunrae well and efficiently; the farm was more profitable now than it had ever been.

As the house came into view, a low white building sur-rounded on three sides by a veranda, James heaved a sigh that was part relief and part pleasure. He loved Dunrae with every fibre of his being. His father, Rolf, had built it with his own hands when he had claimed the rich pastureland thirty-five years ago. Here, as a child, he had played amongst the clucking chickens and waddling ducks, here he had sat his first pony, clutching excitedly at the animal's bristly mane as

Rolf paraded him around the paddock on a leading rein. He had happy memories, too, of Mia-Mia, his mother's old home on the Paramatta river on the other side of the mountains, where he had spent many long and exciting holidays with his grandfather, Andrew Mackenzie, and where Rolf and Regan, James's mother, now lived. But it was Dunrae that held a special place in his heart. Dunrae, more than any other holding in the Mackenzie/Hannay empire, was not only his home. For James it symbolised his heritage.

As he turned his horse, Tarquin, into the cobbled yard a small dark-haired boy emerged from the stable block and came running towards him.

'Papa! Papa! You're home!'

'Duncan! What are you doing out here at this hour? It's long past your bedtime.' James brought Tarquin to a halt and dismounted, bending to rumple the little boy's thick curls.

An impish face grinned up at him, grey eyes, the exact same colour as James's own, wide and innocent. 'It's still light.'

'Only just,' James said sternly. 'Are you hiding from Martha again?'

'No!' Duncan returned indignantly, then added sheepishly: 'Well, not now, anyway. She's gone back to her own house to get Mr Henderson's supper.'

James sighed. Matt Henderson had been his overseer until chronic rheumatism had forced him into retirement, and Martha, his wife, was supposed to keep an eye on Duncan when James was out on the land. But James knew that Duncan led her a merry dance. The boy was growing wilder with every passing year – hardly surprising when he had no mother to discipline him.

'She gave up looking for you, I suppose,' he said, loosening Tarquin's girths. 'It's very bad of you, Duncan. Martha isn't a young woman any more and you know you tire her out with your mischief.'

Duncan pulled a mock-chastened face, then brightened once more, producing a small box from his pocket.

'Papa, look, I caught a beetle!'

James hid a smile. Tired he might be, cross with his young son he certainly was, but Duncan never failed to raise his spirits. For all the trouble he caused, never a day went by but James thanked God for him.

'A beetle, eh! Let me see.' He lifted the saddle from Tarquin's back and bent to examine the fat black specimen Duncan was proudly holding up to him. 'Well, a fine fellow he is too. But now I've seen him, I think you should let him go.'

'Oh, Papa, why? I want to take him to bed with me!'

'He's far too big to be kept in that little box,' James said firmly.

'I made air holes,' Duncan offered. 'In the lid. See?'

'And that was good. But it's no substitute for freedom. How would you like it if we locked you up in the pantry and left you there?'

'Mm.' Duncan thought about it for a moment with all the studied concentration of a six-year-old. 'Oh, all right,' he said at last.

He crouched down on the cobbles, opening the box and watching regretfully as the beetle scurried away.

'Good boy.' James rumpled his hair again approvingly. 'Now let's get Tarquin stabled and you to bed.'

Duncan knelt on the bright rag rug at the side of his bed, wriggling his nose above his folded fingers. He hated having to say his nightly prayers. It was so tedious! All the *God Blesses* to be recited, and then the Lord's Prayer, which he always gabbled through as fast as he could. He didn't know why Papa made him do it every night; he'd once heard Papa saying to Uncle Philip that he didn't believe in God. Duncan could only suppose it was because Mama had always said prayers with him before singing him to sleep and Papa tried to do things as she had. Not that Papa sang him to sleep. Not that he'd want him to. Papa didn't have a very tuneful voice.

'I think you should ask to be forgiven, Duncan, for leading Martha such a dance,' Papa's voice broke into his thoughts. Duncan screwed his eyes shut and muttered obediently.

'Dear God, I'm sorry for leading Martha such a dance.' His eyes flew open again. 'Will that do, Papa?'

James sighed. 'Yes, Duncan, that will do. Into bed now, and do try to be a better boy tomorrow.'

'I'll try.' Words cost nothing. Then, as James tucked the covers around him all the bravado went out of him. 'Papa, you won't put out the candle, will you?'

'No, Duncan, I won't put out the candle.'

It was the same every night. When the moment came for him to be left alone Duncan the scamp, Duncan the wild, who swam like a fish in the cold creek, who climbed effortlessly to the top of the tallest tree and who rode his pony, Jim, with such lack of fear that James sometimes wondered how he had not come to break his neck long ago, became a small frightened child. Duncan was terrified of the dark – not outdoors, where he could see the moon and stars and there was always a glimmer of light even when it was cloudy – but in the house.

James knew the reason why, though it was a weight around his heart that he did not care to think about. Duncan associated darkness with death. When Lorna, his mother, had been lying in her coffin in the parlour he had wandered in. James had been alerted by his screams and rushed to the room where all the curtains were drawn in respect for the dead, to find Duncan cowering in a corner.

'Why won't Mama speak to me?' he had cried, beating at James with his small hands when he tried to take the child in his arms and comfort him. 'Why is she so cold?' And then the question that had haunted him ever since. 'Why is it dark? Mama doesn't like the dark!'

'Mama doesn't know it's dark,' James had tried to explain gently. But Duncan would not be pacified until James lit a candle to leave with her.

Thereafter the little boy who otherwise knew no fear could not sleep unless he, too, had a candle in his room, and James blamed himself for it, as he blamed himself for so many things. He should have taken more care that Duncan did not find his mother like that. His only excuse was that he had been so distraught at her loss that he hadn't been thinking clearly. But it was not good enough for him.

He had failed Duncan then, he thought, pulling the bedroom door half-closed behind him, and he was failing him now. What would Lorna say if she knew Duncan had still been out roaming the grounds at this hour?

He stood for a moment on the landing, listening until he was sure Duncan was asleep, then he clomped downstairs to the big comfortable kitchen where his two younger brothers were sitting over the remains of their evening meal. Philip, a slimly built serious-looking man of twenty-seven, pored over a book that he had set close to the lamp, whilst Cal, three years younger, rangy and handsome, sprawled feet up nursing a mug of tea.

'What in the name of heaven were you two thinking of leaving Duncan to run wild at this time of night?' James demanded, throwing himself down in his chair and reaching for the platter of cold pork.

'We didn't know he was out.' Philip closed his book, keeping his finger in the page to mark his place. 'I could scarce believe my eyes when you brought him in.'

'We thought Martha had put him to bed,' Cal agreed. 'There was no sign of either of them when we got in and . . .'

'And you didn't think to make sure.' James was beginning to be angry. Bad temper came easily to him since he had lost Lorna. 'Good God, he could have been anywhere! Suppose he'd wandered off?'

'Oh, he knows better than that,' Cal said lightly. 'No harm came to him, did it?'

'Not this time, no.' James reached for the knife to cut

himself a hunk of bread. 'Oh, I don't know what I'm to do with him. I can't be here all the time, and Martha . . . she does her best, I suppose, but it's just not good enough. The truth is he's too much for her.'

'She has got her own husband and home to care for,' Philip said, a little sharply. He was fond of Martha and in his opinion James expected too much of her. 'Bad enough that she has to cook our meals and make sure the convict women keep the house clean without having to care for Duncan as well. Perhaps it's time, James, that you made other arrangements.'

James speared a piece of pork with his fork and Philip with his eyes.

'What do you mean? You're not going to suggest again that Duncan should go to live at Mia-Mia, I hope? Because if you are, I have to tell you I shall never change my mind and agree to that. I know Mother offered to have him when Lorna died, but she's not getting any younger and in any case his place is here. I've lost my wife – I'm not about to lose my son too.'

'That wasn't what I had in mind,' Philip said. 'I know you don't want Duncan to go to live with Mother and Father at Mia-Mia and I can understand your objections. No, my suggestion is that we should employ a housekeeper. Someone to live in and take care of Duncan too as part of their duties. Someone young enough to keep him out of mischief when we're not here.'

'A fine idea!' Cal stretched his booted legs and grinned. 'And if she's young and pretty she can keep me out of mischief too!'

James shot him a glance. 'Get you into mischief, more like! Isn't it enough for you, Cal, that half the girls in the district dance to your tune? If you think I'm going to install one here so you have only to creep along the landing at night to take your pleasure you are much mistaken. That's not the kind of home I want my son raised in.'

11

'Oh, James, what a killjoy you've become!' Cal lamented.

James merely grunted, chewing ravenously on his pork without tasting a single mouthful.

'It is the sensible solution, James, you must agree,' Philip said, ignoring his younger brother's flippant remarks. 'Duncan needs a woman's influence. Without it, he'll run wild, I fear.'

'I fear so too,' James agreed. 'Very well. Let me think about it.'

Philip flipped his book open again and pulled it towards him.

'Don't think for too long, will you?'

When James had finished his meal he poured himself a glass of malt whisky, added the merest splash of water, and carried it out onto the veranda.

It was a soft autumn night, the moon and stars very bright in a velvety black sky and a gentle breeze rustling in the branches of the mimosa trees. The scents of the day lingered in the still-warm air, but tonight James scarcely noticed them.

It was another scent that was in his nostrils, the remembered sweetness of Ashes of Roses more real to him now than the night-scented stocks in the small flower plot beneath the veranda.

Ashes of Roses – Lorna's favourite perfume. She had been wearing it the evening he had met her at a grand reception in Sydney hosted by some of the wealthiest businessmen in the colony and attended by the Governor himself. The fragrance had hovered around her in a soft haze, and that night, when he was unable to sleep for thinking of her, it had seemed to him that the scent was a part of her, not something she had splashed behind her ears and on her throat as part of her toilette.

Beautiful Lorna, whom he had loved so much. Staring into the darkness he saw her, too, as she had looked that long-ago evening – fair ringlets falling about a face that might have belonged to a china doll with her perfect ivory complexion and her small even features. But her eyes had been unmistakeably alive, sparkling with fun, and blue as periwinkles.

Fragile Lorna, slender and delicate in her gown of palest blue silk and lace that had come from the finest seamstress in Sydney. That gown still lay, folded in tissue, in the big oak chest in the room she and James had shared. Though he had disposed of most of her things on a bonfire the night she had died in an effort to exorcise some of his anger and grief and guilt, he had not been able to bring himself to toss that gown into the flames. It embodied too many precious memories.

From the moment he set eyes on her, James had pursued Lorna like a man possessed, knowing he would never rest until he had made her his own.

And in doing so, he thought wretchedly, he had killed her.

Lorna was a town girl, used to an endless round of socialising. She had hated the isolation of the farm, where visitors were rare and she had to spend long hours alone whilst James and his brothers were out managing the stock and the lands. James had seen the light die from her eyes day by day, and the harsh sun and wind dry her fine complexion as the solitary existence dried up her spirit.

She longed to be back in Sydney, he knew. Though he took her to Melbourne whenever he could spare the time, it wasn't the same. Sydney, for all that it had been the first landing spot for the convicts, was also where the Governor resided and it had culture and style that Melbourne lacked.

When Duncan was born, James had hoped the child would help to restore the sparkle Lorna had lost, but the birth was a long and difficult one and Lorna grew even paler and more wan. Duncan was a colicky baby who fell asleep and refused to feed whenever he was picked up, and cried fretfully whenever he was put down, and lack of sleep put huge dark circles around Lorna's blue eyes.

Just when he had begun to suspect she was losing her mind, James could never be sure. It happened so gradually. Sometimes Lorna would go silent for days on end, as if to speak at all required an effort that was beyond her; sometimes there were bouts of wild weeping when she would beg him not to go out to work on the farm and leave her alone. And sometimes – though admittedly the occasions were very rare – he would come home to find her excited as a child on Christmas Eve, high spots of colour in her cheeks, bright as a whore's rouge, hair tangled, playing some wild game with Duncan whilst they both shrieked with laughter.

James had been at a loss to know how to deal with these mood swings. Perhaps, he thought, it was normal female behaviour. He had no sisters to compare her with and the women in his world were few. Certainly Regan, his mother, had never behaved so. In the whole of his life he had only seen her cry on a handful of occasions, and that was generally as a result of losing her temper. But Regan was spirited and a little wild. She had, after all, run away with Rolf, his father, when she had been pregnant with James. The two women could scarcely have been more different.

Bemused and anxious, James had tried not to think about what was happening to Lorna. There was, after all, nothing he could do about it. Briefly he toyed with the idea of asking his great-uncle, Alistair Mackenzie, if there was a job for him in Sydney, where Alistair had business interests, including a fleet of three clippers, but dismissed it. He was a farmer, his place was here at Dunrae, which would one day be Duncan's heritage. And as his wife and Duncan's mother, Lorna's place was here too. She would get used to it in time. She would have to!

Except that she never did.

One night when the madness took her, Lorna had run weeping from the house. At first James had decided to let her be. She couldn't go far, and she would come back when she calmed down. But a storm had come, one of the sudden violent downpours that erupted from time to time, and he had begun to grow anxious. He had gone out to look for her, and when he was unable to find her in any of her usual haunts he had run back to the house, soaked to the skin, to ask Philip and Cal to come and help him.

It was almost two hours before they found her, bogged down in the mud banks beside the swirling river. Afterwards, it had occurred to James to wonder if she had intended to take her own life but lacked the courage. Whatever, the water had risen above the top of her boots and her thin gown was soaked through. Her golden ringlets dripped rain water to mingle with the tears on her cheeks. The only words she would speak were: 'I want to go home.'

'I'm taking you home, Lorna,' James had said, scooping her up into his arms. But she began to beat at him with her fists.

'No, *home*! I want to go *home*! she wept, and he realised what she meant. She wanted to go back to Sydney.

Despair filled him.

'Well you can't,' he said brusquely. 'Not tonight, anyway.'

He carried her into the house and stripped off her sodden clothing whilst Philip filled a bath with hot water from the copper. She stood, not helping him but not resisting either, those eyes that had once sparkled now dead and staring. He put her into the bath, not daring to leave her for a single moment, and when at last she stopped shivering he lifted her out, towelled her dry, slid a clean nightgown over her unprotesting body and put her to bed.

He slept little that night. There was nothing for it, he would have to take her back to Sydney. Keeping her here at Dunrae when she was so unhappy was little short of cruelty. Tomorrow he would contact Alistair Mackenzie and ask him to set things in motion.

It was not to be. Lorna contracted rheumatic fever as a result of her soaking. Too late she found the will to live; her heart, never strong, was unable to take the strain and she died a week later.

James was totally distraught. Not only had he lost his beloved wife, but he blamed himself for her death. It was he who had brought her to this isolated place, it was he who had failed to listen when she told him how unhappy she was. And it was he who had let her run out of the house that fateful night of the storm and not gone after her until it was too late. If only he had searched for her sooner! If only he had taken her back to Sydney. If only . . . if only . . .

For months he tormented himself, throwing himself into his work to ease his grief. And he had promised a God he scarcely believed in, and himself, that never again would he give his heart to any woman, never take on responsibility for another's happiness, for which he was so clearly unfitted, never lay himself open to such loss and terrible guilt.

But at least he still had his son. James worshipped the little boy, lavishing on him all the love that he was no longer able to offer Lorna.

Now, sitting on the dark veranda sipping his whisky, James knew a decision must be made. He hated the thought of bringing a woman into the house to care for Duncan. It seemed to him that by doing so he was somehow usurping Lorna's ghost. And he worried, too, that a bond might form between the two of them that would come between him and Duncan. This woman, whoever she might be, would be the one to put the little boy to bed and cook his meals, clean the dirt from his scraped knees and comfort him when he was sick. Duncan would come to look upon her as a mother figure, and the very idea of it caused revolt in James's heart.

But by the same token they couldn't go on as they were. Philip was right, Duncan was too much for Martha. It wasn't fair on her to expect her to take responsibility for the growing boy when the three brothers were away. It wasn't even fair

16

on Philip and Cal to expect them to share his responsibility. Duncan was his son, and he should provide proper care for him. Paid help, someone who was always there, a steadying influence. It was the only real answer.

He had failed Lorna. He must not fail Duncan too.

James tossed back the remainder of the whisky in one healthy gulp.

There was nothing for it. Tomorrow he would set out for Melbourne and see about finding a housekeeper and nanny.

Two

The unmade streets of Melbourne were alive with noise and bustle. Two-wheeled gigs and sulkies wove their way between bullock teams drawing wagons piled high with wool, meat and hides which threw up a cloud of thick choking dust as they passed. The footpaths were no more than a layer of gravel punctuated by the stumps of trees that had been felled in order to build the roads, but they thronged with people, some prosperous-looking, some sun-bronzed but clad only in dirty rags. A good many had the look of the East about them, and indeed that was where they hailed from. They were the Chinese immigrants who had flocked to Victoria when the news that gold had been discovered there spread like wildfire around the world.

As he passed the old red gum 'Separation Tree', so named to commemorate the separation of the colony three years earlier, James slowed Tarquin to a walk. There was too much traffic to canter or even trot safely and in any case he sensed that the great black horse was as tired and thirsty as he was.

Well, they would both find rest and refreshment soon enough now. The Imperial Hotel in Collins Street was the best establishment in town; it would provide a bed with clean sheets, a tub of hot water and a good hot meal for him, and nearby there was stabling and a trough of fresh water for Tarquin. James always stayed there when he was in Melbourne, though it held too many memories of the times he had brought Lorna to town, too many ghosts, for him to be truly comfortable.

It was late afternoon by the time James had stabled Tarquin, booked in, washed off the dust of the better part of three days' travel, and changed into clean shirt and breeches. He checked his pocket watch, wondering if any of the Ladies Committee would still be at the Women's Refuge where he intended to begin his search for a suitable housekeeper, nanny and governess for Duncan. If they were and he could sort the problem out tonight, so much the better. He and the successful candidate, whoever she may be, would be able to make an early start in the morning for the long journey back to Dunrae.

It was worth a shot, he decided. He had nothing else to do in the hours before supper and bed.

The Women's Refuge was in O'Donnell Street. It had been set up by the town dignitaries to put a roof over the heads of destitute women who had nowhere else to go. There were enough of them, God alone knew, widows in desperate poverty and women who had been deserted when their menfolk had been consumed by gold fever and rushed off to the diggings. One of them, surely, would be only too glad to take up his offer of employment at Dunrae.

He started out, this time on foot. O'Donnell Street wasn't far, as he remembered it. Nothing was yet, though judging by the number of new buildings that were being erected, Melbourne would soon grow from the small township it now was.

He found the Women's Refuge easily enough – a couple of shanty-type buildings which had been vacated by a trading company when they had moved to a new purpose-built store. The door stood ajar, to let some air in during the heat of the day, he imagined. He rapped on the peeling woodwork and pushed it open.

The room inside had been set out as an office of sorts with a table, two or three straight-backed chairs and an old oak bureau. A woman was seated at it, poring over a meticulously kept accounts book. She turned a little impatiently and James guessed she had been midway through totting up a column of figures when he had interrupted her.

'Yes?' Her voice was brusque; it matched her appearance, all tightly-corseted propriety. Iron-grey hair was swept up from a jowly face in which small eyes and tight mouth looked almost lost, and on the end of her pinched nose she wore pince-nez which she removed now with a plump white hand. 'What do you want?'

'Are you in charge here?' James asked by way of reply. He was already feeling sympathy for the unfortunate destitutes who had to answer to such a dragon.

'I am.' She didn't add that she was merely one of a rota of volunteers, stalwarts of the church, who took turns at supervising the refuge. 'I am Mrs Alice Munroe. Who are you?'

'James Hannay.' He saw her little eyes narrow a fraction more and knew she had recognised the name. A subtle change in her attitude towards him confirmed it. James suspected Mrs Alice Munroe had little time for men as a species and less for the ones she considered to be beneath her. But the name of Hannay was known and respected throughout Victoria and New South Wales. She would not be averse to a little social climbing, given the chance.

'I'm pleased to meet you, Mr Hannay,' she said now. 'In what way can I be of assistance to you?'

'I am looking for a housekeeper,' James said directly. 'Someone who can also help to look after my six-year-old son. I wondered if you had anyone staying here who might fill the position.'

Alice Munroe raised her eyebrows and her whole pudgy face assumed an expression midway between disapproval and disbelief.

'I don't know, Mr Hannay, that any of our residents would be suitable.'

James frowned. 'Why not?'

'Do I have to spell it out for you?' Alice Munroe folded

her hands in front of her ample waist. 'The women we have here are destitutes – poor immigrants at best, former convicts, for all I know, at worst. Many are no better than they should be. I, personally, have had to show the door to more than one who has abused our hospitality by using the refuge to ply her trade – and I'm sure you will know what I mean by that.' Her lips pursed in an expression of righteous disgust and her chins wobbled in sympathy.

'Perhaps they have no other way of earning a crust,' James suggested shortly.

Alice Munroe sniffed loudly. 'No decent woman would ever sell her body,' she said with dismissive certainty. 'I know I would rather die of starvation than defile myself so.'

Had James not been so angered by her pompous and judgemental attitude he knew he might have seen the amusing side of this statement.

In the first place, from the size of her, Alice Munroe had no idea what it was to go hungry; in the second he could not imagine there was a man alive who would pay for her favours, no matter how desperate he might be.

'I find it hard to believe, Mr Hannay, that you would want such a woman under your roof, much less entrust her with the care of your child,' she went on censoriously. 'But if you will leave your details with me I will make enquiries amongst the respectable families of my acquaintance to see if I can find a willing girl more suited to your requirements.'

'I haven't the time for that,' James said. 'I was hoping to start back for Dunrae first thing in the morning. Surely there must be one amongst the refugees who would be prepared to come with me?'

'Prepared to come with you, I'm sure!' Alice Munroe laughed shortly. 'Prepared to let you keep her, yes. But prepared to do an honest day's work – I doubt it.'

James's patience was at an end. 'It seems to me you have a very low opinion of the women you are supposed to be helping,' he said abruptly. 'I would have thought you would be only too happy to give one of your charges the chance of a better life. The authorities would be glad, surely, to know that they have one less mouth to feed, and wouldn't be best pleased to know that you are doing your best to talk me out of it.'

'I'm only thinking of your good – and the good of your child,' Alice Munroe said, bristling. 'I am certainly not obstructing you. I simply don't think any of them are suitable.'

'Let me be the judge of that. Can I not at least interview some of them?' James asked impatiently.

'Very well. If you insist. I'll call some of them down. If you'll just wait here . . .' Alice Munroe moved stiffly to the doorway, clearly deeply affronted.

What a woman! James thought when he was left alone in the office. No doubt Alice Munroe called herself a Christian, but he suspected that her only motive in helping out at the refuge was to be seen as an upright citizen. No doubt she also gained a good deal of satisfaction from feeling superior to the poor unfortunate women she was so ready to malign. James knew his own grandmother had been forced to sell herself in order to provide a home for Rolf, his father, and on her behalf and that of all the others like her he resented Alice Munroe's sanctimonious attitude.

More than ever he hoped one of the women would be suitable for employment at Dunrae. Not simply because he needed someone to look after Duncan, but because he desperately wished to prove the ghastly woman wrong.

An hour later, however, James was forced to admit that Alice Munroe's judgement, harsh though it might be, was not entirely at fault. Of the women she had brought down from the upper rooms not one had met James's expectations or requirements. One had been older than Martha, a wizened hag who was nothing but skin and bone with more hair on her chin than her head. Another had coughed throughout the interview, a harsh tearing sound that wracked her body – James thought it likely she was suffering from consumption. The next had been unable to utter a single sentence without a peppering of choice swear words which would not have disgraced a gathering of the roughest convicts, whilst a fourth was brassy bold, with a painted face and a gown that was barely decent. There was no way he would have had any of them under his roof, let alone entrusted his son to their care.

'Well?' Alice Munroe demanded as he dismissed the last of them. 'Which one will you take?'

There was a note of spiteful triumph in her voice and it crossed James's mind to wonder if she had deliberately chosen the most disreputable of the inmates in order to prove her point.

'Is there no one else?' he asked in despair.

'Plenty.' Alice Munroe folded her plump hands together with a tight-lipped smile. 'They are all of the same ilk, however. You may as well make your selection from the ones you've seen already.'

James stood up, unwilling to let her emerge the victor, yet having no option.

'I'll sleep on it, Mrs Munroe,' he said grimly. 'Maybe when I come back tomorrow you'll have thought of someone more suited to the position.'

He crossed to the door, burning with frustration and wanting only to get out of the airless room before he said something he would regret to the infuriating woman.

Outside it was growing dark. James strode along the badly made footpath, barely noticing where he was going, the irritation simmering under his skin like heat rash. What now? He'd wasted a precious hour and he was no nearer to finding a housekeeper and nanny. Nor would he be if he returned to the Refuge tomorrow, he was sure, if Alice Munroe had anything to do with it. He'd made an enemy of her and no mistake – though he suspected that Mrs Munroe considered any member of his sex an enemy. Heaven alone knew what her poor husband had to put up with – if she still had one. Doubtless she'd seen the poor fellow into his grave long since!

Well, there was nothing for it, he supposed, but to place some notices advertising the position in some of the stores and hope it was not too long before the applicants began to contact him. It would be pointless to return to Dunrae before he'd had the chance to interview them. But the thought of the delay made him impatient and worsened his already black mood. There was so much that needed his attention on the farm and he dreaded to think of the mischief Duncan would get up to in his absence.

As he approached what looked like a sly grog shop James saw an unruly gaggle of men milling about. Dirty, ragged and unshaven, they were also clearly drunk. A group of goldminers who had struck lucky and come into town to spend their earnings, James guessed. And making a thorough job of it, too. Their noisy whoops carried clearly on the evening air.

James stepped into the road ready to make a detour round them. Then as he drew nearer he realised the cause of their noisy excitement. In the midst of the group, and hidden from his view until now by their bulky bodies, was a young woman.

Disgust twisted in his gut. One thing for a woman of easy virtue to ply her trade in private, quite another to cavort in the street with this bunch of drunken animals, allowing them to paw her. Then, at almost the same instant as this thought crossed his mind, he realised he was mistaken. The girl wasn't cavorting willingly, she was screaming and hitting out at the men who tore at her clothing, laughing and whooping in delight as they did so.

Just as he drew level her flailing fingers caught one of the men in the eye. The man staggered back, swearing, his hands covering his face, and she broke free, plunging wildly through the gang of men and cannoning into James. He put out a hand to steady both himself and the girl and she pushed him away with a desperate thrust, no doubt thinking he was yet another of her tormentors. Then she ran blindly into the street, crossing it at an angle. A gig was approaching at a fast canter. James realised that in her panic she was quite unaware of it. He shouted a warning and raced after her. There was no way the driver of the gig would be able to stop his horses in time, and the girl was right in their path. James did the only thing he could think of to save her from the pounding hooves and spinning wheels. He dived at her, low and fast, yanking her towards him with such force that they both fell, rolling together in a heap at the side of the street. He heard the thunder of hooves and thought for a moment it was the end for both of them. Then the carriage wheels passed by, inches from his head, and came to a jolting halt.

The driver yelled out, his words punctuated by angry oaths. 'What do you think you are doing?'

James ignored him, concerned only for the young woman who lay half beneath him. She was gasping painfully, the breath knocked out of her body by the crashing fall, but already she was trying to fight him off once more, her face a mask of terror.

James caught her wrist, warding off her blows. 'Don't fight me. I'll not harm you. Don't fight me, I say!'

Something in his voice must have got through to her for suddenly she went limp, collapsing onto the rough road.

'It's all right,' James said reassuringly. He glanced over his shoulder. The group of men were dispersing now, sobered by the near disaster that had been of their making, slinking off in twos and threes. 'They'll not bother you again.'

He got up and helped the girl to her feet. She was painfully thin and her cheap calico gown had obviously seen better days, but he was struck immediately by the sweetness of her face, framed with a cloud of dark curling hair, and the clear blue of her eyes. She raised a trembling hand to brush that mane of hair away from her face, leaving a dirt streak down her tear-stained cheek, and he noticed that her arm was badly grazed and bleeding.

'You're hurt,' he said roughly.

She glanced down at her arm as if she had not realised before. Then she gave a small shake of her head.

'It's nothing.'

'It needs attending to.' Blood was trickling down to her elbow, dripping onto her dust-stained skirts. 'Do you live nearby? I'll see you home.'

'No – no – you've done quite enough already.' She swallowed hard. 'You saved my life.'

'I'll not leave you here,' James said decisively. 'There may well be other gangs of ruffians on the razzle. It's not safe for a lady to be out in these streets alone. Where are your menfolk?'

Her chin came up. 'I have none.' There was defiance in her tone, though her voice was still shaky. 'I can take care of myself.'

'So I saw,' he said wryly. 'No more argument now. I'm seeing you safely home or I'll not rest easy in my bed. Where do you live?'

For some reason she seemed unwilling to answer.

'Is it far?' he pressed her.

'Not far. I'll be fine on my own, truly.'

'I thought I said no more argument.' He pulled a clean kerchief from his pocket and offered it to her. 'Wrap this around your arm. It will help to stem the bleeding.'

The girl looked at him uncertainly for a moment, then she took the kerchief and obediently wound it around her arm.

'Thank you. You are very kind.'

'Not at all. I just don't like to see a lady in distress.' Even as he said it James recognised the irony of the words and flinched inwardly. Lorna, his own wife, had been in distress, and he had chosen to ignore it. 'So tell me where you live,' he said, the painful memories making his voice rough.

Again the hesitation, the unmistakable reluctance. What

was it with her? Was she still afraid of him? Afraid, perhaps, that if he accompanied her home he might force his way into her house and have his way with her? James felt the beginnings of the impatience that flared so easily in him these days. Then, all of a rush, she said: 'The Women's Refuge. But I don't want to go back there like this. Not until the women of the Ladies Committee have gone home. They're tyrants; they'll say I brought it on myself . . .' She broke off, her lip trembling.

James stared at her in amazement. It was almost beyond belief that this girl shared accommodation with the hags and harlots who had been paraded for his inspection. Thin she might be, poorly dressed she might be, but she was a different kettle of fish entirely. Clearly it was shame that had made her unwilling to tell him where she lived and he could scarcely blame her for that – nor for her reluctance to face the indomitable Alice Munroe and admit what had happened to her. He could well imagine the sanctimonious lecture, the lack of sympathy, the humiliation Alice would delight in heaping upon this poor unfortunate girl.

He looked at her small face, tear-stained but determined, at the blood already soaking through his kerchief bound around her arm, and made up his mind.

'There's nothing for it, then,' he said. 'I'm staying at the Imperial Hotel in Collins Street. You'd better come back there with me.'

Again he saw the look of horror in those blue eyes.

'Oh no, I couldn't do that!'

'I'm not going to seduce you,' he said impatiently. 'Or harm you in any way. Come on now. What choice do you have?'

She stared him out. 'Just as long as you know I'm not . . . *that* kind of woman.'

'I never for one moment thought you were,' he said, taking hold of her good arm. 'Come on now. We've wasted enough time arguing. Let's get that arm of yours attended to before it turns septic.'

As if all the fight had gone out of her suddenly the girl allowed him to lead her along the street.

Back at the hotel, Annie Hargreaves behind the reception desk gave James a straight look of surprise and disapproval when he walked up the steps and into the lobby with the girl.

'Mr Hannay . . .'

He knew at once that she had jumped to the wrong conclusion. What she wanted to say, but dared not to a client of his standing, was that the Imperial was a respectable hotel and the owner did not approve of his rooms being used for immoral purposes.

James experienced another stab of the all-too-familiar irritation. Surely she could see this girl was no common prostitute? Surely she knew him better than to think he would want to cavort with one?

'This young lady has been injured in a street accident,' he said brusquely. 'Kindly have warm water and bandages sent up to my room, and a glass of brandy too.'

'Oh, certainly, Mr Hannay.' Annie looked relieved and a little shamefaced too. 'What happened?'

'Never mind what happened. Just do as I say.' His hand under her good elbow, James led the young woman up the stairs.

The room that had been allocated to him was large and comfortably furnished. Besides the bed, a chest and a wash stand with its gaily coloured china jug and basin there was a small writing bureau with paper, quill and ink and two chairs, one upright, one easy. James led the girl to the easy chair.

'Sit down. You look as though you need to.'

She was, indeed, very pale. The streak of dirt and another of blood on her cheek stood out garishly. She sank into the chair gratefully and it crossed his mind to wonder if it was hunger as well as shock and fright that was making her faint.

Certainly, thin as she was, she looked to possess no reserves of strength. Perhaps he should offer her a good square meal. But first things first. Her injured arm needed attending to.

The jug of hot water, the bandages and brandy he had asked for arrived in the room almost as soon as they did, a measure of the respect in which the hotel management held James.

'Is there anything else, Mr Hannay?' the young porter who brought them enquired solicitously.

'Thank you, no. You can go.' James placed the glass of brandy in the girl's shaking hands. 'Sip this,' he told her. 'It will make you feel better and ease the pain when I clean your wounds too.'

She sipped obediently, coughing a little as the strong liquor trickled down her throat. Clearly she was not used to drinking alcohol, he thought. Another indication that he was right in his assessment of her. She was no loose woman.

He poured the hot water into the china basin and gently unwound the kerchief from around her injured arm. Then he took a washcloth, dipping it in the water and beginning to cleanse the dust, gravel and blood from the wound.

She winced as he did so and took another quick sip of the brandy.

'I'm sorry if I'm hurting you,' he said. 'But I must get the dirt out.'

'Sure, I know. Go on please. Don't take any notice of me.'

For the first time he noticed that there was an attractive lilt to her voice. Irish, he thought.

'You seem very practised at this sort of thing,' she went on with a small strained laugh, gritting her teeth against the burning pain.

'Oh, I am,' he assured her. 'I have a little boy of six years old. He's always falling over and grazing his knees.'

'Ah, I knew it!' She smiled in spite of herself. Glancing up from his task he saw the way her thin face lit up and the merest hint of a sparkle in those blue eyes.

29

'But does his mother not tend him when he hurts himself?'

'His mother is dead,' James said shortly.

As always, voicing the words was painful for him but they also served to remind him of the mission that had brought him to Melbourne. All that had happened in the last hour had driven it from his mind. Now, suddenly, it occurred to him that perhaps he had happened upon the solution to his problem.

By her own admission this girl had no menfolk, which might very well mean she was alone in the world. She lived at the Women's Refuge, the very place he had gone to seek a housekeeper and nanny for Duncan. But she was in quite a different class to the women he had seen there. Again it occurred to him that Alice Munroe had chosen the least likely candidates to present to him out of deliberate spite. 'All of the same ilk,' she had said. But this girl certainly was not. Could it be that she was the very person he was looking for? Had fate arranged it so that their paths crossed? Not that James believed in fate, any more than he believed in God. But that wasn't going to stop him at least mentioning it to the girl.

'You are not in the market for employment, I suppose?' he said as he tied the bandage around her hurt arm. Her forehead wrinkled in a small frown and he hurried on: 'I came to Melbourne seeking someone to live in on my farm. The duties would be looking after myself and my two brothers, and taking care of my son when I am not there to do it myself. We would expect the person we employ to do a certain amount of cooking and other domestic chores, though the bulk of the cleaning and washing is down by the convict women.'

The girl's blue eyes were sharp suddenly in her pale face. 'Your farm, you say. Where is that?'

'Almost three days' ride from here.' He hesitated, remembering how Lorna had hated being so far from civilisation. 'It's very isolated, I'm afraid. Quite cut off, for the most part,

30

from the outside world. Whoever takes the position will have to be prepared for that. We have few visitors and it can be a lonely life for someone not used to it.'

Her hand went to her injured arm, cradling it protectively, and her eyes fell from his for a moment. Then she looked up at him again.

'Are you by any chance offering *me* the position?'

He nodded, surprised by the swiftness with which he had reached the decision. 'I suppose I am.'

'But you don't know me,' she said. 'You would trust your child to the care of a stranger?'

He raised an eyebrow. 'Put like that, I suppose it might seem unusual to you. But I like to think that I am a good judge of character. I have to rely on my instincts, given the life I lead. My impression of you is that you are determined and respectable, for all the circumstances I found you in. I am in a hurry to fill the position and get home again. And I think that you would suit our needs admirably.'

'Don't you even want to know if I can cook?' she asked with what might have been a mischievous twinkle.

'I'm sure your skills will be good enough for us,' James said easily. 'We are not fussy eaters, and what you don't know you'll learn soon enough. Well, what do you say?'

The girl hesitated for a moment. James could see a multitude of unreadable thoughts chasing one another around behind those blue eyes. 'Put in by a smutty finger', he had once heard someone say, though he had never before seen anyone whose eyes fitted the description so perfectly. He pushed the thought away.

'You need time to think about it, perhaps,' he said. 'You've had a shock and a fright and this is all too sudden . . .'

'I'll take the position,' she interrupted him.

'You will?' He felt his heart leap with unspeakable relief – and something else. Something he could not put a name to, and was unwilling to try. 'Well, in that case I dare say it is time to introduce myself. I should have done so before now. I am James Hannay.'

She nodded, smiling faintly. 'Mr Hannay, yes. I heard them call you that downstairs.'

'And you are?'

'My name is Tara . . .' She hesitated again, bowing her head for a second. Then her eyes came up to meet his and she said in a firm lilting tone: 'Reilly. My name is Tara Reilly.'

Three

A s the Cobb coach bowled along the dusty street beside the Yarra river, Tara settled herself back against the plush upholstery, preparing for the first stage of what she knew was going to be a long journey.

Even now she could scarcely believe the turn events had taken but at least she was leaving Melbourne behind with the chance of a fresh start far from the goldfields ahead of her. Tara slipped her rosary out of her reticule, unnoticed by the other passengers, gripped it tightly between her hands in the folds of her skirt and recited a silent Hail Mary to thank the Holy Mother for answering her prayers.

It was the first time since she had accepted James's offer of a home and employment that she had had a moment to herself to do so, the first chance she had had to sit quietly and reflect on what had happened. From the time she had agreed to go to Dunrae, every moment had been filled, for James was not a man to waste time once a decision had been made.

'We may as well collect your belongings from the Refuge right away,' he had said that first evening. 'There's no need for you to spend another night under their roof. I'll arrange a room for you here at the Imperial Hotel and tomorrow I'll book you a place on the next Cobb coach out of town.'

'I don't have very many things,' she had said hesitantly. 'Nothing worth going back to that place for. I always carry the things I value with me. If I left them there they would only be stolen.'

'Yes, I can imagine.' He had pulled a wry face, remembering the unsavoury characters Alice Munroe had introduced him to. 'But your clothes . . . you'll want to collect them, surely?'

Hot colour flooded her cheeks. She was ashamed to admit she had nothing but what she stood up in.

James saw her flush and assumed it was the quality and condition of her gowns that was causing her embarrassment. Well, he couldn't have a nanny for his son who wore nothing but rags.

'Perhaps it would be best if we saw a seamstress and arranged a new wardrobe for you,' he said briskly. 'Once you get to Dunrae there will be precious little opportunity for shopping for anything but the most basic items. We'll attend to it first thing in the morning. If you are quite sure there is nothing you want from the Refuge.'

'Nothing. It's all here,' Tara said firmly, patting her worn reticule and running a mental inventory of its contents. Her rosary, her mother's wedding band, and a locket which had been passed down through the family and which contained a lock of her mother's hair and a tiny likeness of Mary that had been painted by a travelling artist long ago when she had been young. Sometimes Tara had wondered if perhaps the artist had been the father she had never known and of whom her mother would never speak. Lovely as she had been as a girl, there was something more to the little portrait than a simple likeness. Tara couldn't help feeling it had been painted with love. But perhaps she was just a fanciful romantic to think so . . . Whatever, the likeness was one of her most treasured possessions, a last link with her beloved mother and perhaps with her father too if she was right in her suspicions. Lastly, in the deepest corner of her reticule, lay her own wedding ring.

'I think, then, before we embark on any other plans, we should eat,' James said. 'The food here at the Imperial is first class and I, for one, am hungry.' He did not add that Tara looked in desperate need of a good square meal, but indeed she was.

As they entered the dining room the aroma of cooking meat made her empty stomach rumble and though that night she had been unable to do justice to the fine meal that was laid out before them she had certainly made up for it in the two days that had followed. Steaks, seafood, succulent roast lamb, pork with wonderful crispy crackling, tasty, flavourful vegetables and mountainous bowls of fresh fruit – Tara had scarcely realised such wonderful food existed, much less feasted on it. To begin with the surfeit had made her stomach ache, but already she was getting a taste for it.

And not only the food! After the hardships she had endured, the other luxuries the Imperial Hotel had to offer seemed like heaven on earth to Tara.

Oh, the bliss of soaking in a tub of hot water in the privacy of her room! Oh, the comfort of a soft mattress and clean lavender-scented sheets! For all the thoughts whirling around in her head, for all the fears, the guilt for the past and the anxiety for the future, Tara had fallen asleep the moment her head nestled into the deep feather pillow and slept as she had not slept for as long as she could remember.

The following day James had taken Tara to visit a dress-maker's shop in Bourke Street, where he ordered several new gowns for her.

'Miss Reilly is to leave on the Cobb coach the day after tomorrow,' he informed the little woman. 'We shall want at least one of the outfits ready by then. The rest can follow by bullocky if necessary. Can you manage that?'

The dressmaker nodded. 'Certainly, Mr Hannay. I'll set my girls to work on it right away. Which one would you like it to be?'

'Miss Reilly?' James looked at her. 'The choice is yours.'

'Oh, I don't know!' Tara's head was spinning. Never, in all her life, had she owned clothes such as these, nor expected to. For besides the two or three calicos, suitable for the working day, James had also insisted on ordering her a promenade gown in pink and black and a carriage dress of deep blue silk with an overskirt and yoke of plaid taffeta.

'Surely if your farm is so isolated I won't need such finery?' she had protested, for much as she coveted the gowns she could not help feeling guilty about the amount of money he must be spending on her. But James had merely laughed.

'We do entertain visitors on occasion, Miss Reilly,' he had told her. 'When we do, I'm sure you would like something pretty to wear.'

Still she hesitated, spoilt for choice, and he made the choice for her.

'The carriage dress, I think. Kindly have it delivered to the Imperial Hotel the moment it is finished. Now, Miss Reilly will also need a good warm cloak and bonnet. Winter is only just around the corner. And we'll take a straw, too, for what warm days are still left to us. The sun can be merciless out in the country.'

And so it had gone on. Tara could not imagine why he was spoiling her so – she had certainly done nothing to deserve it! But she could not find it in her to complain.

Anxious though he was to get back to Dunrae, James had refused to leave Tara alone in Melbourne. He would set out, he told her, when he had seen her onto the Cobb coach. From then on the coachman would be held responsible for ensuring her safety whilst he, James, would ride on ahead, making more speed than the coach, to prepare for her arrival at Dunrae. He would meet her when she disembarked at the nearest township, he told her, and take her by gig the rest of the way.

Tara settled back now, watching the outskirts of Melbourne roll past the windows of the coach and silently counting the beads of her rosary. By the time she had finished they had left the town and its bustle behind. The coach was bowling along a road that was little more than a dirt track, all ruts and hillocks, and Tara thought that the swaying motion was more nauseating even than the rolling of the ship that had brought her to Australia.

The memory was sharp in her suddenly, so that she could almost smell the cuddy of the *Gazelle*, the odours of rancid food mingled with the stench of unwashed bodies, and taste the salt in the air. She swallowed hard at the knot of tears that suddenly constricted her throat. Dear God, surely she wasn't going to cry now! She had thought she had no more tears to shed.

But with the tastes and smells of the ship had come back all the love and hope with which she and Patrick had set out on that voyage – yes, and all the misgivings she had felt too. And how well justified those misgivings had turned out to be!

Tara glanced at her fellow passengers in the coach, hoping they had not noticed her sudden lack of composure. It seemed they had not. The burly, well-to-do-looking gentleman, silver watch chain stretched across his full, waistcoated chest, was nodding drowsily; the farmer, boots caked with dust, stared out of the window. And the only other woman, fair, thin and middle-aged, had her hand pressed against her mouth as she attempted to prevent her stomach rebelling against the swaying of the coach.

Don't think of the past, Tara told herself. *Think of the future*.

James Hannay had given her hope for that. He had rescued her just when her fortunes had been at their lowest ebb and provided her with a means of escape.

A farm far away from civilisation. A family to look after, a child to care for, and James himself, kind, prosperous, straightforward – and as ruggedly good-looking a man as one could wish to meet. No doubt, given that he was a widower, half the women in the district would fancy their chances with him. Tara might have done so herself if she had not had enough of men to last her a lifetime – and a husband of her own already, in name at least. James would be a good employer and more than fair, she was certain. Why, already his generosity had amazed her. Perhaps, working for him, she would at last be able to find some peace and happiness. Yet for all the good omens, somehow Tara doubted it. Too much had happened, too many ghosts inhabited her world. The best she could hope for was the safety which isolation could give her and the chance to work hard enough to keep her thoughts occupied by day and send her to bed tired enough to sleep at night.

And how long would it last? How long would it be before she was thrown out into the harsh world once more to fend for herself? The guilt that she could never escape for long wracked Tara. James had asked her nothing about herself. He had followed the unwritten laws of this wild and often lawless country – curiosity about another was frowned upon. A person's history, good or bad, was their own business and if they chose not to tell it, then no one asked.

But if he knew the truth about her, would he want her to live under his roof and care for his child? If he knew why she was alone, frightened and destitute in Melbourne, would he have given her so much as a second glance, let alone offered her a position of such responsibility?

No, he would not, Tara thought. Most definitely he would not. And the knowledge was just an added weight around her heart. As the coach bowled along through the rich green pastureland, Tara let her thoughts slip back to all that had happened since she had arrived in Australia.

'There it is, Tara, me darling! The new country, our new home!'

Patrick's voice rose with excitement as at last – at last! – land hove into view, rising out of the endless ocean.

He slipped his arm about her waist and they stood together at the rail, watching the coastline take shape. After the long months at sea, Tara thought it was the most welcome sight on which she had ever feasted her eyes.

The water of Melbourne harbour sparkled clear and blue beneath an even bluer sky, clippers and smaller ships rode at anchor and on the wharf people of every nationality, it seemed to Tara, milled about.

'Oh, Patrick!' she whispered. 'Patrick, we've arrived! Dear God, there were times when I thought we never would!'

He laughed aloud with delight. Never, for one moment, had he entertained such doubts, she knew. Patrick was the eternal optimist, and now his eyes were alight as he thought of the fortune he was so certain he would find in this rich earth.

'It won't be long now, sweetheart, before you have all the things your heart desires, all you deserve. Fine clothes, jewels, a carriage . . . Oh, Tara, we are going to be rich beyond our wildest dreams!'

A small cloud passed overhead, casting its shadow on Tara's pleasure in his delight. He had promised all those things to Mary, too, and she had not lived to see them. Was it fools' gold they were chasing? No, she mustn't think that for even a moment. But there would be hard times ahead of them before they reached the crock at the end of the rainbow whatever Patrick might think, she felt sure. And he would need her wholehearted support.

Tara rested her head against his shoulder and smiled up at his eager face. Perhaps he would make a fortune for them, and perhaps he wouldn't. It scarcely mattered one way or the other. They had each other and they had their love. That was the only thing of any importance.

And at least now their journey was at an end. Or so Tara foolishly thought that bright shiny day as she walked unsteadily down the gangplank and stepped for the first time onto Australian soil. But oh, how wrong she had been! About that . . . About everything.

'Patrick, I don't think I can go on much longer.'

The sun beat down relentlessly on the narrow track along which they were struggling. Patrick pushed a handcart into which their few belongings were packed, Tara walked alongside. But her legs didn't seem to work properly any more, the muscles, weak and wasted from the months of incarceration on board ship, ached mercilessly, and her feet were covered in bleeding blisters. The sun bonnet she had tied over her head kept some of the burning heat off her face, but all the same, her skin was scorched high on her cheeks, and her lips were cracked and swollen. They had been on the road for almost a week and it felt like a lifetime.

'It can't be much further.' Patrick pulled the handcart into the side of the track as a wagon approached, laden with provisions and drawn by a team of sweating horses. Lucky the people who could afford to travel in such luxury! Dirt thrown up by the flying hooves spattered the pair of them as it passed by and the cloud of choking dust made Tara cough. 'Look! See over there? Those tents and shacks? That must be a miners' camp!'

Tara's heart sank a little more. It was good to see signs of a settlement, yes, but oh, how her aching body cried out for a proper bed, good washing facilities and a good square meal instead of the salt pork they had purchased in Melbourne and the endless smoky beans boiled up in a billy can over a campfire! But this was what she must get used to, she supposed. And really she had no one to blame but herself. Patrick had suggested she should stay in Melbourne whilst he went off to the diggings, as most of the goldminers' womenfolk seemed to do. But Tara had not been able to bear the thought of saying goodbye to him and remaining alone in a bustling town where she knew not a single living soul.

There was something else, too, an even more important reason why she wanted to be with Patrick. Tara had begun to suspect that she was with child. If that were so, then having him by her side meant far more to her than any hardships she might have to face in the goldfields.

An ache niggled now, low in her stomach, just one of many aches and pains yet somehow different to anything she had experienced before and all the more significant because of it. Tara felt a moment's trepidation. She longed for children, of course. She and Patrick had often talked of the day when they would be a proper family. But here, without so much as a roof over their heads, in this wild country? Now, when they scarcely had two beans to rub together? Later, yes, when Patrick had found gold and they had something to offer a child, there was nothing she would rather have than a child of her own. But for the present . . .

Well, at least she had made it to dry land before falling pregnant, Tara comforted herself. One of her secret fears when they had set out was that she might be with child and have to give birth on the high seas. At least that had not happened and for that she was eternally grateful. One poor girl on board the *Gazelle* had been taken to bed as they had tossed wildly in the gales that had beset them around the Cape. The baby had survived only a few hours and word had spread that the mother might never walk again.

'Come on, m'vourneen, you can do it!' Patrick, young, strong and fired-up with anticipation of the moment when he would run earth through his hands and see gold gleaming there, squeezed Tara's arm encouragingly, gripped the handles of the rough cart and set off again.

Wearily Tara trudged after him, gritting her teeth against her bodily aches and pains and the excruciating throbbing of her blistered and bleeding feet.

Patrick was right. There were signs of a settlement of sorts on the horizon. They had come this far; just a few more miles and they would reach their destination. Somehow she would steel herself to make it.

Tara lay beneath the rough canvas shelter desperately trying to sleep. She was bone tired and the moment they had finished their evening meal – the inevitable smoky beans – and she had washed the billy can in water from the creek she had told Patrick she was going to make an early night of it.

She had thought she would fall asleep the moment her head touched the sacking pillow but it hadn't happened. Instead her thoughts raced round and round in relentless circles as she thought over the events of the day and worried about what was to become of her, Patrick, and the baby she was now certain she was carrying.

It was more than two weeks now since they had set up camp alongside some of the other hopeful diggers on the flat lands around Ballarat, and they were no nearer to making their fortunes.

On the very first day after he had spent a guinea of their precious savings to buy a month's licence to dig, Patrick had come running back to the shelter to show her the grains of gold he had found in his pan, and her hopes had soared. But in spite of working from dawn break until the gun was fired in the evening from the Commissioner's tent to signal the end of the day's digging, his yield had been small and his share of the payout when the Government escort arrived to take the gold back to Melbourne had been paltry indeed.

'We might fare better if you could help me,' Patrick had suggested. 'It takes me so long to pan alone. If I were to build a cradle, I could shovel the washdirt in and all you would have to do is dipper in the water and rock it. Who knows, you might bring me luck! We might find some nuggets in the sieve amongst the stones!'

But of course they hadn't. Nothing but the fine dust caught in the riffles.

'It's early days,' Patrick had said, his enthusiasm undimmed. He still saw nothing but a golden future, Tara thought worriedly. Not the felled trees and violated pastureland of the once-beautiful flats, not the tragedy of clear creeks clogged now with tailings and sludge, and certainly not her exhaustion and the curious looks of the other miners she was forced to endure as she worked, a woman in a world of men.

They were a strange lot, the miners. Some were huge men, like great bears, in their cabbage-tree hats, with long bushy beards that covered every bit of their faces and joined up with their matted, uncut hair. Some were wiry monkeys, their loose blue shirts and trousers splattered and caked with clay and earth. Some were British, some Chinese, some native-born Australians or former convicts. But all had that same curious light in their eyes – the lust for gold.

When work was done for the day they gathered around the camp fire, spinning yarns or singing songs, drinking – if their earnings allowed it – and fighting. Even now, as she tried desperately to sleep, Tara could hear the scrape of a fiddle mingling with the incessant barking of the dogs – those huge, half-wild beasts that many of the miners kept to help them safeguard their meagre possessions from the thieves and vagabonds who abounded. The mournful sound of the fiddle reminded Tara of home, and as a bittersweet tide of emotion swept through her she turned over, trying to stop her ears to it.

Oh, if only they had never set out on this wild-goose chase! They had been poor and they had been hungry, but at least the air they had breathed had been soft and sweet, not filled with choking dust. At least there had been the rolling mountains and the sparkling lakes, not this flat landscape scarred with mine workings and dried out by the relentless sun. The people had been friendly and concerned for one another, not ready to loot and kill in the lustful madness that came with the elusive promise of riches. And there had been the church where she could always find peace kneeling before the statue of Our Lady, lighting a candle and whispering a heartfelt prayer. Was the Blessed Mother here with her now? It didn't feel like it. But perhaps if she said a rosary . . .

Tara turned onto her back again, feeling the ground hard and unforgiving beneath her shoulder blades, and reached for her rosary. In the darkness her fingers found the beads, numbering them as her lips moved soundlessly.

'Hail, Holy Queen, Mother of Mercy, hail . . .'

A sudden commotion made her eyes snap open. No sweet

sad fiddle now, but the roar of men's voices, all shouting one against the other in a cacophony of sound. For a moment Tara lay listening, her rosary forgotten. What in heaven's name was going on?

The baying roar rose again and Tara felt a twinge of alarm. Patrick was out there somewhere; suddenly she felt she had to find him. She thrust the blanket aside and pulled herself up, her stiff limbs protesting. Her shawl lay nearby; she wrapped it around her shoulders, for the night air felt chill on her sunburned flesh, and left the cover of the tent.

It was a bright starry night. In the distance she could see gums that had not yet been felled reaching their ghostly arms to the dark sky. She turned her back on them, making her way between the makeshift dwellings in the direction from which the commotion was coming. Embers of camp fires glowed at her feet and she picked her way carefully between them.

A great gaggle of men had gathered in a clearing. Tara made her way towards them, all the while looking round anxiously for Patrick. She could see no sign of him, nor could she make out what was happening beyond the great crush of bodies, but the roar, she recognised now, was one of encouragement. None of the gathering of men took the slightest notice of her as she stood there, craning to see between the mass of bodies, then, suddenly, she was propelled into the crush and her blood ran cold as she realised what it was that was holding their attention and exciting them to such fervour.

A bare-knuckle fight!

In the centre of the clearing two men, stripped to the waist, were pounding one another with their fists. By the light of the moon and the torches that had been staked into the ground she saw that both were covered in blood which streamed unchecked from gashes and grazes around their eyes, and their bunched knuckles too looked raw and swollen.

Tara gasped, pulling her shawl tightly around her and trying to turn away. This was not something she wanted to witness.

44

She had heard of bare-knuckle fighting, of course, but never before had she actually seen it taking place. Sickness rose in her gut and she pushed against the mass of bodies in vain. Not one was going to give way and risk losing his vantage point.

Another roar went up. Against her will Tara half turned to see what had happened. One man was staggering helplessly, his guard dropped, whilst the other rained blows on his defenceless face. As Tara watched, too horror-stricken to tear her eyes away, he went down, very slowly, sinking to his knees like a great sack of grain. She pressed her hand to her mouth, sickened by the raw brutality, and the victor raised his bloody fists aloft in triumph as the cheers from the crowd half-deafened her. She heard the chink of a money purse thrown into the makeshift ring. The victor bent to retrieve it and kiss it before holding it above his head for all to see.

'Tara!' A familiar voice punctuated the roar, a hand gripped her arm. She whirled round, weak with enormous relief, to see Patrick beside her.

'Tara, what are you doing here? I thought you were abed!'

'I heard the uproar,' she said weakly. 'I came to see . . .'

'This is no place for a woman.' Pushing some of the men aside he dragged her through the sweating, swearing mass of bodies and back in the direction of their tent.

It was the first time since they had come to this godforsaken place that he had said anything of the kind, though nothing about it was suited to a woman, and, in spite of her disgust and the raw fear that the bare-knuckle fight and the men's enthusiasm for it had generated in her, Tara felt comforted by his concern. His arm was about her waist as he hurried her along and she felt closer to him than she had at all during these last weeks when he had seemed to have no thought beyond finding gold.

Perhaps this was the moment to tell him about the baby, she

thought. And to reveal all the anxieties she had been keeping to herself about bringing a child into this tortuous life.

'Into bed – you're cold,' he said when they reached the tent.

Obediently Tara slipped beneath the blanket and watched as Patrick took off his own clothes. How muscular he had grown! she thought. In the shadowy light of the moon every sinew seemed to stand out in clear relief. The hard work had honed his body to the kind of perfection she remembered when she had first seen it, long ago, when they were both very young. A spark of the desire that she had been too tired and too sore to feel these last weeks stirred in her and when he slid beneath the blanket beside her she nestled against him, feeling the warmth and hard strength of his body bringing her every nerve to singing awareness one by one until she was yearning for him, body and soul.

He kissed her and his mouth tasted good in a way she had almost forgotten it could. Then his hand was bunching up her skirts, burrowing between her legs for the secret places between.

'Oh, Patrick,' she whispered, all else but her crying need of him forgotten for the moment.

His weight came on to her, pressing her into the hard ground, and she sobbed with desire as he entered her.

Oh, it was good, so good, to be together as man and wife once more! So good to love and be loved, to be borne upwards on this rising tide of urgency, to have his flesh within her, filling her, stroking her to new heights of ecstasy. She moved with him, relishing every delicious tingle of awareness, every sensuous response of her body to his. Then, too soon, it was over. He rolled away from her and she wanted to weep with the sharp sense of loss.

'Patrick . . .' She moved against his side, trying to prolong the sensations she had been experiencing, knowing instinctively that there was more, more, that she had never yet experienced.

But it was no good. The moment was slipping away from her. Again Tara felt like weeping as the knife edge of unfulfilled passion ached within her. Then, as her breathing became more regular and her pulses resumed their normal rate, she was left only with the sadness to which she could scarcely put a name.

This was how it was for women, she supposed. Men spent their passion with their seed; women could only wonder what it felt like to reach that joyous climax. But there were compensations. The warmth, the closeness, the feeling of being so desired . . . and the bearing of children. That, Tara felt, for all the discomforts of pregnancy and the pain and dangers of childbirth, was a very special privilege.

She lay silent for a moment, her bare arm resting across Patrick's chest, then she said softly: 'There's something I have to tell you, Patrick.'

'Mm?' He sounded drowsy, as if he was already half asleep.

'I am going to have a child.'

'What?' He was instantly wide awake again. 'Tara, are you sure?'

'Almost sure. I know my courses aren't always as regular as they might be, but it's more than two months now. And I feel . . . different.'

'Sweetheart, that's wonderful!' Patrick sounded excited as a small boy, then his tone became anxious. 'But – we just – I just . . . it won't do any harm, will it?'

She laughed softly, pleased at his delight and concern. 'No, I don't think so.'

'It's great news, Tara! I was beginning to wonder . . . well, if perhaps we were never going to be blessed. I never said anything for fear of worrying you, but there was nothing to worry about, was there? Oh, I can see that I'll have to take especial care of you from now on. No more shaking that heavy rocker for you! I'll go back to working the sieve by myself. Unless maybe I could find a partner. There's a new lad just arrived from Donegal. He seems a decent enough sort.'

Tara bit her lip. 'Patrick, I was wondering if perhaps we should give up the search for gold altogether.'

'What?' he said, sounding puzzled. 'What are you talking about?'

'I've been thinking.' Tara raised herself on one elbow. 'This is no life to bring a child into, Patrick. It's no life for anyone. If we were to return to Melbourne I'm sure you could find work of some sort. With everyone running off to the diggings labour is bound to be in short supply and you are young and strong and . . .'

'Give up the chance of making our fortune?' he said disbelievingly. 'But it's the whole reason we came to this country!'

'And it isn't working,' Tara said. 'What have you found so far? Nothing but a few grains of dust.'

'It's early days,' he protested.

'For us, maybe. But look at some of the others. They've been prospecting for years. Why some even came from the diggings around Sydney. And what have they got for their pains? Nothing. Nothing except that the fever has made them no better than wild animals.'

'Fortunes *are* being made!' he argued. 'Look at the new buildings that we saw going up in Melbourne, and here in Ballarat too. Look at the fine carriages and the jewellery the women wear. It's all come from gold.'

'Only for the few,' Tara said, despair lending her voice a raw edge. 'Can't you see, it's the officials and the landowners who are growing rich, not the likes of us. Oh, Patrick, please think about it. We might never be wealthy, but at least we'd have a regular wage coming in. At least we'd have a proper roof over our heads.'

Patrick placed both hands behind his neck, staring out at the stars that glittered in the night sky with a faraway expression on his handsome face.

'I don't want to be a labourer all my life, Tara! I don't want to be a farm hand or a pot boy in some tavern. I want wealth of my own. And now that I know we are to have a child I want it more than ever!'

'But Patrick . . .'

'And I'll get it, you'll see. Wealth such as you never dreamed of. You'll want for nothing, sweetheart. I know it's not easy for you now, but I'll make it up to you, I swear. Why, tomorrow could be our lucky day! By the time the baby comes we could be living in a grand house with servants of our own. Trust me, m'vourneen. It's all I ask.'

Tears suddenly pricked behind Tara's eyelids. What could she say to make Patrick see that it was hopeless? He was so carried away by his dreams that he simply would not listen. It had been one of the things she had loved about him, that boundless optimism that brimmed over no matter how difficult things might be. Now, for the first time, she realised that what she had thought of as his great strength was, in reality, his weakness too. Patrick had never seen things as they really were, would never accept defeat even when it was staring him in the face. Especially now, with this madness upon him . . .

'That's all very well,' she said, trying just once more to make him see the seriousness of the situation. 'But what are we going to do for money if you don't strike lucky soon? We spent almost every penny we had on your picks and shovels and the other equipment. Not to mention the licence. That will be due for renewal soon – another guinea. And everything is so expensive here! Are we to starve to buy a new sieve that might never turn up anything but a few grains of dust?'

'We'll find the money, never fear. Why, if the worst comes to the worst I can always fight for it. Do you know how much was in that purse tonight? Enough to buy the licence and keep us in food too for a month or more. And I could have beaten the man who won it with one hand tied behind my back.'

Tara's despair turned to sharp horror. 'Bare-knuckle fighting? Patrick, you can't mean it!'

He shrugged, full of youthful confidence. 'Why not?'

'Why not? Because it's degrading – and dangerous!' Her voice was rising. 'If you think I'd stand by and see you beaten to a pulp . . . Oh no, Patrick, not that. Not that!'

'Very well, then, have it your way,' he said hastily. 'Now, can we get some sleep? I need a good rest if I'm to make an early start in the morning. And you need to sleep too to make sure you're doing the best by the little one you are carrying.'

Tara bit her lip hard. He was right. They both needed some rest and all this argument was getting them nowhere. But she knew that, worried and upset as she was, it would be a long time before she could relax enough to fall asleep.

Four

The idea came to her at some time during that long night as she ran the argument over and over in her mind.

'Everything is so expensive here,' she had said. And why was it so expensive? Because it was in short supply.

It wasn't only those who owned the land or were lucky enough to find gold who were making money, it was the merchants too. Those who sold the picks and shovels and sieves – and those who provided the essential supplies – at the best prices they could get. There might not be a great demand for soap here where men went unwashed for days and weeks on end, but everyone had to eat. Everyone needed candles and oil for their lamps. Everyone needed *something*.

Well, supposing *she* supplied it? If she was to set up a store selling necessities at better prices than the competition, surely she would still be able to make enough profit to keep them in something like comfort whilst Patrick worked the notion of making a fortune out of his system? It was something she could continue to do after the baby came, too. The little one could sleep quietly in the shade and later on run around nearby whilst she carried on her business.

There was only one snag in the plan, and even enthused as she suddenly was, Tara could see it was a very big one. To set up a store required stock, and they had no money with which to buy it.

Well, there was nothing for it, Tara decided. She would have to find someone to back her venture and lend her the money to get started. And why not? A loan repaid with interest would be a good investment – always provided she could convince her backer that she was enough of a businesswoman to make a go of it.

Dawn was breaking before Tara fell asleep at last. She was only dimly aware of Patrick kissing her forehead; when she woke fully he had already left for the diggings, early, as he had said he would, and alone. Tara sat up, rubbing the sleep from her eyes. She was glad he had gone; if she had told him what she planned he might have tried to talk her out of it. As it was, if she was lucky, she could have it all arranged before he came back this evening.

She washed herself quickly and dressed in the better of the only two gowns she possessed. It was a little creased, she thought critically. There was no way here of ironing laundry after washing it in the only creek that was not polluted with waste from the diggings. But at least it was clean and carefully patched. She combed her luxuriant dark hair and tied it back with a ribbon, and pinched her cheeks and lips to give them a little colour. Then she set out on the long walk to the Commissioner's office, hoping against hope that she would find him there.

Commissioner Henry Dupont sat back in his chair and looked thoughtfully at the young woman who sat opposite him across his desk.

'Well,' he said in his silky voice, 'what you have put to me is a most interesting suggestion.'

And not only as a business enterprise, he added mentally as a quick eager expression brightened her pretty face. The girl was a beauty, and that in itself was a rare pleasure. There were few enough women here in the goldfields and most of them were plain as pikestaffs, their hair matted, their clothes dirty and a gaggle of urchins hanging around their skirts, as like as not. Henry Dupont missed female company sorely. He was a man whose appetite for women was as healthy as his liking for exerting his authority over those with less power, and his contempt for the men who left everything to come to the diggings in the false belief that their fortune lay in the next handful of earth they swilled through their sieves. There were always the Fallen Angels of Esmond Street, of course – the girls who had been forced into prostitution when they were unable to find the domestic employment they had hoped for – but when he considered the dirty, unkempt and diseased men who were their clients he found his desire for an hour with one of them diminishing rapidly.

But this girl was something quite different. Her gown, though it had clearly seen better days, was at least clean, and the flower-sprigged calico fitted snugly over full breasts and a small waist. As for her hair, that was not only clean, but luxuriant too, the sort of hair that begged a man to run his fingers through it. Henry Dupont had a sudden vision of it falling about her face – and his own – a thick silken curtain to titillate and excite.

He reached for his kerchief and mopped at the beads of sweat that were gathering on his brow. God, but it was hot already, and stuffy too in this office of his. Nowhere it seemed was there any escape from the fierce heat of the sun out here in this godforsaken place, and precious few comforts either. But there were compensations. There was always money to be made from turning a blind eye to a sly grog shop – alcohol was illegal in the goldfields – or from taking a healthy cut when payments came in for the gold that had been taken back to Melbourne by the Government couriers. Henry rather thought that he was looking at one of the other compensations at this very moment.

'You think you could make a store pay, do you?' he enquired now, dragging his thoughts back to the matter in hand.

'I think so, sir.' Her voice had a soft Irish lilt to it. Henry ran his tongue over his fleshy lips.

'And do you have any experience of this kind of thing?'

'I have to confess I do not. But I have plenty of experience

53

as a customer. I know the things that are needed, that would sell well, and I've a good head for figures.' Her pretty mouth puckered into a determined line. 'Prices are terribly high in most of the stores. They have overheads, I know, but mostly they're just profiteering. I don't want a purpose-built building. I want to be able to set up a stall in front of my tent and move it on if the population moves. That way I could afford to undercut the Ballarat traders. Although,' she added thoughtfully, 'I have noticed that some of the diggings look quite permanent hereabouts.'

'The shafts that are being dug, you mean,' he said. 'That's coalminers from Wales and tinminers from Cornwall. They think they know a bit more about mining than most, and maybe they're right.'

'They work such long hours,' she said. 'Well, they all do. I'm sure they'd appreciate a store within easy reach to buy their provisions.'

Henry nodded thoughtfully. 'You may well be right. You'll need a licence, though, you know that, don't you? At a cost of forty pounds a year.'

Tara bit her lip. Henry could see that he had shocked her.

'Oh, I didn't realise it would cost as much as that . . .'

'The State authorities set the licence fees, not I,' he said. 'I am simply required to collect them. And then there's the little matter of stock to sell. How do you propose to pay for that?'

A slight tinge of rosy colour rose in her cheeks. 'That was really the reason I came to see you, sir,' she said. 'I didn't even know I needed a licence, but I did realise I don't have the money to pay for enough stock, to begin with at any rate. And it occurred to me to wonder if you might come in with the venture. If you would lend me the money I'd repay it with interest and a cut of the profits too. If it does as well as I intend it should I think you would find it a good investment.'

A faint smile curved Henry's fleshy lips, though he quickly hid it. The girl had a brain as well as being a beauty, and she had a silver tongue too. Perhaps she had kissed the Blarney stone before she left Ireland!

'And what makes you think I have money to invest so?' he asked silkily.

She hesitated for only a moment. 'A gentleman such as yourself . . .'

'Quite.' He half-smiled again. 'And would there be any other benefits on offer to me? Besides the interest on my loan and a cut of the profits as you mentioned?'

Tara frowned. 'I'm sorry, I'm not sure I understand you.'

'Surely, my dear, I don't have to spell it out for you?' Henry mopped his brow again. 'Could you see us being partners in something beyond the business aspect?'

The rosy spots of colour in her cheeks heightened, blue eyes suddenly sparked frosty fire, and her hands clenched to tight balls in the folds of her calico skirts.

'I think you misunderstand me, sir. I am a respectable married woman, and I want to run a respectable business.'

For some reason her fiery response only served to excite him the more. 'Indeed. But you will not blame a man for asking, I hope?'

'Sure you can ask,' she returned tartly. 'But I wouldn't like you to think I have any intention of showing my gratitude in any way but financial return. I hope you'll decide that is sufficient incentive for you to back me, but if not . . .' She rose from the chair, a small dignified figure in spite of the darns and patches on her cheap gown.

Henry spread his hands imploringly on the desk top. 'I did not mean to offend you, my dear. I can well see you are no loose woman. Now sit down again, I beg you, and we'll talk some more about this enterprise you plan. Unless, of course, you have decided not to proceed with it.'

She stood for a moment as if undecided and he waited. Unless he was much mistaken she was not one to give up so easily, at the first hurdle, a plan which clearly meant so much to her.

And neither was he, he thought, a smile twisting his fleshy lips. He wanted Tara Murphy in his bed, and by God he would have her. It would just be a question of biding his time until the right opportunity presented itself. And the prize would be all the sweeter for the wait.

'Well?' he said, his eyes resting speculatively on her lovely face. 'Do you want me to back your venture or not?'

She moved decisively back to the chair. 'Yes, sir, I do.'

Within a couple of weeks Tara's store was up and running. With the Commissioner's credit to back her she was able to order supplies of goods to sell – tea, coffee, sugar, jam and bottled fruit, candles, tobacco, cheese and even some baby clothes to fit the small children who ran ragged around the camp. It all arrived by bullock cart and Henry Dupont allocated Tara a small room in his headquarters to store it.

The safekeeping of her stock was one of the problems that worried Tara. She couldn't be continually running back and forth to the Commissioner's office, but neither could she leave goods in the insecure tent. She had no doubt that she would be robbed the moment her back was turned. A guard dog seemed the best solution, and she acquired a bull mastiff named Cain from one of the miners who had decided to give up the life of a prospector and return to Melbourne. Cain was a huge bad-tempered beast who prowled like a lion on the end of his chain, growling and baring his teeth menacingly when approached. But he seemed to take to Tara, licking her hand and following her around, as far as he was able, and his ferocity towards others certainly had the desired effect of keeping thieves at bay.

Soon Tara was doing a roaring trade. Miners and their womenfolk flocked to her store, grateful to have provisions within easy reach. Some of the men tried to persuade Tara to sell sly grog under cover of her respectable trade, but she refused point blank. There might be a good deal of money to be made from the sale of illicit liquor, but Tara did not think it a risk worth taking. The troopers who enforced law in the goldfields were an over-zealous lot. If a dishonest one discovered she was selling sly grog he would blackmail her, as like as not, whilst an honest one might exercise his right to burn down her tent and impose a heavy fine. Either way would spell disaster and Tara had no intention of being the author of her own downfall.

As trade boomed Tara was able to start repaying what she owed Henry Dupont, together with a share of the profits. She hated the weekly trip to his office, when they would go over the accounts together. Henry always insisted they share a glass of Madeira whilst they pored over the figures and Tara was all too aware of the lascivious way he looked at her and the proximity with which he drew his chair to hers, so close his arm sometimes brushed hers and she could smell the sweat that trickled down his neck and burly torso. But she steeled herself to endure it. At least her precious takings were safely locked away in his safe out of reach of bushrangers and thieves. And at least, for the first time in years, she and Patrick were well enough off to be able to live comfortably.

And how she loved the feeling of being self-sufficient! Tara began to plan for how she would one day expand the business. In her mind's eye she saw a chain of stores all over the goldfields, proper stores, with assistants and a frontage that bore her name, not simply a table in front of a tent. But that was in the future when she had paid off her loan, and when the baby had been born and was big enough to allow her some freedom.

For the moment she was well content with things as they were.

Patrick, however, was far from content. Tara was noticing a change in him and it was worrying her. His had always been such a sunny nature, now he was often dour and silent, and where once he had been a rock to her, someone she could always rely on and to whom she could always turn for comfort, now she felt as if he had gone away from her. He held her in his arms less often. Where once he had never let her fall asleep without at least a tender kiss, now he was often snoring the moment his head touched the pillow, and if she reached for him, longing for a tender embrace, he would push her away with a muffled: 'I'm bone tired, Tara. Leave me be.' He snapped at her easily too, something she had never known him do in all the years they had been together.

He had teamed up now with Seamus Flaherty, the lad from Donegal, and the two of them had become great friends. But though he laughed often when he was with Seamus, the fun seemed to have gone out of him when he was with Tara and instead she was treated to frequent displays of ill temper.

One evening when he returned from the diggings and found her still busy sorting a new consignment of calicos that had been delivered that day his face darkened and he growled at her: 'Why is my supper not ready? I've worked my fingers to the bone all day and come home to find you've not even begun to cook something for me to eat.'

'I'm sorry, Patrick, but I've been working hard too,' she said.

He snorted and aimed a kick at Cain, who had come sniffing up to greet him.

This was too much for Tara. She was tired out from a hard day's work, too, as she had told him, and her temper was no better than Patrick's.

'Don't take it out on the poor dog!' she flared. 'It's not his fault. What's the matter with you, Patrick? You never used to be so mean.'

Patrick threw down his pick and shovel with a clatter. 'Perhaps in the old days I had no reason to be. Perhaps in the old days I had a wife to come home to.'

'And what is that supposed to mean?' Tara demanded. 'Why, I swear I feel sometimes as if I can do nothing right. You'll have your supper. By the time you've had a wash and changed out of those filthy clothes it'll be on the table. There's cold beef and salt pork and plenty of it, and I would remind you it's thanks to me working all day in my store that you'll eat so well.'

He whirled round on her, his face like thunder. 'And you wonder, Tara, why I'm in an ill humour these days? Well, there's your answer. How do you think it feels for a man when his wife throws it in his face that he's unable to keep her? I should be the one putting food on the table, not you!'

Her anger died then in a rush of protective love. She hadn't stopped to think before how his pride must be suffering; now she could see it all too clearly, written all over him.

'Oh, Patrick, I know,' she said. 'But what choice do we have? If you struck gold I'd give it all up tomorrow, but . . .'

'But I don't, do I?' Patrick said bitterly. 'Day after day I work, until my back is breaking and my hands are raw. And all for nothing. Nothing!'

It was the first time she had ever heard him come close to admitting defeat, and a tiny spark of hope flared in her.

'Do you know what happened at the diggings today?' he went on. 'The troopers came by, checking licences. We tried to warn one another as we do, shouting out "Trap!" and "Joe!" so the men in the shafts would lie low, but it did no good. They caught one poor fellow, John Garratt – the one with five children and another on the way – you know him? He had no licence, he'd spent the money on food for his family – at your store, no doubt – and he couldn't afford to renew the licence. The troopers dragged him off and paraded him through the diggings, and now he's chained up to a tree in front of the government buildings until he pays his fine. Five pounds! Where can he find five pounds? God alone knows what will become of him and the little ones.'

'Holy Mother of God, that's dreadful!' Tara felt a wash of sympathy – and guilt, too. Only this afternoon she had refused Mrs Garratt credit when she came to beg for tea and beans. Giving credit in a place such as this was no way to run a business, but all the same . . . Knowing the family would be going hungry tonight when her shelves were stocked with food made Tara horribly uncomfortable. And on top of the shame of John being in the lock-up too! Suddenly the indignities and hardships of the godforsaken place seemed too much to bear. Oh, she and Patrick might be managing quite well now, thanks to her store, but what was it doing to them and their marriage? And she didn't want her child growing up here, surrounded by violence and degradation and despair. She could feel the baby now moving within her, just a tiny flutter beneath her ribs but a unmistakable movement all the same. Her child. Hers and Patrick's. He – or she – deserved so much better than this.

'Let's give up, Patrick,' she begged. 'Let's get away from this awful place.'

For a moment he was silent, staring into space, and the hope sparked in her again. Had what had happened today tipped the balance? Had he realised at last how hopeless it all was?

Tara ran to him, taking his hands in hers. 'We could have a much better life in Melbourne,' she said eagerly. 'Perhaps we could open a little store there! I'm versed in it now, and I'm learning all the time. Just think of it – a proper store, and our customers would be people who could afford to pay good prices for their requirements, people with money in their pockets, not paupers asking for credit. I'm sure we could do it!'

'No!' His voice was raw with anger and resentment and he pushed her away bad-temperedly.

'But, Patrick . . .'

'Sure, haven't I made it clear I won't be kept by my wife?' he snapped. 'What kind of a man do you think I am?'

Tara swallowed hard, stung by the viciousness of his tone, yet determined to press her point.

'I wouldn't be keeping you, Patrick. It would be *ours*. We'd run it together . . .'

'And what do I know about running a store?' he demanded. 'By your own admission you're the one with the experience. You'd be the one to make all the decisions. What would I be? No better than hired labour. Hired labour to my own wife.'

'No!' she protested. 'You'd learn too. And then you could take over and leave me to the house and children.'

'I don't think so.' There was a hard look in his eyes. 'You'd never be content to turn your enterprise over to me, Tara. You'd be forever interfering and thinking you knew best. It's not only I who have changed. You've changed too.'

Tara bit her lip. Perhaps he was right, perhaps she had changed. But only out of necessity.

'If you were the breadwinner, Patrick, I'd willingly go back to being just a wife and mother,' she said earnestly.

'And I will be a breadwinner again, better than that. But not from being a poxy storekeeper.' The light that came from the lust for gold was back in his eyes again, sparkling like the will o' the wisp he chased daily. 'I can't let all the work I've put in here go to waste, Tara. I'll make a fortune for us, never fear. And in the meantime, by hook or by crook, I'll find some way to bring my share into the coffers.'

Tara turned away, her own eyes sparkling with unshed tears. She was having no more success in persuading him away from this place than he was in digging a fortune from the earth.

'I'll go and make supper,' she said resignedly.

Tara awoke with a start. She lay for a moment, bemused, yet with the unmistakable feeling that something was amiss. She reached out for the comforting warmth of Patrick's body, but found nothing but cold sacking. The bed was empty. He was not there. And then she heard it, the roar of men's voices as she had heard it before, the same roar as when they raced horses. Or cheered on the contestants in a bare-knuckle fight.

Instantly Tara was wide awake and trembling. It couldn't

be a horse race, not in the dark. It must be a fight. And suddenly she was remembering with mounting horror the things Patrick had said earlier, his self-loathing at not being able to provide for her as a husband should, and the suggestion, longer ago, that he could make good money if he won the purse in a fight.

Fear coursed through her. Oh, he wouldn't, surely? He'd heard about the fight and just gone to watch. But she couldn't rid herself of the awful feeling that it was more than that. That it was Patrick himself who was out there pounding a man's face to a pulp and being pounded to a pulp himself for the entertainment of the baying crowd.

Tara pushed aside the blanket and got up, reaching for her gown and doing it up with fingers that trembled so much they fumbled clumsily on the fastenings. Then, stopping only to thrust her feet into her worn boots and snatch up her shawl, she ran through the encampment towards the clearing where she had witnessed the previous fight. Her heart was pounding, her breath coming in shallow painful gasps, but this time when she reached the edge of the crowd she did not wait for an opening but rushed straight in, pushing through the mass of bodies and sobbing with breathless desperation.

'Let me through! Let me through!'

The crowd parted, grumbling, swearing and staring, and she sobbed again as she saw the contenders.

She had been right! Oh, Sweet Holy Mother, she had been right! It was Patrick in the makeshift ring, Patrick stripped to the waist, his face bloodied, Patrick dancing and staggering alternately as he landed blow upon blow on the head of his opponent and then took sickening punishment himself in return.

'No! No!' she squealed, her hands flying to her mouth as the other man's fist cracked into Patrick's face, sending him reeling. But no one took the slightest notice of her, least of all Patrick. There was a wild expression on his face that she had never seen before, his swollen lips drawn back from his teeth in a snarl that reminded her disquietingly of Cain raving on the end of his chain when strangers came too close.

As she watched, Patrick's opponent's fist smashed into his battered face. Patrick staggered, then brushed his nose roughly with the back of his hand and returned to the attack, fists raised high to defend himself, jabbing with a ferocity that showed he was not yet beaten. But oh! what chance did he stand? The other fighter was a giant of a man, his face and chest covered with a thick mat of curling black hair, his fists the size of the hams that the bullocky brought to her store. Though Patrick was landing blows the big man brushed them away as if they were no more than the petty irritations of a dozy fly. Tara could only watch helplessly as he stood there, immovable as a mountain, awaiting his chance. Then a huge fist powered out, catching Patrick on the side of the head, and as Patrick's guard dropped the other fist smashed into his face, sending him reeling.

Tara screamed, the sound lost in the roar of the crowd, and the man hit Patrick yet again. Patrick went down to his knees like a felled tree, then gamely tried to rise. But as he did so the man's boot caught him with a sickening thud. He fell again, rolling over onto his back, knocked senseless.

For a moment that seemed like a lifetime Tara stood motionless, rooted to the spot in horror. Then she dashed headlong into the ring.

'Here's another prize for you!' someone shouted to the big man who stood, legs spread wide, hands raised above his head and the jeering crowd took up the chant.

'The purse and a pretty woman too!'

'Have you enough energy left to satisfy her?'

'I'm fighting next if that's the booty!'

Tara scarcely heard them and took less notice. She had eyes only for Patrick, lying motionless on the hard ground. Dear God, was he dead? She fell to her knees beside him.

'Patrick! Patrick, can you hear me?'

He stirred slightly and her heart leaped with relief. Seamus

Flaherty and another man who had been acting as seconds for Patrick emerged from the shadows.

Seamus placed a hand on Tara's shoulder. 'Leave him to us, m'vourneen. This is man's work.'

Between them they hauled Patrick to his feet and man-handled him with one unresisting arm around each of their necks out of the ring. Tara followed, white faced, and the crowd parted to let them through, craning curiously to see how badly injured he was.

'We'll take him straight back to the tent,' Seamus told Tara. 'Run on ahead and have water ready.'

Tara hesitated for only a moment before doing as he bid. Water was in short supply – the last remaining creek was muddied with silt and fresh water was now being shipped in and sold by the bucketful. Praise be she had some set aside!

In the tent she hastily ripped an old petticoat into strips and poured some of the precious water into a tin bowl. By the time the three men staggered up she was outside and waiting for them.

By the light of the lamp she could see just how raw and bloodied Patrick's face was. His handsome features were almost unrecognisable, his eyes puffed and his nose misshapen. Tara gasped in horror.

'Bring him inside, quickly!'

Patrick was beginning to regain consciousness, groaning and muttering groggily. Tara bit back the reprimand that sprang to her lips and set to work with cloths and water. Seamus went to the doorway of the tent, taking a quick look round to make sure no troopers were lurking, and pulled a flask from his pocket. Tara caught a whiff of sly grog as he put the flask to Patrick's lips.

The strong liquor revived him a little and he squinted up at Tara through half-closed eyes.

'Sweetheart, what happened?'

'You've taken a beating, that's what,' she replied tartly. 'What were you thinking of, you stupid, stupid man?'

'You . . . I was thinking of you . . .'

'And what good have you done with your foolishness?' she demanded. 'You frightened me half to death – and you'll be fit for nothing tomorrow.'

'I'm sorry, Tara,' he groaned. 'I thought I could make us some easy money.' He turned towards Seamus. 'Have you some more of that liquor, my friend? It eases the pain.'

'Put it away!' Tara snapped. 'All we need now is for the two of you to be caught with sly grog and taken in chains to the lock-up . . .'

She broke off suddenly, catching her breath as a sharp pain knifed through her stomach.

'Tara? What's wrong?' Seamus asked anxiously.

'Nothing . . .' But there it was again, making her double up with its intensity. 'Oh, Sweet Holy Mother,' she whispered. 'My baby! Oh, it can't come yet! It can't! It's been inside me for less than half its allotted time!'

Patrick made to try and rise. 'Tara . . .'

'It's all your fault!' she sobbed at him. 'The fright you gave me, and all the running and the . . .' Another pain stopped her outburst. When it subsided she finished brokenly: 'If I lose our child, it's all your fault!' And she was going to lose it. She knew without a shadow of a doubt.

She was right. Before the long night ended and dawn broke over the diggings the baby she had carried with such hope and love was gone. Tara was left with nothing but flat emptiness and a heart that felt as if it were breaking.

Five

As soon as she was fit to leave her bed Tara threw herself into working at her store with even more vigour than before. She had to have something to fill the emptiness, make her forget her grief for a little while, and work was the only thing that helped.

Certainly Patrick was no comfort to her. If he had been moody and withdrawn before, now with the guilt that came from knowing he had been the cause of Tara miscarrying their child he was a thousand times worse. And in any case Tara found herself quite unable to forgive him.

'You shouldn't blame him,' Seamus told her. He seemed to be spending more and more time with them these days. 'Sure an' it's breaking his heart you are.'

Tara tossed her head. 'He doesn't give a fig what I think, Seamus. Nothing matters to him any more but finding gold. And to tell you the truth, I don't give a fig for him.'

She saw the shocked expression on Seamus's ruddy face and experienced a tiny sharp barb of satisfaction. That was telling him! Such a short time ago she could never have imagined thinking such a thing for even a moment, much less saying it, but everything had changed. Why, sometimes she almost felt as though she hated Patrick! She no longer cared that he did not kiss her and hold her as he had used to do – it was a relief, for she did not think she would be able to conceal her lack of desire for his touch. Whenever she looked at him she could see only the puffed and bloody face that had shocked her so on the night of the bare-knuckle fight, and the once-straight nose, now forever crooked, was a constant reminder of the disgust and fear she had felt – and the tragic consequences they had brought about. And so, where once she had cuddled into his embrace to fall asleep now she often rolled as far as possible from him in the makeshift bed so that their bodies did not touch. And all the while she wept silent tears for her lost child, tears that seemed to freeze to a brittle icy coating around her heart.

Under her driven care the store flourished. Tara and Patrick exchanged their tent for a shanty, built of timber and tar paper, and Tara ordered new bedding to be delivered from Melbourne along with some bits and pieces of furniture. But for everything that she was able to provide she saw Patrick grow more bitter and resentful and could no longer find it in herself to care. He left early every morning for the diggings with Seamus at his side and she was glad to see him go and be left to her own devices. He was obsessed, she knew, with the lust for gold, but she could no longer share his dreams. She lived her life whilst he lived his.

High summer was turning now to autumn. Soon the bitter winds would blow in from the sea and down from the mountains and Tara was glad that they had been able to exchange their tent for the shanty. She was glad too that she was able to buy herself some warm flannel for petticoats and woven wool for a gown, and often she sat sewing late into the night when she returned from the store and Patrick snored, exhausted, in their new bed.

And then disaster struck.

The weather broke suddenly with thunder that rolled menacingly and lightning that first flickered over the distant mountain ridges, then lit the dark sky so that the camp was illuminated bright as day. The rain swiftly followed, a torrential downpour that bounced off the sun-baked earth and soaked the tents and everyone who sought shelter in them. By morning the creeks were on the point of bursting their banks and when Tara heard the talk of flooding her heart stood still.

The land on which the goldfields and the camps had sprung up was pancake flat. If the creeks overflowed the water would rush over it unchecked. There had been precious little rainfall the previous winter and throughout the hot dry summer the risk of flooding had not crossed her mind. Now she watched anxiously as the river rose higher and higher and the dark and stormy skies promised yet more rain to come.

Bad enough for the tents and shacks to disappear under silty flood water, but what of her precious stock? Why, a new consignment had arrived by bullocky only a day or so ago . . .

As the day wore on Tara made up her mind. Something would have to be done. She squelched her way across the now sodden ground to the Governor's office and was mightily relieved to find him there – unwilling, no doubt, to be out and about in such weather.

His small beady eyes lit up when he saw her.

'My dear Mrs Murphy, what a pleasant surprise! But you are soaked to the skin!'

Indeed she was. Water streamed down her neck, her hair hung in dripping strands and her skirts were sodden and smeared with mud at the hem. But it was the least of her worries.

'Never mind that,' she said shortly. 'And I've no time to waste on small talk either. I need to hire a cart to get my stock to higher ground. If it stays where it is much longer I fear it will be ruined by flood water.'

'Dear me! Is the situation so serious?' Henry Dupont sounded surprised.

What had he been doing all day that he had failed to notice the impending danger? Tara wondered. 'It certainly is,' she said shortly. 'Some of the tents are already awash and if the men don't soon come up from their shafts they'll drown like rats in a trap. But that's their concern, not mine. I just want to ensure my stock is safe.'

'Indeed.' He nodded, grinding out a cigar butt in a silver

ashtray which would have looked more at home in some fine drawing room than here in the shanty town. 'It wouldn't do for you to lose your stock. You could be ruined. I'll see what I can do. Wait here.'

He threw on a greatcoat and went out. Soon he was back, dripping water into puddles all over the floor.

'You're right, by God. There'll be trouble if the rain doesn't soon let up. Now, I've arranged to have a cart put at your disposal. It's horse-drawn, I'm afraid. All the bullocks are otherwise employed. But if you work quickly . . .' He took off his greatcoat and shook it. Water droplets splattered Tara. 'I've asked the carter to go straight to your store and I've instructed two troopers to come and help you load it.'

'Thank you. I'd best get back at once.' Tara did not trust the troopers to load her precious stock with her not there to supervise. Given the chance they would fill their pockets with whatever they could carry and rob her blind, as like as not. The troopers were a motley crew, recruited hastily to police the goldfields. Some were former convicts, some military pensioners from Van Diemen's Land. Mostly they were brutal and corrupt, not above using violence and bribery to better their standard of living. Without more ado, Tara pulled her sodden cloak up over her head and hurried out.

Henry Dupont watched her go, smiling slightly to himself. God, even soaked to the skin she was a sight to behold! The weeks of working with her had only increased his desire to have her in his bed but as yet, in spite of her regular visits to his office, the opportunity had still not arisen. He must tread carefully with her he knew; she was spirited as well as beautiful and as cool and remote as a nun. But one day . . . one day . . . That useless husband of hers was growing madder by the day with the lust for gold. Why, he had allowed himself to be beaten senseless in a bare-knuckle fight, or so Henry had heard, and been unable to work for the best part of a week. Madness indeed! Yes, Henry was certain his chance would come soon enough and when it did he would relish every moment of his triumph.

The cart was loaded to the gunnels with every bit of stock that Tara possessed – and not a moment too soon, she thought as she saw flood water inching its way across the flats. How many days would it be before she could open her store again? The thought of the lost business galled her, but she had had no choice. Better to shut up shop and ensure her precious stock was fit for sale when the flood waters receded than to risk seeing it all ruined.

'Make haste!' she snapped at the troopers, who had begun to drag their heels. They were a sullen pair, none too pleased at being singled out for this detail. Why should they have to break their backs in the pouring rain whilst others sat around in their camp, drinking tea and waiting for the weather to improve? was their attitude. Especially for the woman who was, it was rumoured, the Commissioner's floozy.

'You'll have to walk,' one of them said to Tara. 'We'll be lucky to get the cart across this boggy ground as it is without your weight to add to it.'

'You'll have to help us push, like as not,' the other added with relish.

They set off along the rutted road and all too soon it became clear that this was likely to prove no idle threat. Several times the wheels became bogged down almost axle deep in mud and it took the best efforts of the three of them along with the straining horses to free the cart.

Soaked to the skin, her boots heavy with squelching caked mud, Tara found herself wondering angrily why Patrick was not here to help her. Surely he couldn't still be digging in this weather? Surely he should have realised she would have trouble on her hands with the river breaking its banks? But Patrick had no thought or care these days for anything beyond his still-fruitless search for gold. It simply would not have entered his head that she might need him.

She shook her head impatiently and a strand of wet hair went into her eye. At the precise same moment her foot found a deep rut and she sank into mud up to her knee.

'Oh!' she squealed, trying in vain to free herself. She could not, and the indignity of having to be yanked out by one of the troopers added to her woes and bad humour.

'There's water on the road ahead,' the trooper warned as they set off again. 'The floods have overtaken it by the look of things.'

Tara's heart sank even lower, if such a thing were possible. The trooper was right; the road ahead and the flats around it were indeed under water.

'We'll just have to get through it somehow,' Tara said tersely.

The troopers exchanged glances.

'What choice do we have?' Tara demanded. 'We'll just have to hope it's not too deep.'

The horses were hesitating, unwilling to venture into the swirling water. Tara took the bridle of one of them. 'I'll lead, you push,' she instructed the troopers. 'Come on, quick as you can now. Are you ready? Let's go!'

She started forward determinedly and at first it seemed that by their concerted efforts they were going to make it. Then disaster struck. One of the horses stumbled, the cart lurched violently and came to a halt at a crazy angle. Some of Tara's precious stock, piled precariously high, toppled and slid with a splash into the water. Tara squealed in dismay.

'That's done it!' one of the troopers said. He sounded secretly pleased.

'Come on! We have to get moving again!' Tara snapped. There was no way to salvage the sacks of sugar and flour they had lost but more would follow unless they righted the cart, and quickly. 'Push, damn you! Push!'

The trooper shook his head, smirking.

'We'll never do it, missus. Twenty men and a team of four would be hard put. Two men, two horses and a . . . lady . . .'

He hesitated, sneering over the word. 'No, I'd say this cart is going nowhere.'

'Oh, dear God!' Suddenly Tara was close to tears. 'We can't just give up and leave it here! We have to do *something*! A wedge, perhaps, under the wheel . . .'

She began to look around wildly for something to serve the purpose – a thick branch from a fallen tree, perhaps. But there was nothing, nothing but the swirling water, which seemed to be growing deeper by the second.

One of the troopers began to laugh.

'What's so funny?' Tara flared.

The trooper drew the back of his hand across his streaming face. 'You, missus. How in the name of heaven would we get a wedge under the wheels, even if we had anything to hand? That cursed cart weighs a ton. No, you've gambled and lost this time, I fear. The best we can do is take the horses and get out of here before we all drown.'

He was right, Tara reluctantly acknowledged. Much as she hated to admit it, there really was nothing to be done. 'Oh, Holy Mother!' she whispered. But even as she said it she knew that this time there could be no heavenly intervention to come to her aid.

The troopers were loosing the horses and leading them back to the higher part of the road. As they did so the wagon gave another violent lurch and overturned. The remainder of Tara's precious stock spilled out into a sad untidy pile half submerged beneath the ever-rising flood.

There was nothing for it but to turn her back upon the disastrous sight and trudge back along the muddy and rutted road, tears mingling with the rain on her face.

Losing everything for which she had worked so tirelessly drained the last of the fight from Tara. The store and the effort she had put into building it up had been her antidote to all she had endured – the dire conditions under which she was forced to live, the growing alienation from Patrick, her terrible grief at the loss of the baby she had carried. Now, it seemed to her, the remnants of her hopes and dreams and all of her will to survive and prosper had been lost with the candles and rolls of fabric, the sugar and flour and tea, beneath the raging flood.

Though as she waited for the water to subside she tried to force herself to formulate plans for the future, the thought of starting all over again was enough to send her spirits plunging. Start again. But for what? Just so that she could watch Patrick depart for the diggings each day with that curious mad light in his eyes? Just so that she could lie beside him at night holding herself stiff so that their flesh did not touch, and driven mad by his snoring? Just to continue living in this hell-hole where men fought and dogs barked and children cried and troopers beat senseless anyone who dared question their authority? And what guarantee was there that all her efforts would not come to naught again? The creek had flooded and burst its banks once – it could do so again. Gangs of armed marauders could rise and loot her store, and how could one dog, however ferocious, stop them? Anything could happen out here in this wild and lawless land.

I can't bear it, Tara thought. If I don't get away from this cursed place I shall go as mad as some of the miners seem to.

Once more she tried to talk sense into Patrick, once more she met the same implacable response as before. He had invested too much of himself in his search for gold to give up now. He would go on and on to the bitter end until he either made his fortune or lost his life in the process, she thought, and it was the final straw.

'If you intend to go on with this madness, then I'm leaving you, Patrick,' Tara said.

Even now, after all she had been through, even now when she felt devoid of any love or even affection for him, yet actually speaking the words was painful, the death knell for a whole part of her life, a final goodbye to all the hopes and dreams of her youth.

Patrick stared at her blankly.

'Don't you understand what I'm saying?' Tara flared at him. 'I won't stay in this godforsaken place any longer. And if you won't come with me to try and build a new life, then I'll go alone. The coach leaves tomorrow afternoon, and I shall be on it, with or without you.'

Even now she entertained a faint hope that perhaps she might shock him into agreeing to give up this insane quest for which he had sacrificed everything. But with his resigned shrug that last hope died.

'As you wish, Tara,' he said indifferently.

'You mean you'll let me go,' she said. 'Just like that?'

Patrick shrugged again. 'If your heart's set on it I can't stop you, can I? I've never been able to stop you doing what you wanted.'

'And I can't stop you, it seems,' she flared, hurt more than she would have believed possible. 'Nothing matters to you but this damned dream of riches. You'll never find them, Patrick. You'll sink lower and lower into the mire. Well, I won't be dragged down with you.'

He said nothing, simply staring into space in that dreamy way that she had grown to dread.

'Patrick,' she said, more quietly, but with slow deliberation. 'You do understand what this means, don't you? I intend to go to Melbourne and you will be left here. Alone.'

His blue eyes came up to meet hers.

'Oh, but I won't be alone. I'll have Seamus.'

For a moment Tara stared at him uncomprehendingly. She had thought for some time now that Seamus meant more to Patrick than she did and been jealous of the closeness that came from their shared lust for gold. Seamus understood when she did not the importance this vain quest had assumed in Patrick's life. His were the same hopes and dreams, the same disappointments. Together they worked and planned, urging one another on, comforting one another. Seamus was Patrick's only real friend in this world of avarice and greed, rivalry and violence and Tara had told herself she should be glad he had him.

But now, with a twist of disquiet, she found herself remembering all the times when she had seen them with their arms about one another's shoulders, laughing together. The gentle way Seamus had tended to Patrick when he had been beaten senseless on the night of the bare-knuckle fight; the dreamy look in Patrick's eyes as he and Seamus shared a noggin of sly grog – that same dreamy look she so often surprised upon his face. And she thought too of the way he had changed towards her, how seldom now he kissed or held her. Because of her altered feelings for him she had put the omission down to weariness and been glad of it. Now, with a sick jolt, she wondered if there might be another, unmentionable reason why Patrick no longer seemed to have any interest in her, or in making love to her . . .

Such things happened sometimes, she knew, though they were never talked about. But she couldn't believe it of Patrick and Seamus. Wouldn't believe it. Wouldn't think of it even. And yet . . . And yet . . .

'Pat – where are you?' As if her imaginings had conjured him up she heard Seamus's voice, calling through the half-open door of the shack. 'Pat – come on, man! It's a beautiful morning! We don't want to waste it now, do we?'

'Sure an' I'm on me way.' Patrick collected his pick and shovel. In the doorway he stopped, looking back at her. For a moment she felt that he was really seeing her for the first time in weeks – months. That he was reading her half-formed thoughts and doing nothing to deny them.

'You'll do what you have to do, m'vourneen. And so will I,' he said. Then he turned and went out.

Tara stood for a moment as if turned to stone, then she ran to the door, looking after him. The two men were striding together along the track between the dead embers of camp fires, so close their shoulders almost touched. Tara's heart came into her mouth. She watched until they were out of sight, then she went back into the shack, threw herself down on the bed they had shared, but never made love in since the day she had bought it, and sobbed as though her heart would break.

'My dear Mrs Murphy, I'm not sure I follow you.' Henry Dupont was covering his dismay with a great show of bluff good humour. 'You have come to ask me for what?'

Tara drew herself up tight. She was in no mood for Dupont's word games.

'I thought I'd made myself perfectly clear, sir. I want the money you've been keeping safe for me. My share of the profits from the store.'

The minute she had recovered from crying herself dry, Tara had set about making ready to leave for Melbourne. She had no wish to still be in the shanty when Patrick returned from the diggings.

Into a canvas holdall she packed her toiletries, her underwear and a change of gown, settled her rosary around her neck and slipped her mother's wedding band onto the third finger of her right hand. Then she had set out for the Commissioner's office to collect her savings. They were meagre enough, God alone knew, but at least they would pay for her passage to Melbourne on the Cobb coach and tide her over for a night or two's food and lodging until she could find herself paid employment.

But the Commissioner, now that she had asked him for the money, was pretending to be irritatingly obtuse. His small beady eyes met hers with something like a sneer.

'What makes you think, my dear Mrs Murphy, that you are due money? There are no profits from the store. The store is no more.'

'I know that!' she snapped. 'Didn't I see all my stock washed away before my own eyes? But I *was* making a profit before the flood. You know I was. We went carefully over the figures each week and I left what I didn't need to live on for you to look after for me. In your safe, locked away where robbers couldn't find it. Ready for the day I would take it to Melbourne to open a bank account. Well, I want to do that now, today!'

His small eyes narrowed until they were little more than slits in his paunchy face. 'And you don't intend to return, I assume.'

'My intentions are none of your business,' Tara returned tartly. 'But as it happens you are right. I've had enough of goldfields life and I'm going to make a new life in Melbourne. That's why I need my money and I shall be grateful if you'll give it to me now so that I can be on my way.'

The Commissioner dug his hands into the pockets of his jacket, looking at her speculatively. 'Well I'm sorry, my dear, but I really don't think I can do that.'

She stared at him, frowning. 'What do you mean?'

'Surely you realise that you still owe me on my investment?' he said silkily.

'But that was paid off long ago!' Tara protested.

Henry Dupont smiled sadly, shaking his head.

'I think not. The *initial* investment, maybe. But I've put up money since then. You did not pay in full for the stock that was lost in the flood, if I remember rightly. I made up the balance on that out of my own purse as you did not have the correct money to pay the carter . . .'

'That was a handful of sovereigns only! Just loose change!' Tara interrupted.

'I would have recouped that when the goods were sold and we accounted for them in our ledgers,' he went on as if she had not spoken. 'And I've had no share of the takings this last week or more – part of our agreement, if you remember.'

'There have been no takings to share!' Tara retorted. She had begun to tremble. 'I can't believe, Mr Dupont, that you mean to refuse to hand over to me money that is rightfully mine!'

Henry Dupont took a step towards her, a half-smile twisting his fleshy lips.

'You don't have to continue to call me Mr Dupont, my dear. I've told you often enough to call me Henry. We have been partners for some time and . . .'

'Partners, yes! And now you seek to rob me as surely as if some thief had come to my house and stolen the money from me while I slept!' Tara flashed. 'Mr Dupont, I beg you. Don't do this to me!'

'Henry,' he reminded her with a smile. He opened a drawer of his desk and drew out his bunch of keys, dangling them enticingly in front of him while his eyes devoured her lasciviously. 'As I say, my dear, I really think the flood disaster has effectively eaten up what profits you may believe you made. But I would be willing to concede you something, provided you are willing to concede something to me in return.'

Tara's eyes flashed. 'I thought I made it clear from the very outset that ours was to be a business partnership only,' she said, striving to keep her tone level though her heart had begun to race erratically.

'Circumstances change though, do they not?' He had the whip hand, he knew, and it was exciting him unbearably. All those times when he had looked at her and desired her, all those times when he had told himself the opportunity would arise one day if only he were patient . . . Now, he thought, the time had come. 'I think I could be persuaded to open the safe for you Mrs Murphy – Tara. And I think you know just how to persuade me.'

Tara drew her shawl protectively around her, holding his gaze defiantly. 'I may know the way, Mr Dupont, but I assure you I have no intention of acting upon it. How dare you use my own money to coerce me so?'

Dupont smiled again. Oh, but with her temper up Tara was magnificent! If anything he wanted her more now than ever before. He swung the keys so that they jangled together.

'The choice is yours, my dear. Find it within yourself to be friendly towards me and you shall have your money. Every penny of it.'

'Never!' Tara snapped. 'Why, it would make me no better than a common prostitute! I'd starve first!'

'No, my dear, I don't think so. When you are hungry enough you'll sell yourself to some other man. In Melbourne – or wherever you fetch up. Don't you think it might as well be me? We know each other well after all, and . . .'

'Oh, I know you right enough!' Tara flared. 'I know you are a scheming, lecherous rogue! Well, you won't get away with it. When I get to Melbourne I shall go straight to the authorities and tell them how you've cheated me.'

'And you think they will believe you?' Dupont's lips twisted unpleasantly. 'The word of a Queen of the Diggings against that of the appointed Commissioner? I doubt it very much.'

'We'll see.' She turned and flounced to the door.

Henry Dupont moved swiftly for such a big man, planting himself directly in her path. Something had snapped in him. He had invested time and money in this young woman, he had lusted after her for too long. He wouldn't let her walk away from him now.

'Don't think you can make a fool out of me, my lady,' he snarled. His hand shot out, imprisoning her wrist and pulling her roughly towards him.

Tara gasped, caught off balance and taken completely by surprise, and he grabbed her other arm and held her fast, so close that she could smell his sweat and desire. Before she could move a muscle he forced his mouth onto hers. She gagged at the taste of stale cigars and fetid breath as his teeth raked her lips hungrily, and fought to tear her mouth away. Useless. One brawny arm went around her buttocks and Tara squealed as he swept her off her feet, thrusting her to the ground and throwing himself down after her. His weight squashed the breath from her and before she knew what was happening he had yanked both her arms above her head, wrenching her shoulders painfully as he forced them together, holding them with just one of his huge hands. Tara squealed again in pain and outrage as his free hand tore at the neck of her gown to expose her breasts, then moved down to bunch up her skirts.

Dupont was not a tall man but he was thick-set and sturdily built. Beneath his weight Tara thrashed helplessly like a butterfly caught on a pin. Oh, dear sweet Holy Mother, this couldn't be happening to her! She wouldn't let it, she couldn't let it! But what could she do?

Dupont raised himself slightly, unbuckling his gun-belt and letting it fall to the ground beside him, and suddenly she knew. If she could distract him for a moment, get the gun . . . Another moment and he would be undoing his breeches and it would be too late . . .

'Henry,' she whispered. Her voice was a croak of fear; desperately she tried to make it sound like passion. 'Oh, Henry, not here! Take me to bed. Make love to me properly!'

For just a moment he hesitated, relaxing his grip on her wrists. It was enough. She freed one hand, not even noticing the pain in her shoulder as she willed herself not to fight but to slip it around his thick neck, squeezing, caressing.

'Oh, Henry, Henry, take me to bed . . .'

He groaned deep in his throat. Somehow Tara overcame her revulsion and kissed him on the lips, gently probing with her tongue as her heart raced with the fear that her ploy might not work. Perhaps his pleasure came from raping a woman in his power. Perhaps what he wanted most was to take her here on the hard bare floor. If so she was done for.

But already her pretended acquiescence had altered the flavour of the assault. Henry Dupont was basically a sensuous man, not a violent one – and he was vain into the bargain. Tara saw a slow satisfied smile curve those hateful fleshy lips whilst his eyes glittered greedily.

'Come then,' he muttered thickly, raising himself and extending a hand to pull her up too.

Tara half rose, still forcing herself to smile and hold his eyes with a false look of tantalising promise. Then, the moment she saw her chance, she acted. Her hand flashed out to snatch the gun from the gun-belt, levelling it at him and releasing the safety catch in one swift fluid movement.

The shock on his face was a picture. If her situation had not been so deadly serious Tara might have taken pleasure in it or even laughed. As it was she simply grated at him through gritted teeth: 'Keep away from me, you animal!'

Dupont's amazement turned to fury that she had tricked him so and his prize was about to be snatched from his grasp. With a snarl of fury he lunged towards her.

And Tara pulled the trigger.

The bullet caught Dupont full in the chest. Again his expression became one of total surprise, his hands flying to the wound. Then he swayed, his knees buckled beneath him and he went down. For just a moment his arms and legs threshed wildly whilst an awful guttural sound gurgled with the blood from his mouth.

Tara knelt motionless, the gun still clutched tightly in her hand, the muzzle still pointed at the crumpled figure of Henry Dupont. Her eyes were wide with terror, her pulses racing, the blood thundering at her temples and in her ears. She was ready, more than ready, to pull the trigger again and again if needs be. But after a moment or two that awful gurgling sound stopped and the flailing arms and legs twitched erratically and then were still.

Tara's breath came out on a long shuddering sigh. She scrambled to her feet, her eyes never leaving him, the gun still trained on his crumpled form.

'Move – just move – and I'll shoot again!' she grated. The words sounded unreal to her own ears.

He did not move, and realisation began to break through the haze of terror and blind determination.

Dear Holy Mother, he was dead. Sweet Holy Mother, she had killed him. The gun dropped from her suddenly numb and shaking hand, her knees turned to rubber and almost gave way beneath her.

She, Tara Murphy, had killed a man in cold blood. She had meant to do it. She had wanted him dead. And given the same circumstances she would do it again. But, oh, dear God – what now? At any moment the troopers could arrive on the scene and she would undoubtedly be arrested. They wouldn't stop to ask why she had done what she had done, and why should they care? She had murdered the Commissioner, that was all that mattered. After only the briefest of trials they would hang her from the tallest gum, retribution for the slain official and a warning to anyone else who might be tempted to take the law into their own hands.

A fresh wave of fear washed over Tara, not panic this time but cold dread – a dread which somehow cleared her whirling thoughts and filled her with grim determination. She had been going to leave in any case, now she must go right away, before she could be arrested and sentenced. But she was not going to leave without what was rightfully hers. Nor could she afford to. She needed at least twenty-five shillings for her coach fare, and something to tide her over when she reached Melbourne.

The bunch of keys Dupont had dangled tantalisingly in front of her lay on his desk. Tara grabbed them up, searching for the one that unlocked the safe. She ran to it, almost stumbling over Dupont's body in her haste. Pray God it was a simple lock, not some obscure combination . . .

Her prayer was answered. The door swung open the moment she turned the key in the lock. Tara drew out the cash box. Another key, and she was able to lift the lid.

The box was full of sovereigns. Tara opened her reticule and emptied the sovereigns into it. There was no time for counting out her dues, and in any case she was past caring. Any moment someone might come in and find her here with

Dupont's lifeless body and the open safe. They would think she had killed him in order to rob him. She would have no defence, none at all.

The thought sparked an idea in her racing mind. A robbery. Perhaps if she were to make it look as if Dupont had been killed by some bush ranger or a desperate miner turned robber it would help to divert suspicion from her and enable her to get away. It was a long shot, but Tara grasped at it like the terrified animal she had become. In a frenzy she grabbed a few of the valuables Dupont had put in the safe for reasons of security – a signet ring, a few bits and pieces of silver and a jewelled pin – and dropped them into her reticule on top of the sovereigns. Then, leaving the safe door swinging open, she returned to his body. Steeling herself against the feeling of revulsion which turned her stomach she unfastened the chain of the pocket watch which stretched across his burly chest. The watch followed the other items into her reticule. Then Tara ran to the door, opening it carefully and peeping out.

For a wonder there was no one to be seen. No troopers watering their horses, no traps or native police idling away an hour playing dice, no offender in chains outside the lock-up. They must all be out in the goldfields, she realised. No wonder no one had come running at the sound of the shot. Thanking heaven that at least in this fortune was on her side Tara pulled the door closed after her and set out for her own shack to collect the holdall she had packed with her few belongings. It was all she could do to keep from running, but to run would be to attract attention to herself and in any case her knees felt so shaky she was not sure she could have run even if she had tried.

Tara passed scarcely a soul on her way back to the shack and somehow she managed a nod to those she did. She had to look normal, as if nothing had happened, she told herself. Otherwise when Dupont's body was found someone would say, 'I saw Tara Murphy coming from that direction and she looked very flustered and strange,' and then the troopers might come after her.

As the door of the shack closed behind her Tara leaned heavily against it, taking deep steadying breaths. But the shock of what had occurred was catching up with her now, she felt faint and sick to her stomach. She poured herself a glass of water and sipped it, then splashed some onto her face. The skin burned where the Commissioner's stubble had grazed her chin, reminding her all too clearly of his disgusting attack – and what had followed. Somehow, Tara forced herself not to think about it.

It must be almost time for the coach to leave, she realised, panicking again suddenly. She must not miss it. But neither did she want to stand in the main street too long where everyone could see her waiting for it.

She tore open her reticule with clumsy fingers, searching in it for the Commissioner's pocket watch. A man of his standing would be certain to own one which kept good time. As she checked it the sudden clatter of galloping hooves on the track outside brought her heart into her mouth with a sickening jolt and the reticule slipped from her nerveless fingers, spilling some of its contents across the floor.

Oh, dear God, the incriminating evidence in her possession! But there was nothing she could do about that now, except conceal it beneath her underwear in her canvas holdall. No time to find a hiding place for it here in the camp that would not point the finger at some innocent soul if it was discovered. Tara scooped up the scattered pieces and shoved them into the very bottom of the holdall together with some of the sovereigns. Too much money in her reticule might attract unwelcome attention of one sort or another.

Time to go. Tara took one last look around the shack that had been her home, and which she had furnished with such hope and love. There was nothing else she wished to take with her. Patrick could have it all. Patrick and Seamus. But the thought failed to hurt her now. It was as if all her emotions had been tormented and stretched so far that she was left empty and bereft of any feeling beyond the desperate desire to be away from this place.

Tara slipped her reticule over her wrist, picked up her bulging holdall and went out, closing the door behind her for the last time.

The Cobb coach was already waiting in the main street, the fresh horses pawing the ground impatiently. The coachman stood beside them. He turned as Tara approached.

'Melbourne-bound?'

'Yes,' she said, surprised at how level she was able to make her voice sound.

'You have the fare?' the man asked suspiciously. 'It's twenty-five shillings.'

'I have the fare.' Tara set down her holdall, opened her reticule and counted them out for him. Twenty-five shillings – twenty-five weeks' worth of wages for most poor souls.

'Shall I stow your bag for you?'

Tara picked it up quickly, clutching it tightly. 'No, I'll keep it with me if there's room.'

'There's room. Though I wouldn't trust the passengers.' He nodded towards the interior. Tara saw that three rough-looking men had already taken their places – miners, no doubt, who had struck lucky and were going to Melbourne to spend their gains on the high life that was to be found there. Already they looked well in their cups, laughing and swearing loudly and passing a flask of sly grog between them.

'Perhaps you'd better stow it,' she said. The last thing she wanted was for them to decide to turn out her belongings. No doubt they would think it great fun to explore her underwear and wave it about and if they did they would uncover the other items she had hidden beneath it.

The coachman took the holdall from her and helped her up the step.

'We leave in five minutes.'

Tara nodded and took a seat as far as possible from the

rough and rowdy men. They stared curiously at her.

'Company of a lady! Well, who'd have thought it!'

'Maybe she won't be averse to us starting our carousing early!'

'You just watch yourselves!' the coachman warned them. 'First sign of trouble and I'll put you out on the road. I'll not have shenanigans on my run. And mind your language too,' he added grimly.

Tara settled her skirts, staring out of the window anxiously for any signs of troopers looking for the murderer of the Commissioner. There were none, but the stench of liquor was making her feel sick again and she wondered how in heaven's name she would hold onto the contents of her stomach when the coach started swaying too. Concord coaches were notorious for their easy springing.

At last the coachman climbed aboard and took up the reins. At last the coach pulled away, and Tara's heart pounded with relief. They were on their way!

As they passed close by the Government Square, however, her breath came fast again. Something was going on! Two or three riderless horses were tethered outside the Commissioner's office, the door was open and men were running in and out. His body had been discovered then!

The blood drained from Tara's face. Now that Henry Dupont's body had been found the troopers would tear the camp apart looking for the culprit. She was fairly sure no one had seen her leaving the office, but as Dupont's business partner, she would almost certainly have come under suspicion. Thank heavens the coach had been prompt in leaving! She was on her way, but not a moment too soon.

Briefly Tara found herself hoping that no one was wrongly blamed for what she had done. But she couldn't see any reason why they should be. Though there were many who bore the Commissioner a grudge, and would not be sorry to see him dead, there would be not a scrap of evidence to pin the blame on them. Every bit of that was stowed in her holdall and by nightfall would be well out of reach of the most zealous of troopers. But she was still consumed with terror of discovery all the same.

Only when the ugly workings and the scattered tents on the outskirts of the goldfields gave way to grassy plains where sheep and cattle browsed did Tara allow herself to relax a little.

Two days' travelling and she would be in Melbourne. What lay ahead of her she did not know. But of one thing she was certain. It could not be worse than the hell-on-earth she had left behind.

Six

N ow, settled into a corner seat of another coach, bound
for a new life on a farm called Dunrae in the employ of
a man she scarcely knew – Mr James Hannay – Tara found
herself remembering her flight from Ballarat and thinking
back over the miserable weeks she had spent in Melbourne
since that day.

She had told herself that whatever befell her could not be
worse than what she had endured on the goldfields, and she
supposed it hadn't been. But it certainly hadn't been any
better either.

The first few days she had stayed in the relative comfort
of a lodging house, paid for with the sovereigns she had taken
from the safe in the hateful Henry Dupont's office – money
she thought of as hers by right. It would tide her over, she
hoped, until she could find employment. But employment was
harder to come by than she had imagined. Though vacancies
for men abounded – vacancies created when blacksmiths and
farriers, teamsters, labourers and pot boys left their workaday
lives to join the rush for gold – there were more than enough
women left behind to fill the posts of domestic servants,
barmaids and shoe binders. Seamstresses and milliners still
needed assistants, it was true, but Tara's meagre skills were
not good enough to satisfy them when they had the choice
of the cream of experienced needlewomen. The sovereigns
were running out and Tara was beginning to wonder if she
would have to do the unthinkable and dispose of the items
stolen from Dupont in order to eke out a living when she

returned one day to her lodgings to find her room rifled and her holdall and its illicit contents gone.

Tara wept bitter tears at the loss of her few possessions, but she could not find it in her to mind about Dupont's treasures. To profit from the terrible thing she had done would have gone against the grain; the thief, whoever it might be, had, in taking them, relieved her of the decision to pawn or sell them herself.

As the sovereigns dwindled and no opportunity to earn more presented itself, Tara was forced to leave the lodging house. For two terrible nights she slept under the stars, huddled with other down and outs around the embers of a brazier they had managed to beg, borrow or steal. And then she had heard about the Women's Refuge. It was a dire place, run by a rota of women Tara called the 'O-be-joyfuls', who gave themselves airs and considered themselves vastly superior to the poor homeless wretches they purported to help. A good many of these women had, like Tara, come to Melbourne hoping to find work. Some had been abandoned penniless when their menfolk had run off to the goldfields. There were those among them who earned a little money by selling themselves on the streets as the Fallen Angels of Esmond Street in Ballarat did, but Tara was determined that come what may she would never sink to such depths. The revulsion she had felt when Henry Dupont had tried to force himself on her had made her even more certain that she could never shut off her mind and her emotions as they did whilst some stranger used their body for his own pleasure.

Every day she made herself as presentable as she could and trudged out looking for work. And every night she returned, empty-handed and ready to weep with despair. What was to become of her? She didn't know. Hungry, cold, destitute, she existed from day to day. And always hanging over her was the fear that the police would come and arrest her for the murder of the Commissioner. Once, she had thought Melbourne was far enough away from Ballarat to be safe. No more. If the thief who had stolen her bag pawned the valuables hidden in it, if Dupont's pocket watch or signet ring were identified, the finger would point directly at her. Almost certainly the thief would admit to stealing them from her rather than be charged with murder himself. She would be dragged back to Ballarat, summarily tried, and no doubt hung for what she had done, for no one would believe her story that he had been trying to rape her. Tara trembled at the thought, praying each night for deliverance, though she was beginning to doubt that anyone was listening to her.

Sometimes, in more positive mood, she thought about how she could get a store of her own again, here in Melbourne. But all too quickly the realities came crowding in, dispelling the brief moments of hopeful planning. If no one would even give her a job what hope did she have of finding someone to put up the money to get her started? And to seek out a backer would be to draw attention to herself, the woman from the goldfields whose store had been backed by the Commissioner and who had died for his involvement with her.

And then, just when all had seemed at its blackest and most hopeless, James Hannay had come into her life like a knight on a white charger and offered her a job, a home and hope for the future. He had fed her, bought her new clothes such as she had never dreamed of owning and paid for her passage on the Cobb coach.

But most important of all, Tara thought, James Hannay's farm was way out in the wilds, far from Melbourne, far from Ballarat. If the troopers were searching for her they would never look on a farm in the middle of nowhere, and the few people she was likely to meet would never have heard of Henry Dupont, much less know of his murder. But she had taken the precaution, all the same, of using her maiden name when James had asked her what it was.

Tara Reilly. Dear God, in another life she *had* been Tara Reilly, young, innocent, full of hope. Perhaps using that name again now would change her fortune, for certainly little had gone the way she had hoped since she had become Tara Murphy.

Yet the knowledge that she was deceiving her rescuer nagged mercilessly at Tara. Mammy had brought her up to be honest and tell the truth at all times; failure to do so meant a visit to the confessional. Tara couldn't remember the last time she had lied about anything. Now the weight of what this one little untruth was concealing from James Hannay bore unbearably on her conscience.

He would never have hired her, never, if he knew what she had done. A murderess and thief, living under his roof and taking care of his child – unthinkable! And however she liked to wrap it up, whatever excuses she made for herself, that was what she was, Tara thought. She had taken a man's life, shot him with his own gun and stolen his valuables whilst he lay dead in the room. That was what she had to live with for the rest of her life, that was her terrible secret. And a secret it must remain, borne alone and agonised over.

Perhaps, Tara thought, that was part of her punishment, that and the knowledge that she was betraying and deceiving those who trusted her.

Dunrae. As the gig carried her up the drive where the autumn sun glinted in sharply piercing rays through the gums and mimosa trees which lined it, and Tara caught sight of the low white house for the first time, she thought that never, since she had left Ireland, had she seen anything so beautiful.

The Cobb coach had deposited her in the nearest township and James Hannay had been there to meet her, driving the neat gig drawn by a pair of matched bays. After the stomach-churning confinement of the coach it was sheer pleasure to feel the wind in her hair as the gig bowled along the arrow-straight track that ran amidst rolling open pastureland, which, James told her, all belonged to Dunrae.

He must be very wealthy, Tara though, and wondered briefly how he had come to have so much when so many in this new land had so little. But she felt no bitterness. Jealousy had no place in Tara's nature. She accepted the order of things for what it was. And she was only grateful that at last her fortunes seemed to have turned for the better and glad that Dunrae was so isolated, so far from civilisation and anyone who might connect her with the death of the Commissioner.

She felt a twist of nervousness now, however, as the gig rounded the house and came to a halt in a wide yard surrounded by stables and outbuildings. So far she hadn't thought beyond the fact that she would have a roof over her head and the chance of a new life; now suddenly she found herself wondering how she would cope with her duties. She'd never had to keep house or cook proper meals – at home in Ireland Mary had taken care of those things and life in the goldfields had not given her the opportunity to learn. A two-roomed shack was a far cry from this impressive house which looked more like a mansion to Tara, and slicing salt pork and boiling up beans in a billy can hardly constituted cooking. As for looking after a little boy – she knew nothing whatever of children. What would he be like, her new charge? James had said he was a scamp, in danger of running wild. Supposing she was no better able to control him than the overseer's wife had been? Why, James might send her packing in no time at all and look for someone with more experience to fill the position.

As for James's two brothers, Philip and Cal, how was she going to get along with them? How would they react to a strange woman sharing their home? Tara felt as if her stomach were tying itself in knots.

'Here we are then.' James loosed the reins and glanced at her. 'You look ready for a cup of tea, Miss Reilly. You've had a long journey.'

Tara forced a smile. 'Sure, I can't say I'm sorry it's over.

But I wish you'd call me Tara, Mr Hannay. "Miss Reilly" makes me feel about a hundred years old.'

His lips twitched. 'Very well – Tara. But only if you agree to return the favour and call me James. Being called Mr Hannay has much the same effect on me.'

Tara's forced smile became a natural one. 'It's a deal.'

A small wizened man, his face wrinkled and tanned nut-brown from years of exposure to hot summer suns and biting winter winds, emerged from one of the outhouses and hurried to take the bridle of one of the bays. Was he an ex-convict? Tara wondered. James had told her he had several in his employ, one of whom had worked for his grandfather, Andrew Mackenzie, at Mia-Mia, and been with the family for most of his life.

'Thank you, Dickon,' James said. He sprang down from the gig, coming round to hand Tara down too. 'Bring the lady's bags in when you've stabled the horses, will you?'

'I was looking for Master Duncan,' the little man said. His eyes were faded blue in his weathered face. 'But I'll see to the horses first if that's what you want.'

James's face darkened. 'What do you mean, you were looking for Master Duncan? He's in the house surely?'

'No, sir, he's not,' the little man replied. 'Well, not that Mr Philip could find him, leastways. He's gone to see if Master Duncan is down by the creek, and he told me and the other men to have a good look in the hay barn and outbuildings to see if he's hiding himself there.'

'The little devil!' James grated. 'I expressly told him he was to stay indoors until I got back. I'll teach him to disobey me!'

'Mr Philip said you wouldn't be best pleased,' the little man said mildly. 'I wouldn't worry too much if I were you. Boys will be boys, and he'll come home when he's hungry.'

'Hungry or not, he'll go to bed without his supper,' James fumed. He turned to Tara. 'I'm sorry about this. I wanted him here to meet you. Now you can see why I'm beginning to despair of him. The moment my back is turned the boy does as he pleases.'

'Don't be cross with him on my account, please!' Tara begged. 'Sure I don't mind, honestly.'

'But I do.' James's mouth was a hard line. This was a side to him she hadn't seen before, Tara thought. When he had rescued her in Melbourne he'd shown her nothing but kindness. Now she saw a flash of what might well be a fearsome temper and a steeliness that surprised her. 'I won't have wilful disobedience and I won't have rudeness. Not being here to greet you is rudeness in the extreme.' He turned briefly to the little man once more. 'Carry on searching for him, Dickon. And when you find him bring him to me by the scruff of his neck. I'll take Miss Reilly's bags into the house myself.'

He swung her brand new carpet bag, a dressmaker's box and a hat box from the back of the gig and began to stride towards the house so fast that Tara almost had to run to keep up with him. She felt more nervous than ever now. This wasn't a very auspicious start . . .

James led the way up a short flight of steps edged by beds which were, in summer, bright and fragrant with asters and night-scented stocks, but had now been stripped for winter. They crossed a narrow white-painted veranda, and he threw open the door. It led directly into a large homely kitchen where a range glowed a welcome and the table was set ready for an evening meal. A rotund elderly woman in calico gown and all-enveloping apron turned from the range where she had been stirring a pot of something which filled the room with the delicious aroma of cooking, regarding Tara with a curious and not altogether friendly expression.

'We're here, Martha,' James said unnecessarily. 'This is Tara Reilly who will be relieving you of all this hard work once she's settled in. Tara, meet Martha Henderson. Her husband is overseer here.'

Tara was surprised that a man old enough to be this

woman's husband was still working as an overseer for the young and virile James, but she hid it, approaching Martha with a smile and holding out her hand. Martha ignored her.

'Master Duncan has run off again,' she said shortly to James, waving her cooking spoon to emphasise her words. 'Mr Philip is out looking for him.'

'Yes, Martha, I had heard,' James told her.

'The boy is nothing but a scallywag and a ruffian in the making. If I was a few years younger and he was mine I'd give him a good hiding to show him the error of his ways.' Martha glowered furiously, her concertina of rubbery chins wobbling their agreement.

'You won't have to worry about his mischief for much longer,' James soothed her. 'Tara is going to be responsible for keeping him in line.'

Martha cast a withering glance at Tara and snorted derisively. 'She's welcome to the job, I'm sure.'

It occurred to Tara that her appointment might have ruffled the old woman's feathers. Little as she wanted the responsibility of cooking for the family and looking after an unruly six-year-old, she didn't like being replaced either. Perhaps it made her feel old and useless.

'Sure an' I'll be looking to you for advice,' she said earnestly. 'I hope you'll tell me about all his little ways and how best to deal with them.'

Martha snorted again but the tight line of her mouth softened a little and Tara hoped she had gone some way to mollifying the older woman. Ill-feeling was something she could well do without, even if Martha wasn't actually part of the household.

'Is there hot water in the copper?' James asked. 'I'm sure Tara would like to freshen up after her journey.'

'There was – if Mister Cal hasn't used it all.' Martha turned back to the range as she spoke and resumed skimming the scum off what Tara realised must be a stew. 'He came in half an hour ago covered in muck and dirt and trekked half of it across my clean floor. I had to wash it all over again. As if I hadn't enough to do.'

'Do I hear someone taking my name in vain?'

The voice, light and amused, came from the doorway which led to the rest of the house. Tara turned towards it and saw a strikingly handsome young man standing there. That he was James's brother was instantly obvious. Though whippier and less muscular, he was of similar height and he had the same slate grey eyes and thick dark hair. But where James's features were slightly irregular, his were classically proportioned, and where James's face already bore the deep lines of experience – and exposure to the elements – his was still smooth and youthful. He was, Tara guessed, closer to her own age.

'I was just telling Mr Hannay how you trekked dirt across my clean floor,' Martha said. Her tone was as sharp as ever but there was a twinkle in her eye that said it all. Martha had a soft spot for Cal Hannay.

'I know. I did say I was sorry.' Cal's eyes were on Tara, appraising and appreciative. 'So this is our new housekeeper is it, James? Well, I must say you've done well. She appears to meet all our requirements.'

Though she had not been privy to the conversation between the brothers on the night Philip had first suggested taking on live-in help, there was no mistaking Cal's meaning. Tara felt hot colour rushing to her cheeks. She glanced at James and saw that same darkening of his expression as when the farm-hand had told him Duncan was missing.

'Yes, this is Tara Reilly,' he said shortly. 'And I hope you will treat her with the respect she deserves.'

'Would I do anything else?' Cal's face assumed an expression of total innocence but the grey eyes sparkled wickedly. 'Welcome to Dunrae, Tara. I'm Cal – known as the rake of the family, which is why my brother casts aspersions. Take no notice of him, is my advice.'

In spite of herself, Tara couldn't help laughing. There was

something very likeable about Cal Hannay that had nothing whatever to do with those striking good looks.

As if the sudden rapport between them had touched a nerve, James moved impatiently.

'Cal, can I leave you to take Tara's bags and show her where her room is?' he said. 'I'm going out to find Duncan. Excuse me,' he added to Tara.

Then without another word or a backward glance he strode out of the kitchen.

The room Cal showed her to was large and sunny. A patchwork quilt covered the bed, matching curtains hung at the windows, and bright rag rugs were scattered across the bare board floor. A large ornate wardrobe occupied one corner and a china jug and basin stood on the marble-topped washstand.

Tara gasped with pleasure. After the conditions she had been forced to live in for so long the room looked like a little bit of heaven.

Cal smiled. James had told him of the hostel and it was well known that goldfields life was rough and ready to say the least.

'Will this suit you then?' he asked.

'Oh, yes!' Tara ran her hand across the counterpane. It was all she could do to keep from collapsing onto it and rubbing her cheek into the fine cotton.

'I'll leave you to unpack,' Cal said. 'Martha will bring you some water as soon as it's hot so that you can freshen up. Supper will be as soon as that scamp Duncan shows his face again, I expect. I'll be just downstairs if you want me.'

Again that cheeky look. Tara was forced to smile. Cal was a womaniser, not a doubt of it, but he was no Henry Dupont. She couldn't imagine he had ever forced himself on a woman in his life, or needed to. But she was determined to keep him in his place all the same.

'I'm sure I have everything I need,' she said demurely.

'For the moment, perhaps.' He grinned broadly, showing perfectly even white teeth.

'For a very long time I should think,' Tara returned. 'Your brother has been more than kind to me.'

Cal nodded, his face turned serious. 'James is a good man and life hasn't always treated him kindly. If he's a little short-tempered sometimes that is the reason why. But he's told you, no doubt, how he lost his wife.'

'He said he was a widower, yes,' Tara confirmed. 'How did she die?'

'Of rheumatic fever.' Cal's voice was sombre now, with no hint of his usual bantering manner. 'James worshipped her. He's never got over it.'

'How dreadful for him.' Tara knew enough about heartache to feel genuine sympathy.

'It's changed him utterly.' Cal was silent for a moment, then he grinned again, reverting to his easy good humour. 'Philip is a bit of a sobersides, too. But don't worry, I more than make up for the pair of them.'

'I'm sure you do,' Tara said wryly.

'I'll leave you, then.' Cal placed the carpet bag beside the wardrobe, stacked the dress box and hat box on a chintz-covered stool and turned to the door. As it closed after him Tara pressed her hands to her face, looking at the delightful room over the tips of her fingers. Then she did what she had been longing to do ever since she had set eyes on the inviting bed. She lay down on it. And felt something hard and lumpy in the small of her back.

Puzzled, Tara rolled over and got up again, turning the quilt back and then the sheet.

Apples. Her bed was full of small mis-shapen green apples. Tara almost laughed out loud. It didn't take a great stretch of the imagination to guess who had put them there.

So her young charge had prepared a dubious welcome for her. Well, it could have been worse, a frog or a spider or even a snake. The worst these miserable-looking apples would have to offer would be a maggot or two and no doubt they were all nestling safely in the cores and gorging themselves there.

Tara removed the apples, took them to the window and dropped them out onto the lawn below. She wouldn't say a word about this. The last thing she wanted was to get Duncan into more trouble. If she was to build any sort of relationship with him she didn't want him to think of her as someone who would run to his father telling tales. And in any case it would be quite amusing to see how he reacted when she didn't so much as mention it . . .

James Hannay strode purposefully across the stable yard. He was fuming with annoyance that Duncan had run off again but he had a fair idea where he'd find him. He didn't think the lad had adventure on his mind this afternoon. His absence was all to do with Tara's arrival. Duncan had reacted with defiance when James had explained he was going to Melbourne to try to find someone to take care of him, and when James had galloped into the yard on Tarquin this morning his delight at seeing his father had quickly turned to sulkiness when James told him his mission had been successful and Tara would be coming in on the Cobb coach later that very day.

'I don't want her here!' he had said, scowling.

'What you want, my lad, has nothing to do with it,' James had replied sternly. 'Martha can't cope with you any more and your uncles and I can't be here all the time to keep an eye on you.'

'I don't need anyone to keep an eye on me.' Duncan's small face was puckering angrily. 'I'm not a baby any more. I'm all grown up.'

'That's a matter of opinion, Duncan,' James told him. 'If you were really all grown up you'd have known better than to lead Martha such a merry dance. You won't trick Tara so easily.'

'Tara?' the little boy repeated scornfully. 'What a stupid name!'

James sighed. 'She comes from Ireland, on the other side of the world. She's very pretty and she's much younger than Martha – younger than me, even – and you'll like her, I'm sure.'

Duncan scowled. 'I won't. I'll hate her.'

'Very well, have it your own way,' James said wearily. 'But if I catch you being impolite to her I shall put you across my knee and spank you. Is that clear?'

Duncan stared his father out. James had never so much as laid a finger on him and never would and Duncan knew it.

'I mean it, Duncan,' James had reiterated. 'Things are going to change around here unless you learn to behave yourself. Now, I am going to take the gig and go to meet the coach. Do you want to come with me?'

Usually Duncan was eager for a drive in the gig. James would let him sit between his knees and take the reins and the little boy loved to pretend that he was driving it all by himself. But today the carrot had failed to have the desired effect.

'No. Don't want to come.'

'Are you sure now?'

'Don't want to come. I said.'

'Very well, the loss is yours. But I want you here clean and tidy and in a better mood by the time I get back with Tara. No running off somewhere and no getting yourself filthy. Do you understand?'

Well, he'd known that a better mood was a tall order, James thought as he strode towards the stables. But this outright defiance of his instructions was something else altogether. What Tara must think – that he couldn't control his own son – James dared not imagine. A feeling of shame fuelled his anger and he pushed the stable door wide and went inside.

It was dim in the stables and the smell of hay and dung was overpowering, but sweet to James's nostrils. Tarquin whickered as he passed his stall but for once James ignored him, making for the end stall where Duncan's pony Jim was stabled. The door of the stall was closed and no sound came from within.

'Duncan, come out! I know you're there,' James said sternly.

Still there was no sound and no movement except Jim shifting slightly, poking his nose over the door. James felt a moment's alarm. Perhaps he had been wrong. If so he would hardly know where to begin looking for Duncan. Could it be he had been so fed up at the thought of having a nursemaid to look after him that he had run away? James wouldn't put it past him. But no, if he had run away, Duncan would have been sure to take Jim with him. He adored his pony, he would never run off and leave him behind.

'Duncan!' he said sharply. 'Come out this minute or it will be the worse for you!'

And then he heard it. A muffled sniff and a gulp that might have been a sob. Duncan was there all right, and he was crying. James's heart turned over. Duncan scarcely ever cried, but when he did it tore James to shreds.

He pulled the stable door open. In the dim light it was almost impossible to see the little boy. No wonder Dickon Stokes had not discovered him there. His eyes were not as good as they'd used to be, nor his hearing, come to that. But there was nothing wrong with James's sight, and he could just make out the shape at the very back of the stall.

'Come out of there at once, Duncan,' he said. 'And gently, too, if you don't want Jim to kick you.'

'Jim wouldn't kick me.' Duncan's voice was thick with tears.

'You don't know that. Come on now.'

The little boy came, crawling between Jim's sturdy legs.

'What are you doing in here when I told you to be ready and waiting for Tara?' James demanded sternly. 'I'm very disappointed in you, Duncan.'

Duncan hung his head. 'Is *she* here?' he muttered.

'If you mean Tara, yes she is. And I was very ashamed when the first thing she heard when she arrived was that you had run off again. Why did you do it, Duncan?'

The little boy was silent, scuffing at a heap of straw with the toe of his boot.

'Because you didn't want to meet Tara, I suppose,' James said. 'Well, it won't work. You can't avoid her for ever. She's here to stay, whether you like it or not. Now, we're going into the house and you are going to have a wash and brush-up so that she doesn't think you are a complete ragamuffin.'

'Don't care what she thinks!' Duncan burst out suddenly. 'Don't want her here, Papa!' His voice wobbled suddenly. 'I want Mama . . .'

James's heart contracted. He bent down, putting his arm round his son's quivering shoulders.

'Oh Duncan, we all want Mama! But Mama isn't here any more. And she'd want someone kind to take care of you now that she can't do it herself, don't you think? Tara will cook your meals and brush your hair and tuck you into bed at night. And you can show her your favourite places and . . .'

Duncan looked up at him, interrupting. 'She won't wear Mama's clothes, will she? Or sleep in Mama's bed? I know she's in the Blue Room tonight, but . . .'

'Of course she won't!' James said with feeling and wondered if that was what was concerning Duncan – that Tara was somehow a replacement for the mother he had lost. 'No one can take your Mama's place, ever,' he went on fiercely. 'So don't worry that they might. Come on now, let's go inside.'

As if he recognised the ring of sincerity in James's voice and was reassured by it, Duncan rubbed the last of the tears out of his eyes with his knuckles and allowed James to lead him out of the stables and towards the house.

Seven

S upper was a pleasant enough meal, though Duncan was quieter than usual, pushing Martha's delicious stew around his plate. Several times James caught him looking slyly at Tara and wondered what was going on behind those guarded grey eyes. But at least he had shaken her by the hand civilly enough and not been downright rude as James had feared he might be. Cal had been his usual charming self, and the only awkward moment had come when Philip had questioned Tara about her past.

'So you came to Australia from Ireland,' he had said, spooning another helping of tender beef onto his plate. 'It's a long way.'

'Indeed it is,' Tara had agreed.

'And did you make the voyage alone?'

James could see at once that the question made Tara uncomfortable. He had encountered the same reluctance when he had attempted to find out something about the young woman he had brought to Dunrae, and he wondered about it. But Australia was full of people reluctant to talk about their past and it was regarded as taboo to press them.

'Like all of us, Tara no doubt has some unfortunate experiences that she would prefer to forget,' he said easily. 'It's the future that matters now, not the past.'

She flashed him a look of gratitude, and something sweet and sharp twisted deep within him, startling him with its suddenness and intensity. He was as curious as Philip as to how she had come to be in the dire situation in which he had found her but now, looking at her lovely haunted face, he wanted only to protect her from whatever it was she preferred to forget.

'Do you ride, Tara?' he asked, changing the subject.

Pink colour flooded her cheeks and she shook her head.

'But you must ride!' Cal said in astonishment. 'I thought Ireland was full of horses!'

'For those with money, yes. We didn't have much money. And in any case . . .' She laughed, a little embarrassed. 'I've always been a little afraid of horses.'

'Oh, we'll soon change that!' Cal declared confidently. 'Horses are a necessity out here in the bush. I'll have you riding like an old stockman in no time!'

Tara bit her lip; again her vulnerability made that certain something twist deep within James.

'You'll do no such thing, Cal,' he said authoritatively. 'Tara doesn't want to ride like a stockman, do you, Tara? If horses make her nervous the best thing is for her to learn to drive the gig – at least then she doesn't have to sit on one. And I'll teach her myself when she feels ready.'

'Oh, I couldn't put you to so much trouble!' Tara protested.

'The master of Dunrae has spoken, Tara. It doesn't do to go against his plans.' Cal was grinning as he said it but there was just a hint of bitterness beneath the jovial tone that suggested for a brief moment some hint of unspoken rivalry between the two brothers.

When the meal was over and it was time for Duncan to go to bed James wondered if he should suggest Tara came up with him to see where the little boy slept and wish him good night. But he decided against it. Given Duncan's reluctance to have a woman here to look after him it was best to take one step at a time.

'Say goodnight to everyone then, Duncan,' he said.

Duncan did so, but he was still unusually subdued and there was none of the usual chatter or even protest as he folded his clothes and got into his nightshirt. Then, when he was kneeling beside his bed for his nightly prayers, he looked up at James from behind folded fingers.

'Papa . . .'

'Yes, Duncan?'

'I don't have to tell everything bad that I've done today do I?'

James frowned. 'Hiding in the stables, you mean?'

'Yes . . . and . . .'

James regarded him sternly. 'What else have you done, then?'

There was a small pregnant pause, then Duncan shut his eyes tightly and surreptitiously crossed his fingers.

'Nothing.'

James shook his head despairingly. He was anxious suddenly to be downstairs again, to ensure that Philip hadn't taken advantage of his absence to question Tara, or Cal to flirt.

'Get on with it then, Duncan. And ask God to help you to be kind to Tara.'

The little boy's lips moved silently and James had no way of knowing that what he was in fact praying for was that he would find a way to get rid of her. And the sooner the better.

Soon after Duncan had gone to bed Tara rose and began stacking the plates together.

'If you don't mind I'll get the supper things cleared away and have an early night,' she said. 'I'm very tired and I do want to be fresh for my duties tomorrow.'

'Indeed, we intend to work you to death!' Cal joked, propping his booted feet up on the chair she had vacated, and Philip said seriously: 'You'll certainly need all your energy to deal with young Duncan.'

James, however, took the pile of plates from Tara's hands. 'Leave them and go to bed now. We'll clear the table and the convict women can wash the dishes in the morning. It's what we usually do.'

Tara frowned. 'But it's my job now I'm here. I'm not a guest.'

'Tonight you are,' James said. He had seen her eyelids drooping several times over supper. 'Tomorrow as Cal promised we'll work your fingers to the bone. But tonight . . . you look exhausted.'

'Well, if you're sure . . .' Still she hesitated, her eyes, dark in her pale face, meeting James's own with a directness that stirred something in him once again.

'Quite sure,' he said firmly. 'No more arguments – off you go.'

When their goodnights had been said and Tara had left the room Cal laughed softly. 'You picked a winner there and no mistake!' He reached for his drink. 'I wouldn't complain if she mistook the rooms and I found her in my bed! And if I don't, I might make a mistake myself and find myself in hers!'

'Try a trick like that, Cal, and you'll have me to answer to,' James flared.

'It was but a joke!' Cal protested.

'Not one that I find in the least amusing.' James's face was like a thunder-cloud. 'Tara is not the sort of woman to take advantage of.'

'It was a joke I tell you, man!' Cal was beginning to sound irritated himself. 'Why, I do believe you fancy her yourself!'

James swung round, banging down the pile of dishes he had been clearing onto the table with such force that the cutlery leaped and rattled. So furious did he look Philip thought he was going to strike Cal.

'James, for the love of God, what has got into you?'

For a moment James remained motionless, frozen into the hunched posture of a fighter about to attack. Then he straightened, flexing his bunched fists.

'I'll forget you said that, Cal. You know that Lorna was the only woman for me. There will never be another.'

106

He turned on his heel and strode to the door.

'Well!' Cal exclaimed as it closed after him. He looked a little shaken by his brother's outburst. 'That was a fine display and no mistake!'

'You should know better than to rile him,' Philip said evenly. He ran a hand through his thick auburn hair, inherited from his mother, though like his two brothers he too had his father's slate-grey eyes. 'You know how touchy he can be on the subject of women – how he blames himself for Lorna's death and how he is determined to honour her memory.'

Cal raised an eyebrow. 'Maybe. But I can't help feeling our brother doth protest too much. I touched a raw nerve, Philip, and not just his grief and guilt for Lorna. It's my opinion that James has feelings for our new housekeeper, whether he'll admit to them or not!'

As she crossed to the bedroom window to draw the drapes Tara heard the raised voices coming from downstairs. Though she was unable to make out what they were saying her heartbeat quickened and she felt a tug of dismay. Coming so close on her leaving the kitchen she couldn't help feeling that whatever it was it had to do with her. But what? Were Philip and Cal opposed to James having given her the job? They had seemed friendly enough, particularly Cal, but one could never be sure. Tara's experiences had taught her to trust no one.

She bit her lip anxiously. It was so important to her that this should work out. But the last thing she wanted was to cause trouble between the three brothers.

She heard the slam of the kitchen door immediately beneath her window. It was open a little to let fresh air into the room and though she dared not open it wider Tara pressed her nose against the pane, trying to see which of them had stormed out.

The moment he came into her line of vision she could see it was James. In the light of the moon he cut an impressive

107

figure – tall, dark, muscular, the hero of a thousand penny romances, every woman's dream. Except hers, for she had no dreams left. For a moment Tara felt almost regretful, aching with nostalgic sadness for the young girl she had once been. But that girl and her youthful innocence had gone for ever. There could be no going back. She was on her own now and that was the way she would stay.

She stood at the window, watching James cross the stable yard. There was barely controlled fury in every movement, every line of his body. Where was he going? she wondered. Surely he was not going to take a horse and ride out at this time of night? He had reached the stable now. But he did not unlatch the door. Instead he stopped, standing for a moment, head bowed as if in thought. Then with a suddenness that startled her, he brought his fists up, hammering on the wall before leaving them there and bending his head again to lay it against the rough stone between his crooked arms.

Tara felt a rush of pity and alarm and she wished she had not remained at the window. There was nothing worse than witnessing a man's loss of composure, particularly when he thought he was giving way to his feelings in private. It made her feel like a Peeping Tom. But somehow she was quite unable to move away. For endless minutes, it seemed, James stood there and Tara watched him, mesmerised. Then he threw his head back, staring up at the stars, and although his back was towards her Tara imagined she could see the agonised look on his rugged face.

She did move then, tearing herself away from the window and swishing the drapes shut. There was a heaviness in her heart that had nothing to do with her own troubles and when she had undressed and lain down she could see him still in her mind's eye.

To the outside world James Hannay was strong, decisive, ice-cool, maybe even a little hard. But she had just glimpsed a side of him that few, if any, others were privileged to see. She had witnessed a man in torment, and it tore at her heart.

*   *   *

Next morning when Tara came downstairs everything had returned to normal. Whatever the brothers had quarrelled about last night, it seemed to have been forgotten now. And James's mask was firmly back in place.

'Martha has said she'll come in to acquaint you with everything,' he said, piling cold ham for a hearty breakfast onto his plate.

Tara's heart sank. There had been no mistaking the fact that the older woman resented her.

'There's really no need. Duncan will point out everything I need to know, won't you, Duncan?' She glanced at the little boy who studiously avoided meeting her eye.

'Well, if you think you can manage . . .' James said. 'I think Martha might well put in an appearance, all the same. She hates to admit it's all got too much for her. It's the same with Matt, her husband.'

'Yes, I was wondering about him,' Tara admitted. 'If he's your overseer he must be a good bit younger than her I should think.'

James laughed. 'No, he's not any younger. In fact I think he's older, and he's an overseer in name only these days. Philip, Cal and I run things perfectly well between us. But Matt has been with us so long I haven't the heart to tell him he's no longer needed – and not up to it in any case. I pay his wage, he potters, and everyone is happy.'

'That's uncommonly generous of you,' Tara said.

'Not a bit of it.' James speared a piece of ham on his fork. 'Matt's more than earned his retirement over many years of faithful service. And Martha too. And no one likes to feel old and useless. She'll be here to put you through your paces, mark my words. And in spite of appearances to the contrary she'll be enjoying every minute of it.'

Sure enough, Martha put her head around the kitchen door even before James had finished his breakfast. She began busying about, ignoring Tara.

109

'I'll get things started, Mr Hannay.'

'Perhaps you could show Tara what to do,' James suggested tactfully.

'I will. All in good time. Best she just help me for the moment.' She shot a look at Tara. 'There's mutton for a pie for tonight's supper. Can you make pastry?'

Tara felt a moment's panic. She hadn't made pastry since she was a little girl helping Mammy on baking days. But she was not about to admit it.

'I make very good soda bread,' she said stoutly. 'Why don't you make your mutton pie, Martha, since putting it on the menu was your idea, and I'll make soda bread to go with it. I'm sure there's room for us to work side by side.'

'Oh!' For a moment the wind dropped out of Martha's sails, then she puffed herself up again. 'Perhaps it would be best if I did it myself. Mr James always says my pastry is the lightest in the whole of Victoria. Isn't that right, Mr James?'

'Indeed it is, Martha,' James agreed, doing his best to hide an amused smile.

Tara heaved a silent sigh of relief. At least she'd wriggled her way out of that one – and won the first round at the same time, she rather thought.

'When the convict women get in you'd best leave me to deal with them,' Martha said, tying a huge apron round her portly frame.

'Why?' Tara enquired innocently.

'Because they're a pair of insolent lazy galumphs.' Martha's chins quivered beneath her tight lips. 'If you don't keep them in their place they'll run rings round you.'

'I'm sure. But I'll be firm with them, have no fear,' Tara said.

Martha was not about to give up so easily. 'They'll take it better from me.'

Neither was Tara. 'Nevertheless, the sooner they come to realise that I'm in charge of them now the better,' she said firmly.

Again James hid a smile. 'I'm sure Tara will be more than a match for Dora and Lizzie,' he said. 'But she'll be glad of your advice for today at any rate, won't you, Tara? After that, though, I'm sure you'll be only too glad to take things easily, Martha. Matt is looking forward to you being able to spend more time with him in your own home, I know, and you'll be able to visit your son down river more often too now that Tara is here.'

Relieved, Tara realised she had an ally. If Martha had her way she would have turned Tara's role into something no better than a kitchen-maid, Tara realised. But for all his tactful approach James wasn't going to let that happen.

He seemed in no hurry to go out either. Both Philip and Cal had left to go about their duties on the farm but James was still hanging around the house. Although he explained himself by saying he was supervising Duncan's lessons until Tara could manage to do that as well as her domestic duties, Tara could not help wondering if the real reason was that he wanted to be there to keep the peace.

The convict women, Dora and Lizzie, arrived and, good as her word, Tara set them to washing last night's supper things before instructing Dora to clean the house and Lizzie to make a start on washing some of the heap of dirty linen that was waiting to be laundered. They were an ill-matched pair, Dora thin and sullen with a narrow face and weasly eyes, Lizzie big and raw-boned with enormous front teeth which protruded beneath her upper lip and as fine a moustache as Tara had seen on any man.

As midday approached Martha departed for her own home to prepare Matt's meal and soon afterwards James came into the kitchen with Duncan.

'He's worked hard at his lessons,' he said, rumpling the boy's hair. 'I think he's earned a break. And so have you, Tara. Would you like to go for a bit of a walk, have a good look round outside and get your bearings? The wind is cold, but the sun in shining.'

'Sure, that would be great,' Tara said.

'And Duncan will act as your guide, won't you, Duncan? There's no one knows every inch of Dunrae better than he does.'

To her surprise Tara felt a stab of something that might almost have been disappointment. She had thought James was going to show her round himself. But at least it would give her the chance to get to know the little boy better if they were alone, she thought, pushing the disappointment to one side. It was so important for them to get on well if she was to be responsible for him and so far he seemed to view her with suspicion and dislike. She smiled at Duncan; he only scowled back.

'I'll get my shawl.'

As she returned she heard James telling him to behave himself and not play any tricks on his new governess. She smiled slightly. She had a little surprise of her own up her sleeve for Duncan . . .

Tara let Duncan show her the stables, where his bad grace improved somewhat as he introduced her to each of the horses by name, and the outhouse full of farm implements, then, as they headed for the front of the house, she said: 'Oh, by the way, Duncan, I'd like to thank you for the welcome you prepared for me yesterday.'

The little boy looked up at her, guilt and confusion written all over his small face, yet still unable to stop a small satisfied smirk.

'It was very kind of you,' she went on. 'The apples were delicious, just right for when I woke in the night feeling hungry.'

The smirk disappeared; his eyes widened.

'You didn't *eat* them?' he said before he could stop himself.

'But of course!' Tara said, feigning astonishment. 'Why shouldn't I? Wasn't that why you left them there?'

'Oh . . . yes . . .' She had totally wrong-footed him, but

even so he couldn't keep from asking: 'Haven't you got a tummy ache?'

'I've never felt better!' Tara smiled brightly. 'Why, do apples give you tummy ache, Duncan?'

'No.' He kicked at a small stone, which scudded ahead of them up the drive. In a pen alongside it, ducks quacked and strutted and hens clucked.

'Then you must have some too! Why don't you show me the orchard where you got them and we can both fill our pockets. Is it this way?' Tara asked.

'Yes, but . . .'

'Come on then!' she urged him.

The orchard was beyond the paddock. Duncan had no choice but to lead her to it. The trees, of course, were bare now; all the choicest fruit had been harvested and stored away in barrels in the barn.

'So where are these apples then?' Tara asked. 'Oh, I see, here they are – all lying in the grass.' She bent and picked up one small knobbly faller, the very same as the ones he had put in her bed. 'Look, you have this one. I'll see if I can find another for myself.'

Reluctantly he took it from her. His small face was very red now.

'Tuck in!' she urged him, wondering how he would wriggle out of this one and half expecting him to hurl the apple away. But Duncan was made of sterner stuff. As she watched he gulped, took a deep breath, and went to bite into the apple.

Horrified, Tara shot out a hand to stop him.

'Duncan no, you don't have to. I was only teasing. Sure, I might be Irish, but I know the difference between an eating apple and a cooker, and so do you. So let's stop playing games, shall we?'

He nodded slowly, glad not to have to eat the horrible sharp little faller, but feeling incredibly foolish.

'Can't we be friends, Duncan?' she pleaded.

He shrugged, the defensive look coming back to his face.

Tara sighed. She might have scored a point, but there was clearly some way to go yet before she won him over.

'It must be nearly time to eat,' she said. 'All this talk of apples has made me hungry. Shall we go back and see what we can have for dinner?'

Duncan nodded, and together they went back towards the house.

Eight

Winter came in with a vengeance. Rain fell from a leaden sky, waterlogging the pastures and turning the tracks to quagmire, and the wind blew stronger and colder, bringing down the last of the leaves and whipping them into swirls of dun brown flecked with orange and yellow.

Life at Dunrae had settled into a pattern for Tara. By day she carried out her household duties, prepared meals and supervised Duncan's lessons. At night she lingered with the brothers over coffee, sang along with them whilst Philip played the piano or joined in a game of three-card brag, then fell into bed exhausted. But sleep refused to come easily – her guilty conscience saw to that – and when it did she was all too often plagued by nightmares.

It had happened again tonight and it had begun in the way it always did. She was trapped. To begin with, Tara was never sure of the circumstances, just the horrible panicky feeling of a bird caught in a snare. Something bad was going to happen. She knew it. She must wake up in order to escape. But she couldn't. Her eyelids were heavy as lead, every muscle paralysed. And then *he* came to her, Henry Dupont, leering, determined to have her. Always she found the gun in her hand, always the fear and revulsion slicked her body with a fine sheen of sweat, always she felt the terrible inevitability of what she was about to do. And yet, when she pulled the trigger, he still kept on coming towards her, even as the blood turned his shirt scarlet and bubbled on his thick fleshy lips. And he taunted her. '*You can't stop me so easily, Tara. You'll*

never stop me. And you'll never be free of me either . . .' As
he reached for her with his flabby dead hands she screamed
and the scream woke her. She lay, eyes wide with terror, still
unable to bring herself to move a muscle. The dream was still
too real, flooding over the border from unconscious mind to
conscious and losing nothing in the process. He was still there
beside her. If she unfurled a finger, wriggled a toe, she might
encounter clammy cold flesh or congealing blood.

'Oh, Holy Mother, help me!' she prayed. 'I know I've
sinned grievously. I know I am unconfessed. But have pity
on me, please!'

As if her prayer had been answered the worst of the terror
began to subside. But the aura of the dream lingered like
a thick sea mist, cloying, suffocating. Tara lay a moment
longer, gathering her courage, then with a sob she pulled
herself up, her hands and feet encountering nothing but cool
lavender-scented sheet.

Soft moonlight, creeping in at a crack in the drapes, made
huge menacing shadows. Henry Dupont's dead face seemed
to leer at her from every corner. With trembling hands Tara
pushed aside the covers and got out of bed. She had no clear
idea of what she intended to do, only that she did not want to
go back to sleep, not yet. She was too afraid the nightmare
would begin again.

The heavy wrapper that James had bought for her in
Melbourne along with the other clothes lay across the back
of the upright chair beside her bed. Tara pulled it on, then lit
the candle she had snuffed out before going to sleep. Such a
tiny flame, too small to banish the demons. They danced more
gleefully than ever in the flickering shadows and she seemed
to hear their laughter in the creaking of the creeper that clung
to the wall outside her window as it stirred in the wind.

Taking the candle Tara crossed the room, opened the door
softly and went out on to the landing. The house was silent
but for a board settling now and then, silent and sleeping.
She crept along the landing away from the bedroom where

116

Henry Dupont's ghost lingered and down the stairs, making for the big friendly kitchen.

A drink. She'd warm herself some milk and tip a measure of James's whisky into it. Perhaps then she would feel ready to brave her bedroom again and even be able to sleep peacefully. The fire in the range still glowed comfortingly. Tara fanned it to life, poured some milk into a pan and set in on a trivet over the heat. Then she shrank down into one of the big comfortable chairs, drawing the wrapper tighter around her shivering body while she waited for the milk to come to the boil.

Oh, would these nightmares never stop? In the day, busy with her duties, surrounded by people who knew nothing of her past, she managed to avoid thinking of what she had done. But at night when she was defenceless in sleep the horrors lay in wait for her hand she suspected they always would. There could be no escape, never, as long as she lived. She might have avoided the rough justice that would be meted out to a murderer on the goldfields, but she could not escape her own conscience.

Tears pricked at Tara's eyes and a lump began to grow in her throat. *You had no choice*, she told herself but a small insistent voice replied all the same: *There is always a choice*. So many choices, and all of them leading inexorably to where she was today.

Oh, if only she had left the goldfields without going to the Commissioner for her savings . . . If only the floods hadn't washed away her stock . . . If only she hadn't gone into partnership with Henry Dupont in the first place . . . If only she and Patrick had stayed in Ireland . . .

Useless to have regrets now but she couldn't help thinking of how happy she and Patrick had once been and wondering what he was doing now. Was he with Seamus? Were they laughing together? Strange how even now the thought of the closeness the two men shared could hurt her. And there was so much more besides. Every sadness she had ever known

117

was weighing down on her, the memories flying about her like the mischiefs released from Pandora's box. Mammy's death – *'Oh Mammy, Mammy, why did you have to die?'* . . . the baby she had lost . . .

Oh, the baby! That was the worst pain of all. The tears welled and Tara wound her arms around her flat empty stomach, remembering how it had felt to have a new little life growing inside her, the hope, the love, the fierce instinctive need to protect it . . . and the awful realisation that she could not. Oh the baby . . . *her* baby . . .

A sudden explosive hissing and spitting made Tara jump almost out of her skin. The milk! She had forgotten all about it. Now it was boiling over. She leaped to her feet, sending a stool flying across the kitchen and diving for the milk pan without stopping to pick up a pot holder. The handle seared her palm and she screamed, dropping it again. More milk fizzled into the flames and the smell of burned milk filled the kitchen. Tara grabbed the pot holder and pulled the pan from the trivet. Like the last gasp of a dying volcano it dribbled a stream of milk on to the hearth before subsiding.

What a mess! And her hand was burning too. Suddenly it was all too much for Tara. The tears began to flow in earnest. She sank onto the rag rug before the hearth burying her face in her hands and sobbing so that her whole body shook.

'Tara?' The voice from the doorway startled her; she jumped, brushing her eyes with her fists, turning to see James's tall figure silhouetted in the dim light.

He came towards her, concerned. He was wearing a robe, hastily pulled on. Beneath it his feet and legs were bare.

'Tara? What's wrong?'

'Nothing . . . I couldn't sleep . . . I tried to make a drink and the milk boiled over . . .' Her voice was thick with tears. 'I've made a terrible mess.'

'Never mind that,' James said roughly. 'You're crying.'

'No, no, I'm not . . .' How stupid to deny it when her face was wet with tears! The thought brought a short hysterical bubble of laughter, the laughter unleashed the tears once more. Tara fought to control them but there was no way her wobbling chin and streaming eyes would obey. As she sobbed bitterly James looked down at her in concern, then he dropped to his knees beside her, pulling a handkerchief from the pocket of his robe and thrusting it into her hand.

'Tara, whatever is the matter? Aren't you happy here?'

For a moment she couldn't answer. She *was* happy here, happier than she had been in a long while, as happy as she ever could be again.

'It's not that.'

'Then what?' He hesitated, wondering if he was stepping beyond the pale, then took the chance. 'Is it something in your past? Someone you left behind?'

Again she couldn't answer him. She wasn't crying for Patrick, not really, but for all they had had and lost.

'Look.' James gesticulated helplessly. 'I don't know what happened to you before I found you in Melbourne, but I do know you'd had a hard time of it. If you want to talk – tell me about it – well, it might help, Tara.'

For a brief foolish moment she wished she could tell him. There was something so strong, so solid, so comforting about him she felt as if by confiding in him she could somehow purge her guilt, lessen the pain. But even as she thought it she knew it was an illusion. No one could absolve her of her sins and if James knew he would certainly send her away. However kind, however strong, he wouldn't want a murderess under his roof, caring for his child. She shook her head, swallowing at the tears.

'I don't want to talk about it. I want to forget.' She gulped, her lip tremoring. 'But I can't . . .'

James looked at her, this beautiful girl, so spirited and yet so vulnerable, and felt as helpless as he had felt when he had watched Lorna descend into black depression. What had she suffered in the weeks and months before he had found her? What was it that was tormenting her so now? If she wouldn't

119

tell him there was no way he could help her. Nothing he could do, except . . .

Without any thought in his head beyond comforting her, acting purely on instinct, James took her in his arms. His shoulder beneath her cheek was reassuringly solid, he held her gently but firmly. It was so long – so long! – since she had had any physical comfort from another living soul that the sympathy and tenderness and his concern for her, passing between them without the need of words, started her tears again, the soft snuffling sobs of emotions laid bare.

'Oh, Tara, Tara, don't! Don't cry!'

His hand went to the nape of her neck, stroking it gently, and shame for her weakness suffused her. She tried to summon the will to pull away, to dry her eyes, apologise, and could not. It felt too good, too safe, here in the circle of his arms, a place the demons could not reach.

Then, as the sobs subsided, Tara began to be aware of other things which crept seductively into her consciousness. The curling chest hair at the open neck of his robe tickling her nose, the clean male smell of his skin exciting her senses, the hard muscular lines of his body, the strength of his arms . . .

Something sharp and sweet twisted deep within her, her sensitised flesh seemed suddenly aware of him, creeping deliciously with a life of its own. She froze, scarcely daring to breathe as she examined the sensations. Holy Mother, she wanted him! Not just as a comfort but as a man! The realisation shocked her. She knew she should push herself away, put a stop to these forbidden longings that had begun so unexpectedly, yet she remained motionless, relishing the awareness of every nerve ending, the dizzying desire that danced in her veins, as powerless to overcome her sudden need for closeness as she had been to control her tears.

There could be nothing between them, Tara knew. She was a married woman who had made her matrimonial vows in the presence of God. The fact that she had run from Patrick didn't release her from those vows. Only death could do that. But surely, surely it would do no harm to stay here in his arms for just a few minutes longer? Surely it wasn't so wrong to . . . ?

Without knowing she did so Tara nestled a little closer. And then, quite suddenly, James held her away.

'Better now?' There was a rough edge to his voice.

Tara nodded, though the loss of the contact, the closeness, made her want to cry again. 'I'm so sorry . . .'

'There's no need. I'll pour you a brandy. It will help you sleep.'

He crossed the kitchen. She watched his every move, feeling her cheeks turn hot with the newly awakened awareness of him. She could scarcely believe the torrent of emotions his nearness had awakened in her. James poured brandy into two glasses; Tara's hand trembled as she stretched it out to take one of them. Then as the crystal touched her scorched palm she winced. With all the other sensations assailing her she had quite forgotten it.

'I burned my hand on the pan handle,' she explained shakily.

'Let me see.'

She turned her hand over. An angry red weal ran across the palm.

'I'll get you something for that.' James crossed to the dresser and returned with a small bottle of carron oil and a clean white rag. 'Dab this on. It will take away the burning.'

Tara did as he bid.

'Now drink your brandy.'

Again she obeyed, as if she were in a dream. The smell reminded her of the day he had found her in Melbourne and given her brandy in his hotel room, and the golden liquor ran a fiery path down her throat and into her veins.

'More?' he asked as she finished it. He had already drained and refilled his own glass.

Tara shook her head. 'Oh no, I mustn't! I'm not used to it. I'll be disgracing myself!'

Even as she said it she was struck by the irony of her words. Sure, hadn't she disgraced herself already?

'Perhaps you should go back to bed, then, and try to sleep.' The rough edge was still there in his voice.

'Yes, yes, I'll do that.' But she knew that sleep had never been further away. The dull burning pain in her hand, her racing thoughts and most of all the throbbing awareness which ached in every inch of her body would make sure of that.

She crossed the room, paused in the doorway looking back at him. In the half light his face was all planes and angles, strong – and remote once more. Hard to believe that a few minutes ago she had been in his arms, her face against his shoulder, her lips almost tasting his skin. But every one of her singing nerve endings remembered. Her heart remembered. If it never happened again, Tara knew she would never forget.

'Thank you,' she said, her voice husky. Then she turned quickly and hurried from the kitchen.

As the door closed after her James drained his brandy glass and refilled it yet again. God in heaven, he needed that! He was as tense as a tight-stretched drum skin! He tossed the liquor back and crossed to the window, looking out at the moonlit stable yard and seeing only tumbled dark curls and a small tear-stained face.

What in the world had got into him? For a moment just now as he had held Tara in his arms he had been overwhelmed with the desire to kiss her. And not just kiss her. He had wanted to tear off her wrap, touch her silky soft skin, run his hands – and his mouth – over the swell of her breasts. The desire had been so sudden, so unexpected, he had very nearly succumbed to it. Only a massive effort of will had allowed him to push her away. And thank God it had! Another minute and his yearnings would have got the better of him. He would have pushed her back onto the rag rug and taken her . . .

At the thought James's body stirred again and he slammed the brandy glass down onto the table. Dear God, even now he wanted to follow her up the stairs and into her bed! He, who had threatened Cal when Cal had suggested much the same thing, he who had sworn to be faithful to Lorna's memory for the rest of his life.

Perhaps that was the trouble, he thought grimly. He had been too long without a woman. He had thought he could do without, live a chaste life. Monks and priests of the Catholic church did it, why shouldn't he? But in the end he was a man, with a man's appetite. His reaction to Tara tonight had shown him that. Perhaps he should ride into town and find some saloon queen to satisfy his needs. That would be infinitely preferable to risking losing control with Tara and upsetting what was turning out to be a very satisfactory arrangement.

Or would it . . . ? He didn't want a whore, dammit! He wanted Tara! And no one else would do.

It came to him as suddenly as the desire to make love to her had come, a blinding revelation that shook him rigid. It wasn't just frustrated male needs that had made him want her so. Somehow, without his realising it, she had crept under his skin and into his heart. The girl he had promised Duncan would never take his mother's place. The girl with secrets in her past that made her cry in the middle of the night.

A board creaked above his head. The kitchen was directly beneath Tara's room. For a brief moment he allowed himself to imagine her getting into bed, her hair fanning on the pillow, drawing the sheet up over those delicious curves. Then, with a supreme effort of will, he pushed the thought away.

This foolishness had to stop, and quickly, before people, including Duncan and himself, were hurt, and the applecart was well and truly upset. Either that or he must lay to rest the vows he had made to honour Lorna's memory and set out to win Tara in a way that was both honourable and decent.

For the present James was incapable of deciding which it was to be.

123

Nine

A week passed by and James was no nearer to making up his mind. For a man who normally prided himself on his decisiveness this dilemma was proving uncommonly difficult.

In the first place Tara seemed to be avoiding him. Though she still went about her work quietly and efficiently, since that night in the kitchen there had not been one single occasion when they had been alone together. Perhaps she had sensed the desire he had felt for her and was making sure the opportunity didn't arise again, he thought. If this were the case and he propositioned her then perhaps he would drive her away altogether.

On the other hand, he simply could not get her out of his mind. Busy as he was she was always there, invading his thoughts, playing havoc with his emotions. As he rode out on the farm he found himself making excuses to get back so that he could see her again; when he was in her presence the longing to hold her again was so strong he swung between bouts of elation and frustrated angry despair.

He simply did not know what to do and the unaccustomed indecision was driving him mad.

Perhaps the first thing to do was to find out how Duncan now felt about her, he thought. The little boy had to be his first priority; if he still hated her that would have to be the end of it. But Duncan seemed to have been remarkably well-behaved of late. He hadn't once gone missing at bedtime and he seemed to be working hard at his lessons.

That night, when James went upstairs to say his prayers with him, he decided to take the bull by the horns.

'How are you getting along with Tara now?' he asked.

Duncan shrugged. 'She's all right, I suppose.'

'Just all right?' James pressed him.

'Yes, all right.' Ever since the incident with the apples when Tara had called his bluff but said nothing to give him away to his father, Duncan had had a grudging respect for Tara. More than that, it was actually rather nice to have a woman about the house again, one who wasn't as old as Methuselah and as bad-tempered as a dingo with toothache. Duncan rather liked the warm feeling she gave him. But he was not about to admit that to anyone, least of all his father.

James sighed, realising he would get no more out of Duncan. This was a decision he was going to have to make on his own. And that, he supposed, was the way it should be.

James was not the only one in turmoil. Tara, too, was unable to forget that night in the kitchen and the emotions it had awakened in her.

Unlike James, however, she knew exactly what she must do. She must ensure that such a thing never happened again. Even if James returned her feelings there must be no further contact between them. She was a married woman and even allowing herself to think about him in that way was against the laws of the Church and God. If she allowed things to go further Tara knew that she would have no choice but to leave Dunrae and that was unthinkable. In the short time she had been there she had come to love the place and the people she shared it with. Quiet, solid Philip. Cal, with the wicked twinkle in his eye and a girl in every township within a hundred-mile radius. Duncan, the imp with whom she had now at least reached a truce. And James . . . Tara's heart contracted whenever she thought of him, her pulses beat faster whenever he was near. But she must keep the feelings she had for him under control. She must master them. The alternative was a return to the sort of hardship she had endured before he had brought her here – and worse. In the world outside the safe environs of Dunrae the authorities would still be seeking the killer of the Commissioner. Perhaps already suspicion had fallen on her. If ever she was found she would have to face the brutal justice that would be meted out. Tara had no doubt what that justice would mean. Incarceration and death.

A week or so later James announced that he needed to go to Melbourne to finalise some business deals. Tara's heart came into her mouth. Supposing it was just an excuse and his real purpose was to try to learn something of her history? He had grown curious about her, she knew; though he never pressed her there was something in his eyes that told her it was so. Not that he would discover anything from the Women's Refuge – the O-Be-Joyfuls there knew no more about her than he did. Unless of course the authorities had come searching for her in the meantime . . .

Tara trembled at the thought. Would she never feel safe? But she comforted herself that her fears had no basis in reality. She was just allowing the demons to torment her again. And when she saw James ride off down the drive on Tarquin the heaviness of her heart at knowing that it would be long days before she saw him again told her that for all her efforts she was having little success in subduing the feelings she had for him.

'I wish I could have gone with Papa,' Duncan said wistfully as the figure on horseback was lost in a cloud of dust on the long straight road. 'I love Melbourne. It's very exciting there.'

'You think so?' Tara returned drily. 'Well, perhaps your Papa will take you with him next time.'

'I shouldn't think so.' Duncan kicked a small stone which scudded along the drive in front of them. 'He wouldn't want me along when he's talking business. Unless you came too, Tara. Then I could stay with you while he was with all his boring old friends.'

Tara laughed – partly with delight that Duncan actually thought her company not such a bad idea, partly at the irony of him suggesting she should go back to Melbourne, and partly because she had never sat a horse in her life.

'I can't ride, Duncan,' she confessed.

'Oh no, I remember now. You said so the first night you came. And Uncle Cal said he'd give you lessons, and Papa said no, he'd teach you to drive the gig.'

Tara gazed at him, surprised he had remembered.

'But he hasn't, has he?' Duncan went on. 'Why hasn't he taught you, Tara?'

'He's been too busy, I expect,' Tara said. But she couldn't help wondering if there was another reason . . .

'Uncle Cal could teach you,' Duncan said. They were back in the stable yard now where Cal was standing idly, hands on hips, one booted foot resting on the mounting block, talking to Dickon Stokes. 'He's not nearly as busy as Papa is.'

'No, I can see that,' Tara said wryly.

Duncan ran towards his uncle.

'Uncle Cal! Tara wants to learn to drive the gig. Will you teach her?'

Colour rose in Tara's cheeks. 'I never said that. It was all Duncan's idea,' she tried to explain.

'You should learn to drive all the same,' Cal said. 'And yes, of course I'll teach you. Why don't we make a start right away? It's a lovely morning, and there's no time like the present.'

'Oh, I don't know about that!' It occurred to Tara that the reason Cal was anxious to begin her lessons was because James was out of the way for a few days. There was a certain rivalry between the brothers – perhaps Cal wanted to put one over on James. And that could only lead to trouble. 'I've got a lot to do in the house, and Duncan should be at his lessons.'

'Duncan can get on with his work without you there to look over his shoulder,' Cal said airily. 'And if dinner's a little late, what does it matter? I'll get the gig ready.'

Tara could see that he was not in the mood to take no for an answer. And in spite of herself she couldn't help thinking that it would be rather fun. Fun was something there was precious little of in her life.

She took Duncan into the house and settled him with his books, though he seemed less than pleased at being left behind. No doubt he had suggested the driving lesson in the hope that he would be able to go along too. By the time she had asked the servant women to keep an eye on him and returned to the yard Cal had the pair of matched bays in the shafts and the gig turned to face down the drive.

'Ready then?' he called when he saw her.

'Oh, I'm not sure about this . . .' The horses looked so big and powerful; Tara's mouth was suddenly dry.

'Come on, it's easy!' He handed her up into the gig. 'Just watch me to begin with. I'll show you how it's done.'

As the gig bowled down the drive and out onto the track Tara began to relax. Cal had control of the horses; all she had to do was to sit back and enjoy the countryside.

The first of the autumn rains had already turned the sere brown scrub of summer to luxuriant green; under the brilliant blue sky it stretched as far as the eye could see, broken only by tree ferns and ghost gums. Compared with the mine-scarred flats around Ballarat it was unspoiled paradise, vast and beautiful. They passed grazing cattle and flocks of sheep, already sprouting jackets of thick snowy wool that would soon be stripped from them in the winter shearing.

'Surely they need their coats till spring comes?' Tara protested, but Cal merely laughed.

'We have to take the wool when it's at its best. They'll survive.'

Tara bit her lip, imagining the poor creatures shivering in the bitter winds. Farming seemed such an idyllic way of life but there was as much cruelty here as in the rest of the world when one scratched the surface.

She soon forgot about the sheep, however, as Cal pointed

out the wildlife to her – a lyre bird perched on a tree fern displaying his beautiful tail while he mimicked the cries of other birds one after the other, an emu running as fast as its legs would carry it, a kangaroo sitting on its haunches at the roadside to watch the gig pass with alert curiosity. Tara realised that in all the time she had been in Australia she had never before been so aware of the natural wonders it had to offer. Until now she had always been too preoccupied with her own survival.

After a while Cal pulled the trotting horses to a halt.

'Would you like to try driving them now?'

'Oh!' Tara realised with a shock that she had been far too interested in the surrounding countryside to have taken the slightest notice of what Cal had been doing. But then, he didn't seem to have been doing very much at all, just sitting there beside her with the reins held loosely between his big, sun-bronzed hands. The delicious feeling of freedom, the wind in her hair and the sun on her face seemed to have dissipated her fear and made her bold. 'Sure, I'll try!' she said recklessly.

Cal passed the reins to her; she held them awkwardly.

'Just give them a little flip,' he instructed, and, to the horses: 'Get along then, my beauties!'

To Tara's amazement the horses started forward once more. Perhaps it was Cal's firmly spoken order, perhaps it was just that they were enjoying themselves, whichever, she was sure it was not her doing. But the illusion that she had controlled them was an exciting one; she laughed out loud at the feeling of power it gave her.

'There you are, it's easy, is it not?' Cal said. 'But you're holding the reins all wrong. You've no real control like that. Here, let me show you . . .'

He leaned across, changing her grip on the ribbon of leather. At first, deep in concentration, Tara did not notice anything amiss, then she suddenly became aware that his hand was still on hers and his thumb stroking the back of her hand. Colour that had nothing to do with the wind on her face rushed to her cheeks. Oh, she must be mistaken, surely! But how could one mistake something like that? And he had moved closer to her on the driving bench, she was sure. The whole length of their bodies seemed to be touching now, and his arm was brushing her breast.

'All right, let me do it by myself,' she said, a little breathlessly. It was the only way she could think of to get him to resume a comfortable distance. Still his hand covered hers.

'You think you can manage?'

'I said so, didn't I?' she snapped.

If Cal had been less sure of himself, less used to getting his way with any and every girl who crossed his path, he might have been discouraged by the sharpness of her tone. As it was he had fancied his chances with the beautiful Irish colleen from the moment James had brought her into the house, and now he meant to make the most of this opportunity. And why not? he thought. He wasn't treading on anyone's toes. Neither of his brothers had staked a claim on her. James was still too obsessed with guilt and grief over Lorna's death and Philip . . . well, he'd never known Philip to show any interest in a woman. Not since he'd been turned down by that prim and prissy Dorinda Fairley over at Calgary, anyway. He lived like a monk these days. They both did. Which, in Cal's book at any rate, left the way clear for him.

'I think first we should practise stopping,' he said. 'That's as important as getting on the move – more so, really, if you don't want to end up in the middle of the bush.'

His tone was so light, so careless, that again Tara wondered if she was misreading his intentions.

'Pull on the reins – like so – and say *Whoa, my beauties . . .*'

Tara tried to ignore the pressure of his hands on hers and as the gig came to a halt she experienced a quick flush of pleasure. He was right; it *was* easy. And it was so exhilarating to have these huge beautiful beasts respond so instantly to the slightest command.

'I did it!' she exclaimed triumphantly, turning to Cal

bright-faced. Then gasped as his one hand tightened on hers and the other slid about her waist.

'Cal!' she protested sharply. It was the only word she had time to say before his mouth was on hers, silencing her.

For a moment shock rendered her immobile. Her eyes flew wide open, her lips parted too into a small surprised 'o' and the tip of his tongue flicked between them.

It was the first time any man had kissed her since the hateful Henry Dupont and suddenly all her memories of that dreadful afternoon were rushing in, crowding around her like a flock of flapping birds after a crust of bread. Panic rose in her in a great wave, she wrenched herself away, dropping the reins and hitting out at him blindly. As her open palm caught his cheek he let out a shout of pain and surprise, rocking back on the bench. And at that very moment the horses, startled by the sudden furore, took it into their heads to bolt.

As the gig plunged forward Tara screamed; her scream only served to panic them more.

'*Do* something!' Tara cried as the gig gathered speed, rocking wildly.

'Dammit, I'm trying!' Cal had recovered himself now, but the reins were flapping uselessly around the horses' rumps and thundering legs.

Desperately he tried to reach them, levering himself so that he was half hanging over the front of the gig. The horses, frightened still more, veered wildly to the left, the wheels hit a rut, bouncing crazily, and Cal's precarious balance was lost. He toppled, in slow motion, it seemed to Tara, hanging for a long moment in a pose that might almost have been comic had she not been so terrified, his legs flailing wildly, then he was gone, falling with a sickening thud onto the track, rolling over and over, and Tara was alone in the gig. She screamed again, hanging on with all her strength as it plunged forward, jolting and bouncing, at breakneck speed. Dear Holy Mother, what now? Another rut threw her from her seat; she landed awkwardly on her knees in the well of the gig, sobbing with fear.

A deep drainage ditch ran alongside the track; the wheels of the gig skirted it perilously. Dear God, a few short inches and it would be in and over! Then the horses veered again, away from the drainage ditch by some miracle and off the track into the scrub. The gig jolted more violently than ever. It was all Tara could do now to hang on. There was a fallen gum up ahead; the horses leaped it in unison and the gig bounced after them, flying through the air. Then, as it landed again, the wheels slammed against a length of shattered branch and came to an abrupt halt. The horses reared, whinnying, and the harness creaked alarmingly so that it seemed the gig would be torn apart. But it had stopped! Heaven be praised, it had stopped!

Tara pulled herself up and tumbled out into the scrub. She had no intention of remaining in that terrifying contraption a second longer. She hit the ground awkwardly, falling forward onto her knees with a painful lurch, and remained there for a moment gasping and sobbing in shock and fear. She was trembling from head to toe; she had the ridiculous notion that if she tried to stand, her legs would refuse to support her. But she couldn't stay there forever, cowering like an idiot. She had to get a hold of herself. She didn't want anyone seeing her in such a state. Her pride wouldn't stand it.

Not that there was anyone to see. As she struggled to her feet Tara looked back towards the track, hoping vainly to see Cal's tall figure making his way towards her. But the wide vista was empty of any signs of life except the birds and silent but for the noisy blowing of the horses, who stood now tossing their lathered heads between the remains of the shafts.

A new wave of panic washed over Tara like an icy flood. Cal had taken a crashing fall. Dear Holy Mother, if he had landed on his head he could easily have been killed! And even if he wasn't dead he might be badly injured. She had to find him and quickly, though she had no idea of what she would do when she did.

Tara took a quick look at the gig, its wheels firmly anchored in the branches of the fallen tree. That wasn't going anywhere. Even if the horses took it into their heads to set off again there was no way they would be able to budge it. She picked up her skirts and began to run across the scrub towards the track, her ankles twisting painfully on the rough ground. She had no idea how far back Cal had fallen. The whole runaway nightmare seemed to have lasted forever and yet been over in a flash.

She reached the track and started down it in the direction they had come, screwing up her eyes against the glare of the sun. So bright was it the track seemed to disappear in a shimmering haze. Then her heart came thudding into her mouth as she made out something that looked like a bundle at the roadside.

It couldn't be, could it? It was just a mirage, wasn't it? But there was no sign of Cal coming to look for her, and that still bundle wasn't something that should be there . . .

'Cal!' she sobbed, breaking into a run again. 'Cal! Oh, don't be dead! Please don't be dead!'

It seemed to take forever to cover those long rutted yards towards the motionless bundle, and with every one Tara was more and more sure. It *was* Cal. Her breath came in painful gasps, her feet faltered momentarily. Oh, she didn't ever want to see another dead man – any man, and especially not this one. Laughing, wicked-eyed Cal, James's brother, who had helped to make her feel so at home at Dunrae. If he *was* dead then she had killed him as surely as she had killed Henry Dupont. Oh, he shouldn't have tried to kiss her. But that was Cal all over, irrepressible womaniser that he was. If only she hadn't slapped his face, if only . . .

Tears of fright started to her eyes. Somehow she forced herself on. And then she saw him move.

At first she couldn't believe it; she thought it was just wishful thinking. But no. The bundle was taking on the shape of a man, pulling himself up to a kneeling position before collapsing again in a heap.

'Cal!' From somewhere Tara summoned up a new burst of

133

energy, running as fast as her bursting lungs and trembling legs would allow. 'Cal!'

'Tara.' His clothes were covered in dust and grime and his face was white with pain. But unbelievably he was grinning. 'Tara, you're all right!'

All her fear and anxiety exploded into white hot rage. 'No thanks to you!'

'Oh come on, Tara! You can't blame a man for trying . . .' His voice tailed away as he was gripped again by fierce cramping pain. He closed his eyes, gritting his teeth against it, and Tara's anger died as quickly as it had come.

'What have you done, Cal? Where are you hurt?'

'My hip.' As the wave of pain subsided he let his breath out on a long sigh. 'I can't move.'

'It's not broken, is it?' She dropped to her knees beside him. One of his legs was twisted at an awkward unnatural angle. She touched it gingerly and was startled and alarmed by his sharp cry of pain. 'Oh my goodness, what are we going to do now?'

'Where is the gig?' Cal asked as the pain subsided.

'Stuck fast in the bush, a long way back. The horses ran off the road and we hit a fallen tree. I don't know how I managed not to be killed. I was jerked to flinderjigs as it was!' Tara broke off. Going on about it now would do no good.

'Couldn't you pull it out and lead the horses back here?' Cal suggested.

Tara tutted in exasperation. 'It would take a couple of strong men to do that. It's stuck fast, I tell you.'

'Couldn't you at least try?' Cal pressed her.

'Even if I could do it I shouldn't think it's drivable after the battering it took,' Tara said. She was beginning to feel quite desperate.

'Well, it's either that or you'll have to walk home and get help,' Cal told her. 'We can't stay out here for ever.'

'Oh, fiddle-de-dee!' Tara pressed her hands to her mouth, thinking of the long way they had driven – and at a fast canter too. Heaven only knew how long it would take her to walk back to Dunrae and then there might be no one there to help her but wizened little Dickon Stokes and old Matt Henderson. Why, even they might have gone out to do some work on the fences or the land. The only one she could be certain of finding at Dunrae was Duncan . . .

Duncan! With a cold rush of horror Tara remembered that the little boy she was supposed to be taking care of was alone in the house but for the two servant women. It was one thing to leave him for an hour or so, quite another to be gone for the best part of the day. Why, it would be dinner time soon and he would have nothing to eat! Oh, why had she let herself be talked into this outing? How could she have been so stupid and feckless? And what was going to happen now?

Tara realised she was trembling again, tears of guilt and fright pricking behind her eyes. There was nothing for it, she'd just have to try and free the gig as Cal had suggested. Perhaps it wasn't stuck as fast as she'd thought. And then she'd have to overcome her fear of the horses and lead them back here.

'Very well, I'll see what I can do,' she managed, getting a grip on herself. 'You stay here.'

Even when the words were out she didn't realise just how foolish they were until Cal laughed grimly.

'Don't worry, Tara, I won't be going anywhere.'

'It's not a laughing matter!' she snapped, his irrepressible good humour that she usually found so engaging only irritating her now.

By the time she reached the spot where the horses had gone off the road Tara was breathless again and great patches of sweat were staining her already dusty gown. Her face, too, was dirt-streaked from where she had rubbed it with grimy hands, and her hair was falling down from the pins with which she had secured it. She scrambled over the rough ground to the gig, going down on hands and knees to look at the obstruction that had brought it to a halt. Maybe if she broke off some of the bushy branches she could free the wheels and then if she could make the horses go backwards she could turn it.

For long minutes Tara worked. The tree must be newly fallen, she realised, for the branches were still tough and supple with sap, not brittle as she had hoped. She tugged and pulled, with twigs scratching her hands and arms until they bled, and once a piece of branch snapped back, catching her a stinging blow across her cheek. But at last the wheels were free of the worst of the tangle. Now for the horses.

They were standing now as quietly as two aged nags in a paddock so that it was hard to believe they were the same animals that had careered out of control such a short time ago. But they still looked terrifyingly big to Tara. Nervous but determined, she went around and grasped the bridle of one of them.

'Come on now! Back – back!' she urged.

The horses refused to move so much as an inch.

'Back!' Tara tugged on the bridle with all her might. The nearest horse merely tossed his head so unexpectedly and violently that it scared the life out of her, but steadfastly refused to respond to her urging.

'Oh, please!' Tara wailed. 'Back, please, for me!'

It was useless. The horses remained stubbornly immobile. Tears of despair and exhaustion pricked Tara's eyes once more. What in the name of heaven was she to do now? Tara laid her face against the neck of the nearest horse weeping with frustration and anxiety.

Oh, if only James were here! Suddenly she wanted him with every fibre of her being. He was so strong, so capable, there wasn't a single situation she could imagine that he wouldn't be able to cope with. If James were here he would have the horses back on the road in no time and repair any damage to the gig, if damage there was. If James were here he would take charge of everything. The longing for him was an ache within her that grew and swelled until she thought she would burst with it.

But James was not here. She was alone, just as she had always been alone at every crisis in her life.

'Oh, Holy Mother, what am I to do?' Tara wept, and the tears made pale streaks down her dirt-encrusted cheeks.

The thunder of hooves on hard ground impinged gradually on her awareness and she raised her head, listening. A horse and rider somewhere out on the track! The matched bays had heard it too, their ears were pricked. Hope leaped in Tara. Was someone coming this way? For the moment she couldn't be sure, for the sound seemed to echo all around without direction. But surely it was louder now than it had been a moment ago?

Like a flash Tara picked up her skirts and ran to the track. Oh, praise be! A cloud of dust shimmered above the bright road. Her prayers had been answered! As horse and rider began to take shape, Tara wondered wildly if it might indeed be James and her heart gave a great leap into her throat. But that was ridiculous, of course. James would be half way to Melbourne by now. Then another thought struck her – supposing the approaching rider wasn't friendly at all but a bushranger out for all he could get? She and Cal would be sitting targets. But she would just have to chance it. She had to enlist the help of this man, whoever he may be. Without it, heaven alone knew how she and Cal would get back to Dunrae.

Nearer and nearer horse and rider came and Tara stood in the centre of the track waiting. Nearer and nearer, still at a fast canter. The horse, the rider, she recognised them! Surely, oh surely, it was Philip!

As the horse came to a skidding halt, Tara was weeping again this time from relief.

'Tara! What in the name of heaven . . . ?'

'Oh, thank God!' Tara whispered. 'Oh, Philip, I'm so glad to see you!' Never, in all her life, had she spoken a truer word.

Within the hour they were back at Dunrae, Philip driving the gig – which miraculously had not suffered any major damage

– with Pluto, his gelding, tied up behind. Every jolt had made Cal grit his teeth in pain and even cry out sometimes, but Tara's sympathy for him was in short supply now. All this was Cal's fault, including her desperate anxiety for Duncan. Supposing he had got up to some mischief whilst he was alone – run off again, even, as she had heard he was prone to do. If any harm had come to him James would never forgive her – she would never forgive herself!

The moment they were in the stable yard she jumped down from the gig leaving Philip to attend to Cal, and ran into the house. There was no one in the kitchen.

'Duncan!' she called. 'Duncan, where are you?'

There was no reply, no sound of footsteps on the stairs. Frantically Tara ran from room to room but there was no sign of the little boy.

The convict women were in the wash house, mangling a pile of clean steaming linen – though Tara suspected they had been taking their time and stopping for a gossip until they had heard her approach. Their laziness was the least of her worries just now, however.

'Have you seen Master Duncan?' she asked abruptly.

Dora shook her head but Lizzie smirked slyly. 'I think I saw him go out in the yard.'

Tara's heart sank. Without another word she hurried back outside. Philip was manhandling Cal out of the gig with the help of Dickon Stokes. 'I can't find Duncan,' Tara called to them. 'I think he may have run off again.'

Cal swore – whether from pain or annoyance at his young nephew Tara could not be sure.

'We have to find him!' she said with agitation.

'Master Duncan?' Dickon Stokes straightened up with a grin. 'Oh, I can tell you where you can find him!'

'You can? Where?' Tara could hardly believe her ears.

'He's with Matt and Martha if I'm not much mistaken,' Dickon told her in his slow country voice. 'It's past his dinner time, and that boy does love his stomach.'

'Oh, thank you, thank you!' Without a backward glance at the three men Tara hightailed it across to the Henderson quarters. Philip and Dickon were more than capable of getting Cal into the house and arranging for whatever medical treatment he required. Her only concern was Duncan.

She ran up the three rickety steps of the Henderson home and rapped on the door. It was opened at once by Martha who stood, hands on hips, facing Tara squarely.

'You've decided to come home to your duties then,' she said sourly.

'We had an accident . . .' Tara broke off. Over Martha's shoulder she could see Duncan sitting at the kitchen table and tucking into a huge plate of meat and fried potatoes. 'Oh, Duncan, I'm so sorry.'

'And so you should be!' Martha stood her ground, refusing to let Tara into the house. 'You'll let the child have his meal in peace, I hope? Though looking after him is what you were employed to do, as I recall.'

Tara bit her lip. She felt guilty enough already without Martha rubbing it in. But she deserved to be chastised, she knew.

'And what's more, you look a disgrace!' Martha went on triumphantly. 'Your face is filthy and so is your gown. I suggest you go and tidy yourself up before you do anything else.' And with that she shut the door in Tara's face.

For a moment Tara stood staring at it, totally flummoxed. Then, without really knowing the reason why, she burst into gales of uncontrollable laughter.

Everything was all right. Miraculously, nothing terrible had happened as a result of her irresponsible behaviour. Except that Cal was hurt, of course, but he had only himself to blame for that. Tara sent up a prayer of thanks and at the same time made herself a promise. It would be a very long time before she behaved so foolishly again.

Ten

James was furious. Tara had never seen him so angry and she hoped fervently that it would be a long time before she saw him so angry again.

'In God's name what were you thinking of?' he demanded of Cal, who was resting on a daybed in the kitchen, still unable to put any weight on his leg, though Philip had come to the conclusion that nothing was broken and the damage was merely severe muscular pain.

Far from being abashed, Cal yelled back angrily and defensively. 'Don't take that tone with me! And don't treat me as if I were Duncan's age, either!'

'How can you blame me for that when you act as though you were?' James demanded. 'Why, my back cannot have been turned but ten minutes before you took off like some ten-year-old skipping lessons, leaving Duncan here all alone! If it hadn't been for Martha heaven alone knows what he would have done!'

'I'm the one to blame for that,' Tara said, stepping into the fray. 'Duncan is my responsibility.'

'Yes, he is.' James turned to glance at her and the look in his eyes intensified her shame. 'I have to tell you I am disappointed in you, Tara. Though, knowing my brother, I dare say he left you little say in the matter.' He swung back to continue his attack on Cal. 'How did you come to lose control of the gig, anyway? How did it happen?'

Tara held her breath wondering what Cal would say. If he admitted the truth – which was more than he had done to Philip – she knew James would be more incensed than ever. Hurt leg or not, there might be fisticuffs right here in the kitchen!

'I was distracted,' Cal offered. 'Tara was driving – she was doing so well – and something startled the horses. It all happened so quickly. I wasn't to know she'd drop the reins out of my reach.'

'Dammit, man, you should have been concentrating! Ready for anything! You very nearly caused a catastrophe by your infernal carelessness. You could both have been killed!'

'Well, we weren't,' Cal interposed.

'And one or both of the horses could have broken a leg,' James went on, ignoring him. 'Don't you know what a matched pair like that are worth?'

'More than I am, clearly,' Cal said wryly.

'A damned sight more than you!' James agreed. 'If they had harmed themselves they would have had to be put down – unlike you. Though I must say in my opinion that wouldn't be such a bad idea at that.'

'Thank you very much for that kind sentiment, brother,' Cal said sarcastically.

'Stop it, the pair of you.' Philip rose from his chair, doing his best to act as peacemaker. 'As it happened no harm's done.'

'No thanks to Cal.' James was not about to let go so easily. 'If you hadn't happened to be riding out that way to check on the stock heaven alone knows what would have happened to Tara. Or to Cal, if it comes to that, though I can't say I'm overly concerned about him. A day and a night lying on the hard road might have done something to cool his blood.'

Hot colour rushed to Tara's cheeks. Had James guessed the real cause of the accident?

'Please don't blame Cal,' she heard herself say. 'It's as he said, it was all my fault.'

James instantly rounded on her once more. 'So you are

taking his part now, are you? Have you fallen under his spell like all the rest?'

'No, I haven't!' Suddenly Tara's eyes blazed blue fire. 'I haven't fallen under anyone's spell, nor am I likely to. Give me more credit than that.'

Even as she said it she was struck by the irony of her own words. Not fallen under anyone's spell – oh, that was rich! Not fallen under anyone's spell, when she couldn't get this handsome, angry man out of her head no matter how she tried? Wanting him, needing him, as she had when she had struggled with the obstinate horses, seemed to have unlocked all kinds of forbidden emotions. At night she had lain awake remembering how tenderly he had held her that night in the kitchen, how good it had felt and how the smell and feel of him had awakened her senses. By day she had found herself constantly watching and waiting for his return, aching simply to see him again, to be in his presence. Well, now he was here, and in such a fury as she had ever seen. Was his anger really just because they had left Duncan alone and Cal's irresponsibility had put his precious horses in danger? Or did it run deeper? Did he really think there might be something between her and Cal, and if so, could it be that he cared?

The thought heightened the colour in her cheeks to a fierce fiery blush. Holy Mary, it was madness to think such a thing even for a moment. Worse, it was wrong. Bad enough that she should be consumed with thoughts of James, but when she began imagining that he might conceivably feel the same way then it was time to put a stop to it and quickly. There could be nothing between them and she would do well to remember it. But for the moment there was no way she could remain in the same room as him and retain her composure. Why, even now she was afraid Philip might be putting two and two together. He was looking at her narrowly, taking in those flaming cheeks that no will on earth could hide, looking at her in a way that seemed to see right inside her head – and her heart. Of the three brothers, Philip was the shrewd one. Philip was the one she would be least able to fool.

'I'm going to see what Duncan is up to,' she said with all the dignity she could muster. 'You two can insult one another all you like, it's none of my business. But I won't stay here so that you can insult me too.'

For a moment as she swept out of the room there was complete silence as all three brothers stared after her, surprised by her outburst. As she mounted the stairs she heard the argument begin again and closed her ears to it.

Tara very definitely had other things on her mind.

'Tara, I'm sorry.'

James came into the parlour where she sat mending a tear in one of Duncan's shirts whilst he worked quietly over his books at the table.

She glanced up, her face growing hot again. 'For what?'

'For implying . . .' He broke off, his eyes going to his son. 'You've done enough work for one day, Duncan. You don't want to strain your eyes. Run out and play for a while.'

The little boy did not need telling twice. He was down from the table in an instant and running to the door.

'Not too far away, though!' James cautioned him. 'It will be supper time soon.'

Tara bent over her sewing, not daring to look at James.

'I'm sorry if I offended you,' James went on as the door closed after Duncan. 'I lost my temper. I shouldn't have done.'

'You had every right,' Tara said steadily. 'I know how concerned you were about the horses.'

'Damn the horses!' James said roughly. 'It's you I was concerned about. You could have been killed and well you know it.'

The needle ran into her thumb, drawing blood. She jammed it in her mouth, sucking. 'Well, I wasn't,' she managed.

'That's beside the point.' James crossed the room to stand

143

by the fireplace and she was very aware of him, so tall, so good-looking. Even with the width of the hearthrug between them she could feel herself drawn to him, all her skin prickling like her thumb where the needle had pierced.

'Cal was right about one thing, though,' James went on, seemingly unaware of the tumult he was causing in her. 'You should learn to drive the gig. I promised to teach you and I've done nothing about it. My mind has been on other things. I'll put that right. If the weather holds I'll give you a lesson myself tomorrow.'

Tara's eyes snapped up to meet his. 'Oh, no . . .'

James smiled briefly. 'I know you must feel nervous after what happened,' he said, 'but I'm not Cal. I shall ensure no harm comes to you. And the sooner you get back in the driving seat the sooner you'll regain your confidence.'

Tara bit her lip. How could she tell him it wasn't just the thought of being in the gig again that was alarming her? That she wasn't sure she could trust herself alone with him?

'In an isolated spot like this you need to be able either to drive or ride,' James went on. 'And you need to get out of the house too on your own sometimes. Why, I don't believe you'd been further than the stable yard since you arrived here until yesterday. If you're cooped up with only Duncan and the three of us for company you'll go stark staring mad.'

Tara smiled thinly. Oh, she was on the verge of going stark staring mad all right, but not for the reason he was implying.

'What about Duncan?' she asked. 'I don't want to leave him alone again.'

'Cal won't be going far for a day or two,' James said. 'Or I'm sure Martha would look after Duncan for a few hours. For all her moans she's very fond of him and I think she misses having him around.'

Tara nodded, remembering the scene in Martha's kitchen on the day of the accident – Duncan sitting comfortably at the table tucking into his midday meal, Martha fussing around him like a mother hen. Martha clearly did think the world of the little boy and he thought the world of her. It seemed the last of her objections had been answered. There was no other single excuse she could think of to get out of James's proposal.

'Tomorrow, then,' James said.

He strode out of the room. But it was a long while before Tara could bring herself to concentrate on her sewing.

'I'll take you a different way today,' James said. 'Then at least you won't have to pass along the same stretch of road where you had the accident.'

Tara nodded without replying. It was another glorious autumn morning and as good as his word James had arranged for Martha to look after Duncan, harnessed the horses and settled Tara in the gig. Tara had noticed how carefully he had checked over both the beasts and the carriage, raising each of the eight elegant legs to check fetlocks and shoes, tugging on straps and buckles, testing wheels. His attention to detail was not only routine for him, it was also intended to reassure her, she knew. But nothing could still the hammering of her heart.

Now, as the gig bowled gently down the drive between the eucalypts and mimosa trees she did her best to ignore it. But it was far from easy, with James sitting so close beside her. Involuntarily she glanced at him, at the strong, work-hardened hands which held the reins with easy confidence, at the long muscled thighs clad in close-fitting buckskin. Why, with his legs spread slightly to maintain his balance that thigh was almost touching hers. The slightest jolt and she would feel it through the fabric of her gown . . . Biting the insides of her cheeks in an effort to banish the tantalising but unwelcome thought, Tara surreptitiously moved a fraction further away from him.

At the end of the drive James turned the horses to the right. Though in many ways the track was almost identical, straight and rutted, running between swathes of pastureland, the vista was completely different. Instead of the flat lands that lay towards Melbourne and Ballarat, facing in this direction it was not long before the mountains came into view, rising majestically against the azure blue of the sky. The lower slopes were lushly green but on a clear day such as this the snow-covered tips were clearly visible on the horizon.

'Oh!' Tara gasped. 'It's beautiful!'

James smiled at her pleasure. 'We think so, yes. Have you not seen the mountains before?'

Tara shook her head. 'We landed in Melbourne and travelled directly to Ballarat.'

'Then you've seen nothing. One day I'll show you.'

Tara experienced a moment's heady bittersweet joy. Then reality came rushing in. *Don't allow yourself to think like that, even for a moment. Don't read anything into James's words. There can never be more between you than there is now, today . . .*

'How much did Cal teach you?' James's voice interrupted her thoughts.

'Not a great deal,' Tara admitted.

'I thought not,' James said grimly. 'If I know Cal it was not driving the gig that he intended to give you lessons in. Well, I'm here to put that right. Take the reins – carefully now – and remember every move you make sends a message to the horses. Their mouths are soft – I broke and trained them myself.'

For the next half hour or so Tara made every effort to concentrate all her attention on her driving lesson. James was an excellent teacher, calm and patient, and before long she had mastered the rudiments of handling the team. As James had said, they were instantly responsive when they received the correct signals and today they behaved so impeccably it was hard to believe they were the same animals that had taken her on the headlong terrifying flight. But then of course today they had been given no cause for alarm, James made sure of

146

that. At last he took control of the reins once more and pulled the gig into a shady clearing.

'We'll take a rest for a while and give the horses a rest too. You've done well, Tara. I'd go so far as to say you're a natural.'

Tara flushed with pleasure. Contrary to all her expectations she had actually enjoyed handling the horses – though she knew it was only James's steadying presence that had given her the confidence. And she had been concentrating so hard on doing as he said – and doing it right – that she had actually been able to forget that the man who could make her pulses race like an adolescent was sitting so close beside her in the gig.

Now, however, she became aware of him again all of a rush. Beneath his broad-brimmed hat his profile was craggy and weather-beaten. The deep lines etched into his sun-bronzed skin between nose and mouth started a fluttering inside her rib cage. Resolutely she ignored it.

'Sure, I'm Irish, aren't I?' she said lightly. 'Didn't you know the Irish are supposed to have a special way with horses?'

He tipped his hat and stretched his long legs. 'So I've heard. And other things besides.'

'Like what?' she challenged him.

'Oh, that many of you have kissed the Blarney Stone – though I don't think you've done that . . .'

'Well, thank you!' she interposed.

'. . . and that you believe in elves and pixies for all that you go to church on a Sunday and pray to the Blessed Mother and all the saints.'

'The little people, you mean,' she said with a smile.

'The little people, yes.' He looked directly at her, his grey eyes shrewd. 'You don't go to church on Sundays, Tara. Are you not a Catholic?'

'Indeed I am!'

'Then is it not a mortal sin for you to miss the Mass?'

The sun seemed to go behind a cloud. It was a sin. But there were others, worse. She had killed a man. The worst sin of all. Unless she confessed she would never be able to go to Mass again. And she would certainly go straight to hell when she died. And sure, wasn't she on the verge of committing other sins too? Sins she was committing in her heart this very minute?

'There's no church for me to go to, is there?' she countered quickly.

'The nearest is a good two hours' drive away,' James agreed. 'But once you've mastered the gig I'd be happy for you to go there on a Sunday if you wished it.'

Tara felt a lump rise in her throat. He was so thoughtful, so good to her. And she was so undeserving.

'You don't go to church either,' she said, trying to shift the conversation.

'No,' he returned bluntly.

'Are you a non-believer?' She didn't understand why it was important that she should know.

'I ceased to believe a long time ago,' James said shortly.

'But when you look at the trees and the birds and all this beauty, don't you see the hand of God in them?' she pressed him.

'Maybe I did once.' His face was shadowed. 'And then I looked on the face of my dead wife. She was young and beautiful and the mother of a little boy and she died a horrible death. Where was the hand of God there?'

Tara felt a rush of sympathy and also a sudden burning desire to share some of her faith. It had never wavered, not through all the terrible things that had happened to her, and she was glad of it. She may be beyond redemption but this good kind man certainly was not.

'Such things are not for us to understand,' she said urgently. 'We can't know why they should be part of God's plan. Maybe they come to test us, I don't know. But I do know that if you only believe, comfort is never far away.'

He shifted impatiently. 'Father O'Hara came by when Lorna died and tried to give me the same eyewash. I sent him packing.' His eyes met hers and though they were still grave, a corner of his mouth quirked. 'I won't send you packing, Tara, never fear. But I'd be obliged if you'd spare me the sermon.'

'Oh!' The quick colour started to her cheeks. 'Well, it was you who raised the subject in the first place!'

'So it was.' The quirk became a smile. Tara was always ready to bite back, no matter how wrong-footed she might feel. 'Come on, let's walk. It would do us good to stretch our legs and there's a creek I'd like to show you. I'm sure you'll feel close to your God there.'

He swung down onto the springy turf, looping the reins of the gig around a branch of a nearby tree, and Tara followed suit quickly, not giving him the chance to come around and help her down.

To the left of the spot where the gig was tied up the ground sloped away in a series of shelves, dotted with tree fern and the occasional ghost gum. As they reached the lowermost shelf the undergrowth became thicker, with clumps of trees, and far below, down the last steep slope, Tara could see the creek sparkling and bubbling as it trickled over the stones.

'It's low at the moment,' James said. 'We've had a long dry summer out here. But when the winter rains come the water level will come right up to where we're now standing, maybe even higher. Once, when I was a boy, I remember the whole valley flooding.'

Tara shivered, remembering the floods at Ballarat that had swallowed all the stock from her little store and left her ruined. 'That must have been dreadful.'

'It was serious, yes. My father was out day and night moving livestock to higher ground. We still lost a good many head. The corpses were being washed up for weeks.'

'Ugh.' She shuddered again. 'The poor beasts!' Then another thought struck her. 'This is still Hannay land, then?'

'Of course.' He smiled at her surprise.

'How do you manage to farm so far out?' she asked.

'There's a small homestead a mile or so further on up the track. We have a farm manager there. But the size of the farm is the reason why the three of us still live at Dunrae,' he explained.

'And it stretches just as far the other way,' she said wonderingly.

'It does. Would you like to go down to the water's edge? It's crystal clear, as you can see, and I can vouch that it tastes delicious.'

Tara frowned, looking at the steep slope. 'I'm not sure I can manage it without going ass over tip.' The old expression was out before she could stop herself. As James shouted with laughter she blushed in confusion. 'I mean I'll fall over,' she said quickly.

'Oh, I know what you meant.' He was still laughing. 'It's just so funny to hear you use such an unladylike expression, Tara.'

'My Mammy used to say it sometimes,' she protested defensively.

'Well, that's all right then, isn't it?' He stretched out his hand, taking hers before she could draw away. 'Come on, I'll help you.'

Still flustered, she scrambled after him down the steep slope. His hand felt so good on hers, strong, sinewy, just a little calloused. Tara's breath quickened.

They were almost down when suddenly her ankle turned on a loose clod and she stumbled, squeaking with shock.

'Oh!'

Quick as a flash he turned to catch and steady her, swinging her down the last few feet to the dry bank of the creek. As her feet touched the sandy earth she gasped again, but not this time from fear of falling.

James's arms were about her waist, his mouth was inches from her face. Quite suddenly Tara forgot the creek, forgot the sparkling green and blue day, forgot everything. Except that she was closer, far closer, than she should be to James. And in all her life she had never wanted anything so much as to stay right there.

As he first steadied Tara, then lifted her down what remained of the slope, James's senses suddenly began to swim. Beneath his hands her waist felt tiny, taut and neat, and her hair, brushing his chin, smelled sweet as new-mown hay.

Desire rose in him in a tide as remorseless as those floods of his boyhood and even more unexpected. Oh, it wasn't the first time he'd wanted her, of course. Since that night in the kitchen when he'd found her crying and comforted her there had been plenty of other times when he had looked at her and felt his blood warming and his groin hardening. Such unexpected times, too. When she was cooking a stew over the range, her face pink from the steam from the pot. When she was helping Duncan with his studies, leaning deep in concentration over the table so that all he could see of her was her taut back and the nape of her neck where tendrils of hair that had escaped from the pins lay in feathery strands. When she laughed at something outrageous that Cal had said, her lovely face lighting up with a brightness to rival the sun on a fine spring morning. But he had thought he could wait until the time was right – and as yet, he had decided, it was not right. She was still too close to whatever it was that had happened in her past, whilst he was still too tortured by guilt and memories of Lorna. But now, in this one careless moment, all his best intentions were scattered to the four winds. He wanted her now with a fervour that would not be denied, wanted her with every fibre of his being.

He heard her gasp but he did not take his hands from her waist. Instead he drew her closer, brushing that sweet-smelling hair with his lips, then pressing his forehead to hers. For a moment they stood motionless and the world seemed to stand still with them. Then, very gently, he tipped her chin so that her face was lifted to his, and kissed her.

Her lips beneath his were soft and responsive. He could feel the firm but yielding swell of her breasts pressing against the hard wall of his chest. He drew her closer still, so that their lips merged and his longing for her took on a new urgency.

'Oh, Tara . . . Tara . . .' he murmured and then he was kissing her again, parting her lips with his tongue, tasting her sweetness whilst his hands explored her straight narrow back from the ridge of her shoulder blades to the flare of her hips and beyond. He was no longer thinking, only responding to his pent-up needs, too long denied. 'Oh, Tara . . . Tara . . .'

She pushed him away with a suddenness that shocked him. Through narrowed eyes he saw an expression close to panic on her pretty face and tears sparkling on her long dark lashes. His first thought was that he had frightened her with the intensity of his passion. But that didn't make sense. He hadn't imagined her response to his kiss, he was sure.

'Tara?'

She half-smiled at him, touched his arm lightly with her fingertips, then withdrew it as though she had touched something searingly hot.

'I think it's time we were going back.'

'What's wrong, Tara?' His voice was rough.

'Nothing. I can't, that's all. It's not your fault.'

'But why?' he pressed her.

'Nothing, I say! Don't ask, please.' She turned away as if to scramble back up the bank. 'Are you going to help me or do I have to manage by myself?'

It was clearly meant as a joke, to lighten the mood, but it came out sounding tart.

'Give me your hand,' he said.

Passion had died now. He felt nothing but overwhelming frustration and confusion. What was it with her that lay so close beneath the surface? Why was she fighting him – and

152

herself? For he felt sure in that moment that was exactly what she was doing.

Amidst all the puzzles, all the uncertainties, he was sure of only one thing. He wanted her more than ever.

Back in the gig Tara sat with her hands pressed tightly together to try to stop them trembling.

Oh, Holy Mary, how she wanted him! How close she had come to surrendering herself to him completely and utterly! The one thing she must not do. How she had found the strength to push him away she would never know. His arms had felt so good around her, his mouth tasted so right. Everything in her had been crying out for him, every nerve had been alive and singing, every inch of her flesh yearning for his touch. And he wanted her as she wanted him. She was in no doubt of that now and it just made resisting her longings all the harder.

James climbed into the gig and made to hand her the reins. She shook her head. 'You drive. I've had enough for one day.'

'As you like.'

As he turned the horses back in the direction of Dunrae the sudden thought occurred to her: what was it about a drive in a gig that brought out the romantic side of a man? She almost laughed aloud hysterically. But of course, it wasn't the gig. It was because it was a rare opportunity to be alone. And the realisation of the totally different way in which she had reacted to the two brothers sobered her again.

Cal's advance had been unwanted. Dashing he might be, handsome he certainly was. But he didn't affect her as James did. She glanced at him and even now, in spite of herself, felt her stomach knotting with desire for him.

Stop it! Stop it at once! It cannot be!

There was an awkward silence between them now. It made Tara want to weep. Would they never reach Dunrae? All she wanted was to be able to run up to her room, throw herself down on her bed, and weep for what might have been.

At last – at last – there was the drive up ahead. James turned into it and Tara heaved a sigh of relief. Then, as they drew into the stable yard, a small frown puckered her forehead.

A little sulky was drawn up there, a sulky she had never seen before, and a young woman was supervising as Dickon Stokes unloaded some bags and stacked them in the yard. A tall young woman, of slightly bold appearance, brown-haired and blue-eyed, in a striking coat of scarlet and black.

'Elizabeth!' James said softly, sounding pleased. Then, more loudly, a shout of delight. 'Elizabeth!' He drew the gig to a halt, leaped down and ran to the girl.

'James!' A bright smile lit her pretty face and she ran to embrace him.

A knot of jealousy so enormous it felt like a mountain boulder twisted in Tara's gut as she watched them hugging and smiling at one another.

A moment earlier she had been praying for salvation from her tumultuous feelings for James. Perhaps, she thought, this girl was the answer to her prayers. But if she was, Tara had to admit she did not like it one little bit.

Eleven

'Tara! Come over here and meet Elizabeth!'

Tara, who had climbed down out of the gig and was hanging back awkwardly, could do nothing but accede to James's request. As she drew nearer the stranger turned towards her and with a slight shock Tara realised that she was older than Tara had at first thought. For all that her figure was as trim as a girl's, there was no mistaking that she had seen at least thirty summers and maybe more. But the blue eyes were wide and sparkling and her hair, drawn up into a chignon, was thick and glossy.

'This is Tara, who looks after Duncan – and us as well,' James was saying. 'Tara, this is Elizabeth Greenstreet. We've known one other since we were children.'

His hand was on Elizabeth's waist in a gesture that was both affectionate and intimate. Tara tried to ignore it and could not.

'James was more of a child than I. I can remember him as a baby, I'm afraid,' Elizabeth said with a smile, confirming Tara's assessment that she must be into her thirties. 'My father was overseer to James's grandfather at Ballymena. And I have to confess I was more than a little in love with Rolf, his father, before he was even born!'

'It's true that for a time Elizabeth was like a big sister to me,' James admitted. 'How things change! I caught you up and overtook you, Elizabeth. Don't even try to deny it!'

'As if I would! I know a compliment when I hear one,'

Elizabeth said with a coquetry that was in no way unbecoming. 'I hope you don't mind me descending on you like this, James. But I've been in Melbourne and I couldn't be so close and not drop by to visit.'

'I was in Melbourne myself a day or so ago!' James said, surprised. 'If I'd known you were there too . . .'

'Oh, I was on business.' Elizabeth pursed her lips and threw him a mysterious look. 'You were staying at the Imperial Hotel in Collins Street, no doubt?'

'Well, of course. I always do.'

'Not for much longer, I hope. I'm buying a hotel in Melbourne myself. One of the smartest new buildings in town. I shall be mortally offended if you don't patronise my establishment.'

James shook his head, smiling. 'Elizabeth is a business-woman, Tara – and a very successful one,' he explained. 'She already owns some of the finest hostelries between here and Sydney. But what are we doing, talking out here in the yard? Let's go inside.'

He picked up one of Elizabeth's bags, called over his shoulder to Dickon to bring the others, and started towards the house, his arm still about Elizabeth's waist. Tara followed, feeling a little left-out and ridiculously, insanely jealous.

As they went in through the kitchen door Duncan, who had been playing with some lead soldiers at the table, jumped up so excitedly that he knocked them flying. He threw himself at Elizabeth, and even Martha, who was enjoying a cup of tea, beamed a welcome.

'Miss Elizabeth! What a lovely surprise!'

For all her efforts to appease Martha, Tara had never been able to get a friendly word out of her, and her jealousy grew. Fine clothes, a brand new sulky, a string of hotels from Melbourne to Sydney, good looks, an open, friendly nature that seemed to draw everyone to her like bees to a honey-pot – why this woman seemed to have everything! Except a ring on her wedding finger.

156

Now why should that be? Tara wondered. And did not care for the explanation that suggested itself to her. Could it be that the man Elizabeth Greenstreet had set her heart on had been married to someone else? And was he now free? Tara bit her lip, tried to tell herself it was no business of hers, and failed miserably.

The other Hannay brothers were just as delighted to see Elizabeth as James had been. Cal, when he heard the voices, came swinging in on the crutches Philip had fashioned for him out of fallen branches and kissed her hand with exaggerated gallantry, and Philip's serious face became wreathed in smiles when he returned home and found her there.

'It's good to see you, Elizabeth,' he said, and there was genuine warmth in his quiet voice. 'It's been far too long.'

In a way Elizabeth could not have chosen a better time to visit, Tara thought. She had so much to do. Preparing the guest room, heating water for her to freshen up, and making adjustments to the evening meal to make it stretch to an extra mouth kept her busy, and Elizabeth's lively presence was a distraction from the emotional tension that would certainly otherwise have been there between James and herself. As it was, every time she looked at him she was aware of her pulses quickening and hot colour tinging her cheeks. But he – praise be! – was so absorbed in talking to Elizabeth that he seemed not to notice. Or perhaps he was just better at hiding his feelings than she was. She didn't know. After all, she scarcely knew him at all, she reminded herself.

As for Elizabeth, she was a complete enigma. Covertly Tara watched her, trying to decide which of the brothers, if any, she was interested in. But Elizabeth, like James, was giving nothing away.

They spent a pleasant enough evening, lingering over the meal which Tara had prepared and which – in spite of her lack of cooking skills – was quite palatable. She was improving, Tara thought, pleased, as the roast lamb disappeared from the men's plates and they came back for more. At least with her new-found expertise that was one area where she could, in all likelihood, outdo Elizabeth. She couldn't imagine this self-possessed, evidently successful businesswoman had ever had need to learn how to cook or keep house. She would certainly have staff to do that for her. But for all that, she didn't treat Tara as a servant as she might well have done.

'So you look after Duncan,' she said, drawing Tara into the conversation. 'He's quite a handful, I should imagine.' As she said it she cast a sideways smile at the little boy, and winked.

'No, I'm not!' Duncan objected. 'I've been behaving myself really well since Tara came, haven't I, Papa?'

'You've improved,' James agreed. 'Having Tara here has worked wonders.'

Tara felt her cheeks burn again as he glanced at her and momentarily their eyes met.

'I imagine having a woman around the place has worked wonders for you all!' Elizabeth said mischievously. 'What did you do before you came here, Tara? You're not native-born Australian, that much I can tell. And you're not Scottish. James's grandparents on his mother's side were Scottish – the Mackenzies of Mia-Mia. But you've heard of them, no doubt.'

'A little,' Tara admitted.

'My father worked for Andrew Mackenzie and I grew up with that Scottish burr in my ears. And I don't think you're English, either. No – don't tell me – let me guess. You're Irish.'

Tara nodded. 'Indeed I am.'

'And what brought you to Australia?' Elizabeth asked.

'You left Ireland because of the potato famine, didn't you, Tara?' James interposed. It was one of the few things he knew about her, since she was always so reluctant to talk about her past and he hoped it might satisfy Elizabeth's curiosity. She would have none of the men's inhibitions about asking awkward questions. But Elizabeth was not to be palmed off so easily.

'The potato famine!' she exclaimed. 'That must have been terrible! People starving . . . ooh!' She gave a small shiver. 'But what made you choose Australia? Many went to America, did they not, and it's not nearly so far.'

'We came for the gold,' Tara said.

James pricked his ears. '*We* came for the gold.' She had not come alone then.

'Isn't there gold in California?' Elizabeth asked.

'I don't know,' Tara said. The questions about her past life were making her uncomfortable. 'Certainly there are plenty of miners from England, Ireland and China even in the surrounds of Ballarat.'

'So you actually went to the goldfields?' Elizabeth said. Her blue eyes were sharp with interest. 'Tell me, is life there as bad as they say?'

'Yes,' Tara said shortly.

'And how do they get the gold from the ground?' Elizabeth asked. 'I know in the beginning it was all panning, but there are shafts now aren't there? Dug by men wise in the ways of mining? That's the way to strike it rich, isn't it?'

'Good heavens, Elizabeth, you're not thinking of going into the business yourself, are you?' James asked, meaning to lighten what he could tell was a conversation Tara would prefer not to be having.

'I don't know,' Elizabeth said. 'With the right investment, who knows? I might well make a killing. And it might be fun. Hotels can be very tedious when you see nothing else year after year.'

Suddenly Tara was trembling. How dare this woman talk about life on the goldfields as if it were a game? The hardship, the heartache, the sheer hell she had endured was suddenly as sharp and clear as if she were still there, battling to survive amongst the half-mad diggers. She felt again the greed, the lust, the despair; saw the gravel pits and the sludge-filled creeks; heard the roar of blunderbusses, the incessant barking of the dogs, the crying of the children, the curses of the men.

Before she could stop herself, Tara had pushed back her chair and was on her feet.

'Fun?' she blazed. 'You think the diggings fun! Sure, you have not the first idea of what it is like out there and you should thank God for that. For if there is a hell on earth, be sure you'll find it there!'

Elizabeth's eyes widened in shock at the outburst and a faint pink tinged her cheeks. 'Why, I didn't mean . . .'

'Fun!' Tara cried again. The word seemed to have burned itself into her brain. 'This world is a crazy place indeed when what is life and death to the poor and starving is *fun* to the privileged who have never wanted for anything in their whole pampered lives. Oh, you may have fine clothes and jewels. You may have your hotels to play with. But you haven't a brain in your silly head if you think the diggings are *fun*!'

'Tara!' James rose, touched her arm. 'Elizabeth meant no harm.'

She brushed him off. There was a huge lump in her throat, a lump of fury and bitterness and, yes, shame that she had lost control of herself in this way.

'Then she should not have said it.' Her voice tailed away. Blinded by tears she turned and ran from the room.

For a moment they all stared after her in stunned silence. Then James gesticulated helplessly. 'I apologise, Elizabeth.'

Elizabeth gave a small shake of her head. 'It's not your fault, James.'

Cal laughed. He alone seemed to have enjoyed the diversion. 'Tara is a very spirited young woman.'

'She is a very hurt one,' James said. 'We don't know what happened to her before she came to us. She refuses to talk about it. But whatever it was, it has affected her deeply. She had a terrible time, I think. But all the same, I wouldn't have had her speak to you so for the world, Elizabeth.'

'I think I probably deserved it,' Elizabeth said wryly. 'I do run on, I know, and I'm only sorry I upset her so. She's a lovely girl, James, and you are very lucky to have found her.'

'I know it.' James's expression was sober. 'I'll go after her.'

Elizabeth rose. 'Let me.'

'Do you think that's a good idea?' Philip asked.

'I'd like to apologise,' Elizabeth said. 'And who knows, she might be prepared to open her heart to another woman – if she can forgive me.'

'That's true,' James agreed. 'I've tried, heaven alone knows, but there's no way I can get past the barriers she has erected. If only we knew what it is that troubles her so, maybe there would be some way we could help her.'

Elizabeth nodded. 'I'll do my best.' A small rueful smile touched her lips. 'Just be ready to come and rescue me if the fur and feathers start flying again.'

'Elizabeth is a fine woman,' Philip said as she left the room. 'If anyone can reach Tara it's her.'

James looked very tired suddenly. 'For all our sakes I hope you're right,' he said with feeling.

Tara stiffened as she heard the tap on the door. Sweet Holy Mary, what a fool she had made of herself! The Hannays had been so good to her, all of them, and this was how she repaid them – by insulting their guests.

She straightened, brushing the tears off her cheeks and blowing her nose hard. The tap came again and this time the door opened a crack.

'May I come in?' Elizabeth's voice.

Tara tried to answer and could not. The door opened wider and Elizabeth peeped in.

'I've come to say I'm sorry for upsetting you, Tara. You must think me a very foolish woman indeed.'

Again Tara tried to speak; again her vocal cords refused to respond. It was as if her throat had seized up, she thought. If she opened her mouth now she would only begin crying again. What in the world was wrong with her? She wasn't angry any more. A little resentful, perhaps, but not angry.

It wasn't Elizabeth's fault that she knew nothing of the hardships of the goldfields. It wasn't Elizabeth's fault that she had lost everything or that Henry Dupont had tried to rape her. It certainly wasn't Elizabeth's fault that she had shot him dead and been forced to run and hide.

Tara pressed her hands to her mouth, and encouraged by her silence Elizabeth came into the room and closed the door after her.

'I shouldn't have said what I did, Tara,' she said. 'I'm afraid all too often I speak without thinking and it is very stupid of me. I suppose to those of us who have never been there and know nothing of the reality the goldfields seem very romantic. The lure of gold. It all sounds exciting and larger than life. Men in cabbage-tree hats panning in streams, sleeping under the stars, making their fortunes . . . It's the stuff of legend. Perhaps you thought so too before you found out differently.'

Tara nodded slowly, remembering the hopes and dreams she and Patrick had shared, their excitement as they set out on the long trek to Ballarat, and all with no more idea of what lay ahead of them than Elizabeth had.

'You're right, of course,' she said. Her voice, though thick and uncertain, was at least working now.

'You found out the hard way that it was not as you had pictured,' Elizabeth went on. 'Me? Well, I'm the lucky one. I haven't had to be hurt in order to be disillusioned. Just as I've been lucky all my life – in most respects. I had a kind and loving father and the Mackenzies were like family to me. The Mackenzies – James's mother's people – you know? Now . . .' There was a tiny pause and even in her preoccupied state Tara realised there was something Elizabeth was leaving unsaid. 'Now . . .' she went on, 'I have my business. No, I've been very fortunate and I am truly sorry that I spoke so lightly about something which is clearly so painful to you. Will you please forgive me?'

Tara nodded. Her nose needed blowing again. 'I'm sorry,

too, for the things I said. It's just that . . . well, I'm a little raw, I'm afraid. But you aren't to blame for my problems.'

The two women were silent for a moment, then Elizabeth said tentatively, 'Your family – are they still in the gold-fields?'

Tara's head came up. Briefly Elizabeth saw something like panic flare in her eyes. Then she bit her lip hard and her face went shut in.

'I have no family,' she said flatly.

'Ah. I'm sorry.' So this was the defensive wall James had mentioned. For a moment Elizabeth hesitated. Dare she press Tara? Ask who it was that she had journeyed to the goldfields with? No, she decided. This was not the moment. There was something Tara preferred not to talk about. To ask more questions would be to risk the fragile truce.

'Shall we go back downstairs?' she said. 'Just so that I know I really am forgiven?'

Tara hesitated. After Elizabeth's generous gesture in coming after her it would be terribly ungracious to refuse. But the thought of facing them all – especially James – was a daunting one.

Suddenly it occurred to Tara that the things Elizabeth had said did not constitute the whole reason for her loss of self-control. Her emotions had already been in turmoil and mostly it had to do with James. The feelings she had for him. That marvellous sensual kiss at the creek. The strength she had needed to summon to push him away. The longing. The pain of knowing she could never submit to him. And then the arrival of Elizabeth and the fearful wondering if she would have to endure the torment of seeing him with someone else . . . The turmoil of it all had laid her emotions bare.

'Elizabeth,' she said before she could stop herself. 'Are you and James . . .' Her voice tailed away. She could not ask. She must not ask. To do so was not only presumptuous, it would reveal her own feelings.

Elizabeth frowned slightly. 'Are James and I . . . what?'

163

'Oh, nothing.' Tara was overcome now by confusion. 'I just wondered . . .'

'If James and I are lovers?' Elizabeth finished for her.

Tara flushed. 'I'm sorry. I had no right . . .'

Elizabeth smiled faintly. 'James and I . . . ? Oh no, my dear. I'm a businesswoman. I have no time these days for affairs of the heart – or any other kind if it comes to that. It wasn't always so, of course. Once, there was someone. Someone I cared for very deeply. But it wasn't to be.'

She broke off for a moment, her eyes taking on a faraway look. 'He was a young officer on a clipper owned by the Mackenzies. I met him when I was visiting in Sydney. He was the most handsome young man I ever laid eyes on, so dashing in his uniform, so charming . . . I lost my heart, I admit it. For the first and only time since I was six years old and in love with Rolf Hannay, James's father. He broke my heart, too.' Her lips quirked in self-deprecating amusement. 'When he ran off with Regan, James's mother, I thought my world had come to an end. But Regan told me that one day I would meet someone just as nice. And I did. I met Louis.'

'What happened?' Tara asked, her own troubles momentarily forgotten.

'We were going to be married,' Elizabeth said. 'We had a little house in Sydney all ready and waiting for us. Oh, what fun I had supervising the decorating and choosing furnishings! We'd set the date for the wedding, I'd even been to the dressmaker and been fitted for my bridal gown. Ivory silk, it was, trimmed with pink roses. I can see it now, the most beautiful gown I've ever owned – or ever likely to, now I'm nothing but an old maid. Louis had arranged leave for the wedding but there was a bout of fever amongst many of the crew and the clipper was due to sail to the East Indies. The Mackenzies asked him to make the voyage as a special favour and he agreed. We could do with the extra money, he said, to start our new life, and he would be back in plenty of time for the wedding. It's strange, I didn't want him to go.

It was just as if I knew . . .' She was silent for a moment, her eyes sad and faraway. Then: 'He never came back,' she said simply. 'The clipper was lost in a storm and everyone on board drowned.'

'Oh, how dreadful!' Tara whispered, overcome with sympathy for Elizabeth, and shame for herself that she had assumed so readily that the other woman had led a charmed life. 'You must have been heartbroken.'

'I suppose I was,' Elizabeth said thoughtfully. 'I certainly thought my world had come to an end. I think I must have been very difficult to be around in those first months.'

'Well, of course! You were grieving.'

'But one can't grieve for ever,' Elizabeth said matter-of-factly. 'Oh yes, in the beginning I wished I could die too. Then I realised I wasn't going to and I had to do something with the rest of life if I wasn't to go stark staring mad. So I went into business. My father was horrified.' She smiled at the memory. 'He thought I *was* mad – that I'd lost my senses along with my fiancé. In his experience ladies either married or stayed at home. Respectable ladies, anyway. And hotels! He thought, I think, that everyone would take me for a scarlet woman. Which some did, of course. But I proved them wrong, all of them. In the end my father was proud of me, I think. And building up the business was my salvation. It's my life now – husband, children, family.'

'Oh, I am so sorry!' Tara murmured.

'Don't be. It's all a very long time ago now,' Elizabeth said briskly. 'And who knows, one day I might decide to give love another chance.' There was a little twinkle in her eyes – almost, Tara thought, as if she had someone in mind.

'But it certainly won't be James,' she went on, as if she had read Tara's mind. 'Fond as I am of him, James's heart belongs to another.'

'His dead wife, you mean,' Tara said. 'Lorna, her name was, was it not?'

'Lorna, yes. He worshipped her, it's true, but it wasn't

Lorna I was thinking of. I think that like me James has realised that no one can grieve for ever and nor should they. I think he's fallen in love again, even if he doesn't yet realise it.'

A small tremor ran through Tara. 'With whom?' she asked tersely.

Elizabeth's eyes met hers directly. 'Why, my dear, don't you know? With you, of course.'

To Tara it seemed the world had stopped turning. She had recognised James's desire for her in his kiss. But that Elizabeth should think he was in love with her . . . !

'With me?' she echoed faintly.

'Don't tell me you are unaware of it!' Elizabeth smiled. 'Why, to me it's as plain as the nose on your face! I could see it immediately, just in the way he looks at you!'

'But James is a gentleman,' Tara objected to cover her confusion. 'I'm just his housekeeper – an ordinary Irish girl who never had two halfpennies to rub together.'

'Oh, pooh!' Elizabeth said roundly. 'What has that to do with anything? I think you would make a lovely couple. And don't be too hasty in dismissing the idea just because you think his heart still belongs to Lorna, either. He'll never forget her, of course. But that doesn't mean he can't ever love another. Life moves on, my dear, and the heart has an infinite capacity for love. And Duncan is clearly fond of you too.' She clapped her hands together delightedly. 'Oh yes, you and James. A perfect match. He would make you a good husband indeed, and you would make him a wonderful wife. But let's not waste any more time talking up here. Let's go back down and join the others. Are you coming now?'

'Very well.' Tara's heart was pounding painfully, her thoughts running in confused circles. Should she tell Elizabeth that there was no way she could ever be James's wife? If she did, then perhaps Elizabeth would pass on the information and there would be no more misunderstanding, no more awkward moments, no more kisses . . .

166

But even as she wondered Elizabeth crossed to the door and opened it. 'Why don't you wash your face,' she suggested. 'That will make you feel better. And I will see you downstairs.'

With a smile and a wink she was gone and Tara was left alone with her churning emotions.

How she got through the rest of the evening, Tara never knew. Every time she looked at James, or felt his eyes upon her, the hot colour rushed to her cheeks and her pulses drummed a wild and crazy beat. Every time Elizabeth looked at her she saw the knowing smile behind her eyes and heard again her words. 'He's in love with you . . . a perfect match . . .' and her heart felt heavy with knowing it could never be.

After a while – praise be! – Elizabeth suggested she should play the piano and as they gathered around to sing the old favourites which she pounded out with more enthusiasm than finesse, Tara felt less conspicuous. But when at last it was time to retire to bed it was a long while before she fell asleep, and when she did it was to dreams that were even more unsettling and much more sensuously explicit than her waking thoughts had been, leaving an aura that lingered and tantalised far into the next day.

Twelve

Elizabeth stayed another day and night and when she finally left, driving off in her sulky, Tara was sorry to see her go. It had been so good to have the company of another woman of more or less her own age, something she had missed more than she had realised. Why, she had not had a girl friend since leaving Ireland. In all the tumultuous events of the past months there had been neither the time nor the opportunity for friendships.

Elizabeth could easily become a friend, Tara realised. Different though their lives had been, she felt a rapport with the vivacious and self-possessed businesswoman who had endured heartaches of her own yet risen above them.

Tara was not the only one in sombre mood as Elizabeth's sulky bowled away down the drive. Philip was looking unusually downcast too, Tara noticed, and when he turned away to go back to the house and prepare for his day's work it was with a straightening of his shoulders that suggested an inaudible sigh.

Could it be, Tara wondered, it was Philip of whom Elizabeth had been thinking when she had remarked, with a twinkle in her eye, that she might be ready to give love another chance? She was older than him, of course, but perhaps not so much that it mattered. Though she would have been a girl on the verge of womanhood whilst he was still a small boy, twenty years on the difference in ages was far less apparent. People had a way of catching one another up and in any case Philip's serious nature made him older than his years.

168

They were complete opposites too, Tara thought, weighing the arguments, but then didn't opposites often attract? Elizabeth's outspokenness and irrepressible bubbly nature would complement Philip's thoughtful reserve perfectly; his measured good sense would compensate for her impulsiveness.

But perhaps she was quite wrong about them; perhaps pairing them up like this was just so much wistful thinking. It would be so nice to see more of Elizabeth, Tara mused, maybe even have her live under the same roof.

A less welcome thought occurred to Tara suddenly. If Elizabeth were to marry Philip and come to live at Dunrae there would be no reason for her to be employed here any longer! Elizabeth would be more than capable of caring for Duncan when his father was not there and she would certainly want to take over the running of the household.

Well, there was no point worrying about it, Tara told herself. It might never happen. And yet . . . wasn't it bound to at some time? Sooner or later one of the brothers would be sure to take a wife, and when they did . . .

For the first time Tara realised that not once since coming here had she thought about her long-term future. She had been so grateful to escape from the living nightmare of the Women's Refuge, so caught up in day-to-day problems and tumultuous emotions, that she hadn't once stopped to ask herself where she would be five, ten, twenty years from now, or what she could look forward to. Now, with a sinking heart, she realised that it wasn't just James who was unattainable for her, but any sort of family life. Everything she had ever dreamed of was out of reach – a husband, a home of her own, children . . . The emptiness that had consumed her when she had lost her baby that terrible night in Ballarat ached within her again. Tara pressed her hands to her flat stomach, remembering the joy of feeling the new life pulsing beneath her ribs, and wanted to weep with the knowledge that she could never again experience it. Then, angry with herself for entertaining such negative thoughts, she gave herself a small shake.

Just be thankful for what you have, she scolded herself. Just be grateful you have somewhere nice to live, with food on the table and a soft bed to sleep in at night. You could still be in that flea-infested Women's Refuge sharing accommodation with the dirty, the inebriated, the whores. You could be in jail – or worse, lying in a murderer's plot in unconsecrated ground. Take each day as it comes and be glad of it.

And she was . . . she was! Determined not to indulge a moment longer in this stupid self-pity, Tara headed purposefully for the kitchen and the tasks of the day which lay ahead of her.

Duncan came into the kitchen where Tara was up to her elbows in flour.

'What are you making?'

'A pound cake.'

'What's a pound cake?'

'Well, it's a cake with fruit, and you put in a pound of everything. That's why it's called a pound cake.'

Tara rubbed her cheek, leaving a streak of flour behind. She was beginning to wish she hadn't started on this enterprise. She wasn't even sure why she had, unless it was because for the first time for days she had the kitchen to herself – Cal had recovered enough to go out to work on the farm – and she had been fired by some deep-seated need to prove her usefulness. It would be nice, she had thought, to put a freshly-baked cake on the table for James and the others, and surely it was easy enough? Mammy had whipped up pound cakes almost every week in the days before the ingredients had become hard to come by, and Tara had watched her often enough. 'A pound of this, a pound of that,' as she had told Duncan. She could still hear Mammy's lovely lilting voice saying it. The trouble was, it made an awful lot of mixture. And it didn't explain how many eggs should be added, or how much milk. Tara had collected as many fresh eggs as she could find in the hen's run and beaten them up but the bowl of yellow goo now looked daunting to her, and as for working the butter into the flour – why had she been at it for ages yet it was still full of lumps?

'Can I taste?' Duncan asked.

Without waiting for a reply he ran his finger round the edge of the bowl, licked it, and wrinkled up his nose.

'It's a bit . . . ugh . . . it's not very sweet.'

Tara tasted a bit herself and immediately realised. Sugar! She'd forgotten to add any sugar! Thank goodness Duncan had sampled it!

She opened the cupboard and took out the sugar tin. It must be a pound of sugar too, she presumed. She tipped it in, mixed and tasted again. Yes, that was better. Now for the dried fruit. But she still wasn't sure how moist the mixture should be. Oh well . . .

She tipped in the rest of the eggs, gave the whole gooey mess a good stir, and tipped it into the tin which she had greased before she began. The range was good and hot; Tara slid the tin inside, stood looking anxiously at it for a moment, then closed the door with a resounding slam. She couldn't remember how long Mammy had cooked her pound cakes for, either, but if she kept an eye on it, she supposed she'd know when it was done.

'Tara.' Duncan was looking up at her with wide, pleading eyes.

'Yes, Duncan?'

'Can I scrape the bowl? Please? Mama used to let me.'

'Of course you can, Duncan.' Tara passed him a wooden spoon, smiling as he enthusiastically garnered every last streak of mixture, every stray currant.

So Lorna had baked cakes then. Another small piece to add to the picture of the woman who had been James's wife.

When Duncan had finished scraping out the mixing bowl, running his finger around it until it looked as clean as washing could make it, he carried it across to the sink, dumping it in the hot soapy water Tara had boiled to clear up after herself.

'Good boy, Duncan,' she said. 'Perhaps now you'd better do some sums. Papa set them for you, didn't he, before he went out, and he'll expect to find at least some of them finished when he comes home.'

Duncan went off reluctantly and she crossed to the big stone sink to wash the mixing bowl. As she plunged her hands into the water she glanced out of the window, which overlooked the yard, just in time to see a figure disappear into the stables.

Tara frowned. Though she had caught no more than a glimpse of the man she didn't think it was Dickon Stokes. Dickon was small and wizened. She had gained the distinct impression of someone much taller. And it couldn't be Matt Henderson either. He and Martha had gone down river for a few days to visit their son and his family.

Oh, she must be imagining things! Tara told herself. Who else but Dickon would be in the stable yard? But she felt uneasy all the same. She wiped her hands on her apron and crossed to the door, opening it and going out onto the veranda.

The stable yard was deserted, though a horse she did not recognise – a poor, scraggly-looking beast – was hitched up to the rail. Tara's frown deepened. She went down the steps and across the sunlit yard to the stables.

'Hulloa!' she called. 'Who's there?'

There was no reply.

'Who's there?' she called again, pushing the stable door wide open and looking inside. Then she gasped in shock and surprise.

Dim though it was in the stable she could see the figure of a man holding the door of one of the stalls ajar with his back whilst he urged out Conker, one of the matched bays.

'What do you think you are doing?' Tara asked sharply.

For a moment the man made no reply. Then: 'Come to

take your horse to be shod,' he said. His voice was rough and uneducated, the kind of voice she had grown used to hearing at the diggings.

'You mean you're the farrier?' she asked, puzzled.

Out here in the wilds, so far from the nearest township, it was likely a travelling farrier did call from time to time. But neither James nor either of the others had mentioned a horse needing to be shod and there had been so sign of a wagon bearing the tools of his trade in the yard.

'That's right.'

The man was lifting a saddle and bridle from a hook on the wall and the action convinced Tara that he was not telling the truth.

'You don't need to saddle a horse to shoe it,' she said accusingly. 'And Conker is a carriage horse anyway.'

'Is that so?' the man sneered. 'He's a fine beast, I must say. Worth a pretty penny or two, I'll be bound.'

He started along the narrow passageway towards her. Firmly Tara stood her ground, blocking his way.

'I think you are mistaken as to which horse needs shoeing,' she said. 'Kindly put Conker back in his stall and check with Dickon Stokes before you take him out of the stable.'

The man laughed unpleasantly. 'Dickon Stokes. Now would that be the little old bald man?'

'Yes.' Tara was feeling more uncomfortable by the minute, but was determined not to show it. 'He is in charge of looking after the horses.'

'Oh, is he now?' The man laughed gain. 'Well, he's not up to looking after them right now.'

A small icy chill ran up Tara's spine. 'What are you talking about?' she demanded.

'Come on, out of the way,' the man said roughly, not answering her question. 'I haven't got all day.'

'And I told you to put Conker back in his stall,' Tara said fiercely, in spite of her fear. 'I want to know what all this is about before you lay a finger on that horse.'

'Oh, going to be awkward, are we?' His had shot out and caught her roughly by the shoulder, pushing her into Tarquin's empty stall. 'Out of my way now!'

Tara stumbled against the wall squealing with outrage and fright. This man was no farrier. He was a common horse thief as like as not!

By the time she had recovered her footing he was past her, out of the stables and into the yard. She ran after him, fury making her forget her fear.

'Don't you dare to take that horse! Don't dare! Why, this is James Hannay's farm and he'll find you and have you hung from the tallest gum in . . .' Her voice tailed away. Now that they were out in full daylight and she could see the man properly she was struck by the feeling that she had seen him somewhere before. That ugly face with an old puckered scar running from nose to mouth, those narrow eyes scowling from beneath the brim of his hat, his hooked nose and thin lips – all were vaguely familiar. 'Don't I know you?' she said.

'Well, if it isn't the lovely Mrs Murphy!' In full light he had recognised her too and Tara realised where she had seen him before. In Ballarat, at the diggings. He was just one of the hundreds of men who had camped there, but to him of course she was a woman apart. Why, in all likelihood he had purchased provisions from her store, watched her carry Patrick away with Seamus's help after the bare-knuckle fight.

The man laughed now, the same unpleasant mirthless laugh she had heard in the stables.

'Landed on your feet, haven't you, Mrs Murphy? A very nice place you've got here. Perhaps since you've been so furtunate you can find it in your heart to be generous to a poor digger who never found enough gold to buy his supper, let alone get wealthy. I thought a horse would help me on my way. Now I see I've hopes of a great deal more. Have you money? Jewels? Come now, I'm sure you have!'

'You'll get nothing from me!' Tara spat.

The man's thin lip curled. 'We'll see about that! All alone, are you?'

'No, I'm not!' Tara retorted.

'Oh, I think you are. You'd not be out here facing me by yourself if there was a man on the premises. No, there's no one but you and that poor old man, I'll wager. And for your information he's out cold – and likely to be for some time.'

Tara's eyes widened with horror. 'What have you done to him?' she demanded. 'You haven't killed him, have you?'

The man laughed. 'No need of that – though I might yet if he wakes up and starts making trouble. No, a good crack over the head with the butt of my revolver was enough. His skull's as thin as a baby's.'

'You devil!' Tara grated.

'And another crack would lay you out, I'll warrant. But I don't think I'll do that. I'd rather have you show me where the valuables are and I wouldn't want to mar your good looks. It pleasures me, looking on a comely woman. Heaven knows, there are few enough of them in this godforsaken place. And I might do more than look whilst I'm about it.'

He licked his lips and Tara began to shiver inwardly. Sweet Holy Mary, surely history was not about to repeat itself? The same lust she had seen in Henry Dupont's eyes was there in the eyes of this man. Why, out here in this wild and lawless country where clean and wholesome women were so few and far between, that carnal lust seemed to go hand in hand with the lust for gold.

'Lay a finger on me and you'll regret it!' she blazed.

'Oh my, you're fiery!' The man grinned unpleasantly. 'I like that in a woman.' His hand shot out, imprisoning her arm. 'Well, I've laid more than a finger on you, my pretty. What are you going to do about it?'

'You know very well I can do nothing now,' Tara retorted, trying in vain to pull herself free. 'But James Hannay will make you sorry, believe me!'

The evil man yanked on her arm, pulling her towards him.

175

'But he's not here, is he? Now, I've no more time to waste. Let's go into the house and see what baubles you can find for me. Come on!'

Tara lashed out with her free arm but for all his size the man moved fast and sinuously as a snake, sidestepping out of her reach and twisting her arm behind her back so that her shoulder wrenched painfully. A sharp push wrenched her shoulder again and then he was frogmarching her across the yard towards the house. Tara had no option but to stumble up the veranda steps and into the kitchen.

It was full, now, of the delicious aroma of baking, a poignant reminder of the comfortable domesticity that had been so rudely interrupted.

'Something smells good!' the man remarked. 'And God knows, I'm hungry. Get me food, but no tricks, I warn you, or I'll break your pretty neck. Or worse . . .'

He released Tara, shoving her into the centre of the kitchen so that she cannoned into the table, then pulled a gun from the belt that hung low around his waist and trained it on her.

'What have you got? Bread? Cheese? Cold meat? I don't much mind what it is. But no knives. I'll tear it with my teeth. I don't trust you.'

'And what use would a knife be against your gun?' Tara demanded with a coolness that surprised her, since inwardly she was shaking like a jelly. But somehow the sight of the gun, whilst frightening her half to death, had had the effect of sharpening her brain. And the thought uppermost in her mind was – Duncan.

He was in the parlour, doing his sums, with nothing but two flimsy doors and a short stretch of hallway between him and this madman. The very last thing she wanted was for him to hear raised voices and come to see what was going on. Perhaps if she gave the man what he wanted – food, money, an item or two of silver – he would go away and leave them alone. Why, he could take Conker too for all she cared. Just as long as no harm came to Duncan.

176

'There's bread and cheese,' she said. 'I'll get it for you.'

'That's more like it.' The man pulled out a chair and sat down, but his eyes never left Tara as she fetched the loaf and the wedge of muslin-bound cheese, and the gun too followed her every move. 'I'll have a drink too,' he went on. 'Ale, I fancy, if you have it.'

Tara fetched the jug and set everything down on the table before him.

'Now sit down where I can see you.' He motioned to her to take the fireside chair and when she was perched on it he laid his gun down on the table close within his reach and began to eat as if he were starving – which, Tara thought, in all likelihood he was – washing it down with James's good ale.

She sat, tense as a tight-wound screw, watching him and willing him to hurry. Would he never have eaten his fill?

At last he stuffed yet another chunk of bread into his mouth, chewed and swallowed it, and belched loudly.

'That will do for now. You can put the rest in a bag for me.' He pushed it across the table towards her. 'Now, what valuables can you find? He's bought you jewels, I'll warrant, this James Hannay.'

'No, he hasn't,' Tara said. Her eyes were flying round the kitchen. She must find enough to satisfy him without him taking her into the parlour where Duncan was working on his sums. 'There's the little carriage clock, and the candlesticks – they're silver, I'm sure . . .'

'Tara, I've finished . . .' Duncan's voice, from the doorway, fading away in surprise as he saw the strange man in his kitchen. 'Who are you?'

Tara's heart sank. 'Duncan . . .'

'Who have we here?' The man's face split in an unpleasant grin. His hand shot out, grasping Duncan by the shoulder and yanking the little boy towards him. 'Are you a Hannay, my lad?'

'Let me go!' Duncan struggled violently, but to no more avail than Tara.

'A Hannay indeed, I'll be bound! Candlesticks? Carriage clock? Pooh! Your father would pay me a great deal more in return for you, if I'm not much mistaken. I could name my price for you, my lad!'

Tara's blood ran cold. Surely this scoundrel couldn't mean what she thought he meant? Surely he wouldn't go so far as to kidnap Duncan and hold him to ransom? But his eyes were alight with something close to true madness and she knew with chilling certainty that was indeed what he meant to do.

And how could she stop him? Him with his gun and the wiry strength that had come from years of hard labour in the goldfields? Think! Tara told herself. She must think of something!

'Do you want me to pack this food for you or not?' she asked.

The man gave her a quick greedy glance. He had almost forgotten about the food in his excitement at getting hold of the boy.

'There's cake, too, fresh from the oven,' she added.

'Pack it up then and be quick!' he ordered her. 'And cake, yes. It smells good. I don't remember when I last ate fresh cake.'

Especially not as fresh as this, Tara thought. If she remembered rightly it had taken hours for Mammy's pound cakes to cook and her mixture had been much firmer to begin with than the one Tara had concocted. Could she . . . ? Dare she . . . ? It was a desperate idea that had occurred to her – if it went wrong the consequences could be disastrous. But with this terrible man threatening to take Duncan hostage, desperate measures were called for.

With a silent prayer to the Holy Mother, Tara picked up a thick cloth and crossed to the range. As the door swung open the heat came out to meet her in a steamy cloud, almost making her recoil. She pulled the tin towards her, holding it firmly between her hands and refusing to acknowledge it was burning her fingers even through the thick cloth.

'Here we are . . .'

The crust was golden and sparkling, truly delicious looking. But . . .

Please, Holy Mother, don't let it be set underneath, Tara prayed. *Please, Holy Mother, let me do this right . . .*

She carried the cake towards the table, tilting it slightly as if for inspection. The man leaned forward, enticed by the delicious aroma, and quick as a flash, before she could lose her nerve, Tara acted. With all her might she threw the cake full into the man's face.

Praise be, it hadn't set! As the cake hit him the thin sugary crust shattered and thick, scaldingly hot batter exploded over his eyes, his nose, his cheeks. He screamed in pain, his hands flying to his face, and Tara made a grab for the gun, which lay on the table top beside him, with one hand and for Duncan with the other, yanking the startled child out of the man's reach and into the haven of her skirts.

The man had blundered to his feet, still screaming and uttering oaths the like of which Tara had never heard since leaving the goldfields. She levelled the gun at him.

'Get out! Go on, get out, you bastard, or I'll shoot you dead. I've used a gun on a man before and I'll do it again if I have to. Get out! Get out!'

The man roared again in fury and pain, unaware for the moment of anything but the scalding mixture that clung to his skin.

'I mean it – I'll shoot!' Tara cried, her finger tightening on the trigger.

Through the haze of pain and fury the man seemed to register what she was saying, and recognise that her threat was no idle one.

'Whore! Harlot!'

Blindly he stumbled towards the door. Tara followed, keeping a safe distance, the gun still levelled at him. Though her insides felt as if they had turned to jelly her hand was steady. She had meant what she said. She didn't want to have to kill again – God alone knew how she was still tormented by having done so before. But if she had to she would. It couldn't be as bad a second time and she could only be consigned once to the fires of hell.

The door was ajar. The man half fell through it onto the veranda, cannoning into the rail. Then, on the steps, he lost his footing, tumbling head over heels down into the yard.

'Get up!' Tara ordered, standing above him with the gun pointing at his head. 'Go on, get up, take your horse and get out of here!'

Somehow he did as she bid and she followed him at a safe distance to where his horse stood waiting. As he mounted she saw that where the cake mixture had dropped off his skin was scarlet and wrinkled, blistering already as like as not, and she felt a moment's satisfaction.

'Git up!' she shouted, and dared to get close enough to give the horse a hearty slap on his hindquarters. Unnerved by the half-hysterical swearing of his owner and startled by the sharpness of the slap, the horse reared, almost unseating the man, then took off, rounding the corner of the house and racing down the drive in headlong flight.

Tara stood watching, not daring to take her eyes off the man until he had disappeared from view.

'Tara?' Duncan was beside her now. He looked totally awestruck. 'You showed him, Tara, didn't you?'

'I showed him!' she repeated grimly. She was trembling violently now.

'Who was he?' Duncan asked. 'What did he want?'

'He was a bad man. There are plenty of them in this world.'

'But why did Dickon let him into the house?' Duncan asked puzzled.

Dickon! Tara remembered with a sick jolt what the man had said about laying Dickon out. He could be lying injured somewhere, perhaps even dead. He wasn't, after all, a young man – far from it.

She wished desperately she could go to look for him, tend his wounds, or, if the worst had happened, at least afford him the dignity of being laid out and covered. But she dared not leave her place here at the head of the drive. The man might yet come back with vengeance on his mind and if he did he would be doubly dangerous. Until James or one of the other men returned she had no choice but to keep up her vigil. Dickon . . . well, she would try not to think about Dickon.

'I have to stay here and watch the drive, Duncan,' she said. 'You can either go into the house or stay here with me.'

Duncan looked up at her. His eyes were full of admiration. 'I'll stay with you, Tara,' he said.

They were still there, manning the look-out post together, when a horse and rider turned into the drive.

Instantly Tara stiffened, her heart beginning to beat a crazy tattoo. But almost at once she could see it was not the man.

As James came trotting towards them, Duncan ran to meet him.

'Papa . . . Papa!'

'Duncan.' James hoisted him up into the saddle in front of him.

'Papa, you'll never guess what happened!' the little boy burst out, but James scarcely heard him. He was looking at Tara.

She had lowered the gun now, but the sun glinted on it, still held firmly in her hand.

'What the . . . ?' He urged Tarquin towards her and leaped from the saddle, leaving Duncan still sitting aloft. 'Tara! What is it? What's going on?'

'Oh James!' she whispered. 'Thank God you're home!'

Then, and only then, she burst into tears.

Thirteen

Tara sat in the big comfortable kitchen, a glass of James's best brandy clutched between both hands. She was shaking so much she could not trust herself to hold it in only one. But the liquor was beginning to put a little warmth back into her veins and colour into her cheeks.

'Can I have some too?' Duncan asked as she sipped gratefully. He seemed remarkably unaffected by his share in the ordeal, more excited than frightened, and as full of mischief as ever.

'Indeed you cannot!' Tara said sternly, keeping an anxious eye on the door. When she had explained the bare bones of what had happened to James he had taken her into the house, poured her the brandy, and instructed both her and Duncan to remain there whilst he went out to look for Dickon Stokes. But he had been gone a very long time and Tara feared the worst. Dickon was an old man, but she couldn't believe he would have been skulking somewhere all this time if he hadn't been seriously hurt at the very least of it, and through the long hours she had kept guard on the drive she had seen neither hide nor hair of him.

Frustrated in his attempt to taste the brandy, Duncan's eye fell on the cake tin, still lying where it had fallen under the table.

'Oh, look!' He crawled to it on hands and knees, poked his finger into the now cool sludge that remained inside and stuffed a dripping lump into his mouth.

'Duncan!' Tara chastised him, horrified. 'You can't eat that!'

'Why not? It still tastes nice,' Duncan said, scooping out another fingerful.

'You can't eat it *because*!' Tara said. She set down the brandy glass, took the tin from Duncan and fetched a cloth. The mess had to be cleaned up sometime; it might as well be now. It would at least take her mind off wondering what state James had found Dickon in.

She was still on her hands and knees washing the last of the sticky mixture from the flags when James returned.

'What are you doing?' he asked, frowning.

Tara ignored the question, scrambling to her feet with the cloth still in her hand.

'Did you find Dickon? Is he . . . ?'

'I found him,' James replied grimly. 'He's alive – just. He'd been knocked clean out and stayed that way for some time, I should think. He's still floating in and out of consciousness.'

'Oh, I must go to him!' Tara started for the door but James stopped her.

'Matt and Martha arrived back from Springfield whilst I was tending to him. We've loaded him into the gig and Matt has turned straight around to take him back there. He needs the doctor, Tara, and that way he'll see him sooner than if Matt had ridden to fetch him.'

Tara bit her lip, looking at James with suspicion.

'You're not telling me the truth, are you? He's dead!'

'I am telling you the truth, I swear it.' His eyes went to the mess Tara was attempting to clean up. 'I'm not sure you've told me the whole truth, though. Come and sit down, finish your brandy and tell me exactly what happened. Leave that – whatever it is . . . What is it, anyway?'

'It's cake,' Tara said. 'It was supposed to be a treat for your tea.'

'So why is it all over the floor?'

'Because Tara threw it at the man!' Duncan piped up. 'Oh, Papa, you should have seen her! She was wonderful!'

'Tell me,' James ordered.

Between them, they did.

When Philip and Cal came home the whole story had to be gone through again, Tara doing her best to play it down, Duncan embellishing it even more.

'She was so brave! She was just like a dingo! Oh, you should have seen!'

'I had to do something,' Tara said. 'He was threatening to take Duncan and hold him to ransom.'

'The bastard! Let's get out there and look for him!' For all that his leg was still far from back to normal, Cal was on his feet and strapping on his gun.

'There's no point,' James said. 'Not tonight.'

'How can you say that?' Cal demanded. 'When an old man has been beaten senseless and your son damned near stolen away! Not to mention Tara . . .'

'See reason, Cal,' James said. 'No one would like to catch the blackguard more than I and if I thought I could I'd be out there like a shot, believe you me, and I wouldn't give you twopence for his chances when I found him. But we won't catch him. He's long gone, and holed up somewhere, no doubt, to tend to his burns. We could search high and low for a week and not find him. And to do it we'd have to leave Tara and Duncan here on their own again and unprotected. No, the best thing is to report it to the military and hope they can find him for us. From what Tara says, he's likely to be scarred for some time, if not for life, and that should mark him out wherever he goes. And when they do catch up with him, I'll be the first to make sure he gets his just deserts.'

Cal looked unconvinced, but Philip backed what James had said.

'He's right, Cal. Riding out now would be a waste of time. Best leave it to the authorities. Though if we do come across him when we're out on the land, he'll have more than a burning face to worry about.'

'And we must make sure Tara and Duncan aren't left alone until he is caught,' James said decisively. 'One of us – or one of our men – must be here at all times. If he took it into his head to come back . . .' He broke off. There was no need to put into words what he feared might happen should the man come back seeking revenge on the woman who had treated him in such a painful and humiliating manner.

Tara got up. 'I'll see about supper.'

'You'll stay where you are,' James said. 'You're in shock. You need to rest. We'll get the supper and wait on you tonight.'

On the point of arguing, Tara sank back gratefully into the chair. She did feel weak and shaky. But at least, surrounded by the three men, she felt safe – and cherished. It was an unfamiliar feeling, but a very good one.

Tara was finding sleep hard to achieve. Downstairs, lingering after supper in the big warm kitchen in the comforting presence of the three men, the demons of the day had receded; now, alone in her room they were there once again, lurking in every shadow, scraping at her nerves with every creak of the creeper outside her bedroom window. Each time she closed her eyes she saw the ugly face of the man, and little fragments of the terrifying encounter played themselves over and over in her mind.

And not only today's encounter, either, for what had happened had resurrected all the unpleasant memories she had tried so hard to erase. Now, once more, the feel of a gun in her hand was frighteningly fresh and the claustrophobic sensation of being trapped in a room with a man who was threatening her had been reawakened. Why, this man, whose name she did not even know, had even lusted after her, however briefly, as Henry Dupont had done. Perhaps he, too, would have attempted ro rape her if Duncan hadn't appeared and changed the focus of his attention. Tara shivered as visions of what might have happened to both her and Duncan passed in an unending panorama before her wide and frightened eyes.

It was no good, she was never going to sleep. Though she ached with tiredness every nerve was too taut, and her mind refused to stop spinning.

Tara pushed aside the covers and got out of bed. The bare boards as she crossed them felt cold to her feet and her toes cramped. She wriggled them. At least the physical pain was something she could contend with, unlike the shadowy horrors that plagued her emotions.

She pushed aside the window drapes, looking out. In the bright moonlight everything looked still and peaceful. But it was all an illusion. Somewhere out there in the darkness was a man who would surely take a horrible revenge upon her if ever their paths crossed again.

A sudden scream made Tara jump and her overwrought nerves responded, jangling like Chinese wind chimes. What was that? A night bird? Some small and helpless creature being taken as prey by a predator? But the sound had come from within the house, she was sure.

Duncan. It must have been Duncan.

Her own fears forgotten, Tara dashed across the room. Surely, oh surely, the man hadn't returned and stolen into the house to take Duncan? She wrenched open the door and ran on to the landing in time to see a shadowy figure going into Duncan's room. But not the man – oh, thank God – not the man. It was James.

Tara withdrew back into her own room. James, too, must have been disturbed by the scream and hurried to his son. That was all right, then. It was James that Duncan would want, James who could best comfort him. It was unusual for him to cry out like that, though. Usually he slept soundly, not making a sound from the time he went to bed until he woke, full of mischief, next morning. Perhaps he too had been more upset by the events of the day than any of them had realised. One thing to treat the whole horrible episode as an adventure in the full light of day, surrounded by his father and his uncles, quite another – as she had realised herself – to be alone in the shadowy dark. But James was with him now. James would calm his fears.

Tara wrapped her arms around herself and wished desperately that she could look to him for comfort too. But she couldn't. She was a grown woman and a married one at that. She couldn't expect to be afforded such a luxury. She slipped back beneath the covers, pulling them up to her chin, and determinedly closed her eyes. She simply must try to sleep or she'd be good for nothing in the morning.

A tap on the door made her eyes fly open once more. She sat up in bed, as alert and wide awake as ever. The handle turned, the door opened a crack.

'Tara, are you awake?' It was James's voice, low but urgent.

'Yes, I'm awake. What is it?'

James came into the room. In the soft half-light he looked very tall, very broad, and though she could not see his face clearly she could imagine every masculine line of it.

'It's Duncan,' he said. 'He's been having a nightmare.'

'I heard him cry out,' Tara said. 'Is he all right?'

'I think so. He's not as tough as he pretends, though, and he's been more upset by what happened today than I realised. Added to which, his night light had gone out. He hates the dark.'

'Oh, poor Duncan!' Tara had often wondered why it was that a night light was always kept burning in his room but had not liked to ask the reason.

'Anyway,' James went on, 'he seems to have got it into his head that something has happened to you. It was in his dream, I suppose, but he can't seem to shake it off even though he's awake now. And he's afraid to go back to sleep. I don't suppose . . . would you come along to his room and tell him you're all right? Just to set his mind at rest? I wouldn't ask, but . . .'

'Of course I will!' Tara said. She knew all about the way the aura of dreams could spread out destructively into wakefulness.

'I'm really sorry to disturb you,' James apologised again, 'but I don't think he'll settle until he's seen you with his own eyes.'

Tara got out of bed and reached for her wrap, slipping it on.

'It's fine, truly,' she said. 'I couldn't sleep either.'

She followed James along the landing to Duncan's room. James had re-lit the night light; it glimmered now on the table beside the bed, but Duncan was still sitting bolt upright, clutching the covers to him protectively.

'Duncan?' Tara said.

He jerked round to look at her. 'Oh, Tara, is it really you?'

'Who else would it be?' she asked softly.

'But I thought . . . I dreamed . . . that man . . .'

'That's all it was, Duncan – a dream.' She sat down on the edge of the bed and took his hand in hers. 'See, I'm here. Nothing dreadful has happened to me. As if I'd let it!'

He nodded slowly. 'You were so brave, Tara.'

'No, I wasn't,' she retorted. 'I was scared to death and I expect you were too, if only you'd admit it. That man was enough to scare anyone. But it's all over now. We're both quite safe. Your father won't let any harm come to either of us.'

'And that's a fact.' The bed dipped as James knelt beside it and leaned forward on his elbows to encircle them both in his arms.

The touch warmed Tara's chill skin and the glow spread from her shoulders where his arm lay to run through her veins.

After all the horrors of the day that she had been reliving

alone in her room this was like suddenly finding herself in heaven. The scent of Duncan's hair, sweet and clean from his bath, mingled in her nostrils with the musky male aroma of James's body; the softness of Duncan's cheek against hers contrasted with the comforting strength of James's arm around her. It felt right, so right, the three of them there together in the silence of the night, their breathing rising and falling in unison. It was a taste of a happiness and contentment she had never known, no, not since she had been a child herself when Mammy had sat on *her* bed, singing her to sleep with sweet Irish lullabies, and the poignancy of it made her want to weep, in spite of the happiness, because it was just an illusion, all an illusion, a perfect moment stolen out of time, a little vignette of something that could never be.

'Papa,' Duncan murmured, his voice sleepy now.

'Yes, Duncan?'

'Papa, you won't let the light go out again, will you?'

'No, Duncan, I won't let the light go out again.'

'Mm.' Satisfied, he turned his face into the pillow and soon his even breathing told them he had gone back to sleep.

James moved carefully so as not to disturb him and Tara felt a sharp sense of loss. Oh, if only it could have gone on forever! If only they could have stayed like that, wrapped in each other's arms all night! But they couldn't and she knew that she, too, must bestir herself.

Reluctantly she got up. They stood together for a moment, looking down at the little boy's sleeping form, and his face, innocent, cherubic and very young in the flickering golden light. Then James drew her to the door, his arm about her waist. On the landing he pulled the door closed after him and turned to her.

'Thank you.'

'For what?'

'For coming to comfort a little boy in the middle of the night.'

''Twas nothing. I told you. I wasn't asleep anyway.'

She felt less than comfortable suddenly, all too aware of his nearness.

'And thank you too for what you did today. If that blackguard had taken him . . .' James's voice was rough, vibrating with emotion. 'You took a great risk, doing what you did. But you saved him, not a doubt of it. I can never thank you enough.'

'It was nothing,' she tried to say again but somehow this time the words would not come. The muscles of her throat simply refused to work.

'If anything had happened to either of you . . .'

Suddenly, without any warning, he pulled her to him, and taken totally by surprise, Tara was unable to resist.

Stupid to have been taken by surprise, she told herself afterwards. The charged atmosphere should have warned her. But wrapped up as she had been in her own emotions it had simply not occurred to her that he might be feeling the same, that the magic had come about because it was shared. But in that moment Tara did not think at all. She was aware only of James's arms around her, the hard wall of his chest against her yielding breasts, the pressure of his hips and long muscled legs. Instinctively she lifted her face and his mouth came down on hers, covering it so thoroughly that she felt she was drowning in him. With one hand he caressed the nape of her neck beneath the fall of her hair, loosed for bed, and his fingers drew tingling sensations from the very depths of her to prickle on her skin, whilst with the other he held her firmly to him.

Through the thin fabric of her robe she could feel every line, every sinew, every swell of his hard and muscular body. She twined her arms around him and the equally hard lean frame of his back delighted her fingers. And all the while desire rose in her in a flood tide so that nothing in the whole world was of any importance but her desperate need of him. It prickled over every inch of her skin, it sang in her veins, it drew the very depths of her like iron filings to a magnet so that she instinctively pressed her body closer, closer to his, and still it was not close enough.

His hand moved from the nape of her neck, sliding down and around to the neckline of her robe, slipping inside and rasping gently against the soft swell of her breast. Her nipple tingled deliciously and hardened at his touch and she moaned deep in her throat.

'Oh, Tara, Tara!' His lips were on her throat and then on her breast where his fingers had lately been, kissing, sucking, drawing out the heart of her. The robe came loose from its sash and he unfastened it so that it fell open and the full length of her firm young body was revealed, milky in the moonlight.

'Oh, Tara, Tara . . .'

Before she realised what was happening his arm had gone beneath her knees, scooping her off her feet and up into his arms. She gasped, both from a wonderful sense of abandonment and a sense of loss. Heaven to be held like a child in his arms, but she ached still for the feel of his body close against hers. He kissed her face and she buried it in the coarse curling hair of his chest as he carried her effortlessly along the landing.

The door to his room stood open. He carried her inside and kicked it closed behind them. The drapes had not been drawn; soft moonlight lay in a pool on the rumpled bed. James pushed the covers fully back and laid her down, straightening for a moment to remove his own robe. Through eyes hazy with love and desire she saw his magnificent body for a moment in its full masculine glory, then the bed dipped and he was lying beside her, pulling her close once more.

The touch of skin on skin was electrifying, the pressure between her legs a sharp sweetness that was almost painful in its urgency. Tara buried her face in his shoulder, biting at the firm flesh and drinking in the saltiness.

Then, with a fluid movement, he rolled on top of her and

she parted her legs to him in an instinctive response as old as time.

'My love.'

With a quick thrust he was inside her and their bodies moved in unison. Yet still she wanted more. She lifted her hips, every breath a sob of desire. Up, up, as if she were being borne along on a mighty wave. Up, up . . .

With a feeling of distress she heard his breathing quicken, heard his shout of triumph, felt his hot seed spill into her. It was over and she didn't want it to be over. She wasn't ready . . . she wanted more. Wonderful though it was to experience his pleasure she knew from past experience that she was to be left here on the precipice, stranded in the maelstrom of her tumultuous need.

'Oh, please . . . oh, please!' she whispered urgently.

And to her amazement and delight he did not abandon her. For a moment or two longer his body worked in her, then, as it softened and slid away he slipped his hand between her legs, seeking those secret places and moving against them with the same urgency as his body had done.

The wave carried her upwards again, up, up, to a place she had never been, a place of delight she had only imagined. Every nerve seemed stretched to breaking point; she gasped in disbelief that it could be so insistent – and so beautiful.

At the last she cried out, feeling she might die from the sheer intensity of it, then, as the wave subsided, layer upon delicious layer, and the aftershocks ceased, she curled around James's body, languorous and truly satisfied for the first time in her life.

'Oh, that was wonderful!' she murmured shamelessly.

'As it should be. As it always will be for us.' He, too, sounded drowsy.

Tara lay her head in the crook of his arm, savouring the sensual dampness of his skin, and listened to the beating of his heart. It was the last sound she heard before she fell asleep.

Tara woke once in the night, found herself still curled

against James, and revelled in the wonder of it. Then a small frisson of unease crept in. She shouldn't be here in his bed. It was wrong, terribly wrong. Briefly Tara wrestled with her conscience then pushed her doubts aside. She would worry about it tomorrow. For the moment she was going to make the most of every wonderful stolen moment. It *wasn't* wrong, she told herself. She loved him and she felt sure he loved her too. She wouldn't think about anything else.

Laying her face against his shoulder, clutching her dream tightly to her, Tara fell asleep once more.

It was full daylight when Tara next woke, morning sun streaming in through the window and playing on her closed eyelids. For a few blissful moments she lay wrapped in the delicious aura that still pervaded her senses and reached out for James. Her seeking hand encountered nothing but cold empty sheet. Her eyes flew open; he was not there. She was alone.

Dear God, what time was it? Tara sat up, reaching for her wrap which lay discarded on the floor beside the bed, and instantly reality came rushing in along with all the guilt she had refused to acknowledge last night.

What had she done? How could she have allowed this to happen? Oh, she must have been mad. Mad!

She pushed aside the sheet that lay loosely across her nude body, leaped out of bed and pulled on her robe. In the doorway she paused, listening to make sure there was no one on the landing. If she walked out of James's room wearing nothing but her night things and straight into Philip or Cal or Duncan she thought she would die of shame. But the landing was deserted. She fled along it to her own room where she dressed as quickly as her fumbling hands would allow, then hurried to the head of the stairs.

The men's voices came floating up to her, together with the chink of crockery that told her they were at breakfast.

Somehow she had to face them, and she quailed before the prospect. They would know, surely, from her face, that something had happened – if they didn't know already. And James, how in heaven's name could she face James? The memory of the loving they had shared was sharp and clear to her, her cheeks burned dully as she recalled her abandoned behaviour. Bad enough if she had been free to have to see her love for the first time after their frantic coupling in the presence of his son and his brothers. But she was not free. She was a married woman who had sinned in the sight of God. A married woman who had behaved like a brazen harlot.

Somehow Tara forced her unwilling feet down the staircase, somehow she pushed open the door to the kitchen. They looked towards her, all of them, and Tara felt her cheeks glow even more hotly.

'I overslept,' she said. 'I'm sorry.'

'That's hardly surprising after what happened to you yesterday,' Philip said.

For a confused, humiliated moment, she thought he was referring to her night of love. Then she realised he meant her ordeal at the hands of the intruder. He was smiling at her kindly, that gentle smile of his, without the slightest hint of innuendo, as was Cal. But James . . . oh, James was a different kettle of fish altogether.

Though he made no reference whatever to where she had spent the night – as if he would! – his acknowledgement of it was there in his eyes. His glance caressed her, the intimacy of it reached out to touch her and pierced her through with bittersweet pain.

My love, that look said, and the tears formed a lump in Tara's throat so that she had to turn quickly away in order that he should not see it.

And this, she thought, was perhaps the worst sin of all. She had deceived James. Kept from him all the things that he had a right to know. That she was a murderess and a refugee from justice. And most important of all, that there could never be anything more between them.

There must never be a repeat of last night. Never. Though the knowledge made her feel as if her heart were breaking, Tara knew that somehow she must make sure of that.

Fourteen

James came up behind Tara as she piled the breakfast dishes in the sink for washing and put his arms about her waist, pulling her close to him.

'Thank you, Tara.' His lips were against her ear, his breath whispered over her skin and she felt the desire for him begin to tingle again in her veins.

'For what?' she asked, trying to make her voice light in order to hide the tremble in it.

'For last night. And for being you.'

Tears pricked her eyes. It was all she could do not to turn towards him, lift her lips to his and let him kiss away all the pain that was in her heart. Instead she bent over the sink, plunging her hands into the hot soapy water.

'You're not sorry, are you, that we . . .' His voice tailed away and she felt the pressure of his lips on the pulse point in her neck.

'Of course not,' she whispered.

And in part it was true. How could she regret the glory they had shared? It was something she would treasure for the rest of her life. But at the same time she was very sorry indeed because their relationship had gone beyond the point of no return. By allowing him to make love to her she had gained everything – and lost everything. There was no way back to the comfortable state of employer and employee. They had moved on, not only accepted the way they felt about one another but acted upon it. Nothing could ever be the same again.

And she didn't want it to be, she knew that now. Pleasant as it had been at first to have a secure life with decent folk who made her feel at home, a roof over her head and food on the table, as she had become aware of her feelings for James the whole set-up had become sheer torture. To look at him and love him, knowing she had no right, no right at all. To live the illusion, to taste what might have been and know that it was forever beyond her reach. So, she thought, might a starving child feel looking in at the window of a baker's shop, his nose pressed against the glass that prevented him reaching out for the things he craved.

Well, that was all over now. She had known it from the moment she had woken this morning and realised the full enormity of what had happened between them. For one glorious night she had not only looked but tasted and eaten her fill and she could never go back to simply looking again. If she stayed at Dunrae, she would sin over and over again, and it wouldn't only be her that would suffer in the process. Best that she should leave now, before any more harm was done. James might be a little hurt – yes, almost certainly he would be – but not nearly as much as if she stayed.

She had spoiled everything by her weakness, Tara thought wretchedly. Now, somehow, she must be strong.

'I'm taking Duncan out with me today,' James said. 'You saw for yourself how upset he was last night and I think it would do him good to be away from these four walls – help to take his mind off what happened yesterday.'

Tara nodded. 'I think that's a very good plan.'

'And I'll ask Matt to come over and keep an eye on you.'

'There's no need.' Tara steeled herself to turn around and look him straight in the eye. 'With Dickon to look after, Martha will need him there.'

Dickon had recovered full consciousness now, but the doctor had prescribed complete rest for him and Martha had insisted he move into the Hendersons' quarters so that she could care for him.

197

'Don't worry about me, James. If it's just me I can look after myself.'

A faint smile touched his lips. 'Yes, Tara, I think you can. That blackguard is ruing the day, no doubt, that he tangled with you. But all the same . . .'

'He'll not come back,' Tara said with more confidence than she felt. 'Leastways, not today. And if he did . . . Well, I've got his gun, haven't I? And I wouldn't hesitate to use it.'

'Hmm. It seems in good order.' James had picked it up from the shelf where it now lay, examining it closely. 'I think I'd prefer it, though, if you didn't have to use something belonging to that scoundrel to defend yourself.' He crossed to the bureau, selected a key, and inserted it into the keyhole of one of the drawers that was always kept locked. When supervising the cleaning, Tara had sometimes wondered about it, and what the drawer contained. Now, in a flash, she guessed – and correctly.

'This belonged to Lorna, my wife.' James slid the drawer open and took out a small neat gun. Something glinted in the sunlight which streamed in at the window and Tara saw that the handle was set with a pattern of tiny diamonds – a lady's gun, without doubt, and a very expensive one. James turned it over in his hands for a moment, looking at it, and there was a sad and thoughtful expression in his eyes. Then he held it out to Tara. 'It might be small,' he said, 'but it's also deadly. It would be much lighter and easier for you to handle.'

Tara spun round. 'Oh, I couldn't! Not your wife's!'

James smiled ruefully. 'She has no need for it any more, Tara. You do. She would be glad for you to have it, I know.'

He spoke soberly, as if he had thought long and hard about this and come to an important conclusion.

It was, Tara thought, as if the gun was a symbol of a heart locked away. Now it was not just his wife's dainty but deadly firearm he was offering her but all the other things that had belonged to her. His life. His love.

Guilt flooded her. She couldn't let him do this. But how could she refuse? Easiest all round for everyone if she accepted the gun – for the moment. Later . . . her throat closed.

'Thank you,' she said.

James bent to kiss her forehead. 'I have to go. But I'll be back as soon as I can. Just promise me you'll be careful whilst I'm away.'

'I promise.' She swallowed hard.

He made to pull her to him but at that exact moment Duncan came rushing in, dressed for riding, his small face alive with excitement.

'I'm ready, Papa. Are we going now?'

James smiled – a smile that tore at Tara's heartstrings – and rumpled Duncan's hair.

'Yes, we're going now, Duncan. Say goodbye to Tara.'

'Goodbye, Tara.' But it was rushed. Already Duncan was halfway to the door, eager to be out in the open air on his beloved pony at his father's side.

James smiled again, this time at Tara, a secret smile, full of promise, then he too turned for the door.

Tara touched her fingers to her lips and blew a kiss after him but even that small gesture filled her with guilt. She had no right. No right at all . . .

As if he caught something of the wretchedness and confusion she was feeling, he frowned.

'Tara, are you sure you're all right?'

'Sure, I'm fine,' she lied. 'Off you go now.'

But as she watched father and son ride away together down the drive the tears pricked at her eyes and this time she did not even bother to blink them away.

This was the last time she would look on James and Duncan. When they returned she would be gone. It was for the best. It was all she could do, for all of them. But the weight on her heart was almost more than she could bear all the same.

When they had disappeared from view she went to her room and packed together the few things she had brought with her to Dunrae. She wouldn't take anything James had bought for her, she decided – and she certainly wouldn't take Lorna's gun. The one that had belonged to the man who had come here yesterday with robbery in mind and precipitated this whole situation would be good enough for her to protect herself. Tara thrust it into her reticule.

In the bureau in the parlour she found paper, a quill pen and ink. There was no way she could explain to James why she was leaving and it would take longer than she could spare to concoct some sort of story that would hold water. Tara settled for a simple note of thanks for all he had done for her and an apology for taking the gig and horses.

'I will stable them at the Imperial Hotel in Melbourne,' she wrote carefully. 'I am sure they will be well looked after until you can collect them. I am sorry for any inconvenience this may cause you.'

That was it, then. It was done. All that remained was for her to decide how to sign off. Tara ached to write some loving words, telling him she would carry the memory of him in her heart forever, but she knew she must not. To do so would be to give him hope, and that would be very wrong. The break must be quick, clean and final.

With a heavy heart she folded the page, sealed it into an envelope and propped it on the table against a pitcher of winter-flowering jasmine which she had cut and arranged. It was the only gesture of love she dared make. Then she gathered her things together, took one last look around the kitchen where she had found such unexpected happiness, and went out, closing the door behind her.

A young lad, the son of one of the farm workers, was in the stable yard. He had been drafted in to look after the horses until Dickon Stokes was fit to resume his duties. Tara ordered the lad to harness the bays to the gig and make it ready for her. He looked surprised but made no comment.

And why should he? Tara thought. He was not yet of an age to remark on the actions of those he considered his superiors. An employee, too, Tara might be, but she lived in the big house and consorted with the Hannays. Whatever he might think privately, the lad would do as she told him and no questions asked.

The gig was ready. Tara climbed into the driving seat and took up the reins, a little nervous of her ability but full of grim determination. For safety's sake, in case she should run up against the man who had terrorised her yesterday, she took the gun from her reticule and laid it on the seat beside her.

As she trotted the horses down the drive, the sun slanting through the mimosa and eucalypts seemed to mock her. Tara turned onto the Melbourne road and did not dare trust herself to look back.

'Papa, Papa, where is Tara?' Duncan came tumbling down the veranda steps, almost falling over himself in his haste.

James, watering the horses before stabling them, glanced up, puzzled.

'What do you mean, where is Tara?'

'She's not in the house. I can't find her anywhere!'

James felt a stab of alarm. Surely the man hadn't returned and done her some mischief? Dear God, he should never have left her alone today!

He twisted Tarquin's reins around the hitching rail, ran across the yard and took the veranda steps two at a time. Duncan, frightened by the show of urgency, followed.

As the little boy had said, there was no sign of life in the kitchen and no evidence of a meal being prepared either, though it was now well into the afternoon.

'Tara! Tara!' James hurried through the house, throwing open doors and leaving them to stand ajar. Each room was as empty as the one before. 'Tara!'

Even though he had little hope that she was there, he knocked before opening the door to her bedroom. As he had thought it too was empty – and somehow ominously tidy, the pillows stacked, the blankets neatly folded.

What in heaven's name had happened here? He could think of no logical explanation. He hurried back downstairs again and the moment he went back through the kitchen door he saw the note, propped against the pitcher of jasmine.

His stomach seemed to fall away. He reached for the envelope and tore it open. The words leaped out at him from the page, hitting him like hammer blows to the heart, and yet he had to read and re-read the note several times before he could take it in.

Tara had gone. He simply could not believe it. And yet . . .

Dammit, he'd known something was wrong this morning. There had been something different about her, something remote and shut-in, something he could not understand or reach. He had put it down to a slight awkwardness after the abandon of the night they had spent together, or perhaps more likely to the residue of tensions left over from her ordeal of the previous day. He had told himself that she, like Duncan, had been more upset by what had occurred than she was prepared to admit. However bravely she had acted at the time the shock and fear had likely left her nerves in tatters.

Now, James cursed himself for making such a easy assumption. He should have realised there was more to it than that. But what . . . what? Did she regret having spent the night making love to him? That must be it. Nothing less could have precipitated such a hasty departure. But why? It wasn't as if he had forced himself on her – far from it. She had been every bit as eager as he. And afterwards she had slept in his arms, rosy and fulfilled. No, the regret must have come later. But it made no sense. No sense at all.

He re-read the note she had left him and wondered how long ago she had left. He went out into the yard, calling for Edwin, the boy who had been looking after the horses.

'Miss Reilly took the gig for a drive. What time was that?'

202

The boy reddened a little at James's sharp tone. 'Early this morning, not long after you left.' He chewed his lip. 'I thought she'd be back by now.'

James nodded abruptly. It was as he had feared. Tara would be far away by now. But it would be impossible for her to make Melbourne in one day, or even two. She would be forced to stop overnight at one of the small hostelries along the way. On a good fast horse he had every chance of catching her. Not Tarquin, though. Tarquin was already tired from a long day out on the land.

'Saddle Pluto for me,' he instructed the boy tersely.

Duncan had followed him outside, his small face anxious.

'You'll have to stay with Martha until your uncles get home,' James told him. 'I'm going after Tara.'

He took the little boy over to the Hendersons' quarters. Dickon Stokes was lying on the couch in the kitchen – a good sign, James thought – but apart from a cursory enquiry as to how he was feeling James paid him little attention. Dickon was in good hands with Martha. All James's concerns were for Tara, and he was anxious to be on his way.

Briefly he explained what had occurred and what he planned to do. 'Duncan can go back to the house as soon as Philip or Cal get in,' he said. 'But tell them, will you, I'm likely to be gone all night.'

'And what's this lamb to have for his tea?' Martha demanded. 'Or the boys for that matter, if there's no one to get it for them? I can't go over there. I've got my hands full looking after Dickon.'

'They can manage for once,' James said shortly. 'There's food in the house. They'll not starve.'

Martha's lips were pressed tightly together in a grim expression which left no doubt as to what she thought of Tara Reilly for causing so much trouble. Why, she'd let the girl go and be glad to see the back of her if it was left to her. But here was Mr James chasing off after her like a madman!

James, however, scarcely even registered Martha's disapproval.

'Be a good boy now, Duncan.' He rumpled his son's hair by way of farewell. 'I'll be home again as soon as I can.'

'Papa . . .'

'Yes, Duncan?'

'Papa you will bring Tara home with you, won't you?'

James nodded grimly. If there was one thing he was determined on, it was that. How easy or difficult it would be, he did not know, since he had no idea of her reason for leaving in the first place. But somehow he was going to find out. Somehow he would persuade her that running away would solve nothing.

'Oh yes, Duncan, I'll bring her back, I promise,' he said, and refused to even contemplate the possibility that she might not agree to come with him.

Tara had come into his life like the springtime after a long hard winter, bringing warmth and sunshine and new hope. She had touched the heart that he had thought was frozen for all time and made it live again. That she should go away now was quite unthinkable.

Anxious, but driven by grim determination, James went out and crossed the yard to where Pluto was saddled ready and waiting for him.

Darkness was falling, and an exhausted Tara had begun to think she would never see civilisation again when she came upon a few shacks along the side of the road signifying the outskirts of a small township.

'Oh, praise be!'

Her hands were sore from the constant rub of the reins, her arms and shoulders ached and her head throbbed painfully. The concentration required to drive the gig, given her inexperience, had been bad enough. Even worse had been the lowering sun which had been directly in her eyes for what had seemed like hours as she drove due west. Then, as it sank below the horizon, the dusk had descended with the frightening swiftness and Tara had been very afraid she was going to find herself still on this endless empty road in pitch darkness.

She should have stopped at the last hostelry she had passed, she told herself. Driving on, especially with the tiring horses, had been folly. But she hadn't wanted to stop. She had wanted to press on, putting as much distance as possible between her and James. Now, however, she had no choice in the matter.

The hamlet had been built up along either side of the road – some shops, a smithy, a chapel, and a square stone building whose dusty, sun-faded awning proclaimed 'Commercial Hotel'. Thankfully Tara pulled up on the forecourt, looped the reins around a hitching post, and went up the short flight of steps that led to the main door of the hotel.

The low buzz of male voices came out to greet her and as she pushed open the door she saw that the saloon beyond it was full of men. Some were perched on stools at a long bar, some had gathered their chairs round a log fire which blazed invitingly in an open grate. A few were eating, the aroma of the mutton stew on the plates before them mingling with the pungent smells of wood smoke and tobacco. The moment they saw Tara standing in the doorway they fell silent, each and every last one gazing at her open-mouthed.

Tara felt the blood rush to her cheeks but she lifted her chin and walked boldly into the saloon. It was only to be expected that a woman travelling alone in this wild country would arouse interest, and for all that they were roughly dressed the men looked harmless enough compared to the baying hordes of low-life she had been forced to content with in the goldfields. Some were travellers passing through, no doubt – the ones sitting alone at the tables to eat their mutton stew. But the majority were probably townsfolk and farm workers who had ridden in from the surrounding district for an evening's drinking and the company of others.

Behind the bar a tender wearing calico cuffs to protect the

sleeves of his shirt looked up at her enquiringly. There was not even a barmaid, then. Tara was indeed the only woman in the place. She returned his stare boldly.

'I'd like a room for the night if you please,' she said. 'I'd also like something to eat. And I have a gig outside, with two horses who need feeding and watering. I hope you will be able to oblige me?'

The room to which the hotel owner showed Tara was small and a little shabby, but at least it was clean. Tara freshened up and went back down to the saloon where a place had been set for her at one of the small tables.

The hotel owner himself served her with a plate of mutton and vegetables, something which surprised Tara until he lingered beside her chair and she realised it was to give him the chance to ask her all the questions he had not when she had signed her name in his leather-bound register.

'Where are you headed then?'

'Melbourne,' Tara replied shortly.

'Your husband not with you?'

The habit of the past weeks and months was so strong that Tara almost replied that she did not have a husband. Then, very aware of the exclusively male company, she wondered about the wisdom of such an admission.

'No.'

She saw the hotelier's eyes go to her bare fingers and made a mental note to replace her wedding ring at the first opportunity.

'And have you come far today?'

'Quite some distance.' Tara was beginning to feel annoyed by the persistent questioning. 'Would you mind? I'm very tired and I really don't feel like talking,' she said firmly.

Disgruntled, the hotelier withdrew and Tara made a start on her meal. It was palatable enough, she supposed, though not as nice as the ones she had taught herself to make, but, hungry as she had supposed herself to be now that the food was in front of her, she found she had no appetite.

She pushed a piece of meat around her plate with her fork, bereft, unhappy and worried as to what tomorrow would bring. Barring mishaps she would make it to Melbourne. Once there, she would deliver the horses and the gig into the safe keeping of the Imperial Hotel as she had promised to do. But what then? Back to her former existence, she supposed. Back to traipsing the streets day after day in search of a job. Back to sleeping under the stars – or enduring the privations of the horrible Women's Refuge. The thought of it was almost more than she could bear, but what choice did she have?

Well, perhaps this time she would fare better in her search for work, Tara told herself, trying hard to be optimistic. At least now she had a couple of good gowns and for the moment at least she was clean and presentable, not the refugee from the goldfields she had been before. And she had improved her domestic skills too. When applying to prospective employers she would be able to cite her experience as housekeeper at Dunrae and nanny and governess to Duncan.

The thought was a painful reminder of all she had lost. She wouldn't think about it, she told herself. There was no point, no point at all. But all the willing in the world could not stop her wanting James. However she tried to blank him out of her thoughts he still came creeping back. And even when she succeeded in not thinking about him the wanting was still there, an ache around her heart so fierce it was almost physical.

At last Tara gave up the unequal struggle to eat the lamb stew. The moment she put down her knife and fork and pushed back her plate, the hotelier was there at her elbow.

'Nothing wrong with your meal, I hope?'

'No, nothing,' Tara assured him. 'I'm just not very hungry.'

'My, and after you've had such a long day travelling too!'

Tara sensed another barrage of questioning was imminent and sought to forestall it. 'It's true I'm very tired.'

'You'll be going straight to bed then?' His eyes were shrewd, summing her up.

'I suppose so.' The thought of going up to that small shabby room was not an appealing one. Tired as she was, Tara felt sure that sleep would be difficult to come by.

Suddenly into her mind came a vision of the church she had noticed as she drove into the little township.

'I passed a church just down the street,' she said. 'What denomination is it?'

He stared at her blankly.

'Is it Catholic or Protestant?' she asked.

'Catholic, I think.' The hotelier had little interest in religious matters. 'Yes, Father O'Hara, the priest, comes in for a glass of whisky sometimes. Though he's always complaining it's not like the liquor he was used to at home in the Emerald Isle.'

'He's Irish?' Tara cried eagerly.

'He is at that! And anyone would think that no one but the Irish knew how to brew whisky from the way he goes on about it!'

Tara wiped her lips on her handkerchief and stood up. She was aching suddenly for the sound of a voice from home. Oh, the priest wasn't likely to be in his church at this time of night, but his presence would be there amidst all the trappings, and perhaps in the quiet and holy building she would be able to find some peace.

'You're not going there tonight, surely?' the hotelier asked in surprise. 'It'll be all locked up for sure.'

'Not if it's a Catholic church,' Tara said with certainty. 'The doors should always be open in a Catholic church.'

'Well, I wouldn't go there after dark, be damned if I would!' The hotelier was looking at her as if she was stark staring mad. 'It's creepy enough in daylight, what with all those statues looking at you!'

Tara didn't bother to reply. She was filled now with a sense of urgency. It was so long since she had set foot in the house of God. Perhaps she'd be struck down, sinner that she was, for daring to do so now, but what did that matter?

From the outside the church was little more than a shack with a cross over the door – which was firmly shut. Tara felt a moment's misgiving. Perhaps it *was* locked. Perhaps out here in this wild and lawless country it had to be locked at sundown to keep out looters and drunken rowdies who might desecrate it. But when she tried the handle it gave to her touch.

She pushed the door open and at once she was enveloped by the once familiar scents of incense and candle fat and the faint musty smell that came from a dish of holy water. With the ease of long habit Tara dipped her fingers into it and touched it to her forehead, then waited apprehensively to see if she was indeed going to be struck down – a murderess and an adulterer anointing herself with holy water. Nothing happened and she moved slowly and reverently into the church.

The building was full of candlelight. Thick candles burned on the altar and in sconces on the walls, tiny tea lights surrounded a statue of the Blessed Virgin, small penny candles, some mere stubs, some barely melted, stood on the spikes of the votive stand, each one signifying a prayer.

Tears pricked Tara's eyes. Oh, the peace, the blessed peace of the place! How could anyone describe it as creepy? Slowly she crept along the back of the church, her slippered feet making no sound. As she crossed the aisle leading between rough wooden pews to the altar she genuflected, a gesture as natural to her as breathing, then moved to the area in front of the statue of the Blessed Virgin which had been set up as a small Lady Chapel. The flickering candlelight played on the sweet plaster face of the Virgin, softening the garish hues in which it had been painted so that the face seemed to glow in the surrounding darkness. Tara fumbled in her reticule for a coin, fed in into the coin box and took a candle from the basket beside it. She lit it from one of the other candles and fell to her knees in front of the statue, raising her eyes to that beautiful face and reciting the prayers of the rosary.

'Hail, Holy Queen, Mother of Mercy, hail . . .'

The oft-used words sprang easily to her lips but she added no supplications of her own. Lost, lonely, heartsick, Tara had no idea what she should ask for. The deepest wish of her heart was for something that could never be, anything less was not worth praying for. All Tara hoped for was forgiveness of her sins – and peace.

And she felt it. A warming glow that surrounded her, a sense that here in the church she could leave behind the torments and trials of the world outside for just a little while. Tara only wished she could stay here forever.

The soft pad-padding of sandalled feet and the swish of a soutane on the bare board floor caught Tara's attention. Realising she was no longer alone, she looked up. The priest – Father O'Hara, was it the hotelier had called him?

'My child.'

He stood looking down at her, faded blue eyes shrewd yet kindly in a weather-beaten face that looked more as if it belonged to a farm hand than a man of God. His voice indeed had the soft lilt of home and his robes, a little dusty and impregnated with the perfume of incense, smelled hauntingly familiar.

'Father.' She made to rise and he placed a hand on her shoulder, firm yet gentle.

'Don't disturb yourself for me, child. Finish your prayers.'

'Sure, I've finished.' Tara got to her feet, feeling oddly self-conscious.

'You're Irish,' he said, sounding surprised.

'I am Father. And you?'

'Indeed. From County Clare. But I've been here for many years now. We're a long way from home, the pair of us.' He paused. 'I've not seen you here in Edwardstown before, have I?'

'I'm passing through. But I wanted to come into the church.'

Father O'Hara looked at her closely, at the good-quality

clothes she wore, smart but modest, at the clear-featured face – and the haunted eyes. Young as she was, she bore some great sorrow, of that much he was certain, but she bore it bravely. And her devotion to her faith was there, written all over her as she spiked the candle onto a spare holder at the feet of the Madonna and crossed herself quickly and silently.

'Is there anything I can do for you?' he asked softly.

She hesitated, then shook her head. 'No, thank you, Father.'

'You do not wish to make a confession?'

She hesitated for so long he felt certain there was something. Then she shook her head again. 'No, thank you.'

'Very well. I'll be in the sacristy if you change your mind.'

But she knew she would not. Much as she longed to unburden herself and have the absolution of the Church, Tara could not bring herself to do so. She was too ashamed.

But at least for just a little while she had found peace. Tara hoped that it would help her through the long and lonely night ahead.

Contrary to all her fears, Tara fell asleep the moment her head touched the pillow. Once during the night she woke, but in spite of all that was wrong in her world she felt incredibly calm and safe – happy, almost. She wondered at it briefly, curling into the pillow with much the same delicious contentment as she had felt during the previous night in James's arms, and then she was drifting off once more into sweet dreamless sleep.

It was morning when she next woke and, mindful of the long hard day ahead of her, she got up at once, washed her face in the cold water that stood in the jug on the wash stand and dressed herself. Then she went downstairs.

The hotel was quiet this morning, though a fug of stale tobacco smoke and ale fumes hung in the narrow passageway as a reminder of how busy it had been last night.

Tara pushed open the door to the saloon. A couple of lone travellers sat at their tables over breakfast. This morning they scarcely bothered to look up as she went in. Tara took her place at the same table she had occupied last night and a serving wench appeared from the direction of the kitchen.

'Breakfast, madam?'

'Please.' She didn't really feel hungry, but who knew when she would eat again? 'And a big pot of tea.'

She thought briefly of the Hannays, no doubt gathered now around their own breakfast table, sharing their own pot of tea, then pushed the thought aside. *Don't start that now . . .*

The door to the lobby was ajar. Tara glanced towards it and caught a glimpse of a man standing at the desk. His back was towards her, a long muscled back, and above it dark hair curling thickly over the nape of his neck.

A nerve jumped in Tara's throat. It was as if thinking about the Hannays had conjured up an illusion. Why, for a moment she had thought the man at the desk . . .

He turned round and the nerve jumped again, setting all the other nerves in her body jangling with the shock of it.

This was no illusion. His eyes met hers; he came towards her.

'James!' she whispered faintly.

Fifteen

'Tara.'

James crossed to her table and stood for a moment looking down at her. The colour burned in her cheeks, a thousand confused and guilty thoughts chased one another around inside her head, as many emotions churned in her stomach. Only one mattered. A sudden fierce joy. He had come after her.

'How did you find me?' she asked.

'There aren't so many hostelries between Dunrae and Melbourne and this one seemed the most likely given the time you left yesterday.'

'You just got here?'

'No, I arrived late last night. You had already retired for the night. I checked on my horses and retired myself.'

He could hear that his tone was cold and hard and he really didn't know the reason for it when all he wanted to do was to take her in his arms, kiss that pretty flushed face and thank God he had caught up with her before she was lost in the mêlée of Melbourne.

Tara lowered her eyes. 'You're angry with me.'

James could not deny it. He *was* angry with her.

'Why did you do it?' he demanded. 'Why run off like a thief in the night – and with my horses and gig too?'

Tara's heart sank, the joy dying. It wasn't her he'd come after at all. It was his precious horses.

'I'm not stealing them,' she said fiercely. 'Only borrowing them. I left a note to tell you where you'd find them.'

'Two or three days' drive away. Yes.'

'And I did apologise for the inconvenience.'

'Dammit, Tara!' James brought his hand down so hard on the back of the chair that it jumped and rattled. 'If you were so desperate to get away why didn't you say something? I'd have driven you back to Melbourne if that's what you wanted. But to creep away like that when my back was turned . . . Am I such a monster?'

Tara shook her head. 'No . . . no, of course not.'

'Then why? Was it because you were afraid that blackguard would come back? Was that it?'

She shook her head again.

'Then it must have been because of what happened between us. Well, I'm sorry if I misread the situation. Won't you consider coming back to Dunrae? Duncan needs you, we all do. And I promise you it won't ever happen again.'

Tears pricked suddenly behind Tara's eyes. She was the one who had misread the situation then. He hadn't wanted her the way she wanted him. It had been nothing but lust on his part – a lust he was prepared to curb so long as he had the convenience of her there to look after Duncan and supervise his housekeeping. Well, she couldn't control her emotions so easily.

'I can't come back,' she said thickly.

Suddenly she became aware of the serving wench hovering with a tray and listening with barely concealed curiosity to every word they were saying. She nodded meaningfully to James; he turned and addressed the wench in the same clipped tones he had been using to her.

'You can put that down here and fetch another cup for me. I'll take my breakfast with the lady.'

'Yes, sir.' She deposited the things from the tray and scuttled off.

James pulled up a chair and sat down.

'We'll discuss this later in private. We don't want the whole of Edwardstown knowing our business.'

Tara set her lips in a firm line. 'There's nothing to discuss.'

James's face was still dark with anger and determination. 'Maybe not. But we'll discuss it anyway.'

James looked at Tara across the table, at her small set face, at the high spots of colour in her cheeks, at the little wisps of hair that she had failed to catch properly with the pins and which somehow made her look very vulnerable, and cursed himself for the way he had approached her.

It wasn't at all the way he'd planned it – if he'd planned at all. All this way he'd come to find her and persuade her to come back to Dunrae, and when he had found her all he could do was snarl bad-temperedly.

He couldn't understand what it was with her, of course, any more than he had ever understood what it was with Lorna. Women! Puzzling, complicated creatures that they were! He'd been to hell and back with Lorna and he'd sworn never to become involved with a woman again. Now, here he was caught in the same honeyed trap. No wonder he was angry! The best thing he could do was drive her on to Melbourne and leave her there. But . . .

But he had promised Duncan he would bring her back, so somehow he'd better find a way to do just that. But be damned if he was going to let her upset his life again!

When their silent awkward breakfast was over, James took Tara's elbow and steered her out of the saloon. She had no choice but to go with him. They had already made enough of a spectacle of themselves and James's set jaw warned her that if she argued they would soon be making a spectacle of themselves again.

The weather this morning was less bright than of late. A heavy blanket of cloud had blown in and the wind had a sharp cold edge to it. Tara shivered slightly. James glanced at her but did not relax his grip on her elbow. Along the street he propelled her, past a handful of stores and a livery stable, past a few townsfolk going about their business. The built-up area ended abruptly; suddenly there was nothing before them but open countryside as far as the eye could see, and they were alone.

James turned to her, still holding on to her arm, his face still closed in and determined. Tara felt a moment's sharp anxiety. This was a different James, one she did not know at all.

'I compromised you the other night,' he said. 'I realise that now and I'm sorry.'

'No . . .' Tara wished she dared tell him it was what she had wanted too, with all her heart. But she dared not.

'I did. I know it. You're a decent woman, Tara. I know I have no right to expect you to return under such circumstances. But . . .' He broke off, looking at her narrowly. 'Where did you plan to go?'

Caught by surprise she could think of no answer but the truth. 'I don't know.'

His eyes narrowed. 'Back to the life you had before? Back to the Women's Refuge?'

Her chin came up. 'I'll be all right.'

'You can't believe that any more than I do,' James said. 'It's no life in Melbourne for a woman alone. You were happy, weren't you, at Dunrae?'

Tara could not deny it.

'And you could be happy there again, I promise. We need you, Tara.'

She caught her lip between her teeth. 'James . . .'

'I know. Don't say it. I've apologised once, I'll do so again if necessary. But apologies are nothing but words. You and I both know how easy it was to behave – well, as we did. I could promise you, as indeed I did just now, that such a thing won't happen again, but I think we are both aware that it very well might. Which is why I'm about to suggest a different arrangement.' His eyes met hers, steady and surprisingly hard. 'I'm going to suggest, Tara, that you and I should be wed. You'd be mistress of Dunrae and I promise you would want for nothing. If you won't come

216

back to the situation as it was, then I am proposing that you come back as my wife.'

The blood was singing in her ears. She couldn't believe that she had heard aright. James didn't look like a man who had just proposed marriage. His face was too hard, too devoid of any emotion whatsoever. And the situation – nothing even vaguely romantic about grey skies, a cold gusting wind, and the bare autumn countryside. Not a star or a moonbeam in sight, nor likely to be.

Briefly, incongruously, Tara found herself remembering the night Patrick had proposed to her, hidden from the world in one of their special secret places. He had gone down on one knee, kissing her hand, and she had felt both cherished and excited at the same time. And she had accepted him without hesitation. God help her, she had said 'Yes' and not thought for a single moment that she was making a terrible mistake. One that would tie her to him till death them did part.

'James . . .'

He knew from the tone she spoke his name that she was going to refuse him.

'Don't,' he said quickly. 'Don't say anything yet. I've shocked you, I know. Heavens!' He laughed shortly. 'I've shocked myself! But don't say no until you've had time to think about it. Only come home with me, Tara, please. I don't want to lose you.'

Suddenly her eyes were full of tears. Not for a single second did it occur to her that if she were to fail to admit to her status no one, least of all James, would be any the wiser. Tara knew she had already sinned grievously and she would not have entertained for a moment the further sin of bigamy. She lowered her gaze from his.

'I can't.'

'You can't come home with me?'

'No.'

'But in God's name why not? You've nothing and no one

to go to. And I'm trying to show you I wasn't using you as a wanton woman . . .'

'And I can't marry you either.'

He gesticulated helplessly. 'I don't understand.' The anger was returning, the anger born of helplessness. 'Maybe I'm not such a good catch – a widower with a child. But I would treat you well, Tara. You would want for nothing. Why won't you even think about it? Do you find the idea so repulsive?'

The tears overflowed, spilling down her cheeks. It was more than she could bear, to be offered heaven on a plate and to have to refuse it.

'James, I swear to you, there's nothing I would like more in the whole world than to be your wife. But I can't, I tell you.'

He stared at her, totally confused. 'What do you mean?'

'Don't ask me, please,' Tara whispered.

'Why not?'

Tara turned her head away, unable to speak. James yanked her back to face him.

'Tara, you are the most infuriating woman I have ever known. Everything you say and do contradicts what I can see in your eyes. Why shouldn't I ask your reasons for not even considering my offer? Why did you run off in the first place unless you think I'm a monster? Why don't you say "I don't want to marry you, James"? Why do you say you can't?'

Tara drew a long shuddering breath then her eyes snapped up to meet his.

'Very well, if you want the truth you shall have it. I can't marry you, James, because I already have a husband. There, is that a good enough reason for you?'

His face went blank with shock. Whatever he had expected to hear it was not this. And yet why hadn't he thought of it before? He'd known there was something in her past that she was hiding. He'd known that she had not come to the goldfields alone. It didn't take the greatest leap of the imagination to guess that she had come with a man. But that she was *married* – no, it hadn't occurred to him. Not once. How could he have been so stupid?

'I see.' His voice was level, controlled. 'And where is he now, your husband?'

Tara shrugged. 'Still in Ballarat, I presume. He no longer cared whether I was there or not so long as he had his friend—' She broke off. The memory of Seamus and the closeness he and Patrick had shared still hurt too much.

'He left you for another woman?' James asked.

'No – not a woman. He had a mate who shared his dreams when I could not. He told him the things he wanted to hear. That tomorrow, or the next day, they'd strike a rich seam and we'd be wealthy beyond our wildest dreams. They couldn't see the reality, either of them. They went mad with the lust for gold.'

James nodded slowly. That figured. Tara's husband was not the first and he would not be the last to lose his senses to the lure of gold, not the first nor the last to abandon his wife and family, to see nothing as so important as the elusive glitter amid the dross. But to abandon a woman like Tara . . . he must truly be mad.

'So now do you understand?' Tara asked softly. The tears were still wet on her cheeks but she was no longer weeping. 'It's the reason I left in such haste, James, for what was happening between us was wrong.'

'Why didn't you tell me?' he asked.

'And what good would telling you have done? It wouldn't have changed anything. And anyway, I was ashamed of myself.'

'Ashamed? Why?' James asked, frankly astonished.

'Well, what sort of a woman am I? I've walked away from my marriage, I've deceived you from the start, I've let you make love to me when I knew it was a sin—'

'For the love of God!' he exploded. 'There's nothing to be ashamed of in that!'

'That's easy for you to say. You don't go to church.'

'And neither do you.'

'Because I know I am not fit to go! Because I can't bring myself to go to confession.' Tara caught her lip between her teeth. Why, even now she was keeping from him her worst sin of all – that she had killed a man – just as she kept it from the priests who could offer her at least the empty words of the absolution. Only God could forgive her, but she couldn't see that he would, especially when she could not bring herself to admit the truth to any living soul. 'I did go to the church here last night, though,' she went on after a moment. 'I did light a candle . . .'

And you are here. The words hovered on her lips but of course she did not speak them.

James might be here, but nothing had changed. The obstacles were as high now as they had ever been.

'You spoke to the priest?' James asked.

'Yes, but I didn't tell him anything.'

'Well, I think you should,' James said with decision. 'Father O'Hara is a good man.'

Tara's eyes widened in surprise and another tear squeezed out and trickled down her cheek.

'You know him?'

'I know most folk between here and Melbourne. Not that I've ever sought his counsel, of course, but if he's the man I think he is he'd not blame you any more than I do. He's a man of the world as well as a man of God. And perhaps he could help you to come to terms with your situation.'

She hesitated for a moment. 'I couldn't tell him,' she said softly.

'Why ever not?'

'I just couldn't.' Again the greater sin hung before her like a great shadow. 'You don't understand.'

'No,' he said frankly, 'I don't. But I know you can't go on like this, Tara, running away from yourself. Suppose I was to tell him, would you talk to him then?'

'What good would it do? He can't dissolve my marriage. Only the Pope himself could do that, and with good reason.'

'But at least perhaps he could make you see you still have your life to live, Tara . . .' He broke off as a sudden thought struck him. 'You don't want to go back to your husband, do you? You don't . . . still love him?'

Tara shook her head sadly but decisively. 'The love I had for Patrick died a long time ago. And it was never . . .' Her voice tailed away. Like the love I feel for you, she had been going to say, but she knew she must not.

'Then for the love of God speak to Father O'Hara,' James said urgently. 'Will you at least do that? You can't go on running forever. Perhaps you can't be my wife – as long as your husband lives, anyway. But somehow you have to begin living again.'

Tara was silent for a long while and James saw the inner conflict she was facing written all over her lovely face. Then at last she nodded.

'Very well. Perhaps you're right.'

He took out his kerchief and wiped the last of the tears from her face.

'Come on, then,' he said. 'We'll go and find him.'

Tara was trembling from head to toe. She sat in one of the rough wooden pews, head bent, hands folded around her rosary in the fullness of her skirt, peeping shamefacedly from beneath lowered lids at James and Father O'Hara who stood talking quietly together in front of the small Lady Chapel where last night she had knelt to pray.

She couldn't hear what they were saying but she could guess and her face burned with shame. Bad enough to be burdened with so much guilt, but that she should have lacked the courage to confess herself to the priest . . . Tara, proud and courageous, loathed herself for what she saw as yet another example of her weakness.

At last it seemed the conversation between the two men was over. James and Father O'Hara came towards her.

'I'll wait outside,' James said, and the priest moved into the pew beside Tara, sitting down and arranging his dusty soutane around his knees.

'James has told me your situation,' he said gravely. 'Is there anything you would like to add?'

Tara stared down at her rosary. This was the moment she had been dreading. The priest knew only half the story. He couldn't give her absolution unless he knew it all. She drew a long and shuddering breath.

'Yes,' she whispered.

'You want to tell me here, or in the confessional?' Father O'Hara asked.

Tara hesitated. Easier to speak in the confessional looking at nothing but the blank wall, not able to see the priest's face. But she wanted to see his face. It was a kind face, care-worn yet understanding. She wanted to see how he looked when she told him – if he was shocked or if he understood.

'Here, Father,' she said.

'So go on, my child. In your own time.'

'Father – I killed a man.'

There, it was said and there was no taking it back. She looked directly up at the priest. His eyes had narrowed a little, but she saw no condemnation in them. Only pity.

'Tell me about it, my child,' he said gently.

Tara told him. She told him everything, every detail, leaving nothing out. When she had finished he sat silently for a few moments. Then: 'You hold yourself to blame for all this?' he said.

'Well, of course I do, Father! I've sinned grievously, haven't I?'

'From what you have told me there was no evil in your heart. You have had a hard life, my child. In my humble opinion you are more sinned against than sinning.'

'But I've broken the laws of God!' she insisted.

'You have, it's true, but seldom have I seen more genuine repentance. Too many folk come to me and mouth the words without meaning them for one moment. They leave my church and go to sin again.'

Tara swallowed hard. 'And so will I, Father. I know it.'

'You would kill again?'

'If I had to, yes, I believe I would. Why, I almost did . . .' She told him about the man who had come to Dunrae and threatened her and Duncan. 'I would have shot him dead if he'd tried to take Duncan. I would!'

'But you didn't. You were more resourceful than that.'

'I suppose. But there's the other thing. I have committed adultery and I'd do that again too if I went back to Dunrae. I wouldn't be able to help myself.'

Father O'Hara was silent for a long while. Tara peeped at him anxiously from beneath her lowered lids. At last he sighed and nodded. 'Adultery is a sin, of course it is. It is the breaking of a solemn promise made in the presence of God. But He knows, my child, that you are but a woman, with all the needs of a woman. He knows that what you did, you did for love, not lust. It's what is in your heart that matters. And who knows, if you return to Melbourne, what other sins you may commit?' He smiled briefly and sadly. 'There is a saying – Better the devil you know.'

Tara stared at him incredulously. 'Are you telling me, Father, that it is all right for me to go back to Dunrae knowing that I'll never be able to resist James?'

Father O'Hara leaned forward and patted her hand. 'You know I can't tell you that. But if you return to Dunrae and if you sin again then I am here to take your confession as often as you feel the need to make it.'

'Oh, Father . . .' Was he a priest of God or was he an agent of the devil, placing temptation in her way? For temptation it was, without a doubt. Temptation so sweet she didn't know how to resist.

'The love between a man and a woman is a sacred thing,

my child. A benediction from God himself,' the priest said. 'It is best, of course, that it is blessed by Him in His church. But sometimes circumstances make such a thing impossible.' His eyes held hers, worldly-wise and kind. 'I believe you love this man with all your heart. And I have no doubt that he loves you.'

It was the same thing Elizabeth had said to her. It warmed her through with tenderness and hope.

'A word of warning, though,' Father O'Hara went on. 'For love to be pure and holy, there should be no secrets. Does James know everything?'

Tara bit her lip. 'You mean . . . ?'

'I mean does he know about the man you killed?'

Tara shook her head.

'I thought not. I think, my dear, that you should tell him as soon as you can. He will understand, I'm sure, and you will grow the closer for being honest with him. Come now.' He rose. 'I will give you absolution and we will pray together. For the rest . . . you must follow your heart.'

As Tara left the church she felt as if a weight had been lifted from her shoulders. Even the heavy grey clouds had lightened a little and the sun was trying to break through.

She looked around for James and saw him on the opposite side of the street looking in at the window of a small store. There was tension in every line of his body. As she crossed the street towards him he turned to greet her.

'You've been a long while,' he said unsmiling.

'I know. There was a great deal to say.'

'And what was the upshot?' he asked tautly.

Tara half smiled, nervous now that the moment had come. 'I'm coming back to Dunrae. If you still want me, that is.'

If he still wanted her!

James put his arm around her shoulders, felt her soft hair against his cheek, closed his eyes briefly and sent up a silent prayer of thanks to the God he scarcely believed in.

'You know I do,' he said to Tara. And then, impatient to be gone, 'Let's go home.'

Sixteen

In all her life Tara thought that she had never been happier, for at last Dunrae did, indeed, feel like home to her.

In no time at all she had fallen back into the comfortable routine of running the homestead, cooking the meals and tutoring and caring for Duncan, and the days sped by, busy and fulfilled. Philip and Cal made no mention of her running off. They assumed, she thought, that it had been out of fear that the man would return, for she noticed that wherever possible they conspired to ensure she was not left alone longer than was absolutely necessary.

'Sure, I'll be fine,' she assured them again and again. 'Haven't I got Lorna's little gun in the pocket of my apron for protection? And isn't Dickon armed now too, just in case?'

The men exchanged glances. Though he had made a remarkable recovery Dickon seemed older and more frail, as if the vicious blow to his head had aged him overnight and made him aware that he was no longer the wiry but strong man he had once been, but old and vulnerable.

'Just do as you always do and forget about me!' Tara insisted, and they shook their heads, smiling at the glow that seemed to emanate from her these days.

They both knew the reason for it, of course, though they would never have dreamed of mentioning it in her presence. The same reason why James was better-tempered than he had been for years.

Discreet though they were the brothers could hardly avoid knowing what was going on between James and Tara. It was there in the looks that passed between them, in the way the lightest and most accidental of touches was allowed to linger, in the tone of their voices when they spoke to one another.

There were the early nights, too, when one or the other of them would make an excuse to retire, followed, not long afterwards, by the other, and the tell-tale squeak of the floor boards and creak of a door as they conducted their rendezvous in the privacy of either James's room or Tara's. But in the morning both were back in their own beds so that to all intents and purposes everything was as it had been before.

Those hours spent alone together were the cause of their new-found happiness, of that Philip and Cal had no doubt. But for the sake of propriety they made no mention of it. James would tell them in his own good time, they thought, and they lived in expectation of the announcement of a wedding in the family, smiling to themselves as Tara sang softly whilst she cooked or sewed.

In those hours that they spent in one another's arms Tara and James did not only make wonderful satisfying love. They also talked as they had never been able to talk before, sharing the secrets of their hearts.

James confessed the deep love he had borne Lorna, his despair at his inability to make her happy and the terrible guilt he suffered over her untimely death. Tara told James much of what she had experienced in the goldfields.

Only one thing did she keep to herself – the fact that she had killed a man. In spite of Father O'Hara's urging that she should do so she found she was quite unable to bring herself to say the words. The memory was still too painful to her. It was something she didn't want to think about, let alone talk about, and she couldn't bear to spoil the precious moments of intimacy she and James shared. But it was a cloud over her happiness all the same.

Autumn turned to winter, with bitterly cold winds blowing in from the south. The fertile green land turned dark and barren, the men came in from their work on the farm blowing on their frozen fingers and more than ready for one of Tara's warming stews. But the house was cosy, with huge log fires burning in every room and the range providing an oasis of warmth in the kitchen.

Tara drove out now whenever she could. She had learned to enjoy managing the matched pair of horses. Sometimes she went to the nearest township to shop, sometimes she went further afield to Edwardstown, staying overnight in the same hostelry she and James had used that fateful night when she had run away. These visits had one purpose and one purpose only, to make her confession to Father O'Hara and receive the absolution that was so necessary to her peace of mind.

One winter's day when the frost lay heavy on the grass, sparkling in the pale sunlight, Elizabeth came calling. Tara was surprised but delighted when she saw the sulky pull into the stable yard, and ran out to greet her.

Elizabeth was looking rosy and wonderful in a driving gown and cape of midnight blue velvet edged with fur and Tara thought it was difficult to believe Elizabeth was ten years and more her senior.

Elizabeth held both hands out to clasp Tara's, then pulled her close to kiss her warmly on the cheek.

'I hear my prophecies about you and James are all coming true!' she said with a wicked twinkle.

'Oh yes . . .' Tara broke off, staring in surprise. 'How did you know?'

'Oh, I see Philip from time to time,' Elizabeth said airily. 'He keeps me informed.'

'You see Philip?' Tara echoed. She had had no inkling of it, but then she was so bound up in her own life she was quite blind to what was going on under her very nose where James's brothers were concerned. She knew Cal often went to visit his lady friends, of course. He was open and even boastful about his conquests. But Philip was another matter, the proverbial dark horse – though hadn't she once suspected there might be something between him and Elizabeth? It seemed so long ago now it might have been in another life, but little as she had known about the family then it seemed she might very well have stumbled upon the truth.

'Oh yes, we might yet be sisters,' Elizabeth said with the same wicked twinkle.

A shadow crossed Tara's face. Perhaps Elizabeth and Philip would be wed, but she could not look forward to a similar future. It just wasn't possible that she and Elizabeth should ever be sisters-in-law. But she mustn't think about that. She must be grateful for what she had. And she was . . . she was!

'Why are we talking out here in the cold?' she asked gaily. 'Let's go inside before we both turn to icicles!'

'Elizabeth!' Duncan came tearing down the steps, leaving the kitchen door wide open to the elements, and the awkward moment passed.

'So how are your plans for the new hotel coming along?' Tara asked when they were inside the house and she was brewing a pot of tea.

'Plans no more. Practically a fait accompli,' Elizabeth said, drawing off her gloves and unfastening the ties of her cape. 'I was lucky in my choice of builders. They haven't all deserted me to rush off to the goldfields and they are completing the work in record time. I'm having great fun choosing furnishings, and less fun finding suitable staff. If I hadn't learned about you and James from Philip, I might very well have come to try and steal you away from him to be my housekeeper, Tara.'

Tara flushed with pleasure. It was good to think that someone such as Elizabeth considered her suitable for a responsible position, and indeed, if things ever went wrong here at Dunrae she felt she had at least one friend who would help her to make a fresh start. But she hoped and prayed things didn't go wrong. She loved James with all her heart and wanted nothing more than to spend the rest of her life with him and his family.

'Anyway,' Elizabeth went on, 'if everything progresses as it is at the moment I shall be ready to receive my first guests in the spring. There will be a grand opening and I want all of you to come to Melbourne to share it with me.'

'Oh, what fun!' Tara said, but in truth her heart was sinking at the thought of a visit to Melbourne. Her memories of the place were so unpleasant she thought she never wanted to see it again and besides it was a good deal too close to the goldfields for her comfort or safety.

'So tell me about you and Philip,' she begged, changing the subject. 'Are you really in love with him?'

Elizabeth smiled, the happy smile of a woman with a great deal more than a new business to look forward to.

'Do you know, Tara, I am! I can hardly believe it. I was so sure that after Louis I'd never again feel that way about anyone. But with Philip – well, I've found out that I do still have a heart after all.' She glanced around, making sure they were still quite alone. 'We've talked about marriage,' she confided, 'but it's not all plain sailing, of course. We lead such different lives. But I'm sure that we shall find a way to compromise when the time is right. And what about you and James? Has he asked you to marry him?'

Tara hesitated. Suddenly she was wishing with all her heart that she could confide in Elizabeth, but she knew she must not. If Elizabeth and Philip were on such intimate terms, anything she told Elizabeth would almost certainly get back to Philip and it was for James to decide how much his brothers should know about their unconventional relationship.

'It's not all plain sailing for us either,' she said ambiguously.

Elizabeth frowned. 'In what way?'

Again Tara hesitated, but she was saved from answering when Duncan came bursting into the room.

'Tara! Elizabeth! It's snowing! Really, truly snowing!'

'Oh, my goodness, I hope I'm not going to be cut off here!'

Elizabeth cried, but she didn't look as though she thought it was the worst thing that could happen to her.

Tara ran to the window. 'That's not snow, Duncan. That's just sleet,' she said laughing. 'I doubt you've seen proper snow in the whole of your life.'

'But can I go out in it anyway? I want to see if I turn white . . .'

'You'll just get very wet,' Tara said.

'I don't care . . .'

'Go on then, if you must,' Tara agreed. 'And I'd better get the copper on so there's hot water for you to have a bath when you come back frozen half to death and soaked to the skin.'

She winked at Elizabeth and went to light the fire under the copper. By the time it was done Philip had come in, his face glowing with pleasure at the sight of Elizabeth, and as the two of them went into a huddle the awkward subject of the barriers to a wedding between Tara and James had been forgotten. Tara hoped fervently that it would not arise again.

Winter wore slowly on and there were days when it seemed to Tara that it would never end. Shearing was done, and the poor shorn sheep huddled, shivering, beneath the leaden grey skies. The crisp coldness gave way to an unpleasant damp chill that seemed to creep into one's very bones and the wind managed to find every crack and crevice in the sturdily built farmhouse. Sometimes Tara thought of Patrick, enduring the winter in the flimsy shanty on the goldfields, and pitied him. If Patrick was cold and miserable he had no one to blame but himself, of course, but she couldn't help worrying about him all the same. Impossible not to, when once she had cared for him so deeply and shared her whole life with him.

One night, when the wind was whistling eerily in the gums and mimosa and making the ivy around her bedroom window creak eerily, Tara awoke with a start from a bad dream. She lay for a moment wrestling with a deep sense of foreboding and trying to remember just what it was that had upset her

231

so. The details were hazy, all she knew was that something was terribly wrong and it had had to do with Patrick. Patrick was in terrible danger.

Oh, don't be so foolish! she told herself. It was a dream, that's all. You've been thinking about him too much of late and worrying about him and it's preying on your mind. But no matter how she tried to rationalise it, she couldn't shake free of the way she was feeling. Frightened for Patrick. Frightened for herself. Frightened for everything, really, everything and nothing.

She shivered, pulling the covers up over her ears to try to shut out the moaning of the wind that was adding to her unease, but still the anxiety gnawed inside her, more and more insistent, and the ghosts of the past which had not plagued her too much in recent months were all around her again suddenly, hemming her in. Sleep was never going to come, not whilst she was in this mood. And the thought of being alone with her torments through the long hours till dawn was more than Tara could stand.

She wanted James, wanted him desperately, with all her being. To lie in his arms, to feel his strong wholesome body next to hers, to listen to him sleeping. Surely, surely it could not matter if she went to his room just this once? The others would never know – and if they did, so what? Philip and Cal were well aware that she and James were lovers. Only for Duncan's sake should proprieties be observed, and Duncan was fast asleep.

Unable to help herself, Tara got out of bed and slipped on her robe. As she made her way along the landing the cold air chilled her in spite of the thick wool of the robe. She shivered, and the discomfort seemed to resurrect all her forebodings again.

She opened the door to James's room softly and stepped inside. She could see his big form hunched beneath the coverlet, hear his even breathing, smell the intimate scent of his body heat, and her throat closed with longing. She crossed to the bed, pulled aside the covers and slipped in beside him without taking off her robe. Then she snuggled close, curling her body around his.

At once he stirred drowsily, turning to take her in his arms.

'Tara?'

'Sh!' she whispered urgently. 'Go back to sleep!'

For a moment or two he lay unmoving, simply savouring the closeness of her, then gradually his body began to respond. Without a word he felt for the ties of her robe and loosened them. Beneath it her nightgown was fastened right up to her neck. He fumbled beneath the covers, bunching it up about her waist. She made no protest, simply wriggled closer so that their naked bodies fitted together perfectly like the pieces of a jigsaw puzzle.

Beneath his caressing hand her buttocks were full and firm. He pressed against them, holding her to him, and she moaned softly.

He made to move then, to roll on top of her and take her, but instead of lying to submit to him he felt her move away.

'No, let me.' Her whisper was soft but insistent.

She pushed him back onto the pillows and slipped on top of him, straddling him. The covers fell away but neither of them noticed as she raised herself, then slowly lowered, raised again, lowered again. Beads of sweat stood out on his forehead and he groaned at the sheer tantalising delight of it, he who was usually in control now having no say in the matter at all. One moment he was enclosed tightly in the moist warmth of her body, the next bereft and yearning for her with an intensity that made the whole of his body ache.

'You love me?' she whispered, poised teasingly above him so that only the tip of his straining cock touched the soft feathery down that hid her most secret places.

'I love you.' His hands tightened about her waist trying to pull her down onto him again but she resisted. She bent forward from the waist so that her face was close to his, her hair falling about it like a curtain.

'Really truly love me?'

'Yes.'

'No matter what?'

'No matter what.'

She lowered herself onto him then, moving with long slow strokes and at the last, as he climaxed, she drove down on him so hard that it made her gasp. Then she remained there, sitting astride him until the aftershocks had passed and he slipped from her, moist and spent.

'Did you . . .' he asked softly.

'No. But it doesn't matter.'

'It matters. Wait a few minutes, my love, and then it will be your turn.'

She lay above him, revelling in the nearness and in the sticky wetness between her legs, feeling his seed run out between them and grow cold on the sheet. The sweet smell of it was more desirable to her than the most expensive perfume from the East and when she felt him begin to grow hard again she was more than ready.

He took her slowly, deliciously slowly, with all the care of a man satisfied, and she thought she would die with the sensual delight of it. Oh, if this was what Adam and Eve had experienced in the Garden of Eden, then how could they have regretted for one moment taking that bite of the apple? And it was more than simply the physical pleasure, it was the sense of oneness, the feeling of love so complete that they were together as close as any two human beings could ever be. Tara felt her heart would burst with so much love.

When it was over she nestled into his arms.

'Oh, James, I adore you. I can't tell you how much I adore you.'

'And I adore you. My Tara. The light of my life.'

For the first time they fell asleep in one another's arms.

For the moment, at least, the demons had gone away, the sense of foreboding dissipated.

Tara had wanted to take control of their lovemaking as if by doing so she could somehow also take control of every aspect of her life – including the terrors that haunted her – and it seemed as if the ploy had worked.

But when in the first grey light of dawn she crept back to her own room she was disturbed to find that they were still there waiting for her. Not even the power of love could quite extinguish the dreadful creeping foreboding, the certain knowledge that whilst she did not know the reason for it something was horribly, terribly wrong. Tara wondered with a dread that made her blood run cold how long it would be before she found out what it was.

Seventeen

At last, at long last, winter began to give way to spring. As the first buds appeared and the land began to turn from barren brown to fresh and delicate green Tara felt her heart lightening. The change in the seasons alone was cause for optimism and the fact that none of her vague but insistent forebodings had been fulfilled gave Tara fresh hope that perhaps, after all, her life had at last reached an even keel, a plateau of happiness that was as much as she could ever hope for.

Elizabeth visited regularly and Tara found herself forming an ever closer friendship with the woman who was clearly in love with Philip. It was so good to be able to exchange girl talk but Elizabeth kept off the subject of Tara's relationship with James now and Tara wondered if Philip had warned her that it was a topic best avoided.

The hotel was nearing completion now, and one hot sunshiny day when it seemed that not only spring but summer too had finally arrived, Elizabeth drove up to Dunrae in her sulky with the invitation Tara had secretly been dreading.

'I've arranged the grand opening of the hotel for the week after next,' she told them, her eyes sparkling, 'and I hope you'll all be there to celebrate with me. You'll be my guests of honour.'

Philip beamed with pride and Duncan leaped up and down with excitement, but James shook his head.

'Leave me out of it, Elizabeth. You know I don't care for socialising – that's more in Cal's line. He'll be there like a shot from a gun, if I know him, and you'd better make sure all your female staff are warned about him in advance if he's not to leave a few broken hearts behind him when the party is over.'

'Oh, James, you have to come!' Elizabeth pressed him.

But James remained impervious to her pleadings. 'We can't all come and leave the farm unattended. It's by far the best if I stay here to keep an eye on things and leave the celebrating to those who will enjoy it.'

'Oh, you are such a killjoy!' Elizabeth upbraided him. 'And what about Tara? She was so excited about the prospect of coming to Melbourne, weren't you, Tara?'

'Oh, I don't mind, really,' Tara said quickly, but James overrode her.

'Just because I'm not coming it doesn't mean Tara can't. It will do her the world of good to have a change of scenery and some fun.'

'But, James . . .' Tara protested.

'Don't dare to argue with him, Tara!' Elizabeth cut in gaily. 'Look on it as a much-needed holiday. I shall be terribly hurt if you don't come. Heavens, with a repu-tation like mine I *need* a girl friend there to confound the gossips. They like to pretend that an unmarried lady who runs hotels for a living is no better than she should be!'

'If I'm not much mistaken you'll soon be giving them a much better reason to stop their wagging tongues,' James said with a sly glance at Philip.

By the time Elizabeth left the following day it was all arranged. Philip, Cal, Duncan and Tara were to travel to Melbourne in just over a week's time. They would be gone for a week in all and during their absence James would run Dunrae with the help of the farm hands.

'Matt will lend a hand too,' he assured them. 'I think he is quite looking forward to coming out of retirement for a week and getting out from under Martha's feet. And Martha has promised to keep me well fed, so there's no need to worry on that score.'

Tara did worry, however. She didn't like abdicating responsibility back to Martha one little bit since her place in the household had been so hard won. She spent hours in the kitchen baking bread and cakes and boiling up an enormous pan of mutton stew.

'Just remember to bring it to the boil every single day,' she warned James. 'If you don't it will go rancid and make you ill.'

'I doubt it will last long enough for that,' James assured her with a laugh. 'You well know the appetite I have when I come in from the land and with you not here to tell me I'll grow fat I'll doubtless polish off the whole pan in a couple of days at the most.'

'Well, I suppose that's a compliment for my cooking at least,' Tara said. She was proud of her new-found talent for producing appetising food.

Duncan was beside himself with excitement at the prospect of a visit to Melbourne and a party as well.

'Elizabeth said there will be other children for me to play with,' he bubbled enthusiastically.

'Oh, and what children are those?' James asked.

'Why, the sons of her friends and employees,' Duncan replied.

James ruffled his hair. It concerned him that Duncan lacked company of his own age and he only wished he and Tara could be wed and give him brothers and sisters of his own. After their night of unbridled lovemaking when Tara had come to his room back in the cold months of winter he had wondered whether she might become pregnant and if she did how they were going to explain a baby to the censorious wagging tongues in the nearby townships and, more importantly, to Duncan, but it hadn't happened and since then he had taken care that the risk of pregnancy was as small as he could make it. Though he didn't care a fig for himself, he didn't want Tara to have to bear the stigma of being an unmarried mother and he didn't want to have Duncan asking all kinds of awkward questions either.

Now, however, he was delighted to think that Duncan would be meeting up with other children.

'You may find that living in a town they are a bit different to you, though, Duncan,' he cautioned.

Duncan's face fell, then he brightened. 'I'll wager they can't ride a horse as well as I can!' he said.

James laughed. 'I'll wager they can't.'

'Or light a fire with kindling and a tinder box.'

'No, and you're not to show them either!' James said sternly. 'We don't want Elizabeth's new hotel burned down even before the first guests have stayed there.'

In spare moments between all her other chores Tara sorted the men's best linen ready to be laundered and ironed by the servant women and selected two or three gowns for herself that she thought would be the most suitable for the occasion.

'Perhaps whilst you're in Melbourne it would be a good idea for you to visit the dressmaker and order some new ones,' James suggested. 'Choose anything you like and have the account sent to me.'

Tara flushed with pleasure and hugged him. 'You are so good to me, James.'

'I know it,' he teased, then added with a smile: 'But it's because I consider myself a lucky man.'

'No,' Tara said emphatically. 'I'm the lucky one.'

And indeed she was, she thought, far luckier than she deserved, and a great deal happier. She had a good home, an affectionate family and a man who loved her as much as she loved him. And if the shadows came sometimes, then they were the price she had to pay.

But with all her heart she wished she did not have to go to Melbourne, and the closer the day came the more trapped and reluctant she felt. Could she perhaps pretend to be ill and get out of it that way? But they'd suspect something – she was never ill. And Elizabeth would be so upset if she thought Tara had contrived some excuse to avoid her grand opening. No, there was nothing for it but to grit her teeth and live through the next week, and hope against hope that her worst fears about the trip were unfounded.

Melbourne was baking in the heat of a November day. But for all that her skin was warm to the touch and her nose peeling a little from where the sun had caught it on the long drive west, there was a chill in Tara's bones that had begun the moment they had approached the environs of the town where she had been so desperate and so unhappy.

There were unpleasant memories around every corner of the bustling streets, it seemed, and the sense of foreboding and the feeling of being trapped closed in on Tara until she felt she would scream. But somehow she hid her deepest feelings behind a façade of gaiety and neither Philip nor Cal seemed aware than anything was wrong, though Elizabeth did occasionally give her a long thoughtful look.

And really she had no reason now for the way she was feeling, Tara told herself. Now, she had Cal and Duncan for company – Philip was fully occupied helping Elizabeth with preparations for the grand opening – and they alone should be enough to keep her mind off the past. Duncan was so full of excitement that it was impossible not to catch a little of his mood and the irrepressible Cal, tipping his hat and winking at every pretty woman who came within yards of him, was amusing enough to raise a smile in spite of the fact that her lips felt stiff.

As for Elizabeth's new hotel, that was a far cry from the ghastly Women's Refuge. A square, spanking new building, it sat right on the intersection of two busy streets, and just as she had promised, Elizabeth had spared no expense making its interior luxurious. The saloon was furnished in mahogany and rich ruby red velvet, the walls hung with gilt-framed paintings and sketches, and the bedrooms were bright with chintz and gaily-decorated chinaware. Tara's room even boasted an elegant chaise longue, a small rosewood writing desk and a spindly-legged high-back chair whose rose-pink velvet seat exactly matched the blooms that proliferated in the fabric of the drapes and bedspread.

Sinking into her soft feather bed on their first night in Melbourne Tara sent up a prayer of thanks that she was no longer having to share a louse-infested mattress with the most pathetic dregs of humanity, but the memory of it was too sharp for comfort and the wounds beneath the surface still too raw to allow her even a moment's complacency.

All this could turn to dust in an instant, she reminded herself. Like Cinderella at the prince's ball, she might very well be living on borrowed time. For she was a murderess and by now she could be a wanted woman as well. If the authorities had come by any evidence of her guilt, and if she was discovered now, not even being in the company of the illustrious Hannays would save her.

Next day promised to be another scorcher. By the time they had finished breakfast the sun was already high and bright and Cal suggested taking Duncan on a sightseeing tour before the heat became unbearable.

Tara's heart sank. A sightseeing tour was the very last thing she wanted to do, but she could see no way of getting out of it. Elizabeth was far too busy to entertain them as she supervised the preparation of the food for the reception, changed her mind a hundred times about the floral arrangements and chased the army of maids as they swept and scrubbed and dusted every corner of the already sparkling rooms into a state of even greater perfection.

'There might be something I can do to help here,' she suggested weakly, but as she had suspected, Elizabeth would have none of it.

'You are supposed to be taking a well-earned break, Tara! Make the most of it!' she said firmly, and before she knew it Tara found herself climbing into the gig with an exuberant Duncan tucked in between herself and Cal.

'It wouldn't surprise me if Philip didn't move to Melbourne to help Elizabeth with the running of the hotels when they are married,' Cal said as they moved off. 'He seems in his element here.'

Tara felt forced to agree. The last they had seen of Philip he had been supervising the setting up of a small stage on which a quartet would play to entertain the guests, and doing it with more enthusiasm than she had ever seen him display for farming.

'He does seem to fit in remarkably well,' she agreed, and thought that perhaps if things worked out that way it would be for the best. She would miss his quiet sensible presence at Dunrae, but fond as she was of Elizabeth there was rarely enough room for two women under one roof and she had grown used to doing things her way.

'Perhaps they'll make some kind of announcement at the party,' she suggested. 'It would be a really good opportunity and we can have a double celebration.'

'Is Uncle Philip going to marry Elizabeth, then?' Duncan asked, cottoning on a little late to Cal's earlier remark.

Cal nodded. 'I think that's the plan, Duncan.'

Duncan was silent for a moment then he turned to Tara. 'And are you going to marry Papa?'

Tara felt her face flame. 'I shouldn't think so, Duncan.'

'But why not? If you married Papa you would be my new Mama, wouldn't you?'

'And to think this is the boy who didn't want you to come and live with us!' Cal exclaimed. 'You've changed your tune, Duncan.'

'Well, Tara is good fun. And she makes Papa happy.'

Tara turned her head quickly so that her face was hidden from them by her bonnet but not quickly enough to escape Cal's shrewd glance.

'Out of the mouths of babies . . . You do make James

happy, Tara. He's a different man these days. I think Duncan is quite right. You should marry him.'

So James had kept her secret, Tara realised. The others did not know she was married already, and though she was a little surprised he had not confided in them she was grateful all the same.

As they bowled along the all-too-familiar streets Cal pointed out the various landmarks to Duncan.

'See, that's the Yarra River.' And: 'Look, over there is the Separation Tree – the gum that was planted to commemorate Victoria becoming a state.'

'What's a state?' Duncan asked.

'It's all to do with government,' Cal said airily, ducking a more detailed explanation.

'Oh, I thought a state was what Martha used to get into when I ran away!' Duncan said brightly, and laughed at his own joke.

'Those days are long gone, praise be!' Cal said. 'You've become much better behaved, Duncan, I'm glad to say.'

'Leading Martha a dance was good fun though,' Duncan said a little regretfully and they all laughed.

His mood and Cal's was infectious and Tara's depression lifted a little. These might be the same mean streets that she had trudged with such despair but things were different now. She was riding in a fine gig behind a matched pair with Cal driving and Duncan sitting beside her. Why, the people in the streets probably thought they were a happy and prosperous family – which indeed they were, except that she wished with all her heart it was James the passers-by would take for her husband. She was no longer the down-and-out in rags, widowed by the lust for gold. Perhaps it was time she stopped worrying and began to enjoy herself.

'Perhaps we should stop at a store and buy some little memento of our visit,' Cal suggested as they drove along one busy street. 'Would you like that, Duncan?'

'Oh, yes!' His already bright face lit up even more.

Cal looked for a suitable hitching post, climbed down from the gig and wound the reins about the rail. Tara noticed with pride the looks of admiration the fine vehicle and horses drew from the passers-by, some of whom were frankly envious. She couldn't help noticing too that not one of the women wore a gown half as nice as hers and the warm feeling grew. Oh, she had been so lucky and no mistake!

She walked along the street with Cal and Duncan, stopping to look into the shops they passed. There was a provisions store, where sacks of flour and dried fruit were banked beneath a counter laden with cheeses, bacon and cold cuts, then a hardware store with cooking utensils hanging from hooks, tools stacked against the walls and rows of tiny neat drawers, each carefully labelled, concealing their contents of nails, screws and brackets of every kind imaginable. The next shop was a glory-hole of bric-a-brac.

'We'll try this one, shall we?' Cal suggested. 'Look, Duncan, they're selling little figurines of goldminers! Now that's something a bit different to your lead soldiers, isn't it?'

'Oh, yes!' Duncan cried enthusiastically, but Tara felt her mood grow heavy once more as she looked at the little ornaments. Whittled from wood, they were perfect tiny replicas of some of the men who sweated out their life's blood in the search for gold. A digger in a cabbage-tree hat carrying a shovel. A wiry wizened figure bent double over his sieve. A careworn woman with a baby in her arms. The talent that had brought them to life was amazing but to Tara they were far too realistic for comfort. Some poor miner had fashioned them she felt sure, scraping away night after night with his knife after the curfew had sounded, working partly for pleasure and partly in the hope of selling his work to make a little money to keep body and soul together. And much would he get for his pains! The figurines were ridiculously, insultingly cheap, given the hours of painstaking effort that had gone into making them.

244

'Which one do you like best?' Cal asked Duncan.

Suddenly Tara felt as if the shop were suffocating her, the little figures sucking her dry as the lust for gold sucked dry the men in whose image they had been made.

'I'll wait for you outside,' she said.

Cal nodded carelessly, all his attention on the wooden figurines. 'Very well. We won't be long.'

As Tara left the dim musty shop the white heat of the day hit her and she took a few deep breaths to steady herself. Stupid to let such a little thing upset her so! But it had. She walked back and forth on the badly made pavement wishing Cal and Duncan would come and hoping – vainly, she felt sure – that they would have decided against buying any of the figurines that had resurrected such horrid memories for her. She was being selfish, she supposed. The few pence they would so carelessly spend could buy a square meal for the pour soul who had fashioned them. But she didn't like the thought of having to look at them day after day at Dunrae one little bit. And she also found it curiously upsetting that anyone should buy for their own amusement or pleasure something which represented so much suffering and hardship.

A figure walking on the opposite side of the street caught Tara's eye suddenly and she started, her heart beginning to race so wildly that she thought she might be going to faint.

Dear God, he looked so familiar! That stocky figure, that thick curling hair . . . why, for a moment she had thought . . .

As if her gaze had somehow attracted his attention, the man turned, looking directly at her, and Tara's heart seemed to stop beating altogether. As his eyes fell upon her recognition flared in them and was reflected in the startled tensing of his body.

She had been right! Unlikely – impossible! – as it seemed, she had been right!

Tara stood frozen like a statue. With a shout the man started across the street towards her, and for the first time in many long months Tara found herself face to face with Seamus Flaherty.

245

Eighteen

'Tara! Tara! For the love of God, don't run away now!'

As if she could! She stood rooted to the spot and his bulk cast a great shadow over her that seemed to blot out the sun. Tara licked her trembling lips to moisten them but when she spoke her voice was nothing but a dry croak.

'Seamus.'

She could still scarcely believe her eyes. Of all the cruel tricks that fate could play, that she should have happened to be in this spot, at this moment. But wasn't it just what she had feared about coming to Melbourne, that she might run straight into someone who knew her? And yet that of all people it should be Seamus . . . Seamus, who had encouraged Patrick in his madness and replaced her as the one who shared his dreams. And a Seamus who looked even more unkempt and disreputable than he had done the last time she had seen him, if such a thing were possible.

Anger flared in her suddenly. 'What are you doing in Melbourne?' she demanded. 'Have you given up the search for gold? For clearly you haven't found it!' Then, as another thought struck her, she looked around quickly, anxious eyes scouring the busy street. 'Is Patrick with you?'

Seamus laughed shortly, an explosion of anger that matched her own.

'No, he is not. I'm here looking for you to take you back, you worthless bitch. I guessed you'd be somewhere where the living was easy – and I see I was right.'

His dark furious eyes ran scornfully over her fine gown

and fashionable bonnet, the small beaded reticule swinging from her wrist, her pretty slippers. Tara scarcely noticed.

'Take me back?' she repeated. 'But what for? Patrick doesn't want me, does he? He's got you.'

'Patrick *needs* you,' Seamus said shortly.

Puzzled, Tara experienced a frisson of alarm. 'Why, is he ill?'

Seamus laughed again, the same expression of anger as before. 'Would that that is all it were! Oh no, Tara, it's worse than that, much worse. Can't you guess?'

She shook her head wordlessly.

'Don't you know the mess you left behind?' Seamus grated. 'Isn't it what you intended, to make him suffer for your sins?'

Tara was trembling now from head to foot. 'What are you talking about?'

'Didn't you kill the Commissioner?' Seamus shot at her.

Tara's hand went to her throat. 'I . . .' She broke off, quite incapable of speech.

'We guessed at once it was you,' Seamus went on. 'Who else could it have been? Your business *partner* . . .' He laid unpleasant emphasis on the word. 'Your *business* partner dead, his safe rifled and you gone. Even the authorities suspected you, but you were nowhere to be found.'

So she had been right to fear she was a wanted woman, Tara thought. She had been right to fear the worst.

'But what has this to do with Patrick?' she asked, her lips stiff with shock, barely moving.

'They wanted a scapegoat, didn't they? Did you really think the Commissioner could be shot dead and no one made to pay for it?'

'But Patrick . . .' She protested. 'Why Patrick? He was at the diggings with you when . . .'

'Oh yes, and that saved him for a while. But they've never stopped hounding us, looking for a way to pin the murder on him. A week or so back our home was raided.

Looking for sly grog, they said. But you know what they found, Tara?'

She shook her head.

'The Commissioner's signet ring and watch. Hidden beneath that fancy couch you bought and had brought in by bullocky.'

'*What?*' Tara's eyes were wide with shock. 'But . . .'

'Did you leave them there, hoping to divert suspicion on to Patrick if they were discovered?' Seamus demanded.

'No! Of course I didn't!' Tara cried.

Her racing mind was replaying the events of that terrible afternoon and she had a sudden clear recollection of spilling the contents of her reticule as she made her frantic preparations to leave. Had the ring and the watch rolled beneath the couch then? Had she failed to notice them as she hastily scooped the fallen items together? And had they lain there ever since? Patrick and Seamus would never have moved the couch to clean or sweep the floor, so it was possible. Or could it be that the items had been amongst the things that had been stolen from her at her lodgings in Melbourne? Had they come back into the possession of the authorities who had decided to plant them in Patrick's shack in order to be seen to be bringing someone to justice for the murder of the Commissioner when they were unable to find her to answer the charges? She supposed she would never know the answer to that for sure, for she simply could not remember whether she had seen the watch and the ring after leaving Ballarat. But what did it matter now?

'What happened when they found them?' she asked urgently.

'Why, Patrick was arrested, of course. He's in gaol now awaiting trial – but a monstrous charade that will be. He'll be found guilty without a shred of doubt, Tara, and sentence will be passed. You know what that is, don't you? Death. Patrick will be sentenced to die as surely as you and I are standing here. No mercy will be shown to him. None. That's why I came looking for you, you worthless crow. To take you back so you can tell them the truth, that Patrick never killed anyone. He is totally innocent.'

'But of course he's innocent!' Tara cried. 'Seamus, this is terrible! I never thought for a moment . . . I never intended . . .'

'You're his only chance, Tara,' Seamus grated. 'I don't know why you shot the Commissioner, but . . .'

'Because he tried to rape me!' Tara interposed quickly. 'And I took money from his safe only because it was rightfully mine and he was refusing to give it to me. All I wanted was to leave Ballarat and start afresh. I certainly never meant for Patrick to take the blame. You must believe me, Seamus.'

'Then come back and tell them so, or Patrick is a dead man.' Seamus caught her arm, holding it tightly in his huge calloused hand. 'They'll doubtless treat a woman more gently.'

Tara was white to her trembling lips. She did not for one moment believe that the authorities would treat her with any special leniency. An official had died and someone must be seen to pay the price. Her worst nightmare had become reality. Her crime had caught up with her. They would hang her just as surely and with no more compunction than they would hang Patrick. But whatever her fate she must face it. She couldn't let Patrick die for what she had done. To do so would be a sin far worse than any of the others.

'Of course I'll come,' she said, and her voice now was surprisingly steady.

'Thank God and all the saints!' Seamus crossed himself. 'Have you a horse at your disposal?'

Tara shook her head.

'Then take the coach tomorrow. The fare will be no problem for you by the look of it. I'll follow as best I can. I've no money for such luxuries.'

'I'll pay your fare,' Tara promised him. 'We'll go together. I'll meet you at the stage in the morning.'

His grip tightened on her arm. 'You'll not double-cross me? You'll not do another disappearing trick?'

'On my mother's grave, I will not. I'll be there, I swear it.' His eyes lingered on her face whilst he tried to decide how much dependence he could place on her now, and she added softly: 'I loved him once too, Seamus.'

He nodded then, satisfied. 'Very well, Tara. I only hope you mean what you say. For if you don't you'll rot in hell.'

'I know it.' She glanced back towards the store to see Cal and Duncan emerging from the doorway. 'Leave me now, please,' she begged him urgently. 'I'll be there, believe me, but . . .'

Cal, seeing an unkempt stranger holding Tara by the arm, had started to run along the street towards them. Seamus let go of her abruptly.

'You'd better be,' he spat at her. Then he turned and walked away.

'Tara!' Cal reached her, made to pass her and go in pursuit of Seamus. Tara caught his sleeve.

'Cal, don't. Leave him.'

'But . . .' Cal stared after the burly figure, still clearly up for a fight.

'Cal, please!' Tara said again. 'It's all right. I'm all right.'

Cal looked back at her, at her white face and the tiny lines of strain that had etched themselves around her eyes in the space of a few short minutes.

'You don't look all right. Did he try to accost you?'

'No.' Duncan had joined them. His expression, halfway between alarm and excitement at the prospect of seeing Uncle Cal, his hero, beat some stranger senseless, was almost comical. But Tara was in no danger of laughing. 'It was just someone I used to know,' she said.

'A pretty unsavoury looking character for all that!' Cal's face was still dark. 'I shouldn't have let you come out onto the street alone. James will flay me alive for it and I can't say I blame him.'

'I'm all right, truly,' Tara said.

Cal was still looking at her narrowly. But Duncan, sensing the excitement was over, turned his attention to his recent purchases.

'Look, Tara, see what I've got!'

He held up two of the little wooden figurines, the miner with the shovel and the one bent double over his sieve.

'Aren't they the best? Oh, the games I will play with these!'

Tara bit her lip. She hated the figurines now with all her heart. It was as if they had hexed her, she thought, transported her back to her old life and worse. Somehow she forced herself to smile.

'I'm glad you're pleased with them, Duncan,' was all she said.

How she got through the remainder of the day Tara never knew. Throughout the rest of the trip she was mostly silent, though she did make a few valiant efforts at affecting enthusiasm for the sights Cal pointed out to Duncan. The little boy seemed unaware that anything was wrong, though she did notice Cal looking at her speculatively from time to time. But he said nothing. She had, after all, made it plain enough that she did not want to discuss the incident or the burly stranger and in any case, with Duncan sandwiched between them, this was not the time.

'I think I'd like to take a rest,' Tara said when they eventually arrived back at Elizabeth's hotel.

'You do look very tired,' Elizabeth said. 'Aren't you feeling well, Tara?'

'Sure, I'm fine,' Tara said briefly. 'It's nothing but a bit of a headache, brought on by too much sun, no doubt.'

Elizabeth looked at her anxiously for a moment longer, but she was too busy and her thoughts too occupied with the preparations for the grand opening to spare much time worrying about something so apparently trivial.

251

'Pull the curtains and lie down for an hour or so then,' she advised. 'You don't want to be feeling poorly this evening. You'll miss all the fun!'

Tara went up to her pretty room and though she pulled the curtains as Elizabeth had suggested she did not even attempt to lie down. Instead she paced the floor, too distraught to relax for a single second.

Think. She must think! How was she going to manage this? What, if anything, should she tell Philip and Cal? She didn't know, couldn't come to any decision at all. Only the thought of Patrick imprisoned for a crime he had not committed and facing an almost certain death sentence was terrifyingly clear in her tormented mind.

Was he in some airless cell, she wondered? Or chained up outside the government buildings in the glare of the pitiless sun? Whichever, he must be suffering all the terrors of hell and the thought of it was enough to strengthen her resolve. She couldn't let this happen, wouldn't let it happen to any living soul, and certainly not Patrick. As she had said to Seamus, she had loved him once and he had loved her. Now she must do whatever was necessary to save him. And she would, whatever it cost her.

Tomorrow when the Cobb coach left the stage she would be on it. And though she had no doubt whatever that it would be the last journey she would ever make, it did not occur to Tara for one moment to renege on the promise she had made to Seamus.

The reception was due to begin at seven. At six-thirty chaos still reigned, with any number of last-minute hitches to be ironed out. But by the time Tara came downstairs twenty minutes later everything was in perfect order and a radiant Elizabeth, with Philip at her side, was ready to greet her guests.

'Is your headache still troubling you, Tara?' Elizabeth asked anxiously. Though Tara had bathed, dressed herself in the pretty sky-blue gown she had chosen to wear for the occasion and teased her hair into a mass of tumbling curls, there was no mistaking that she was still very pale, and however hard she tried to smile there was a shadow in her eyes.

'A little,' Tara admitted.

It was no more than the truth – she did have a headache and small wonder! She had spent the last hour before preparing for the party in deciding what she should take with her tomorrow when she slipped out to catch the coach, and packing it into her smallest valise. She would have to carry the bag herself so she didn't want it to be too heavy and in any case there was little point taking finery. Just a couple of decent gowns and bonnets so that she could at least appear respectable at her trial. After that . . . Tara's blood ran cold and she cut off the thought. If she looked ahead to what would follow her trial as surely as night must follow day she didn't know how she would find the courage to get on the coach, no matter how good her intentions.

As she packed she thought too, fleetingly, of the other times she had gone through this ritual. The excitement that had gone into packing to leave Ireland for their new life in Australia. The desperation with which she had thrown her few belongings into her bag when she had left Ballarat and Patrick. The heartache when she had run from James the morning after he had first made love to her.

That, at least, had turned out well. Tara's heart lifted even now as she recalled seeing his dear familiar form in the lobby of the hostelry at Edwardstown, and the realisation that he had come after her. But there could be no such happy outcome this time. James was not even within striking distance to come after her and even if he was, there would be nothing he could do to save her.

And would he want to? When he knew that she had killed a man?

Yes, Tara thought suddenly. Yes, I believe he loves me enough to understand. And with all her heart she wished she had been able to bring herself to confide in him. It would not have helped her now – nothing could do that – but at least he would have heard the truth from her own lips. That much she owed him. But it was too late now. She would never see him again.

Somehow, though, she must let him know what had happened, tell him how much she loved him, how sorry she was for the pain she must cause him, how grateful she was for all they had shared. Tara wondered whether she should speak to Cal and tell him the truth about Seamus, but decided against it. For one thing she simply did not know how to begin, for another she was very afraid he might try to stop her from going. And the timing was so bad. She didn't want to do anything to spoil Elizabeth's party – for any of them.

Best to write James a letter, she decided. She would do it tonight when the party was over. And if it took her all night, what did it matter? She couldn't imagine she would sleep a wink anyway and she had to leave at dawn, before any of them were up and about.

At seven prompt the first guests arrived and soon the reception was in full swing. Elizabeth's friends, all dressed up in their finery, mingled with the family and the town dignitaries, all gasping in admiration as they were taken on a guided tour of the new hotel. A huge table groaned under the weight of platters of the most delicious food Tara had ever seen in her life, most of them arranged so that they looked like works of art as well as being succulent enough to tempt the most jaded palate. The quartet played classical music interspersed with clever arrangements of the popular tunes of the day, and when the meal was over and enough wine had been imbibed to loosen inhibitions the dancing began.

The children, meanwhile, were making their own fun. From what Tara could gather they were playing a game of hide and seek through the endless rooms, for she scarcely saw Duncan at all. Pink-cheeked and over-excited, he was having the time of his life and making the most of the rare opportunity to enjoy company of his own age.

'Dance, Tara?' Cal said, and though she protested he insisted on sweeping her onto the floor for a minuet and a waltz that left her breathless.

'Where did you learn to dance like that?' she asked him when at last he returned her to the edge of the floor and brought her a glass of ice-cold lemonade.

'Oh, we might be country bumpkins but social graces were part of our education,' Cal said with a smile. But his eyes were on her face, pale and drawn still even though the dancing had raised high spots of colour in her cheeks, and he looked thoughtful and not a little concerned. 'Are you sure you are all right, Tara?'

'Sure, I'm fine,' she lied.

She was afraid he might be going to press her even so, but at that very moment Philip took the stage, a blushing Elizabeth at his side. Philip held up his hand to silence the quartet and slipped an arm about Elizabeth's waist.

'Listen, everyone, I have something very special to say.' He paused, his eyes twinkling, as if to lend emphasis to the moment. 'Elizabeth has agreed to do me the honour of becoming my wife.'

There was an excited buzz, though Tara guessed that the announcement came as no more of a surprise to most of the others than it did to her and Cal. Elizabeth and Philip were so obviously a couple and had been throughout the proceedings.

'The wedding will take place at Christmas,' Philip went on. 'And I hope you will all be there to celebrate with us.'

Tara managed a fixed smile but her eyes were shining with tears. Heaven alone knew where she would be by Christmas. Certainly not at Elizabeth and Philip's wedding. Maybe not even in this world at all.

Again she caught Cal's eyes on her, and determined not

to spoil the moment for him she caught at his arm with forced gaiety.

'The quartet is playing! Let's dance again! Unless you have your eye on one of Elizabeth's prettiest friends, of course.'

'No one here is half as pretty as you, Tara,' Cal returned gallantly. 'And there is no one I'd rather dance with.'

He whirled her onto the floor and she tried to forget for the moment all her fear and dread, all her heartache and pain and despair.

When Cal decided it was time for Duncan to go to bed, however, there was no way to keep the lump from her throat. She took the little boy to his room, knelt with him to say his prayers and fought to hold back the tears, knowing it would be the last time she would do this.

'God bless Uncle Cal and Uncle Philip . . .'

'And Elizabeth, who will soon be Aunt Elizabeth,' Tara reminded him.

'And Aunt Elizabeth. And God bless Papa. And God bless Tara.' He opened one eye, looking at her by the light of the candle. 'And let her marry Papa,' he added.

Tara was unable to say a single word.

Duncan, who did not want the evening to end, spun his prayers out much longer than usual, insisting on including his pony and every other animal on Dunrae by name, or so it seemed to Tara. When at last he could not think of another single creature to pray for he climbed into bed and Tara tucked the covers around him.

'It was a lovely party, wasn't it, Tara?' he said dreamily.

'Yes, it was a lovely party.' Tara's throat was thick with tears. She bent to kiss his forehead for the last time.

'Tara,' he murmured, sleepy now. 'You can put out the night light if you like. I'm not afraid of the dark any more.'

'That's good, Duncan,' she managed. 'But I think I'll leave it on tonight. Just in case.'

Duncan did not reply and she realised that he was already asleep. She tiptoed to the doorway and stood there for a moment, her cheeks wet with tears. How he had changed in the short time she had known him! And how she loved him! She only hoped he would not be too upset when he woke to find her gone, but there was nothing she could do to change that. Sadly she went back downstairs to rejoin the party.

At last, just when she thought she could not force her stiff lips and aching cheeks to smile for a single moment longer, it was over. She stood on the steps of the hotel with Elizabeth, Philip and Cal to watch the line of carriages carry the guests away and was overcome by a sense of total unreality. When they went back inside the quartet were packing away their instruments and the tired maids were collecting plates, glasses and cutlery from the unlikeliest corners of the big reception room.

'We'll have a drink now, just ourselves,' Elizabeth said. 'I could just do with a glass of brandy, even if it isn't a very ladylike thing to do. What do you say, Tara?'

'I think I'd rather just go to bed if you don't mind,' Tara said. Much more socialising, much more pretending to enjoy herself, and she would go stark staring mad, she thought.

'You do still look very tired,' Elizabeth agreed. 'Off you go then and we'll see you in the morning.'

Tara nodded wordlessly and went upstairs. There she sat at the small bureau in her room and began to pen the hardest letter she had ever had to write in her life.

A tap at the door made Tara start. She froze, then dropped the quill and pushed her epistle to James beneath the blotter just as the door opened softly.

'Tara?' It was Elizabeth. 'May I come in?'

'Yes . . . yes, of course . . .' Tara didn't want to see anyone, but what choice did she have?

Elizabeth came in and closed the door after her. Tara sensed that Elizabeth was surprised to find her still fully dressed and sitting at the bureau, but she let it pass.

'Tara, I felt I had to come and talk to you,' she said, her voice low and a little uncertain. 'Tell me to go again if you like. But you haven't been at all yourself today and I was worried about you.'

'I'm fine,' Tara tried to say for the umpteenth time that day. But somehow the words simply would not come. And to her alarm – and shame – she felt the tears gathering in her eyes again.

'Tara, I know something is wrong,' Elizabeth said gently. 'And I know too that it has to do with what happened this morning. Cal has told me about the man you met in town and how it upset you. And you haven't been right since. We've all noticed it. Oh, I know it's none of my business, but I thought maybe it would help if you could talk about whatever it is. To another woman.'

'Elizabeth . . .' Tara broke off. A tear spilled over and ran down her cheek.

Elizabeth crossed and put an arm around her. 'We all have things in our past that cause us pain, Tara. We talked once before and I told you my secrets. Won't you share yours with me? I promise you I'll never tell them to another living soul if you don't want me to. But talking about it might just help.'

'Nothing can help me, Elizabeth,' Tara said wretchedly. 'I'm beyond help.'

'Surely not!' Elizabeth found a handkerchief and gently mopped the tears from Tara's face. 'Nothing can be that bad.'

'Oh it is, believe me.' Tara was silent for a moment. The urge to confide had never been stronger. And Elizabeth was a good friend – to all of them. Perhaps she would be able to explain to James all that Tara needed to say, and better too than any dry letter for she would have seen with her own eyes just how genuine was her remorse – and how strong her love.

'I have to leave on the stage for Ballarat in the morning,' she said haltingly. She saw the shocked look come into Elizabeth's eyes and put up a hand to stop her saying anything. 'I don't have any choice, Elizabeth. A man's

258

life depends on it – a man who was once my husband – still is, though only in name. If you want the whole story, hear me out, though I warn you it will take some time. And before I begin I must ask you not to try to dissuade me from what I have to do, and please, say nothing to either Philip or Cal until I've gone. Do you promise me that?'

Elizabeth nodded. She was almost as pale as Tara now, her eyes full of shock and concern.

'Afterwards,' Tara went on, 'you can share my story with the others. James knows part of it already, though they do not. But he doesn't know it all. He doesn't know the worst part. I think I would like you to be the one to tell him, Elizabeth. Because you can also tell him how sorry I am. And how I love him. Will you do that?'

Elizabeth nodded. 'Of course I will, Tara. But whatever it is, surely it can't be so terrible.'

'Listen and judge for yourself,' Tara said.

Then she began her story.

Dawn was beginning to paint the sky with rosy fingers when Tara finished.

'Oh, my dear!' Elizabeth was weeping too now, her strong pretty face streaked where the tears had run rivulets through her powder.

'Don't try to tell me I mustn't go,' Tara said. 'I must, Elizabeth.'

'Yes, my dear, I can see that you must,' Elizabeth agreed. 'But would you not like Philip or Cal to go with you?'

'No!' Tara said sharply. 'They're not to know until I've left. You promised, Elizabeth.'

'Yes, and if that's the way you want it, then I shall keep my promise,' Elizabeth said. 'But you shouldn't be facing this alone, Tara.'

'It's my mess and I must sort it out by myself,' Tara said stubbornly. 'I don't want any of you implicated. But you will explain to James for me, won't you? I won't have time now to finish my letter to him and I do so want him to know how

I love him and how happy he has made me. You will be sure to tell him?'

'Of course I will. But is there nothing we can do?'

Tara's fingers found her rosary, the only comfort left to her now. 'You can pray for me,' she said softly.

Nineteen

As the Cobb coach rolled out of Melbourne Tara sat rigid and numb sandwiched between Seamus and a sweating farmer. The reek that emanated from his every pore and the rolling motion of the coach added to her misery. Soon her vague nausea had worsened to a horrible all-pervading sickness and she could think of nothing beyond holding on to the contents of her stomach. Her world had reduced to a living nightmare, unreal, yet holding her fast, its aura bearing in on her like a dense cloud of mosquitos from which there was no escape.

At the second stage after leaving Melbourne armed guards joined the coach. Mean and desperate-looking, they took up their positions, one at the front with the driver, one riding shot-gun at the rear.

'What's going on?' Tara asked, alarmed. For an incredible moment she wondered if it was her they were guarding, a murderess who might try to make her escape.

'Doubtless Cobb and Co. fear the coach might come under attack,' Seamus answered shortly. 'There's trouble brewing in the goldfields.'

'Trouble? What sort of trouble?' Tara asked, her own predicament momentarily forgotten.

Seamus scowled. 'The diggers have had enough of the way they're treated,' he told her. 'You know what it's like out there. Men are continually persecuted and fined outrageous sums for having no licence whilst horse thieves and burglars are left alone to get on with their crimes. Half the police force and damn near all the government officials are as corrupt as a purse full of tin dollars and they'll help themselves to a man's meagre returns as soon as look at him.'

'Don't I know it!' Tara muttered bitterly.

Seamus scarcely seemed to hear her. There was a light in his eyes now, a crusading zeal, and Tara suspected that Seamus might well have been one of those stirring up anger and resentment until Patrick's arrest had given him something else to think about.

'We've no representation, that's half the trouble,' Seamus said, sitting forward earnestly, hands balled to fists resting on his knees. 'Much is talked about the Parliament of Victoria and how it will take this land forward, but what help is that to the likes of us? Most miners don't even have the vote. What can we do to improve our lot? Not a thing! Why, there's no help even for those who want to leave the diggings, for there's no lands for sale to help them to better themselves. And there's no justice either. We'd clear proof of that a month or so back. Young James Scobie was murdered outside the Eureka Hotel. Do you remember James?'

Tara shook her head. There was only one James as far as she was concerned.

'He was just a young digger with everything to live for and Bentley, the publican, killed him,' Seamus went on. 'But did Bentley get the rough justice that would have been meted out to one of us? No, he did not. The presiding magistrate was a good friend of his and the inquest cleared him of any involvement. Clear proof of corruption in high places – as if we needed proof. The mood turned ugly then. They reckon there were five thousand gathered near the Eureka Hotel. Bentley made his escape, coward that he is, but the crowd made sure his hotel didn't escape too. They burned it. Such a roaring blaze I've never seen in my life, and it warmed the cockles of my heart as well as my skin, I can tell you.'

'You were there, then,' Tara said.

'I was, and Patrick too. I wouldn't have missed it for a

crock full of gold.' Seamus laughed lustily at the memory, then his face sobered once more. 'The authorities weren't so pleased though. In fact they took it for what it was, the start of open rebellion. The new Commissioner – Rede – called for reinforcements, British soldiers from Melbourne. And what a load of whey-faced recruits they turned out to be! They took the wrong road to the camp and blundered on to the Eureka Diggings. The miners soon showed 'em what they thought of 'em – shots were fired. Well, what would you expect? The drummer boy got wounded and the military didn't take kindly to that either. I tell you, Tara, it's very near open warfare now. There's monster meetings for the masses, and wildcat action for a few. They'll help themselves to anything that smacks of capitalism. That's why Cobb and Co. are taking no chances, I'll be bound.'

Tara nodded, taking another nervous look at the armed guards. She hoped fervently that no gang of disenchanted miners would try to storm the coach. She didn't want to see bloodshed on any side, and in any case such a raid would delay them. But it was disturbing enough just to learn of all the troubles that had been brewing in the goldfields without her hearing a word of it.

'What does all this mean for Patrick?' she asked anxiously. 'Are they likely to be the harder on him with all this trouble going on?'

'You can thank the trouble for him still having his neck intact, if you ask me,' Seamus said roundly. 'The authorities have enough on their plates at the moment without his trial and execution added to it. And they doubtless think it would stoke the miners' anger more. But the minute they get their chance they'll take it. That's why there's no time to waste.'

His words had started a tiny flare of hope in Tara.

'Do you really think so? Don't you think they might be afraid of starting another riot if Patrick were hanged?'

'Aren't you listening to me, Tara?' Seamus demanded bluntly. 'They'll wait until they have enough reinforcements to make sure it's the diggers who end up with a bloody nose. But they'll do it, don't doubt that for a moment. They want someone's neck for Dupont's murder – and if they can make an example of a digger like Patrick and let the rest of us see who's running the show at the same time, then so much the better. Shall I tell you something? It was right after the burning of the Eureka Hotel they came for Patrick. Doesn't that tell you something?'

Tara's eyes narrowed. Yes. It told her the authorities were not prepared to wait any longer to lay charges for the killing of one of their own and, as Seamus had said, they intended to make an example of their prime suspect, by hook or by crook. Once again she found herself wondering if the items which had been stolen from her had found their way back into the hands of the authorities – and the authorities had used them unscrupulously for their own ends, planting them ahead of their search, or even during it. It certainly made sense – especially if Seamus and Patrick were high on their list of troublemakers.

'So you see, Tara, why I think they might treat you with leniency,' Seamus went on. 'Patrick is one kettle of fish, you are quite another. To hang a woman would certainly cause outrage. I don't think they'd want that at this moment.'

'It's possible, I suppose,' Tara said slowly. 'But if they're simply looking for an excuse to make the miners rise so that they can crush them and call whatever means they employ justified, then I can't see what difference it will make.'

The coach began rocking and she sank back once more, her hand pressed against her mouth. Things at Eureka were even worse than she had thought. Bad enough to have to confess to Dupont's murder and face up to trial and punishment. But to be going into such a welter of trouble too . . .

Tara closed her eyes and forgot about everything but the pressing matter of not being sick.

All along the way, as they neared the diggings, Tara saw more and more evidence of the disturbing way things were shaping up. Units of the military, their arms at the ready, clattered past, alert and watchful, whilst in the small camps and shanty towns bands of men were gathered and it was clear their mood was ugly. The hot air was laden with menace; it would take very little to put a spark to the tinder box that was being assembled.

Was it possible that she, Tara, might provide the spark? The thought made her tremble. But the alternative, she acknowledged, was even worse. Supposing the authorities were to find some opportunity to try Patrick before she and Seamus reached Ballarat? Supposing they were too late? Tara knew that if they were, she would never forgive herself. Oh, she had never imagined when she ran away that it would come to this, but that didn't absolve her of blame. If Patrick lost his life because of what she had done she would have killed him as surely as if she had turned the gun on him instead of the hateful Henry Dupont.

Tara's stomach had grown more accustomed to the rocking of the coach now, and although she still felt queasy she no longer had the urgent need to keep from being sick to divert her thoughts. They whirled and threatened like great black ravens around a piece of carrion, giving her not a moment's peace. And though she still held her rosary beads between her stiff fingers, she found that she was quite unable to pray. She was beyond that. Beyond hope, beyond help.

At last – at last! – the coach rolled into Ballarat. Though it was late afternoon the sun was still strong and high and the shadows cast by the detachments of military as they rode along the street were sharp and threatening. There were few passengers left on the coach – no one with a grain of sense wanted to be heading for this hot spot of rebellion, Tara thought – but the ones who were climbed down gratefully enough into the hot airless street, flexing their stiff limbs and aching muscles.

'Pray God we're in time,' Seamus said, lifting down her bag.

Tara stood for a moment breathing in the hot smell of menace that hung over the small township and trying to still the frantic beating of her heart. Then she lifted her chin. 'It won't be my fault if we are not,' she said, and her voice was firm and full of resolve despite the trembling of her hands which she was quite unable to control, despite the fluttering in her stomach and the weakness of her knees. 'I shall go to the authorities now. Without delay.'

There were more military than Tara had ever seen before in the square outside the Commissioner's office. Some sat in the shade, smoking or playing cards, some paced, their eyes ever-watchful, and like those they had passed on the road, their guns were drawn. The Commissioner feared an attack on his headquarters, Tara surmised. With head held high she marched right through the middle of them.

Seamus, to give him his due, remained at her side, though whether to offer her protection from the leering, jeering soldiers or whether to ensure she did not lose her nerve at the last moment, Tara could not be sure.

Not that he needed to worry on that score, she thought grimly. She hadn't come so far and at such cost to give up and run away now. Straight to the door she marched.

A soldier who was clearly acting as sentry moved sharply into her path. 'Just a minute! Where do you think you are going?'

'To see the Commissioner.'

'Oh, yes, and what about?'

Tara met his gaze defiantly. 'I am Mrs Patrick Murphy. I believe you are holding my husband here on a charge of murder – a charge of which he is wholly innocent.'

'Oh yes?' the guard sneered. 'And who says he is innocent?'

'Why I do!' Tara returned.

The guard laughed unpleasantly. 'All wives would have that their husbands are innocent – unless it's that he's been lying with a whore. But murder, oh, they'll deny murder, every last one of them. What makes you any different?'

Tara stood her ground. 'I *know* my husband is innocent because it was *I* who shot Henry Dupont,' she said boldly. 'Now, will you kindly take me to the new Commissioner without delay?'

'A pretty tale, Mrs Murphy. A pretty tale indeed.' The Commissioner pushed back his chair, folded his arms across his chest, and looked directly at Tara.

The office had changed little, she had noticed, since Henry Dupont's time. The desk, the bureaux, even the safe – now firmly closed – were in the exact same places. Only the rug on which he had fallen had gone, soaked beyond redemption by his blood, she imagined. And the sun, slanting in now at the window, showed one patch of floor lighter than the rest where doubtless it had been scrubbed relentlessly.

The Commissioner too had a different look about him. Henry Dupont had been a flabby bully. There was a hard edge to this man that made Tara realise he would be a cruel and ruthless enemy.

'It may sound like a pretty tale to you,' she said shortly, 'but I assure you it's the truth. Every word of it. Henry Dupont robbed me of what was rightfully mine and then he tried to rape me. Right here in this very room. I shot him to protect my honour, with his own gun. So I know for a fact that Patrick is innocent of any crime whatsoever.'

The Commissioner raised an eyebrow. 'And what do you expect me to do to about it?'

'Well, release him, of course!' Tara cried. 'And arrest me instead!'

The Commissioner smiled slightly. 'If only it were so simple.'

Tara stared at him, frowning. 'It is simple! You have the wrong man incarcerated . . . wherever he is incarcerated. I didn't see him at the lock-up tree on my way in . . .'

267

'He has been moved to a cell for his own safety,' the Commissioner said smoothly.

Tara snorted. 'For *your* safety, more like!' Then, realising she was not helping matters by such an outburst, she bit her tongue. 'I am the one who should be locked up in a cell awaiting trial,' she said passionately. 'You must release Patrick and take me in his place.'

'Oh no, Mrs Murphy, I'm sorry, but I don't think I can do that.' The Commissioner smiled again, a smile which did not reach his eyes. 'You must see this from my point of view. On the one hand I have a suspect in whose home items stolen from the murdered Commissioner were found concealed. A suspect against whom I am confident a conviction can be obtained. On the other, I have a hysterical wife who will say anything, no doubt, in order to save her husband's neck. A wife who thinks that in all likelihood the law will deal with her a great deal more leniently than it will deal with the man she loves. Given the circumstances, and attempting for a moment to be impartial, Mrs Murphy, which one would you believe?'

'But . . .' Tara ran a hand helplessly across her cheek, tucking behind her ear a strand of hair which had come loose during the long journey. Put like that, the Commissioner had made a good case for holding Patrick. But he was wrong – so wrong!

'I killed Henry Dupont,' she said urgently. 'It's the truth, I swear it. And it was I who robbed him – though all I took was money that was rightfully mine and a few trinkets to make it look like a robbery. Patrick had nothing to do with any of it. As for doing this for love of him – I wouldn't if it weren't the truth. Our marriage was over when I left him. The only reason I am here now is because I don't want him to suffer for what I did. Please, you must believe me!'

'I thought I'd made myself clear, Mrs Murphy.' The Commissioner was beginning to display signs of impatience.

'What I believe is neither here nor there. It will be for the courts to decide whether or not your husband is guilty. As far as I am concerned, I am perfectly satisfied with the findings of my investigating officers.'

Tara stared in outraged disbelief. Why wouldn't he listen to her? Why wouldn't he release Patrick and lock her up in his place? But the reason was all too clear. In Patrick, the Commissioner had a troublemaker of whom he could make an example. In Tara, he would have a woman whose courage and loyalty would stir up sympathy amongst the already inflamed mining community. This man did not care about justice. That the right culprit was punished was the least of his concerns, just as long as someone was punished and seen to be punished. Just as long as one of the ringleaders of the unrest was silenced for ever. For Patrick, along with Seamus, had been one of the ringleaders, she felt certain of it. Their Irish blarney had fuelled the fires at more than one meeting, if she was not mistaken. And Patrick was always ready with his fists too . . .

'If that is all, Mrs Murphy, I'm a very busy man,' the Commissioner said dismissively.

Tara looked at his impassive face, at his tight lips and narrowed eyes, and knew without a shadow of a doubt that she would get no further with him.

'Is there anything else I can do for you?'

As if he had done anything at all! she thought furiously.

'Yes,' she said. 'Yes, there is. I would like to see my husband please.'

The Commissioner moved to the door, opened it and called to the sentry. 'Mrs Murphy wants to see her husband. Arrange it, will you?'

Then, with no more ado, he ushered her out of the office and closed the door after her.

Seamus came rushing eagerly towards Tara, but the moment he saw her set face he stopped short, the light dying out of his eyes.

'I got nowhere, Seamus,' Tara said bitterly. 'Nowhere at all.'

Seamus shook his head in disbelief. 'But surely you told him . . . ?'

'Oh, I told him,' Tara assured him. 'It made no difference. He wouldn't listen to a word I said. He *wants* Patrick to be guilty, Seamus. Or at least, that's how it seemed to me.'

Seamus's face darkened. 'That figures. Yes, dammit, that figures! But I never thought he'd have the nerve to send you packing . . . I thought that even he would have to show some respect for the truth when he heard it.' His eyes narrowed suddenly. 'You are sure you made yourself clear? You did take full responsibility? I wasn't there, remember, to hear what you said.'

'Of course I made myself clear!' Tara retorted, stung that he still did not quite trust her – though under the circumstances who could blame him? 'I told the Commissioner that it was I who shot Henry Dupont with his own gun – a fact I couldn't have known unless I was speaking the truth – and I told him I took the trinkets to make it look like a robbery gone wrong. He just smiled and said he was satisfied he had the right man. There was nothing more I could do, Seamus. All that's left to me now is to go through it all again when they bring Patrick to trial, and hope and pray that I'm believed then.'

'Fat chance!' Seamus said bitterly. 'Do you honestly think the Commissioner will allow himself to be made to look a fool like that?'

'Mrs Murphy?' The sentry was approaching them. 'I thought you wanted to see your husband.'

'Oh, yes – yes, I do.'

'Come on then.' The guard was jangling a bunch of keys and indicating a stout stone building that stood a little apart from the others. As Seamus made to follow Tara the guard turned on him unpleasantly. 'Not you. Only the lady. That's my orders.'

Seamus swore and caught at Tara's arm, delaying her for a moment. 'Tell him we'll not let him rot, nor hang,' he said in a low voice.

'What's that?' The guard swung round officiously. 'Any more chit-chat and the lady won't see her husband either.'

'Oh, for pity's sake!' Tara tossed her head and walked past both Seamus and the guard, heading straight for the building where Patrick was incarcerated.

It was the stench that hit her first, the awful stench of raw sewage and unwashed bodies and the sweet sickly smell of blood, all mingling in the stagnant heat. Tara recoiled a step and the guard, who had a kerchief pressed to his own nose, laughed.

'Changed your mind, Missus?'

'No, of course not!' Tara searched in her reticule for her own handkerchief, hating herself for her weakness but knowing that without it she would never be able to step into the foulness of the gaol and not gag. 'How can you keep human beings in conditions such as these?'

The guard shrugged. 'Not very nice, is it? That's why we use the gum tree mostly to chain 'em up to. But there's some prisoners that'd just incite too much trouble. Your husband's one, Roaring Jim Pomerey's another. So we got 'em locked up in here out of harm's way.'

'Jim Pomerey?' Tara exclaimed. A huge bearded giant in his cabbage-tree hat, as much religious fanatic as goldminer, Jim had been a familiar figure around Ballarat where he Bible-thumped more hours than he ever panned for gold. 'Why is Jim Pomerey in this hell-hole?'

The guard shrugged again. 'Refused to renew his licence from what I hear. Not just forgot, or couldn't afford it – refused, point blank. Said it was God's good earth put there for all to share.'

'And for that he's been locked up in this . . .' Tara broke off as the stench hit her nostrils again, making her heave.

'Can't have troublemakers like that on the loose,' the guard

271

said casually. 'Quite a gathering he had round him when he was chained up to the old gum and stirring them like one of those evangelical preachers. Now . . .' He gesticulated impatiently. 'Are you coming in to see your man or not?'

Tara took a last deep breath of good fresh air and marched steadfastly into the prison building.

At first she could see nothing. The only light filtered through a heavily barred gap in the stonework and after the brightness of the sun outside she was rendered temporarily blind. Then, gradually, as her eyes became more accustomed to the dimness, she made out two forms, chained and shackled like wild animals – or slaves of old – to the far wall. One was the huge form of Jim Pomerey. The other . . .

'Patrick,' Tara whispered in a shaky voice. 'Patrick, is that you?'

And heard the familiar lilting Irish voice she had once loved with all her heart.

'Tara! Tara, m'vourneen! You came!'

'Well, of course I came, Patrick!' Tara could hardly speak for the lump in her throat – and the rising sickness. 'You must have known I would.'

'I hardly dared hope . . .'

'And much good it did!' she said bitterly. 'It's you they want.'

'I was afraid so. Aah, I was afraid so.' He sighed heavily.

'Don't give up hope, Patrick!' she whispered urgently.

Hearing the word 'hope' Roaring Jim Pomerey made a sudden movement like a puppet when the strings are pulled. 'Hope! Yea, hope! Our hope is with the Lord Jesus! His rod and his staff shall comfort me . . .'

'Oh, be quiet for the love of God!' Patrick shouted at him. And to Tara he said, more quietly, 'He'll drive me mad, so he will. As if it wasn't bad enough being chained in this stinking hole, to have him ranting all day and half the night . . .'

'Listen, Patrick, I'll work tirelessly to get you released,' Tara whispered. 'I mean to be here when you come to trial so that at least I can tell the judge and jury – if there is one – the truth of what happened. They'll have to listen. They must!'

'I doubt they will.' Unsurprisingly, Patrick sounded like a beaten man. 'Justice is the last thing I've come to expect out here in the goldfields though it's what the men are ready to rise for. Good British justice. We took it for granted at home, so we did. But here . . . Many men will have to die before we get it, I fear.'

'Oh, don't say that, Patrick!' Tara begged.

'It's true, though. Revolt is coming, Tara, and it'll mean big trouble and bloodshed. Seamus is part of it, so he is. Have you seen Seamus?'

'He's with me, yes. He came to Melbourne to find me and bring me back. Didn't you know that?'

'Oh yes, I think I did know.' Patrick sounded vaguely puzzled. 'I must have forgotten. How did I come to forget that?'

'Nothing is surprising when you're locked up in a place like this!' Tara cried. Tears of helpless anger were stinging in her eyes. 'I'll get you out of here, I promise you. Somehow. Oh, and Seamus said to tell you we won't let you rot and we won't let you hang. You must hold on to that, Patrick.'

'Oh, I will. If Seamus said . . . But listen to me now, sweetheart.' He reached for her hand. The smell emanating from him made her gag anew but somehow she managed to control it and not let him see how his touch was revolting her. 'You've got to get away from here, Tara. Seamus should never have brought you here. He should have known it would do no good. And this is no place now for a woman. There's big trouble brewing. Promise me you'll take the next coach out of this place, m'vourneen. I don't want harm to come to you because of me.'

'But harm has come to you because of me,' she said softly.

'Ah, forget it! If I'd been the husband I should have been to you . . . Oh, Tara, such dreams we had, you and I! Didn't

273

we have such dreams? But I let you down badly, didn't I? First it was the gold – I never found enough to even buy you a fine gown, let alone all the other things I promised you. And then . . . ah, sure, sweetheart, I never meant to hurt and betray you. But Seamus understood me where you did not. We shared, you see, Seamus and I, as you and I never could. It's a different love and I wouldn't expect you to understand. We were just children together, you and I, while Seamus . . .'

'Patrick, don't, please,' Tara said shortly. 'I don't want to hear. It doesn't matter now, not one bit. All that matters is getting you out of this terrible place.'

A chink of light fell across his face, bearded, hollow-cheeked, as the guard opened the door once more.

'Time's up, Mrs Murphy. Out you come now.'

'Tara, promise me!' Patrick whispered urgently.

Desperate to be free of his clinging fingers, desperate now to be out in the fresh air, Tara nodded. 'I promise.'

Satisfied, he released her and she stumbled towards the sunlight. But she had not the slightest intention of leaving Ballarat tomorrow. She must finish what she had come here to do. And she would never rest unless she knew that Patrick was safe and would not suffer the death penalty for what she, Tara, had done.

Twenty

That night Tara and Seamus sat late over a noggin of sly grog. Being back in the shanty that had once been her home was a strange feeling. The once familiar now seemed subtly changed.

'You can sleep in the bed. I'll make myself up a couch on the floor,' Seamus had offered and when Tara made a token protest he added drily: 'It's yours anyway. You bought and paid for it.'

But good bed or not, and tired as she was, Tara did not feel like retiring. There was far too much on her mind.

'Oh, I can't bear to think of Patrick in that terrible place!' she groaned. 'Just think of it, he's chained to the wall like a wild animal. There are rats in there, too, I'm sure of it, and the stench was just awful. He'll catch the fever and die of it if he's there much longer. He was a bit rambly this afternoon.'

Seamus said nothing.

'What can we do?' Tara cried in despair. 'Do you think if I went back to Melbourne and lobbied the parliament there it might do some good? Perhaps I could get him tried there and we'd have a better chance of a fair hearing. Do you think it's worth a try?'

'It might be, though I think they'll all stick together. You won't get one official to condemn another. And I doubt there's time in any case.' Seamus reached for the flask of sly grog.

'What do you mean?' Tara asked, alarmed.

'Things are moving here apace. There's another monster

meeting planned for tomorrow. On Bakery Hill.' He poured some more sly grog into Tara's cup. 'The diggers are getting well and truly wound up now and I don't know what it will mean for Patrick if there's open warfare.'

'Oh, Seamus, we must do something. We must get him out of that hell-hole!' Tara cried.

He swigged his own sly grog, staring into the middle distance. 'I've got one or two plans up my sleeve.'

'What?'

'Never you mind. It's best you don't know.'

'You mean you don't trust me?' Tara exclaimed indignantly.

'No, I mean the fewer that know the better. Don't ask me, Tara, there's a good girl. Now drink up that liquor, it'll help you to sleep. And you'll need every bit of rest you can come by with what lies ahead of us.'

Tara did as he told her. The sly grog had a rough taste that burned her mouth and gullet but at least it was buoying her up a little. Worried though she still was about Patrick, things did not look quite so black, quite so hopeless. She couldn't imagine what Seamus had in mind and she couldn't see what she could do except to keep informing anyone who would listen of Patrick's innocence. Yet she was beginning to feel that somehow they would find a way. They had to! That was all there was to it.

With the pearly dawn, however, Tara felt less optimistic. In spite of the sly grog, she had slept badly, tossing and turning half the night, and what sleep she had managed had been racked with horrible, muddled, nightmarish dreams where James and Patrick were somehow fused into one, and always in dire and distressing circumstances. When she finally woke fully she had a burning dry throat and a thumping headache and every time she tried to move she felt horribly nauseous.

'Oh, it will be a long time before I swallow so much as a mouthful of that evil stuff again!' she groaned. 'I'm good for nothing this morning, Seamus.'

Seamus set a cup of strong syrupy coffee down beside the bed. 'Drink this and hopefully you'll feel a bit better. It's the monster meeting, remember.'

'I don't have to come to that do I?' Tara asked. All she wanted to do was to close her eyes and lie perfectly still – though not even that seemed to help much.

'I think you should,' Seamus told her. 'There's going to be trouble, without a doubt.'

'Then surely I'd be better off staying here . . .' she protested weakly.

'That's one way of looking at it. But there's safety in numbers. If things get heated the military might come up here and sack the camp. I wouldn't put it past them. If you were here alone, heaven alone knows what might become of you.'

Tara shivered. It didn't take a great leap of the imagination to know what he meant. Gingerly she sat up and reached for the coffee. 'I suppose I'd better try to be fit to come with you then,' she said resignedly.

The crowd that assembled on Bakery Hill was at least five hundred strong and Tara could tell at once that their mood was ugly.

'They must be serious if they're holding meetings rather than panning for gold!' she said.

Seamus shrugged. 'Small use panning for gold until things have been put to rights.'

Tara screwed up her eyes against the sun. Her headache now had concentrated above her left temple so that it felt as if someone were driving a screw right into the eye socket.

'You mean you've come to realise how hopeless it all is?'

'Hopeless for now, yes!' Seamus said impatiently. 'Hopeless until we can get some rights for ourselves. For until we do the authorities will simply rob us blind and grind us down into the dust.'

Tara grimaced. For all the hardships and dangers Seamus

had clearly not given up on his hopes of finding a fortune. The lure of gold was still strong.

At last the meeting began. As speaker after speaker took the tub and ranted about the injustices they were forced to endure the crowd became more and more inflamed.

'Licences to dig? They charge us the earth for them and what use are they to us?' one orator yelled. 'I vote we burn them and show the powers-that-be what we think of their licences!'

Tara couldn't help thinking of Roaring Jim Pomerey, imprisoned because he had dared to speak out against licences.

'Burn them! Burn them every one!' the orator yelled and the crowd took up the chant.

'Burn them! Burn them!'

Every digger in the crowd who had a licence, it seemed, pulled it from his pocket and waved it in the air. Some set fire to them with the flints they used to light their smokes, some formed a small clearing and started a bonfire. As the flames licked and smoke curled up into the hot still air the mood of the men became jubilant. It was as if this symbolic defiance had somehow solved all their problems at a stroke. They were intoxicated with their own daring, just as last night Tara had been a little intoxicated with the sly grog.

Another man climbed onto the makeshift platform. The crowd roared their approval.

'Peter Lalor,' Seamus told Tara.

'Peter Lalor?' she repeated. It wasn't a name she knew.

'Our Commander-in-Chief. Hush now!'

Commander-in-Chief! Dear God, how warlike that sounded! Was that where this was headed – open warfare? It certainly looked that way. But what would it mean for Patrick? If open warfare came, would the authorities forget about him, locked in his disgusting airless cell? Or would they lose patience and execute him without even the pretence of a trial, thinking the diggers too preoccupied with airing their grievances to notice and anxious to be rid of one more troublemaker? Tara felt the claustrophobic aura of last night's confused dreams closing in once more and briefly closed her aching eyes. Another roar made her snap them open again and she saw that a flag was being run up a hastily erected flagpole. It fluttered bravely in the light breeze that had sprung up, a bold white cross on a blue ground, the four arms and the centre of which each bore a star.

'The Southern Cross,' Seamus said, reverence in his tone. 'Our flag, Tara. *Ours*, do you understand?'

She nodded. Upwards of five hundred pairs of eyes – her own included – were focused on that flag, and the swell of emotion as it reached its zenith was almost tangible.

The man Seamus had referred to as their Commander-in-Chief, Peter Lalor, stepped forward, raising his hand. His voice on the ever stiffening breeze was thin and reedy so that Tara was unable to make out every word he said. But somehow it scarcely mattered. The sense and the sentiment were clear enough.

The Commander-in-Chief was swearing allegiance to the flag of the Southern Cross and pledging to fight for the rights and liberties of every man who took it for his own.

Like everyone else there on Bakery Hill that day, Tara could not help but be stirred by the groundswell of solidarity that came when a downtrodden population united behind a common symbol, a common cause. But she also had the sense to be afraid.

Revolution didn't happen easily. It didn't happen without bloodshed and loss of life. The Southern Cross might be fluttering bravely now, but there might yet be blood upon it. In the hot sun Tara shivered, for she knew instinctively that the rebellion had developed a momentum of its own. There would be no stopping it until one side or the other triumphed, or was defeated. And the toll would be heavy.

Tara was not the only one who anticipated trouble now that the rebellion was out in the open. The men's leaders were only too well aware of how far they had gone and how likely it was that the authorities would act swiftly to put a stop to further defiance. The very next day they began to build a stockade which would afford the rebels some defence against the might of the military.

As she might have expected, Seamus went to help with it, though this time he did not insist Tara go along too.

'You'll be all right in the camp today,' he told her. 'There are plenty of people about, and if the military take it into their heads to come looking for trouble it's the stockade and those of us building it they'll head for. But I dare say you'll be welcomed with open arms if you think to bring up some refreshments later on.'

'I'll do that.' She didn't like the idea of having nothing but her thoughts for company and she felt uncomfortable around the camp, where some remembered her and others looked at her curiously.

But for the most part they were too preoccupied to bother about her much. There were constant comings and goings, and impromptu meetings which started with the men's heads close together and finished with them punching the air with a sort of barely controlled excitement. And there were more weapons in evidence, too, than Tara had ever seen before. Guns, pistols, pikes – every man seemed to be armed to the teeth.

At midday she took cold meats and bread up to the site of the stockade and was surprised to see how much progress had been made. At this rate it would be more or less finished by the day's end.

And indeed, according to Seamus when he came home late in the evening, the stockade was more or less completed. It was certainly at a stage where it would afford good protection for the diggers should the need arise. But to her surprise, as soon as they had eaten, he told her he had to go out again.

'Where are you going?' Tara asked, a little sharply.

'Never you mind.'

'But . . .'

'Just remember what I told you when you first came. There's some things it's best you don't know. Just bolt the door after me and don't let anyone in, do you hear? No one.'

Tara frowned. She was more certain than ever that Seamus was one of the ringleaders of this rising. There was a hard edge about him tonight, something of the same barely controlled excitement she had noticed amongst the gathering diggers, but also a wariness, eyes that darted beneath half-hooded lids, an alertness of muscle and sinew. He had strapped on his gun-belt too, she noticed.

'Am I not to let you in either when you return?' she asked.

'Likely I won't be back, leastways, not until morning. I can always sleep at the stockade. Just bolt the door and don't worry about me.'

Tara nodded, but her pulses had begun to race and her imagination was working overtime. What was it that Seamus was up to this night?

Alone in the shack that had once been her home Tara found herself longing with all her heart for James. She shouldn't, she knew. That part of her life was over and all the longing and hoping in the world couldn't take things back to the way they had been the last wonderful months. James knew now that she had killed a man, and worse, that she had kept it from him. If he could understand the circumstances that had made her a murderess and forgive, he certainly would not be able to understand and forgive the secrecy, the half-truths, the downright deception she had practised, for they made a mockery of the love and closeness the two of them had shared. James had forgiven her for hiding from him the fact that she was a married woman it was true, forgiven her with a generosity of spirit that made her continued deception all the worse. But that had been before they had become lovers. The circumstances were quite different. James would be terribly hurt, Tara knew, that she had kept so much hidden from him whilst sharing his bed and his life, and the hurt would sour his feelings for her, cast a different light on his perception of all they had meant to one another.

Oh, why hadn't she been able to bring herself to share her secrets with him? she asked herself over and over. Now that it was too late she regretted the omission bitterly.

Tara found herself wondering briefly what the others had thought when they had learned the truth. Had they been shocked? Or had they always suspected there was more to the girl their brother had brought home from Melbourne to be their housekeeper than met the eye? She really did not know, but thinking of them all, and especially thinking of James, was an ache around Tara's heart so fierce she could barely stand it.

With an effort she drew her thoughts back to Patrick. She had failed him too. It was all due to her that he was in this terrible situation now. For the moment she couldn't physically do anything to help him, but maybe if she prayed hard enough, and concentrated every ounce of her will, maybe something would turn up.

'Please save Patrick from that awful place,' she whispered over and over. 'Oh, Holy Mary, please save Patrick from that awful place.'

She was still whispering the words like a mantra when she finally fell asleep.

The knocking at the door awakened her. Instantly she was wide awake, every nerve straining. Pale light creeping in at the window told her it was morning. Tara pushed aside the covers and padded across to the door, jumping as the hammering on the flimsy panels of the door began again.

'All right, all right! Who is it?'

'It's me! Open up, Tara! It's all right, it's me.'

Seamus's voice, urgent, demanding. Tara struggled with the heavy bolt, wriggling it back inch by inch. The moment it cleared its holster the door was thrown open.

'Have patience, Seamus!' Tara snapped. 'Didn't you tell me to bolt the door and let no one in?'

'Get your things together quickly, Tara. We have to get away from here.'

'But why? What's happened? Where are we going . . . ?'

'Come on, will you? There's no time to explain. Just get some clothes on, for the love of God.' As he spoke Seamus was upending the bed, rooting under the mattress. To her amazement Tara saw that she had been sleeping on a veritable arsenal of ammunition. 'Oh, will you get a move on!' he shouted in exasperation when he saw her looking at him. 'Unless you want the soldiers to come and take you in your shift, that is.'

That was enough for Tara. She pulled on her gown and fetched a shawl and her bonnet and reticule. Seamus was waiting for her outside, watching the roadway as if he expected the soldiers at any moment.

'Where are we going?' she asked as she hurried alongside him, almost running to keep up.

'The stockade. Come on, save your breath. I'll tell you what's happened when we get there.'

In the early light the stockade looked bleak and alarmingly flimsy. Armed men were stationed at look-out points. They nodded recognition at Seamus but one called out as they passed: 'Get inside! We could be attacked at any time thanks to your night's work!'

The urgency – and resentment – in his voice frightened Tara still more. 'What . . . ?' she began to ask again. Then she broke off, for she had the answer to her question with no word from Seamus.

In a corner of the stockade, half raised against a wooden fencing post and covered with a rough blanket, lay a dishevelled, unkempt figure. Tara stood stock still for a moment, then her breath came out on a gasp. 'Patrick!'

'Aye, Patrick.' The ghost of a smile touched Seamus's lips. 'We got him out, Tara. We brought him here. That's why I had to get you away from the shanty. It's the first place the military will go looking for him. They'll burn it to the ground, most like . . .'

Tara was scarcely listening. She had started across the rough ground to where her husband lay. 'Patrick – oh, Patrick!'

Twenty-One

Patrick opened his eyes a little at the sound of her voice, then closed them again as if the effort was too much for him. Tara dropped to her knees beside him.

Dear God, he looked terrible! Ragged, unshaven, pale as death, with high spots of fever staining his cheeks in an unnatural blush that looked like the painted face of a Dutch doll, and he shivered uncontrollably.

'Jesus, Mary and Joseph!' Tara whispered, crossing herself. 'Oh, he has the fever! Didn't I say he'd get the fever if we didn't get him out of that terrible place?'

'Well, he's out now,' Seamus said. 'All we can do now is care for him as best we can and pray that we can pull him through.'

Tara bit her lip so hard that she tasted blood. She had see too many men – and women too – in this state on the long sea voyage from Ireland to Australia, and few of them had recovered. Perhaps with good nursing care there was a chance, but how could Patrick be given that here in the stockade? There were no physical comforts, and if the military came they would be under siege with no medicines and no fresh water either. Conditions would be as bad if not worse than they had been on board ship.

'I don't know what to do for him,' she confessed. 'I'm no nurse, Seamus. He needs a nurse, or better still a doctor. Isn't there anyone we could fetch to him?'

'You know there's not.' Seamus ran a hand through his hair, looking helpless. 'And even if there was why should any medical man risk everything by throwing in his lot with us? Doctors don't have a bad time of it, they don't share our grievances. And this is going to be no picnic, Tara. We killed three soldiers to get him out. The military will come down hard on us, make no mistake of it.'

'How did you get him out?' Tara asked.

'By catching them off guard,' Seamus said. 'We picked them off silently one by one with a garotte and took the keys. If we'd had to open fire I doubt we'd have made it. Shots would have wakened more men than we could deal with.'

His face was grim and briefly Tara pictured the scene – the sudden vicious deaths, the nerve-stretching tension as they brought Patrick out of his cell, the difficulty of hoisting a man as sick as he was onto a horse. Her stomach clenched and she tried to close her mind to it.

'What about Roaring Jim Pomerey?' she asked. 'Did you free him too?'

'We did not. The man's as mad as a hatter. He'd have woken the sleeping soldiers without a doubt if we'd let him loose.'

Tara nodded. Sorry as she felt for Jim Pomerey, she could see the sense of the argument. Patrick had been Seamus's only concern. It was for Patrick he had risked his life, not some half-crazed fanatic. And he had risked his life, without doubt.

'Thank you, Seamus,' she said softly.

Seamus turned on her almost angrily. 'I did it for Patrick, not for you.'

'I know.' Humbled by the man's love, she touched his arm. 'I'm sorry. I have no right . . .'

'I only wish I'd done it sooner,' Seamus said bitterly. 'But until the stockade was built there was nowhere I could have taken him where the authorities wouldn't have found him. Now . . . Please God I didn't leave it too late.'

Amen to that, Tara thought. It was heartbreaking to see

Patrick in this condition. Even worse to think he might yet die because of her actions.

'And you think the military will come?' she asked, looking down over the countryside that was beginning to wake now for a new day.

'They'll come.' Seamus moved abruptly. 'Will you look after Patrick? I have to help with preparations to repel an attack.'

'Of course I'll look after him, Seamus,' Tara said.

The long summer's day wore on but the soldiers did not come. The men on look-out began to grow restless, sweating in the blistering heat of the sun, but the only movement in the flat valley beneath the stockade was from those diggers and their families who had not retired to it. And there were few enough of those. Within the flimsy stockade more than fifteen hundred men prepared to defend themselves, and the sheer weight of numbers gave them a sense of security and a growing optimism.

For Tara, however, every minute was a living nightmare. She stayed beside Patrick, doing her best to make him comfortable, but he showed not the slightest sign of improvement. If anything, she thought, he was worse. In spite of the heat he still shivered uncontrollably and in moments of consciousness he ranted in delirium or tried to fight off some invisible assailant whom only he could see.

'Patrick, don't! she implored him, trying to restrain his flailing fists. 'Lie still for the love of God! You're safe. There's no one there.'

'Tara?' he whispered once, almost lucid. 'Tara, what are you doing here?'

'Trying to look after you. Now save your strength, Patrick.' She wiped the rivulets of sweat from his forehead with a cloth wrung out in a little cool water.

'Tara . . . I'm sorry . . .'

'Hush now! I'm the one who should be sorry.'

His eyes opened wide and he looked around wildly. 'Where's Seamus?'

Tara swallowed hard. Strange how even now it could hurt to know that it was Seamus he wanted.

'He's not far away,' she reassured Patrick. 'Do you want me to fetch him?'

But Patrick was drifting again, back into that strange fevered world he was inhabiting. By the time Seamus came to see how things were going he was unconscious again.

Towards evening a rustling of impatience began to grow amongst the massed diggers in the stockade. Groups of them began drifting outside the structure and making their way down the rise.

'What's going on?' Tara asked Seamus, who had come once again to check on Patrick. Seamus tossed his head impatiently.

'The fools think it's safe for them to return to their homes for tonight at least. Tomorrow's Sunday. They don't think the military will attack on the Sabbath.'

'Why ever not?' Tara cried. 'How many of them are churchgoers?'

'That's what I tried to tell them. They just won't listen. They can't see beyond the comfort of their own beds.' He swore, then rubbed his own eyes which were aching with tiredness; he had had no sleep himself at all the previous night. 'Oh, I don't know, maybe they're right. I was so sure the military would attack today.'

'I wonder why they haven't?' Tara said, though she was thanking God today had at least been peaceful. It had been bad enough as it was watching over the fevered Patrick; if there had been fighting too it would have been unbearable.

'God alone knows. I don't. Who can tell what those devils plan? I only know I could do with a good bed myself,' Seamus said wearily.

As the sun sank towards the western horizon the trickle of men leaving the stockade became a steady flow. By the time the stars came out and a cool breeze whispered over the scorched land there were fewer than five hundred left in the stockade.

Tara threw another blanket over Patrick and propped herself up beside him.

'You get some sleep,' she said to Seamus. 'They won't come in the dark. And I'll watch Patrick.'

'I think I'll have to,' Seamus agreed, 'or I'll be fit for nothing tomorrow. Wake me, though, won't you, Tara, if there's any change.'

'Of course I will.'

She sat with her shawl wrapped round her, watching Patrick's fevered tossings and turnings, listening to his wild ramblings and felt closer to despair than ever before. Soon, surely, his crisis must come? Soon, surely, the fever would break? At least he was still alive. And yet . . . and yet . . . Oh, he was so weak. So terribly weak. And she was so alone. For all that Seamus slept within arm's reach, so terribly alone. For no one but James could fill the need that ached in her, and James was not here, and never would be again. Weariness tugged at Tara's eyelids, dragging her down. Desperately she fought it.

'Tara!' The sound of Patrick's voice brought her sharply, fully awake.

'Patrick!' she murmured urgently, hope springing. Had the crisis passed? Was he lucid again, and on the mend?

'Oh, Tara, will you look at that lake! Sure isn't it the most beautiful sight in the world with the sun on it and the fish leaping?'

A chill of fear shivered over her skin. 'What are you talking about, Patrick?'

'Why, the lake! And the mountains! Oh, the green – look at the green, Tara! Emerald, all emerald! Oh, praise be! Tara, we're home. We're home at last!'

His eyes were wide open, staring into the blackness of the Australian night. But he wasn't seeing the dark. He wasn't seeing the stars of the southern hemisphere. He was seeing . . .

'Seamus!' Tara cried. She grabbed his shoulder, shaking him awake. 'Seamus! He's really wandering now. He thinks he's at home in Ireland!'

Seamus was up in an instant, kneeling beside Patrick, taking him in his arms.

'Patrick, hold on now! Patrick, hold on! It's me, Seamus. For the love of God don't leave me . . .'

Tara could only sit and watch, trembling with apprehension.

'Seamus!' she heard Patrick say. Then his breathing became odd and laboured. There was a rasp, a rattle. And Seamus sobbed, a loud wail of despair. Tara's blood ran cold.

'He's gone,' Seamus said. His voice was thick with tears. 'Dear God, Tara, he's gone.'

'No!' Tara cried. 'Oh no, no!'

She tried to get to Patrick and could not. Seamus was holding his lifeless body close. Once again she experienced the terrifying loneliness. And then there was nothing but the grief. Grief for the man she had once loved and shared her life with. Grief for a dream turned sour. Grief so black it overwhelmed her. Tara threw back her head, screwed up her eyes, and wept.

The noise of the guns woke Tara. Some time during the long night she must have cried herself to sleep. Now, with disturbing suddenness she was awake again, startlingly, shockingly awake, every nerve tingling, every bit of her body trembling.

Oh, dear God, the guns! And the shouts and the yells and the crashing sounds of metal on metal and splintering wood.

They had come. She knew it in an instant without thinking, without wondering, without doubt. The military had come, rushing in with the dawn in a surprise attack, overrunning the depleted numbers of diggers who had remained in the stockade.

Chaos was all around her. Men lying wounded and dead. Men taking aim with rifles and pistols. Men fighting with pikes and hand-to-hand. Seamus was nowhere to be seen. Patrick lay, his face now covered by the blanket, where he had died.

Tara leaped to her feet, looking around wildly. Between her and the only exit from the stockade was a heaving mass of men. She cowered back against the fence, hands pressed to her face. Feet away from her a man armed only with a pike rushed a soldier, a shot rang out and the man fell writhing to the ground clutching his stomach. Blood oozed scarlet, spreading around him, clotting into the dust.

Dear God, it was massacre! They were all going to be killed! The stockade they had built for their protection had become a prison, they were caught like rats in a trap and outnumbered ten to one.

The mêlée shifted slightly. Tara thought she saw a way through and took it, running in the direction of the exit. She had no idea how she was going to get away, she just ran blindly and for a moment or two it seemed she might just manage it. No one seemed to be taking notice of her, they were all too preoccupied with the fighting. A body lay on the ground in her path. With a sob she skirted it and ran on.

And then, quite suddenly, a heavy hand grabbed at her shoulder and a voice yelled at her to stop. Tara swung round to find herself face to face with none other than the guard who had taken her to Patrick's cell on the day she had gone to see the Commissioner.

'Wait!' he snarled. 'It's Mrs Murphy, isn't it?'

Tara tried to speak but no words would come. Her dry throat worked but only a croak came out.

The guard's grip tightened on her arm. 'Where's your husband?' he grated. 'And that murdering friend of his?'

'He's dead,' Tara managed. Her teeth were chattering.

'He'll wish he was when we find him! I want him alive after what he did to my comrades. I'll make him suffer!'

'Patrick's dead, I tell you!' Tara squeaked. 'I don't know where Seamus is.'

'You'll give him to me, lady. He'll come for you too.' The guard's fingers held her wrist in a vice-like grip. 'If he doesn't then you can pay the price for him.'

Tara sobbed in pain and terror. She had no doubt the guard meant what he said. He would take her instead of Seamus, ringleader, troublemaker, gaol-breaker. She, who had confessed to the killing of Commissioner Dupont. And with Patrick dead they would be happy enough, now, for her to pay the price. An authority that would hang a woman was an authority to be respected and feared.

'Please, no!' She almost spoke the words, then bit them back. She wouldn't demean herself by pleading. She had come back of her own free will to take responsibility for what she had done, and though Patrick was dead now and it was too late to save him, she would still face up to her punishment with every scrap of courage she could muster. But oh, Holy Mary, it didn't mean she wasn't terrified! For she was, she was . . .

'Unhand her!' For all the uproar the yell, loud as a pistol shot, carried clearly on the hot smoky air.

The guard stopped in his tracks, turning towards it, though he did not release his grip on her arm, and Tara too jerked her head round in the direction from which it had come.

A sensation of total disbelief was catching at her heart, a twist of hope and joy that she dared not acknowledge. It couldn't be . . . Not here in the Eureka stockade! She must be going mad. As mad as Patrick, imagining things that weren't there . . .

But she wasn't imagining things. Coming towards them at a run, gun unholstered, face like thunder, was James.

'Unhand her!' he shouted again, the authoritative tone that was used to being obeyed. But the guard was not a farm hand or a convict but a hardened soldier, and his only response was to drag Tara closer to him.

'Who says?'

'*I* say!' James's jaw was set, his eyes were blazing. 'Unhand her or I shoot you dead!'

The guard swore, going for his own gun which he had holstered when he grabbed Tara. And then, it seemed to Tara, everything happened at once.

A shot rang out, whistling past her ear, hot sticky blood and tissue showered her, and she stumbled to her knees. She heard a scream and knew it was her own. But the strong fingers were no longer gripping her arm. She jerked her head around and screamed again. James's bullet had caught the guard full in the face. He lay beside her, features shattered so he was no longer recognisable. Before she could even attempt to rise on legs turned useless by shock James had hold of her hand, jerking her to her feet. She felt her knees almost give way but his hand supported her and pulled at her with rough urgency.

'Come on!'

There was no time to ask, or even wonder, how he came to be here. Tara simply let James yank her through the mêlée. Every moment she expected that a bullet would catch one or other of them, every moment she thought they would be directly confronted by one of the soldiers in their way. But by some miracle they were not. They reached the edge of the compound, James dragging her behind him, and then they were out in the open, running, stumbling on the rough ground, regaining their balance, running again, towards a clump of trees. As they reached it Tara saw the most welcome sight of her life – James excepted. Tarquin stood there, his reins tethered around a low branch, tossing his head restlessly at the sounds of the battle in the stockade.

Tara felt her knees buckle again. A blackness was closing in from the edges of her terrified mind, a blackness that encroached remorselessly no matter how she tried to fight it. A tiny gasp escaped her and she knew she was going to faint.

The very last thing she was aware of was James's arms about her, lifting her into the saddle. And then the blackness closed in completely and utterly and Tara knew no more.

Sun dappled through branches, a creek burbled over stones. Resting against a giant boulder Tara looked up at James, who was watering Tarquin. He looked back at her, unsmiling.

'Feeling better now?'

She nodded. 'Oh, James, that was terrible. Terrible!'

'What do you expect in a place like that?' His tone was cold, grim. 'A tea party?'

Tears pricked her eyes. She still felt weak and after all that had happened in the last hours his aggression was the last straw. Yet his comment could just as well apply to his attitude towards her – what did she expect? She had deceived him, run out on him, leaving Elizabeth to make her explanations for her, returned, for all he knew, to the man who was her husband.

'I'm sorry, James,' she whispered humbly. 'I had no choice.'

He didn't answer.

'But how did you come to be at Eureka?' she asked after a moment. 'When I saw you I thought . . . oh, I don't know what I thought!'

'I was there looking for you, of course,' he said in the same grim tone. 'The minute I heard what had happened I set out for Ballarat to do what I could. I learned from the authorities that your husband had been snatched from gaol and spirited away. It didn't take much imagination to guess where his friends had taken him. I also learned that the military planned a surprise attack at dawn. I guessed it would be a rout. I couldn't leave you there, so I rode with the soldiers.'

'You rode in with the soldiers?' Tara repeated, surprised.

The first ghost of a smile played about his mouth.

'I can be very persuasive – and as devious as you, Tara.' The smile died again. 'Well, I couldn't leave you there, could I? You could easily have been killed.'

She shivered. 'Sure, don't I know it!'

'So I made up my mind to get you out whether you wanted it or not. Did you want to get out, Tara?'

Or did you want to stay with him? The unspoken question hovered in the warm air. Her chin shot up.

'Well, of course I wanted to get out! I never wanted to come back to the goldfields in the first place. I was so happy with you. But I just felt I had to. Now . . . well, there's no reason for me to stay. Patrick is dead, he died in the night. They'll never hang him now for what I did.'

'Oh, Tara, Tara, why didn't you tell me?'

She could see his pain. She reached for his hand, praying that she could make him understand.

'If you'll listen, I'll tell you now. Everything.'

'No more secrets? No more surprises?'

'None.'

'And you want to come back to Dunrae?'

'More than anything in the world. If you'll have me.'

He pulled her into his arms then. She thought it was the most wonderful place in the world to be.

'Then save your explanations for later. I take it you're a free woman now. Let's go home.'

Epilogue

'*Dearly beloved, we are gathered together here in the sight of God and in the face of this congregation to join together this Man and this Woman in holy Matrimony . . .*'

The tiny church in Edwardstown was full to overflowing. Everyone in the district, it seemed, had wanted to be here to witness the marriage of James and Tara. It wasn't what either of them had intended. The only people who mattered to them were in the front pew – Duncan, scrubbed and rosy, smart as paint and looking very grown-up in a new suit, Philip and Elizabeth, themselves recently wed in a grand ceremony held at Elizabeth's hotel, and Cal, with a bonny new belle on his arm. But the Hannay family were too well known in New South Wales and Victoria for folk to let the occasion pass and many of them had dressed in their best and converged on Edwardstown.

Regan and Rolf, James's parents, were there too. They had made the long journey from Mia-Mia, staying for a few days at Dunrae. Tara had liked them at once, especially Regan. James's mother was still lively and spirited though there was a good deal of grey now in her once luxuriant chestnut hair, and in spite of bearing three sons her figure was still trim – the result of many hours spent in the saddle, Tara thought. Regan still loved to ride, according to James, and Tara had made up her mind to learn. She was no longer as afraid of horses as she had been and it would be well worth the effort if it kept her in as good shape as it had kept Regan. Tara had bonded well with

Rolf too, who reminded her very much of an older version of James.

'So you were there, Tara, when a little piece of history was made,' he had said, smiling at her.

Tara had flushed at the reference to the battle of the Eureka stockade, awkward in the knowledge that James's parents knew the secrets of her past.

'You were very brave, Tara,' Regan had said, noticing her embarrassment. 'Not many women would have risked what you did for the sake of doing what was right.'

'I couldn't have lived with myself if I hadn't done what I could to save Patrick,' Tara had said quietly. 'And I would never have got out alive if it hadn't been for James. But what did you mean about history being made, Rolf?'

'Why, they are saying that the miners' stand will eventually change the law in Victoria,' Rolf told her. 'The battle may have been lost but it is making the government take a fresh look at the way things are done. The licensing system will be changed, miners will be able to frame their own laws, and every man will have a vote and representation in parliament. You should fly the flag of the Southern Cross at your wedding, if you ask me, and feel proud of it.'

With the permission of James and Father O'Hara Tara had taken up the suggestion. It was, it seemed to her, a small tribute to Patrick and Seamus, who had died in the fighting that day, and to all the others who had given their lives for the cause. The flag of the Southern Cross fluttered bravely now on the flag pole outside the tiny church.

'*I require and charge you both, as ye will answer at the dreadful day of judgement when the secrets of all hearts shall be disclosed, that if either of you know any impediment why ye may not be lawfully joined together in Matrimony, ye do now confess it . . .*'

Father O'Hara's voice rang through the little church; his eyes rested kindly on Tara and James.

For a brief moment a shadow of the past hung over Tara,

as if even now she could not quite believe that she was free to wed James. But she was free. There was no longer any reason why she and James should not be man and wife.

In the silence she glanced at him and as their eyes met and held happiness filled her. Oh, she had been so lucky, far luckier than she deserved. To be wed to James. To have this wonderful family, a comfortable home, a secure future. And to know too that the next time they were gathered here in the church it would be for the baptism of the baby she now carried inside her. James's baby. A brother or sister for Duncan – who was as excited as any child could be at the way things had turned out.

'*Forasmuch as James and Tara have consented together in holy wedlock and have witnessed the same before God and this company . . . I pronounce that they be Man and Wife together . . .*'

Her hand was in James's hand; his ring on her finger.

Tara smiled, her heart full. And for a moment she sensed another presence there beside them in the church.

'Oh, Mammy!' she whispered silently, remembering the vow she had made so long ago on board the *Gazelle*. 'We never found gold, but I have something infinitely more precious. I did it, you see! I lived the dream for you.'

And she knew she would continue to live it down all the years.